The Seat of The Scornful

A SECOND CHANCE

Also by George W. Cave

October 1980 (2013)

Sufi Poetry (1972)

The Seat of The Scornful

A Second Chance

A Novel By

George W. Cave

ISBN: 1540503895
ISBN 13: 9781540503893
Library of Congress Control Number: 2016919735
CreateSpace Independent Publishing Platform
North Charleston, South Carolina

This novel is purely fictional,
totally imaginary,
and
approved by the Publications Review Board
of the Central Intelligence Agency.

This book is dedicated to agency officers who paid the ultimate price.

Part One

The Plan

Chapter I

Washington. February 17, 1982.

ALAIN DEMBRAY HURRIED through the biting February wind. There had been a dusting of wet snow earlier that was now mostly gray slush. It was the kind of snowfall that threw Washington into a tizzy, causing fender benders and missed appointments. The buildings along K Street were as bleak as the gray, uninviting weather. Alain was oblivious to his surroundings, lost in personal thoughts. He was on his way to meet a former colleague, Kurth von Stiegel.

Kurth was possibly the only close friend he had made during his career with the Central Intelligence Agency. They had been in training together at the agency's principle training base, still referred to by its navy designation, Camp Peary. During World War II, it was a navy base where Seabees were trained. Agency officers refer to it as the Farm. When he and Kurth arrived there in 1955, it had not changed much since its days as a Navy base. For cover reasons, the commander of Camp Peary was an army colonel. The agency junior officer trainees dressed in army fatigues. All of the locally hired civilians thought they were with the army.

While there, they had worked on several training problems together. Their friendship grew during the course of their agency careers. It became very close when they each served in Germany during their final overseas tours. Since both men were divorced and shared some interests in common, they spent a lot of time together there. They continued their friendship after retiring from the Agency. Alain had retired a year ago. Kurth preceded him out the door, retiring in 1980, after they both returned from Germany. Alain hung around for a year but found his headquarters assignment boring so when he was told he had plateaued and retirement was suggested, he took the hint and left.

Alain was born and raised in Baltimore. His family was well off, but not wealthy. His father and mother were respected members of Saint Mark's Parish where Alain went to the Holy Family Catholic High School. His father, Fletcher Dembray, was an independent accountant. Both Fletcher and Alain's mother, Sarah, were deceased. Alain was an only child so the inheritance had been nice to receive, particularly the house which he sold for a very respectable price. His inheritance and his agency retirement allowed him to live well, but not lavishly.

Alain believed that he had not been adequately compensated for the commitment he had made to the agency. His sincere belief that he had been poorly treated galled him and led him to think of ways to even the score. There had been three fairly extensive firings; one was in the mid-seventies when Colby was director, another in the late seventies, and the final one under Admiral Turner. Alain had always had a high opinion of his own capabilities. He thought of himself as a head above most of those who were forced into retirement during the most recent purge, a consideration that irked him to no end.

Alain's agency colleagues respected his intelligence, but most of them found him difficult. He was a brilliant problem solver and a solid operations officer. His people skills were not the best, but what hurt him the most was his lack of political skills. He was termed an oddball by his colleagues, a consideration that was accentuated by his refusal to develop people skills. It was his linguistic skills and very good college grades that had opened the doors of the agency for him. His recollections of the four years he had spent at Johns Hopkins University were clouded by the fact that he met his first wife while there and married her immediately after graduation.

The marriage lasted less than a year. He retained no fond memories from his first marriage and it had soured him on women. He had several affairs during his agency career, but never considered remarriage. They were like wildflowers that blossomed quickly and faded just as fast. Finally, in 1969, while serving at headquarters in Langley, he met Jane Brophy with whom he shared some common interests. She worked in the Directorate of Intelligence as an expert on arms proliferation, primarily the rush on the part of several Third World countries to develop weapons of mass destruction. She and Alain were married in November of that year.

The marriage didn't work out. There were no children. Jane moved to Virginia from their townhouse in Norbeck, Maryland. Curiously, both found they got along better separated than when they were married. Once or twice a month, they got together for dinner, a trip to the Kennedy Center, or to some other event that they both wanted to attend. Their mutual female friends were mystified by this conduct and could only surmise that Jane saw something in Alain that was to them undetectable.

In appearance Alain could be described in one word - average. He was about five feet, nine inches tall and weighed about one hundred and fifty-five pounds. He had blue eyes, light brown hair, and a scar on his left arm - the result of an accident with a hunting knife. He was neither handsome nor unattractive. Some said he would be lost in a crowd of three, that is, until he opened his mouth. There was no subject on which he could not argue trenchantly. His colleagues considered him a sophist, but he thought himself something of a Renaissance man, despite Kurth's insistence that the last Renaissance man died at the end of the 16th century.

When Alain arrived at their favorite restaurant, The Enchanted Cat, Kurth was already there. The first time they ate there, Kurth had wondered if the name of the restaurant in any way reflected the menu. They eventually met the owner who said the name was his wife's idea. She kept several cats in their house. Alain gave his topcoat to the maitre d' and joined Kurth at their usual table. They shook hands.

"How's the executive?" Alain asked with a wry smile.

Kurth returned his smile. "It consumes time. How's the consultant?"

"I had a good job for two weeks at the beginning of last month, but nothing currently on tap."

"How was the job last month?"

Alain was thoughtful. "Not bad. It paid well. I was advising a major corporation on what, in the old days, we used to call escape and evasion. They have a pretty big operation in the Gulf States and are concerned about the war between Iran and Iraq spreading."

Kurth interrupted, "Spreading across the gulf? That seems highly unlikely considering our large naval group now controlling the Persian Gulf."

Alain nodded his agreement. He did so in quick, bird-like movements. The habit was somewhat disconcerting to people who did not know him well.

"Their main concern is terrorism against American interests. I provided some guidance on how to brief their employees and the steps they should take to protect themselves. Just in case, I helped them put together an escape plan and spent some time with two of their security officers advising them on the kind of contacts they should develop locally that would be useful if things started to come apart."

Both fell silent while they studied the menu they already knew by heart. Alain ordered broiled rockfish and Kurth went along with him. Alain ordered a bottle of Chateau Ste. Michelle chardonnay to go with the fish.

"Alain, have you seen Jane recently?" Kurth questioned, a tone of wonderment in his voice. Like others who knew them both, Kurth could not fathom their current chumminess. He wondered if sex was involved but decided not to ask. For the moment, the fact that Alain and his ex-wife spent time together would have to remain a source of wonder. Kurth's question animated Alain.

"Yes, in fact she came over last weekend. We went to a dinner theater."

"Any specific reason?"

"The theater was putting on *Carousel*, one of Jane's favorite Broadway shows. Also, the food's not bad." Alain changed the subject, wondering why Kurth considered his friendship with his ex-wife strange. "Tell me, now that you have been working for a major corporation for well over a year, how do you like it?"

Kurth shrugged his shoulders. "The pay is very good, but I must confess, I don't have much in the way of responsibility, nor am I involved in making any major decisions. My sole corporate responsibility is making small talk with representatives of German companies who come to Washington on business with our company. I've made several trips to Germany with company executives where my only duty is to make intelligent comments in German. The company has gone to some length to build up my prestige. I am beginning to feel like an ornate Christmas tree decoration. I even have an attractive secretary who spends most of her time reading paperback romances or playing solitaire. The company is very serious, not given over to levity. In short, my life in the business world is about as exciting as watching grass grow."

"Don't tell me we are both getting nostalgic for life in the agency?"

Kurth looked like he was far away, recalling the past. He snapped back suddenly and answered, "You have to admit, we had some great times. Mostly, it was routine, business as usual, but there were times when the heart pumped hard and fast as if it couldn't get enough blood to all your parts. The black exfiltration of defectors and the running of sensitive agents were exhilarating experiences you just never forget."

Alain nodded his agreement with enthusiasm and recalled a shared experience. "Remember the time we were sent to the Middle East to help arrange the black exfiltration of that Chinese communist official?"

Kurth answered softly, "I'll never forget it. That was the kind of operation you wish you could relate to your grandchildren." Kurth paused as if trying to visualize grandchildren, then added with a lowered voice, "If we were allowed."

"We kept asking headquarters if we could carry arms and what aggressive actions we could take if we were challenged by Chinese security people. Headquarters avoided answering any crucial questions, particularly our request to carry arms."

"That was twenty years ago. We were young and gung-ho. Remember how our team chief was upset with the response from Headquarters? He said their guidance was as useless as a wooden cock."

Alain nodded, "I remember the last cable our team chief tried to send, asking what we could do if Chinese agents came after us."

"Ah yes, the local Chief of Station refused to send it." Kurth laughed, then turned serious. "He was probably right, but at the time we thought he was more of a politician than an operator."

"He was a very nervous person, always in motion, even when sitting down. He made me uneasy just looking at him."

They finished lunch in silence. When coffee was served, Kurth spoke, "We always talk about the good times we had in the Clandestine Service, but they weren't always good."

Alain tilted his head like a curious bird. "Force of habit. Do you know that the term Clandestine Service is not official, despite all the official references to it?"

"I didn't know that. When I was overseas during our last tour together in Germany I thought I might try to write. You know why?"

Alain looked at his friend quizzically. "I have no idea."

"Remember the surveillance exercise in Petersburg when we were in training at the Farm? We went to that small museum about the Civil War. The weapons were interesting, but what really had an effect on me were the letters on display. I couldn't believe the eloquence in those letters home to mothers, wives, and sweethearts. Teenagers wrote some of them. Now you have a hard time finding someone who can write a simple declarative sentence. Maybe that's what wrong with our society. We lack eloquence."

"It's no longer needed."

"Maybe it should be."

Alain grinned, thinking that maybe it was time to pique Kurth's curiosity about something he had been considering for a while. "They were lucky. They didn't have radio or TV. You know Kurth, I think of it as kind of a waste that we can no longer make use of the skills we learned in the agency."

Kurth's antennae immediately went up. He knew from past experience that when Alain brought something up that required an answer from you and you were uncertain as to his intent, you had best reply with a cautious answer. He did.

"On the whole, I suppose you are right, but I have learned in my brief business experience that an awful lot of what we learned in the agency is applicable to the business world. I suggest to you that the constant assessing of persons as targets while in the agency has served me well in sizing up the people I must deal with."

"I won't argue that. We both had considerable experience in counterintelligence during our agency careers. There is a lot you learn in the espionage business that is useful in private life," Alain countered.

Kurth knew his friend well and he was certain there was something on his mind besides mere conversation. "Agreed, Alain. The counterintelligence and counterespionage disciplines are by far the most difficult and, possibly, the most unrewarding. How many cases were there that, in the final analysis, we could not satisfactorily resolve?"

Alain grimaced. He had a peculiar way of screwing up his face as if he was in serious pain. It was an expression familiar to all who knew him.

"Solving, or rather, resolving a CI case is somewhat like trying to piece together a pile of broken glass."

"Or like trying to pick fleas off of an elephant," Kurth added with a grin.

They finished their coffee and paid the check. As they left the restaurant, they said goodbye to the maitre d'. Once outside, they stopped before going their separate ways. Alain made a parting comment.

"I have been thinking about something which may interest you, a venture which will allow us to make use of our agency-acquired skills and also provide a little excitement."

Kurth was curious. "What do you have in mind?"

"Let me work some things out, we can discuss my ideas the next time we meet."

"Okay, but you have aroused my curiosity."

"So be it."

The two friends shook hands and parted. Kurth watched his old friend walk away. Waving to Alain, he turned and began walking back to his office. Kurth cut quite a figure as he strode down the street. He was over six feet tall and walked with an erect military bearing. He had pale blue eyes and blond hair. Virtually every woman he met considered him handsome and exciting, qualities that played a role in his divorce. He was sophisticated and urbane, everything Alain wasn't. His wife, Ulla, from whom he was divorced but on good terms, once told him he was the living idealization of the classic Aryan man. Kurth merely laughed at the comment but inwardly felt very complimented.

When he arrived back in his office, his secretary passed him a note giving the details of the only call he had received. He made himself comfortable in his office. He reached for the telephone to return the call but withdrew his hand.

Whatever Alain had meant when he suggested they do something to make use of their agency skills made Kurth wonder. He had known Alain for many years and had worked closely with him on several operations. He could tell when his friend was working on the kernel of an idea. With Alain, during his CIA years, this could mean a well-planned operation or one so complicated that it could not be made to work. Finally, Kurth told himself that whatever it was would have to wait until their next meeting. He shrugged his shoulders and reached for the telephone.

⇥⇤

Norbeck.
Alain watched the evening news on TV as he ate a sparse dinner. Sometimes he cooked something approaching a gourmet meal and other times it was soup and a sandwich. After such a big lunch with Kurth, tonight it was the latter. He decided that after dinner he would begin to put his thoughts together on the idea that he hoped might intrigue Kurth. He wanted to put everything on paper, just as if he were planning an operation. He was addicted to putting things in writing. He believed that your thoughts didn't amount to anything unless you could express them effectively on paper.

After eating he went into the spare bedroom he used as an office. He had been toying with an operational idea for the better part of a month. The more he thought about it, the more he considered it a workable concept. He started by writing down the different skills that would be needed, then tried to match the skills to potential candidates. He planned to consider only retired officers who, like himself, felt they were unjustly forced to retire from the agency. To the seventh floor they had been only numbers. Some of those forced to take early retirement had framed their pink slips, reminders of an evanescent debt owed them by the agency. He was concerned about how some candidates would react to an approach, but he was sure he could come up with individuals who would be able to rationalize their participation. He personally knew several retired officers who believed they had been treated unfairly by the agency.

Because of the sensitive nature of his planning, there were some important considerations. He would have to be very careful how he broached his proposal to the persons he had in mind. He was sure his friend would be interested. Kurth was key. Alain trusted his judgment. If Kurth had doubts about the operation after studying the possibilities, then Alain would can it. He was aware that he sometimes got carried away. If Kurth said he thought it was workable, they would go ahead with serious planning. There was also the question of compartmentalization, and how he and Kurth would handle it. He thought he could come up with a plan where only the two of them would be fully aware of the details.

Funding would not be a serious problem. He thought the basic costs could be as much as a hundred thousand dollars or as little as forty thousand, depending on how long it would take them to collect the information crucial to a successful operation. By the end of the evening he had outlined the operation and a list of the capabilities they would need to mount it. He had some ideas on who they might approach, but declined to write down any names for security reasons. He hoped they could limit the number of persons involved in the operation to four, but in any case no more than six. It would be a plus if the candidates they ultimately picked could pony up some of the necessary seed money, but he doubted he could get any funding from some of the persons he had under consideration. Asking them to kick in on the funding would mean that they would have to be fully briefed on the operation. This was something he did not want to do. He concluded that he and Kurth would have to handle the expenses.

He reviewed what he had written and decided to sleep on it. The one remaining question was research. While Kurth was a close friend, he knew he must be able to present a plan to him that was both workable and well researched. He would try an outline of his idea on Kurth the next time they met. He turned off the lights and went upstairs to his bedroom.

Baghdad. February 25, 1982.
Saddam Hussein sat in one of his downtown Baghdad offices. He was there because his ornate office in the Presidential Palace overlooking the Tigris River was

not considered safe. It was early evening and he was staring out of the large picture window at the fading light reflecting off the distant Tigris River. Tomorrow would be Friday and, considering the way the war was going, there would be a lot to pray for at the afternoon prayers. Saddam was infuriated with his military. When his armed forces launched the attack on Iran in September of 1980, he had expected rapid success. Initially, the attack had gone well. Several fair sized Iranian towns had been occupied and his ground forces had crossed the Karun River, but the offensive ground to a halt in the face of fanatical Iranian resistance. His ground forces had not been able to extend their initial successes into Khuzistan in southwestern Iran.

He was particularly disturbed by his intelligence services. They had assured him that the Arabs in Iranian Khuzistan, the majority ethnic group in the area, would rise up against their Aryan oppressors and support the invading Iraqi forces. The General Intelligence Directorate had spent a lot of money on something called the Arab Liberation Front. They had assured Saddam that the Front was a force that would support his territorial aims in southwestern Iran. The occupation of Khuzistan, and more importantly, a large piece of the shoreline, would fulfill a long time Iraqi goal. Saddam's long-term strategic plan for Iraq was to become a Persian Gulf power. In order to achieve this long-held goal, it was necessary to gain control of some of the ports on Iran's southwestern shore. Once in control of the ports, he planned to annex a large part of Iranian Khuzistan. Unfortunately for Saddam and the Iraqi Army, the Arab population in Khuzistan did not rise up in revolt; in fact, fanatical, although inept, resistance by the Iranians confronted and halted the Iraqi invading forces.

Saddam fumed at the failure of his intelligence services to correctly assess the situation in Khuzistan, but the Air Force's performance was even more depressing. Very little damage had been done to the main Iranian oil terminal on Kharg Island. Saddam had punished several senior officers for their inability to capitalize on the initial military gains. He had several intelligence officers executed for their incompetence in analyzing the situation in Khuzistan and their misreading of the capabilities of the Iranian military.

They had assessed Iranian military competence as being severely eroded due to the purges of its upper ranks that were carried out by the Mullahs. The unexpected ferocity of the Iranian Revolutionary Guards made up for their military incompetence. The Iraqis were surprised and forced to make some strategic withdrawals. Despite careful planning, logistics had broken down primarily because the troops were expending ordinance at a rate much greater than had been planned.

The key problem was Khorramshahr. Saddam was elated when his ground forces gained control of the city, one of Iran's busiest ports. Khorramshahr had been fiercely defended. The follow-on target was Abadan Island. Iraqi ground forces laid siege to Abadan, but were unable to capture it. Without Abadan, the capture of Khorramshahr was a hollow victory. His ground forces had been surprised at the spring counter-offensive launched by the Iranians. In April 1981, they crossed the Karun River and, if the situation could not be reversed, Iraqi forces would have to withdraw from Khorramshahr.

At the moment all this did not particularly concern Saddam. He had successfully dunned his Arab allies, primarily Saudi Arabia and Kuwait, for financial support. Some of these funds were deposited in an Iraqi government account in the Banque Suisse. Saddam had arranged to have some of this support siphoned off and deposited in his own Swiss bank accounts. His longstanding friend and comrade, Wafiq Tikriti, controlled the official Iraqi government account in the Banque Suisse. Both he and Wafiq had joined the Baath party shortly after it was founded. Both had participated in the 1959 failed assassination plot against President Abd al-Karim Qassem. They fled into exile in Syria and on to Egypt. They returned when Qassem was assassinated in 1963. As a result of the successful Baath takeover in 1968, Saddam was named Deputy Chairman of the Regional Command Council in charge of internal security. He used the post well in consolidating his hold over the Baath Party and, in 1979, became president of Iraq. Wafiq had been there all along.

Saddam hung up his private telephone. He had phoned Wafiq to discuss how certain items should be handled. He genuinely liked Wafiq, perhaps because he had no political pretensions. Saddam reserved his affection for those who posed no political threat to him. Wafiq was a businessman through and through, and had honestly handled Saddam's interests.

Saddam called for Mustafa Naghshabandi, his private secretary and office manager. Mustafa was elderly, in his sixties, but he was sprightly. When others were present he always agreed with everything the boss said, playing the role of an obsequious servant. In private conversations he could be brutally frank, like a father to a son. When required, he went to Europe on business for Saddam. These trips concerned private affairs and were rare because Saddam did not like him to be absent from Iraq. Saddam started speaking as soon as he entered the ornate office.

"Mustafa, what would you do with my Generals who seem to be working hard to lose the war with Iran?"

"Perhaps they worry too much about fighting a country that is twice as large as Iraq and three times as populous."

Saddam almost smiled. "Maybe I should have made you a general, Mustafa. You couldn't do any worse than the jackasses who are apparently unable to hold the little pieces of Iran that they have managed to capture. Abadan and Ahwaz were the major targets and they remain in Iranian hands. They tell me they were forced to lift the siege of Abadan and have only been able to threaten Ahwaz. It seems the only thing I can rely on is our stock of Scud missiles."

"*Ittikal al-Allah* (Reliance is on Allah)," Mustafa intoned. "In the end Allah will decide the outcome of the war."

"What will Allah do, Mustafa? Flip a coin?" Saddam spit the words out, arrows designed to hurt. He occasionally expressed some displeasure with Mustafa's total faith in Allah and the fatalism he took for granted. His mood changed and he laughed, "Maybe I would be better off with the flip of a coin by Allah than relying on my generals."

Mustafa decided to wait patiently. Saddam did not call him to complain about his generals. He had known Saddam since before the failed assassination attempt on Abd al Karim Qassem. Both he and Wafiq Tikriti had fled to Syria with Saddam and then gone to Egypt with him. Finally, Saddam explained why he had called him.

"Mustafa, I want you to go to Germany to see Wafiq. I just talked to him on the phone and he is involved in some business deals I should know more about. As you know, I cannot leave Iraq. I must be here to whip the jackasses I have for generals into prosecuting the war. Wafiq is too engaged in Europe to come here. I want you to go and pick up some reports he has written about several recent deals and bring them back to me. I also want you to question Wafiq on how he manages the one government account he controls. We must make some new arrangements to handle the funds we will receive from our Arab Allies. Bring me any suggestions he has on how to manage the new accounts that will be opened. Also, question him on any problems we may have. Leave tomorrow and get back as soon as you can."

Mustafa didn't know why Saddam always said he was too busy to leave. He had left Iraq on occasion, notably his trip to Algiers in March of 1975 to sign the agreement with the Shah ending the Kurdish insurrection. In all probability, Saddam rarely traveled because he did not want to give anyone the chance to take his place in his absence. Mustafa sometimes wondered whether Saddam actually trusted him and Wafiq or whether he was just certain neither would dare betray him.

"As you wish. If you have no further orders, I will leave to make my travel plans."

"Allah will be with you."

Mustafa left the room unhappy. The prospect of traveling to Europe to ensure Saddam was getting his share of the Arab money made him uneasy. He wondered when they had stripped off their youthful optimism like old clothes. He had watched as they gradually gained control over everything that resembled economic activity in Iraq. Mustafa, an older, very interesting man, was perhaps the closest thing to a patriot in Saddam's inner circle. He was one of the few who had subordinated his personal aims to his belief that Saddam would improve the lives of all Iraqis. Mustafa rationalized the corruption in the government by noting that more financial benefits trickled down to the majority than in any other country in the Middle East. He was opposed to the invasion of Iran, but had never expressed his opposition to anyone, not even his wife. Now, for the first time since the Baath party assumed power, he was concerned about what the future held for his country.

Chapter 2

Norbeck. February 26, 1982.

AT FIRST HE had just played with an idea. By the time they had lunch, what had started as a vague idea had begun to gel into a plan. Since his lunch with Kurth, Alain had done some serious calculating. Devising the details had motivated him to put the outlines of a plan on paper. When everything began to fall into place, he decided it was time to explain his thoughts to his trusted friend and colleague.

Kurth was crucial. If he perceived some merit in the plan, then they could consider fleshing it out with real people. Alain smiled. He was pleased with himself. If his plan worked, it would compensate him for the shabby treatment he had received from the agency. He smiled again. Maybe someday he would thank the agency for forcing him to retire. The more he thought about it, the more he was convinced the plan would work. His major problem was convincing Kurth. He needed his participation.

Alain had made few friends during his agency career, and Kurth was perhaps the only one whose judgment he respected. He figured that only the two of them would need to have full knowledge of the plan. A first-rate tech would handle the electronics, do concealment, and handle the procurement of documentation. They might have a problem if they needed disguises. It was a difficult specialty to fill. The problem would be finding someone who could handle both disguise and all the technical needs. He hoped he was worried about a problem that might not arise.

Alain had two retired techs in mind. He considered Jack Blanton a good candidate. He had worked with Jack on a couple of operations. He was an electronics wizard and was skilled in making concealment devices, but Alain was uncertain about him. He had never married, and for some reason, had little to do with the female population of the agency, preferring the occasional company of prostitutes. Alain knew that Blanton had been forced to retire due to suspicions that he had dipped into the till. Alain had seen him several months ago and Blanton was pretty bitter about the way the agency had treated him.

There was another recently retired tech, Wayne Goodal, who might have all the necessary qualifications. He was a good tech, but Alain did not know him well. Goodal also had a reputation of being a straight arrow, hardly the kind of person for what Alain had in mind. Kurth also knew Blanton and that was an advantage. He planned to ask Kurth his opinion of Blanton.

They would also need someone who could effectively pose as an Iraqi. Hashem Samara'i was the only one he could come up with. There may be others who had worked in the Near Eastern Division of the Clandestine Services, but Hashem was the only one Alain knew who could fill the bill. He was unsure regarding Kurth's feelings about Hashem, but would question him at their next meeting.

Alain knew Kurth had used several technicians in the German telephone system. He was hoping Kurth could come up with a candidate who would be able to handle the needed telephone tap. Alain figured several months of analyzing material from the tap would be necessary before they could mount the operation. With a little bit of luck their patience would be amply rewarded. Alain reached for the phone and placed a call to Kurth.

⊷➤◉ ◉◄⊷

Hamburg. March 1, 1982.

"Mustafa, I was most pleased to get your call. It is only on rare occasions that old friends come to Hamburg," Wafiq Tikriti said as he ushered Mustafa into his office. Wafiq had been in Hamburg almost two years. Saddam Hussein had appointed him Iraqi Consul, but he did little consular work. His main function was managing his and Saddam's business accounts. He was also executor of the large Iraqi government account in the Banque Suisse. He countersigned disbursements used mainly in paying for arms and related purchases. Both Wafiq and Saddam had profited greatly through this arrangement.

"It is good to see you, Wafiq. Knowing you, I don't have to ask if business is good," Mustafa answered.

"I have ordered coffee. I hope your trip was comfortable enough and the hotel is adequate. It is nearby and very pleasant. I frequently have dinner in the hotel restaurant. It is quite good." Wafiq was interrupted by a knock. A young lady entered Wafiq's office carrying a tray of coffee and cups. She placed the tray on the coffee table separating the two friends. Wafiq thanked her as she left the office.

Wafiq turned to Mustafa, "Ingrid handles our German and English correspondence. She is quite efficient."

Knowing Wafiq, Mustafa wondered if she had other functions. She was also very attractive and Wafiq had a well-earned reputation as a skirt chaser. The coffee was good, better than anything available in Baghdad. He decided to get to the point of his visit abruptly.

"Wafiq, I am here at Saddam's request to explain some new developments. We are in the process of getting large sums of money from our Arab allies in support of the war effort against Iran. Some of these monies will be deposited in the government account under your control. As in the past, whenever there are funds disbursed from this account for arms or related purchases, certain administrative charges will also be drawn from the account and deposited in one of Saddam's personal accounts." Mustafa paused to sip his coffee, but more to note any reaction from Wafiq.

Seeing no abrupt change in Wafiq's expression, he continued, "Because of the amounts involved, three other personal accounts are being opened ultimately for Saddam's benefit. As in the past, we will send individuals from Baghdad whom you will identify to the bank so they can withdraw amounts to cover certain expenses." Mustafa paused to drink more coffee and give Wafiq an opportunity to comment on what he had told him.

Wafiq stared at his old friend. If the new accounts for Saddam upset Mustafa, it was not apparent in his expression. Wafiq felt he and Mustafa were close enough friends for him to ask some pointed questions.

"Three new accounts? Our Arab friends must be coughing up a considerable sum of cash."

"That they are, my friend. A large portion of the money we receive from our Arab supporters will be deposited in the official account which you control," Mustafa smiled. "You must have already guessed that you will not know the details of the new accounts. Saddam is being careful. He is obsessed with the need for security. I do have a question. How do you handle the withdrawals from the official account? The ones we refer to as administrative expenses."

It was Wafiq's turn to smile. "I have found the best method is to take the withdrawals in bearer bonds or, in some cases, cash. There are several moneychangers who buy the bonds from me. Bearer bonds are very valuable to people who wish to move money quietly. I then make a cash deposit in Saddam's account. There is no paper trail from his account back to the government account." Wafiq failed to mention that, in some cases, moneychangers paid him a small premium for the bonds.

Mustafa stroked his beard in deep thought, "Three new accounts, all three in Saddam's two sons' names, will be opened shortly. Saddam wants your suggestions on the best way to withdraw money from the government account and then deposit the proceeds into the three new accounts. Please explain the arrangements you make when someone is sent from Baghdad to make a withdrawal from the government account."

Wafiq thought about Mustafa's question. "I am the custodian of the official account at the Banque Suisse and am well known to the bank manager. Between us we have devised a mechanism we use when someone else is making the withdrawal. Whoever is to make the withdrawal must first come to Hamburg. I make a photocopy of his passport, have him sign his name three times, and I tear a ten mark note in half. I then send these three items to my contact in the Banque Suisse via DHL. I call my contact and give him the passport number and the serial number of the ten-mark note. I also tell him the amount of the withdrawal. He calls back immediately at my private number to confirm my call." Wafiq cut his explanation short. He asked Mustafa, "Do you follow me so far?"

Mustafa nodded vigorously, "Yes, please continue."

"The person making the withdrawal goes to the Banque Suisse in Geneva and asks for my contact. He presents his passport and his half of the ten mark note to my contact. My contact asks him for the exact amount of the withdrawal. If everything is okay, he will have him sign for the money, check his signature against the exemplars I have sent, then make the transaction."

Mustafa rubbed his chin, a bemused expression on his face. "Since it is a cash transaction, there will be no record. But what about large sums?"

"Whoever makes the withdrawal should do what I do. When I make a large withdrawal, I take the amount of the withdrawal in bearer bonds and cash them with moneychangers over a period of time. The cash can then be deposited in one of Saddam's accounts or any other account for that matter. It is all pretty simple, except for the amount of money involved. A million dollars in cash takes up a lot of room. I have a safe deposit box in the bank where I keep the bearer bonds until I cash them. I usually take the withdrawal in bearer bond denominations of half a million dollars. Most of the transactions I handle personally are between two to three million dollars, although on some occasions much more. I then sell the bonds over two or three days, and make the deposits in different branches of the bank in which Saddam has a personal account."

Mustafa wondered just how much money Wafiq had transferred into Saddam's account through this method. "You make it sound like simplicity itself."

"Well it is not all that simple. My only real fear is being robbed while running around Geneva with half a million dollars."

"You might get set up by one of the moneychangers you use."

The same thought had occurred to Wafiq. "That is a possibility, but I think it is somewhat remote. The transfers in question are irregular. The moneychangers never know in advance when I will show up. If the sum is relatively large, I take Ahmad with me as a bodyguard."

Mustafa was intrigued. "Can these bearer bonds be traced?"

"Not really. The bonds will pass through several hands before they make their way back to the issuing bank. Swiss bank secrecy rules would prevent the bank from identifying the original purchaser of the bonds. Even if they did identify me, I have committed no crime."

"Any other precautions?"

"Yes. The Consulate in Geneva is under instruction to support me. I use an armed driver to take me around to the moneychangers and then to make the deposits. I also check out a Browning 9mm automatic to carry during these trips around Geneva. So far, there have been no incidents worth noting."

Mustafa was pleased. "Well, Wafiq, this is all apparently a lot simpler than I thought it would be. I will make some notes and brief the boss when I get back to Baghdad. Now, we have one other subject to discuss that is not at all simple."

--➤═ ═◄--

Norbeck. March 5, 1982.

Kurth had driven his BMW north on 16th Street. He had left his office on K Street to go to dinner at Alain's. He did not know if anyone else was invited. Kurth sometimes wondered about his old friend. To Alain there was no clear-cut division between the rational and irrational. He was capable of following an irrational train of thought long after it should have been dropped as unworkable. He had fooled many people due to his knack of making the irrational appear plausible. Kurth had concluded a while ago that Alain sometimes engaged in such circumlocutions just to see how long he could keep people's attention before they realized what was going on. He wondered if this was a trait common to all extremely intelligent people.

At the intersection of 16th Street and Georgia Avenue, he had turned north onto Georgia. He was glad it was Friday. There would be plenty to drink during an evening with Alain. Fortunately, he could sleep late tomorrow morning. Alain was a very good cook, so it would be a pleasant evening. He drove through the heavy evening traffic. After he passed the intersection of Layhill Road and Georgia Avenue, the traffic thinned out. Alain's townhouse was located on the southwest side of the Georgia Avenue and Norbeck Road intersection. The townhouses in the development were well built, all brick. Alain's had a basement and two floors. The most attractive feature of Alain's house was the huge, well-lit kitchen. As he pulled into a parking space in front of the house, he wondered if Alain had invited his ex-wife, Jane Brophy. Kurth picked up a bottle of scotch from the back seat of his BMW. He had brought the scotch as a present for his old friend.

There was a tree of some kind in the small front yard of the house. Kurth was hard pressed to tell one kind of tree from another. He could see that the tree was beginning to bud. It wouldn't be long before spring, then the long, hot, muggy summer. Kurth rang the bell. Alain opened the front door and ushered him inside. Kurth proffered the scotch and Alain thanked him.

"Let's go into the kitchen to have drinks. I can manage the dinner better that way."

"Okay by me," Kurth replied. When he saw no one else there, he asked Alain, "Is no one else coming?"

Alain smiled mysteriously. "You're it. This is a business dinner."

"What kind of business?" Kurth asked, his curiosity aroused.

"All in good time. What would you like to drink? I'm having a martini."

"A martini is okay by me. What have you been up to?"

Alain answered without looking at Kurth. "It's interesting that you ask. Something happened a couple of nights ago that set me thinking. I began to wonder if we don't in effect become different people at various stages in our lives."

Kurth was immediately alert. He had learned to beware of Alain waxing philosophic. He frowned at Alain. "I'm not sure I agree with your conclusion that we become different people. As we age we outgrow things, we appreciate different things. It is our perceptions that change. What brought on all this philosophizing?"

Alain stared at Kurth for a few moments. "A few nights ago, I went to a birthday party for a guy I hadn't seen in at least twenty-five years. We knew each other in the army. We became close friends. We played chess together. We went on rock climbing trips together and we sailed together. We drank together. Hell, we even chased women together. While it was nice to see him, he was a different person. We had nothing in common but some faded memories. He seemed to be the same guy I knew years ago, but I have to admit, I don't care if I ever see him again. I can't go back in time to recapture some past images. After I left the party and came home and thought about it, I ended up asking myself if I had become some kind of snob."

Kurth laughed in surprise. "That bothers you?"

Alain averted his eyes momentarily and drank some of his martini. "Life has treated my old friend more modestly than me, but he has accepted the hand he was dealt and appears to be quite happy. He was very kind and affectionate to his wife of close to thirty years and I have two failed marriages. Maybe being in the agency made us too elitist."

"Look, Alain, don't be so philosophical. To my way of thinking, the end of philosophy is insanity."

Alain laughed wryly. "Maybe so. Do you remember the old saw about the governor visiting the insane asylum?"

"No, but I'm sure you'll refresh my memory."

"Well, it seems the governor was visiting one of the state's institutions for the insane. At the time, the more violent persons were kept in cells. He noted that one of the cells held a man who seemed relatively calm. The governor stopped and chatted with the man who, from his statements, appeared rational. Finally, the governor asked the man why he was in the asylum. The man replied, 'Because there are more of you than there are of me.'"

Kurth laughed, enjoying Alain's offbeat sense of humor. Since he and Alain were alone, he assumed this dinner was directly related to Alain's cryptic remarks at their last luncheon.

"The last time we met you mentioned something about putting to use our agency acquired skills. What gives?"

"Patience, Kurth. Let me get dinner on the table. Finish your martini." Alain went to the refrigerator, removed two salads, and placed them on the country table. "We'll eat French style, salads first." Alain next withdrew a bottle of Macon Villages from the refrigerator, opened it, and poured two generous glasses.

"What's for dinner?" Kurth asked between bites of his salad.

"It's in the large pot on the stove. It is a recipe I learned in southern France, something like Coq au Vin except much more delicious. The other pot has the rice in it." Alain paused to look at his watch. "It should be ready in about five minutes."

They finished the salads while discussing the Iran-Iraq war. Both commented on the lack of coverage in the American media. Alain mentioned that no one gives a damn as long as it doesn't spread to other countries.

Alain put some steamed rice on two plates, then ladled some of the chicken onto each plate. The dish was made of chicken thighs simmered in red wine and seasoned with finely chopped carrots. Alain had added halved mushrooms and pearl onions late in the simmering process. Kurth looked at his plate dubiously before tasting it. His expression changed with the first bite.

"This is quite good. I should have known you wouldn't cook something that wasn't worth eating. What else is in it?"

"Just a couple of cloves of garlic, salt and pepper, oregano and a bay leaf or two."

Kurth looked intently at his friend. "You really enjoy cooking, don't you?"

"Yes I do. Neither of my two wives were much in the kitchen, although Jane has demonstrated an interest lately. Now eat before it gets cold."

Kurth ignored him. "I have never heard of carrots being used as a seasoning."

Alain laughed. "You learn something every day."

They ate in silence. When they had finished the chicken, Alain brought out some fruit. Kurth recalled that Alain was always a nut on proper diet. Jane had complained to him about having to sneak ice cream when Alain wasn't around. After the fruit, Alain served freshly brewed coffee and asked Kurth if he would like some cognac. Kurth nodded his agreement and Alain fetched a bottle of Hine cognac from his liquor cabinet. He brought the bottle and two snifters back to the table then poured some in each snifter. After Kurth had tasted the cognac, Alain smiled at him and, in a half serious tone, asked Kurth if he had ever given serious thought to robbing a bank. Kurth was visibly startled at the question.

"Not that I recall," he answered, wondering exactly what Alain had under consideration.

--→■◎◎■←--

Hamburg.

Wafiq's concern was clear from his pained expression and his nervous toying with a pen. Mustafa had left after lunch. It was very late but Wafiq could not sleep. He did not like the other business that Mustafa had brought up. Saddam himself wanted Wafiq to take a more active role in the war against Iran. He wanted him to encourage expatriate Iranian organizations to be more aggressive in their opposition to Ayatollah Khomieni's government. Saddam was certain these groups could help undermine Iran's war effort. Mustafa instructed Wafiq to contact and assess all those Iranian exile groups that were actively opposed to the current regime in Iran. Wafiq told Mustafa he did not think any of the various exile groups were in a position to do much harm. Most of them would take Iraqi money that would simply disappear into various pockets, very deep pockets. Mustafa agreed that giving such groups money was akin to shoveling it into a bottomless pit, but Saddam's orders must be obeyed.

There was an exception, the Mojahidin-i-Khalq, a very radical young group of Iranian exiles that was already operating from bases in Iraq. Mustafa had emphasized that they were a special case. On his part, Wafiq thought it unlikely that any of the Iranian exile groups in Europe would want to be identified as supporting the Iraqi war effort. Too much water had gone under the bridge. Iranians and Iraqis despised each other as much as any other two groups of people on the face of the earth. Wafiq knew the leaders of several exile organizations. Most of the organizations were little more than debating societies. Wafiq wondered if support to such groups might also be a vehicle for siphoning off money into Saddam's accounts. He shrugged his shoulders thinking that at least it would be an additional vehicle for his usual commission.

Iranian opposition organizations were not his major concern. Mustafa had told him that Saddam also wanted him to recruit a network of Iraqis loyal to Saddam who would report on the activities of Iraqis opposed to Saddam. Wafiq presumed that some sort of action would be taken against them. One point that Mustafa had emphasized was Saddam's interest in learning if the Central Intelligence Agency was involved in supporting any of the Iraqi opposition. Mustafa told him that Zaki Sa'duni, a key officer in the DGI (Directorate General of Intelligence), was sending one of his operatives to Hamburg to help Wafiq set up a network of informants. Wafiq was not at all happy with this new assignment. In no case did he want to tangle with the CIA. Their support of Mullah Mustafa Barzani in the mid-seventies was still fresh in his mind. He did not like doing dangerous things on someone else's turf. He wondered who from the DGI Sa'duni was sending to help him. He was worried. His life in Hamburg was very simple and very profitable. Wafiq was not the adventurous type. He hoped he could get by with exerting a minimal effort in carrying out Saddam's orders.

Wafiq thought about the war that had started so favorably for Iraq which was now turning into a disaster. Iranian forces had recaptured Khorramshahr in March. The Iraqi generals were concerned about intelligence information indicating that Iran was preparing a major offensive. Meanwhile, the Iraqi economy was suffering, primarily due to the sharp decline in oil production. Before the war, Iraq had been producing about four million barrels of oil a day. The Iranian blockade of the Shatt al-Arab had reduced production to about six hundred and fifty thousand barrels a day. Iraq had appealed to Arab states for assistance and some limited financial help was being supplied by Kuwait. Saudi Arabia had also promised to put together an Arab aid package.

The turnaround in Iraqi military fortunes forced Saddam to figure some political way out of his perilous military situation. Reports from his military commanders describing the fanaticism with which the Iranian Revolutionary Guards were fighting were a source of worry. One proposal being considered was for Saddam to declare a unilateral cease-fire and announce the withdrawal of all Iraqi troops from Iranian territory. Saddam was reluctant to take such a drastic step and ordered his generals to cause as many Iranian casualties as possible in the hopes that Tehran would agree to a cease fire proposed by a third party such as the United Nations. Behind all this thinking was a nagging worry about what the majority Shia population would do if the Iranians launched a successful invasion into southern Iraq. One way or another, Wafiq would need to lay low.

-->=○ ○=<--

Norbeck.

There was a pregnant silence before Alain spoke.

"Kurth, I think we have the necessary knowledge to pull off a major bank robbery. What skills the two of us don't have we can acquire from other annuitants like ourselves."

While Kurth was mildly surprised at Alain's initial question, he was stunned by Alain's proposal. His agitation showed in his voice as he answered Alain.

"Just wait a minute, friend. You've had some off-the-wall ideas in the past, but nothing to compare with robbing a bank. What got you on this kick?"

Alain's expression was smug. "I have devoted a lot of time to figuring out how it could be done."

Kurth was incredulous. "You're serious?" There was an alarmed tone in his voice. "You can count me out. I don't consider robbing banks a pastime conducive to a long and enjoyable life. If the FBI is good at anything, it's catching bank robbers."

"Just hear me out. You may decide to change your mind."

Kurth raised his arms in a gesture of resignation. "I guess I'm dumb enough to listen to anything. But I must warn you, I am at a loss as to why you are suddenly talking to me about robbing a bank. At the moment I am more worried about your sanity than curious about what you have in mind."

"Be patient, I am not talking about just any old bank. I'm talking about the Banque Suisse. Do you recall the telephone tap we had on the Iraqi Consulate in Hamburg? We were particularly interested in what, if anything, the Iraqi Consul, Wafiq Tikriti, was doing in Germany. Our curiosity was aroused by the fact that he was one of Saddam Hussein's closest friends."

"Yes, the Germans put a tap on his private line. The agency was interested in him because we suspected Saddam was using him to fund terrorist organizations in Europe. The Germans took the tap off when there was no indication of support for terrorism."

Alain smiled with satisfaction. "That's correct, but while we had the tap, we also learned that Wafiq controlled an official Iraqi government bank account."

"So what? Knowing that he controls a government account is not much help. We need a lot of information to rob a bank. I might add that inside information is critical where banks are concerned."

"What's happened to you? One of the reasons I always admired you was the way you responded to operational challenges. I'll tell you what Kurth, let me make you a proposition. We sit down over the next couple of weeks and draw up a plan to rob Saddam Hussein of four or five million dollars. If, after a reasonable period of time you can't wholeheartedly support the plan we devise, we'll drop the whole idea. I think it would be an interesting exercise to work out such a plan, even if we never carry it out. What do you say?"

Kurth decided on the spot that he had better agree with his friend. If, after discussing Alain's plan, he concluded it was unworkable, he could at least persuade Alain to drop the whole idea.

"Well if you were working, Alain, I'd say you need a rest. Since you are not working, let's go ahead and plan the thing. It might be good for us elderly gentlemen to get some mental exercise. I suppose we could always use our research to write a book." Kurth laughed lightly, "I assume you are not thinking of an armed robbery since you have already brought up Wafiq Tikriti and the Iraqi account he manages."

"Correct, Kurth. Armed robbery is not worth the effort because you only get access to the cash in the tills. As I said, the FBI has a good record of catching bank robbers. I would imagine European law enforcement does too. Some insiders have drained accounts, but you have to be an insider to do that. What I have been considering is robbing a specific account. In thinking about this account, I became intrigued about the possibility of pulling off a successful operation. Let's call it an operation, not a robbery. One of the most interesting pieces of information from the tap was the clear indication that occasionally others besides Tikriti made the withdrawals."

Kurth grimaced at Alain and sipped some of his cognac. "We're liable to need a lot of this before the evening is over," he said, looking at his snifter. "I do have a critical question."

Alain ignored Kurth's cynicism. "Ask what you will."

"If armed robbery is out of the question, I assume we must in some way obtain the number of the Iraqi Government account, right?"

"Right, Kurth, the account number is key to the operation." Alain reached into his shirt pocket and withdrew a piece of paper that he handed to Kurth. "This is it."

Kurth took the paper and looked at the number written on it. "I'll be a son-of-a-bitch. How did you get it?"

"It appeared on the tap once. I can't recall who it was but someone called from the Banque Suisse and asked for the account number. He seemed upset that

Wafiq had forgotten to give it to him before he left Hamburg. The conversation was in Arabic. According to the transcriber, the accent of the caller was Iraqi."

Kurth studied Alain's expression. "What made you keep the number?"

Alain answered with a smile, "You never know when something like this will come in handy. I thought it was a nice souvenir. It is an official Iraqi government account that is controlled by Wafiq."

"Well, that's one key element in place. Obviously having the account number led you to conclude an operation against the account was a possibility." Kurth toyed with his snifter, trying to decide how to deal with Alain's strange proposal. He thought it best to draw him out. He wanted as much information as possible from Alain so he could punch rational holes in what he thought was an illogical proposal.

"Okay, Alain, this is going to require a lot of research and planning. Any ideas about how we can pull this off and what we need in the way of personnel and material?"

Alain was pleased that producing the account number had piqued Kurth's interest. "You are absolutely right that this operation will require a great degree of intricate planning. I have already given some thought as to how it could be set up. Maybe we both better have some more cognac before we begin discussing details." Without waiting for an answer from Kurth, Alain picked up the cognac and poured some in each snifter. "First, we have the account number without which there is no operation."

Kurth was certain that Alain was attaching too much importance to the account number. "Alain, I hate to pour any cold water on your scheme, but suppose the accounts have been changed?"

"That, my friend, is a chance we'll have to take, but chances are it's the same. As I recall, the number came up on the tap about two years ago," Alain answered while staring at Kurth. "I think our first objective is to get a tap on the Iraqi Consulate, more precisely, Tikriti's private number. According to my recollection, his private number rings in both his office and his living quarters upstairs. We may need several months of take from the tap before we get all the information we need. We need to record an instance when someone else unknown to the Banque Suisse makes a withdrawal. Studying the take should give us some additional ideas on how to access the account, plus any paroles and documentation used by a second party to access the account."

Kurth rubbed his chin while considering what Alain had said. "Don't you think this is kind of a long shot?" Kurth thought there was too much they would have to know before they could mount a successful operation. "I mean we don't have much to go on, except the account number. Anything we can recall from the old tap on Wafiq's private line may have changed."

Alain thought his old friend was being far too cautious. This was not the Kurth he knew from their past association. Kurth had always been one to take operational chances. Lucky for him things usually turned out for the better.

"Look," Alain said, "We have the account number and we know that on several occasions someone other than Wafiq made withdrawals from the account. The purpose of the operation is to determine if this is still the case. My recollection is that Wafiq always made the arrangements for a third party to make a withdrawal from the account. There is also one more key piece of information I recall from the tap. The unidentified Iraqi who called Wafiq and asked for the account number was miffed because Wafiq forgot to give it to him when he was in Hamburg."

"So Wafiq forgot to give him the account number. What's your point?"

Alain frowned at Kurth. "My point is that I suspect anyone coming from Baghdad to make a withdrawal first goes to Hamburg where Wafiq makes the arrangements for him with the Banque Suisse. Unfortunately, I can't remember any specifics from our old tap and we no longer have access to that information. So, our first problem is how to tap Tikriti's private line. I think a month or two of coverage would give us information on how he arranges for such withdrawals currently." Alain paused and calmly drank some cognac while awaiting Kurth's reaction.

Kurth had both elbows on the table. His hands were in front of and even with his face as he slowly tapped his fingertips together. "It might work if we are able to tap Wafiq's line. But there are too many ifs. The big if is the telephone tap, no small accomplishment. What happens if the tap does not reveal anything we can use?"

Alain raised his hands, palms upward, in a gesture of futility. "If after an agreed upon time we don't get the information we need, we pack up and leave."

"Okay, suppose we decide it's worth a try. Specifically, mounting a tap of Tikriti's private line. We need someone that can do the tap. That someone must, of necessity, be in the German Post, Telephone and Telegraph. We also need someone to transcribe the take from the tap. Any good ideas?" Kurth asked, hoping Alain's answer would be some indication of how much he had thought things through.

"I think I have a good choice for the technician, Jack Blanton. He is good for several reasons. First, he has mastered several different technical skills. Second, he is not married so he would be able to relocate easily without raising suspicion. I suspect he is still pissed off at the agency for the way he was forced into retirement. He would also be attracted to the professional challenge involved."

"Have you considered anyone else?" Kurth asked.

"Yeah, I have considered a couple of others like Wayne Goodal, but none of them have Blanton's skills, and besides, they are all married with children."

Kurth nodded his head. He couldn't think of anyone else. "Blanton is an excellent choice. He is a very low profile guy who won't draw any attention. I don't buy him being intrigued by the professional challenge. His interest will be in how much he gets paid. I do not know to what extent he has been exposed to the German intelligence services, but I doubt if he was ever exposed to the local boys in Hamburg. He should be questioned on this point before we make up our minds. If we do get the tap, we will need a transcriber, any thoughts?"

"Just one. I think we should approach Hashem Samara'i. He is very good at what he does and there is no love lost between him and the agency. He is superb at catching nuances from listening to the changing inflections of voices on any taped conversation. Most important of all, he likes to live high on the hog and I know he is not adjusting well to retirement. I think I can count on him. What do you think?"

Kurth took a sip of his cognac. "I have some doubts about Hashem. He is well known to the Iraqis, and is a very high profile man-about-town wherever he goes. Do you have anyone else in mind for the job of transcriber?"

Alain smiled inwardly. He was pleased. Kurth was now talking like he was dealing with an ongoing operation. "I know of no one else, and this isn't exactly the kind of job you advertise for in the local press. I'm willing to consider someone else. What you say about Hashem also concerns me. What I like about him is that he is a risk taker. But what attracts me most is that he has scores to settle with Saddam. Remember, we need someone who can walk into the bank to make the withdrawal. Whatever defects Hashem has, he is a first-rate role player. Let's just consider him for the moment. I'll ask around and see if there is anyone else available that can fulfill our requirements."

Kurth quietly considered what Alain had said so far. The more they talked, the more he thought there was at least a remote possibility the operation could be pulled off. He knew Alain would not take any excessive chances. He would dot every "i" and cross every "t" before he decided it was a go. "Let's get back to the German PTT. Do you have anyone in mind?"

Alain smiled enigmatically. "Why are you asking? You know damn well that the only candidate is the man you dealt with on the tap of Tikriti's private line. I can't remember his name."

"You mean Otto Schmidt?"

"Of course. Can you think of a more suitable candidate? I certainly can't."

Kurth thought that Alain could have brought up a possible difficulty. "I'll grant you that Otto supposedly did some unilateral work for us as our agent. The problem is that I never fully trusted Otto. I always felt he was too willing to take risks. I don't like it when people aren't scared about doing things that should scare the shit out of them."

Alain laughed, but had to admit Kurth had a point. "There was never any blow back from the Germans finding out about any of his unilateral efforts on our behalf, was there?" Alain's head moved in quick, birdlike jerking motions, emphasizing his point. This characteristic unnerved people until they got used to it.

"Not that I know of, but that could be because he was sharing things with the BKA (Bundeskriminalamt) and they chose not to question what we were doing."

"Look, Kurth, the simple case is that we have no other candidates that can access the substations and do the tap. What do you think?"

Kurth considered the possible use of Otto for a few moments. Perhaps it was his German ancestry but he would always think things through before answering. "There is one thing in our favor. Otto is within a couple of years of retirement. He might like a tax-free nest egg to use during his retirement. He is certainly worth considering, particularly since there is no one else on the horizon. One more thing in his favor is his knowledge of the Hamburg phone system. He has got to be one of their most senior technicians."

Alain sat in his chair staring at the ceiling as if he was observing something deserving his attention. "Okay, for the time being let's consider Blanton, Schmidt and Samara'i as candidates. We may or may not come up with a substitute for Samara'i. In the meantime, I might sound out Blanton."

"Do you really think it would be wise to reveal to Blanton what we are considering? Maybe we should think this out a little more before running off half-cocked?" Kurth questioned Alain. He was concerned. Alain was getting ahead of himself. What he had described was hardly a workable plan. In fact, at the moment, it was nothing more than an idea.

Alain smirked. "Hey, have a little faith in my judgment. I think I can talk to Blanton without revealing what we actually plan to do. I intend to tell him the agency is thinking about mounting an off-line operation and are considering using only retired personnel with no current connection to the agency."

It was Kurth's turn to smirk. "You think Blanton will buy it?"

"I doubt it but, as you said, the money will be his most important consideration."

"You're right there. Jack's fascination with money is what got him in trouble. He also really loved the job. I think it was losing the chance to do what he loved that ticked him off the most about being forced into retirement."

Alain nodded his agreement. "Okay, I'll sound out Blanton in the most general terms possible. In the meantime, we'll go ahead with the planning."

"Okay by me," Kurth said as got up from his seat to leave. "Give me a call when you want to get together. Good night and thanks for the stimulating evening." Kurth laughed as he opened the door, left the townhouse, and walked to his car. When he opened the door to his car, he looked back at Alain's front door and wondered if retirement had driven Alain to distraction. He shrugged his shoulders and got into his car.

⇥ ⇤

Washington. April 2, 1982.

"Hello."

"Jack?"

"Yeah, who's calling?"

"Jack, it's Alain. I have to see you about something. Let's have lunch."

"That depends, are you buying?"

"Yes, Jack, of course I'm buying," Alain answered. "Can you meet at Clyde's in Tysons Corner today at twelve?"

Blanton smiled as he answered, "Okay, see you soon."

Alain grimaced into the receiver before hanging up. He had called from a pay phone in the Wheaton Plaza mall. He had decided early on that he wanted no tell-tale phone records if anything went wrong. He thought about Jack. It was nice to know that some things never change. Jack was the same as he had always been, an outsider with a total lack of social sensibilities.

A short while later, Jack pulled into Clyde's and parked his car in the parking lot. He was dressed in casual attire that, on Jack, looked shabby. He was the kind of person who looked unkempt in a tuxedo. He entered the restaurant and noted that he had arrived before Alain. After telling the hostess he would wait for his friend, he walked the few steps to the bar and ordered a beer. Alain walked in about ten minutes later. After shaking hands, they followed a trim young lady who showed them to a table. Fortunately, there were no agency officers within eyesight that either of them recognized. While ordering and eating, they spoke about the agency. When they were served coffee, Alain changed the subject.

"Jack, why didn't you ever marry?"

Jack laughed, "You didn't set a good example. You had two failed marriages that I know of. Was there a third?"

"No Jack, two taught me all of the lessons I needed. Look, what are you doing now? I haven't heard from you in some time. Did you decide to go to work at something else?"

Jack toyed with his coffee before answering, "I thought about a second career, but decided against it. I play a lot of golf and go on a fishing trip every year. I have a cousin who has an electronics repair shop near my condo. I sometimes help him out when he is backed up or has a piece of equipment that is troubling him. It works out pretty well since he pays me under the table."

Same old Jack, Alain thought to himself. Doing things under the table was what got him in trouble with the agency. Alain turned serious and lowered his voice.

"Jack, I'm glad to hear you are not tied down. There is a possibility I'm going to run a unilateral operation."

"I thought you retired?" Jack questioned Alain. His surprise was reflected in his voice.

"No one ever retires from our business. If the operation is a go, I will need someone with your skills. I invited you to lunch for two reasons. First, I wanted to find out if you were available to work. Secondly, I wanted to see if you are interested in making some money."

Jack was pensive. In his case, that meant nodding his head as if in deep thought. He had been involved in a couple of operations with Alain and, to the best of his recollection, Alain, while a little on the strange side, was always pretty straight with the people working with him. Still, he had his doubts.

"Look Alain, I find this hard to believe. The agency would never agree to my being on the payroll."

"This operation, if approved, will be off-line. No one will know you were involved except me. No one will have any current connection with the agency. What makes it nicer is that it's tax-free. What do you say?"

"Say to what? So far you have been very lean with specifics. I'd like to know what I'm going to do, where I'm going to do it, and when. In short, what gives?"

Alain didn't recall Jack being so questioning, but that was when he was on the inside. Now he was on the outside, and obviously not going to commit himself until he had more information. "Okay Jack, the operation, if approved, will require a unilateral phone tap. It will also require a device to conceal both a tape recorder and a voice activator. We may also need some disguises. That's about it."

Jack mulled over Alain's proposal briefly before answering. "I see no problem with the phone tap. I assume it will be in a foreign country. Is that right?"

"You got that right, Jack. It's in a foreign country. When you agree and I have the go ahead, I'll let you know where. Since I'm in charge, based on my past career, you can assume the operation will be carried out in Western Europe, not behind the curtain. Any questions?"

"Yes, if this is an off-line operation in Western Europe, you're going to need someone in the local PTT, unless the agency can arrange the tap for you."

"The agency ain't going to arrange anything. We have an old asset in mind that is in a position to provide the needed information and support. We think we can begin in a month or so, once I have the needed approvals."

"How much would I get for my work on this operation?"

"We will pay you expenses, plus one hundred and fifty dollars a day."

Jack stared at Alain and said, "What about two hundred a day?"

Alain thought, *good, he's on board.* "Don't think so cheap. If the operation is a success, you'll get a bonus of twenty-five thousand dollars. All of it will be tax-free."

Alain saw his eyes light up. Jack didn't hesitate answering, "Sounds okay so far."

"Good, that's as much as we can do today. I'll be in touch when, and if, we get a go ahead. You probably will not hear from me for a month or so."

Jack shrugged his shoulders. "So be it."

⋅→═● ●═←⋅

Hamburg. April 15, 1982.

Wafiq Tikriti was seated at his desk enjoying a second cup of coffee while looking over several offers of equipment that had not been sent to him through the Bundespost but passed to him in an obscure restaurant the previous evening. The equipment was needed to expand the production of nerve gas. He was astonished at the prices demanded for some of the items. The phone rang and forced him to divert his attention. Ahmad was on the other end of the line.

"There is someone here from Baghdad who says you are expecting him. He says his name is Haitham Abd al-Nebi."

Wafiq was surprised. He had had a passing acquaintance with Haitham, but had not seen him in several years. Their paths had not crossed much because Haitham was one of Saddam and Zaki's most prized assets. He was always on the move doing tasks for Saddam. He could make his way through Europe, and the rest of the world, with facility. He had the appearance of a polished, professional businessman, at ease internationally, fluent in several languages.

"Let us find out what he wants. Send him in, Ahmad."

Wafiq got up as Ahmad ushered Haitham through the door of the office, "*Ahlan wa salan* (welcome), Haitham, it has been a long time. But tell me, what brings you to Hamburg?"

Haitham's face registered surprise. "It is always good to see an old acquaintance, but I thought Mustafa Naghshabandi told you I would be coming?"

Wafiq was startled. He found it hard to believe that Haitham was the operative sent by Sa'duni. Haitham had to be over fifty. "Mustafa told me that Colonel Sa'duni would be sending someone, but he mentioned no names."

Haitham was amused and it showed on his face. "I assume you are surprised that Zaki would send such an old man."

It was Wafiq's turn to be amused. "Well yes, given the nature of the assignment, I expected a younger man. But I am pleased he chose you since I know you and know you are reliable."

"Thank you for the kind words. Zaki and I both thought an older business type would create less suspicion among our targets."

"Good point. When did you arrive and do you have a place to stay?"

"That has all been taken care of. I will let you know where I am staying later. In the meantime, as far as the Consulate staff is concerned, I am a logistics officer from the Ministry of Defense who has been assigned here to facilitate the purchase and shipment of crucial military items. While I am being based here because of the port, I will spend a lot of time traveling so I will only be here from time to time. Now, my first question, is about the man who brought me to your office. Is he someone you trust implicitly?"

Wafiq was impressed that Haitham wasted no time getting down to business. This was not the usual practice among Middle Easterners. "Very trustworthy.

He serves as my bodyguard sometimes when I am forced to handle large sums of money, particularly large withdrawals from banks. He is honest and you will soon learn that he worships the ground Saddam walks on."

"Good. There may be a time when we might have to make use of him. If you are not too busy, maybe we can review my assignment here, what the targets are, and some ideas on how we can go about getting the information our superiors in Baghdad think they need."

"When you arrived, I was looking at some offers of equipment. Since the items are embargoed due to Europe's pose of neutrality on the war, the suppliers have raised the prices on key items by fifty percent. Baghdad will not be happy. If the media here is correct, we are in a tight spot as far as the economy is concerned."

Haitham rubbed his mustache with the thumb and forefinger of his left hand. "That's a pretty accurate statement. We are getting some help from some of the Arab states and the Saudis are working on putting together a substantial Arab aid package."

"Mustafa told me in general terms about possible Arab financial aid. Why don't you explain what you intend to do while you are here and what you want me to do to help. We can then go to lunch if you like. I can clean up what has to be done today after lunch."

Haitham nodded his approval. "Good, let's get started. I have been put in control of all Directorate General of Intelligence assets in Europe. The DGI has been tasked by Saddam to monitor all activity by Iraqi groups in Europe that are actively engaged in plots against him. We are to identify all the important opposition leaders and their key personnel. I must provide Baghdad with estimates of the capabilities of the various opposition organizations."

"Identifying everyone may take some time. Estimating the capabilities of the opposition will be easy," Wafiq responded.

Haitham nodded his agreement. "While I do not believe that opposition expatriate Iraqi organizations pose any danger to the regime in themselves, the important point for us to determine is what, if anything, our enemies are doing with these organizations. A prime concern in Baghdad is uncovering any Iranian attempts to manipulate them."

"I had not considered that angle. It could be important. What are your specific concerns?" Wafiq asked.

"We are most concerned about Iraqi Shias. The large Iranian mosque in Hamburg is of interest. We must determine if the Iranians are using the mosque to organize Iraqi Shia against the government. So far, the Iranians have not been successful in their attempts to goad the Shia in southern Iraq to revolt against the government. In the beginning of the war, there were a few assassinations of Iraqi officials by members of the *Da'wa* party, but these efforts did not produce much support for an insurrection against Baghdad. There is an additional critical question. What role is the CIA playing in supporting Iraqi opposition activity in Europe?"

Wafiq was surprised, if not astounded, at the paranoia inherent in what Haitham was saying. "From what I know of Iraqi opposition activity in Europe, it is not worth a barrel of pig shit."

Haitham's laugh was a loud guffaw that must have been heard in the rest of the Consulate. "It is not what you think my friend, it is what Saddam thinks, and he thinks we may have a problem. I will be traveling for a few days to assess Directorate General of Intelligence capabilities in Western Europe. When I get back we will take a hard look at the Hamburg area. I have two Iraqi Shia recruits and I intend to have them spend a lot of time in the local mosque to see if they can uncover anything." Haitham paused and when Wafiq did not offer any comment, he said, "Why don't we have lunch and continue this conversation afterwards."

Wafiq got up from his desk. "Good, I know an excellent restaurant nearby. Ahmad can drive us."

Haitham nodded his agreement as he got out of his chair to join Wafiq. "I am at your disposal." As they left the office, Haitham continued, "You will be receiving instructions by courier regarding how you will fund my activities from the government account."

Wafiq looked at Haitham intently but said nothing.

Chapter 3

Norbeck. April 26, 1982.

ALAIN WAS SITTING at the kitchen table making notes. He thought he was making serious progress. Jack Blanton would be relatively easy to bring on board since he had responded positively to the mention of respectable sums of money. Alain had also put in a call to Hashem Samara'i and left a message on his answering machine. Hashem had called back almost immediately. From their conversation, Alain concluded that Samara'i was not exactly enjoying retirement. Hashem pressed Alain on why he had called but Alain put him off by asking if he was available soon to get together for lunch. When Hashem agreed, Alain ended the conversation by saying that he would call back during the following week. Alain assumed Samara'i had called him from his condo in Virginia. At lunch, he would emphasize to Hashem that he should only use a pay phone. In the meantime, he and Kurth would meet and consider the steps he had taken to date. He picked up the phone and dialed Kurth's office number. When Kurth's secretary put him on the line, Alain told him he had contacted Hashem and would be having lunch with him the following week.

"You seem to have been busy since we had dinner together. What about Jack?" Kurth asked with an unmistakable note of concern in his voice.

"I saw him. We need to talk."

"How about lunch?"

"No, I think it would be better for you to come to my place. How about Saturday night?"

"Wait a minute." Kurth checked his calendar. "I must host a dinner for two executives from Germany Saturday evening. Can we make it Friday night?"

"Okay by me. One last thing, are you planning to travel to Germany in the near future?"

"Yes, I have to go over during the second week in May. Why?"

"We can talk about that on Friday, but I think you can guess."

"Otto," Kurth mumbled. He smiled to himself. "You know, Alain, these Friday night dinners are playing havoc with my womanizing."

Alain made an obscene noise into the phone before continuing, "Keep your libido in check until we pull this off. I'll see you Friday night."

If we even make the attempt, Kurth thought to himself before hanging up.

→→━● ●━←←

Washington. April 30, 1982.

Friday was a beautiful spring day. Kurth quit work early and took a long walk around the reflecting pool in front of the Lincoln Memorial. When he joined the CIA, most of the Directorate of Plans, usually referred to as the Clandestine Service, was located on the south side of the reflecting pool. Judith Coplon, an NKVD penetration of the Department of Justice, had met with her Soviet case officer on a bench by the reflecting pool in full view of any CIA personnel who happened to be looking out of the temporary building windows. Kurth had always thought that was one of the more amusing anecdotes of the intelligence business.

He drove from Washington, stopping only to pick up a bottle of scotch before heading for Alain's townhouse. Alain greeted him at the door and, after accepting the scotch with his usual grace, built them both martinis. Alain wondered why Kurth always brought him a bottle of scotch when he knew Alain was addicted to martinis.

The dinner passed pleasantly enough. Alain had prepared shrimp, mussels, and clams in a marinara sauce served over pasta. Kurth ate with relish, wishing he had taken the trouble to learn the basics about cooking. Kurth had tried to draw Alain out during the course of the dinner, but Alain had insisted that business wait until they were having coffee and cognac. When they had finished eating, Alain brought a pot of coffee to the table, filled two cups, then produced the promised cognac.

After Kurth had a sip of his cognac, he said, "Okay, Alain, what's the current state of your planning?"

Kurth's question hung in the air while Alain smiled enigmatically at him. He could tell that Alain was excited about something because of his birdlike agitation. Finally, Alain said, "I've talked to Jack Blanton. He is on board. As you know, I've also phoned Hashem, but have yet to see him. I proposed lunch and he agreed. I didn't want to go any further until I had the chance to talk to you." Alain paused. "We both have some doubts about Hashem, but I can come up with no alternative. What do you think?" Alain put the onus on Kurth, "If you can't accept Hashem, can you come up with a suitable replacement?"

Kurth grimaced, deep in thought for a few seconds. "I confess I've made little or no effort to come up with a substitute, but then I can't for the life of me think of anyone else we can approach. We need someone to translate Arabic and someone who can pose as an Iraqi. Hashem is the only person I can think of who can perform both functions. I would feel much better about Hashem if I was sure he would maintain operational discipline."

Alain had to admit that Kurth had a valid point. Hashem had a reputation of doing what he wanted to, sometimes counter to instructions from more senior officers. This had led to his encouraged early retirement. Hashem was a man who did not wear his bitterness well. Any conversation with him was punctuated with references to the various assholes that had done him in. On one occasion Alain had tried to get him to look at life in a more positive light, but to no avail.

"I have to agree with you, Kurth. We don't have to make a final decision on him until after you get back from Germany. In the meantime, I'll see him and find out if he is free to work on our project full time. We would want to compartmentalize him from everyone else in the operation except me. If he got to know that you and Blanton were involved, he would be very suspicious."

"Well, Alain, if we have to use him, we have to use him. If we do, you will have to maintain some semblance of control with him. Why don't we forget about Hashem for the moment? I want to hear more about how you think we are going to pull this off." Kurth's tone registered his doubts about the whole operation.

Alain got up from his chair to fetch a pencil and a note pad. He sat down, wrote Otto on the note pad, underlined it for emphasis, then said to Kurth, "On your upcoming trip to Germany, I want you to sound out Otto."

"Fine, I don't think I'll have any trouble seeing Otto. But what do I say to him? 'Hey Otto, you want to rob a Swiss Bank?'"

Alain smiled fleetingly, "Tell him what I told Blanton. You are involved in the planning of a sensitive off-line CIA operation. Emphasize that if the decision is made to go ahead with the operation, those involved will be well paid. Warn him about the importance of security. Because the operation is off-line, it will pay exceptionally well. He will be able to make up to one hundred thousand marks for little work. The key here is security. There is no backstopping for the operation and none of the funds will be vouchered. Explain to him that when the operation is approved, we will pay him an initial ten thousand marks to help us out. You will be the only one seeing Otto. He will be compartmentalized from everyone else."

"That may not be possible. Won't he have to confer with Blanton?"

Alain considered Kurth's question for a few moments. "I don't think so. You and I can relay messages between Otto and Blanton. There is no reason for Blanton to know of your involvement at all. If Blanton and Otto must meet, we'll cross that bridge when we come to it. Wasn't Otto involved in the old tap on the Iraqi Consulate?"

"Yes, but the tap was done with the BKA who worked directly with the local exchange. The BKA passed us copies of the transcripts."

"That's true, Kurth, but Otto should know a lot about the phone lines."

"Alain, this is the first priority. If Otto can't manage the tap, we have no operation. I'm pretty sure we can't do it without Otto's help. It would require an entry into the Consulate. Remember, Wafiq lives on the top floor."

"We need some more cognac," Alain said as he poured some into each of their snifters. "We have one essential element necessary to succeed, the account number."

"If it is still the account number," Kurth interjected.

"I've been thinking about that, Kurth. Usually the only time bank account numbers change is as a result of a merger or a takeover. This hasn't happened with the Banque Suisse."

Kurth stared at his friend. At this point he didn't know whether it would be best to encourage him or discourage him. "Okay, Alain, I suspect the risk that the account number has changed is an acceptable risk. We have been talking about a telephone tap on the Iraqi Consulate. After the account number, telephone coverage of the Iraqi Consulate is the second essential. We must know how Wafiq handles withdrawals when they are executed by someone other than himself."

Alain leaned back in his chair and stared at the ceiling. "Then we agree, the phone tap is the key to the operation. It will provide the information we need." Alain smiled wryly at Kurth. "Without it, we don't have an operation."

"Agreed," Kurth answered. His personal consideration of the operation was not nearly as enthusiastic as Alain's. While the account number was almost certainly still valid, getting the needed information from the telephone tap was a big gamble.

"Okay Alain, let's assume the account number is still valid and we succeed in tapping the line. If we get the necessary information from the tap, what next?"

"That's the easy part," Alain answered, a self-satisfied smirk on his face. "Hashem, or whoever takes his place, will be the one to actually show up at the Banque Suisse to make the withdrawal. We have a lot to learn before Hashem can walk into the bank and pull it off. We don't have the slightest idea of how Wafiq currently handles these withdrawals, but with any luck we should learn enough from the tap."

"If we can get the tap installed," Kurth answered. He was suspicious. With Alain it was sometimes difficult to determine whether you were being convinced or conned.

Alain made a mental note of the tone in Kurth's voice. "Okay, given your concerns, I think it's a good idea that you continue to play the devil's advocate. There is one other role that will be important. One of us will have to pose as Wafiq on the telephone conversations with the bank. I do not recall what language he used when we had the tap. I suspect it was German, as I recall he knows some German. It depends on which one of us can best mimic his voice."

"That's another big problem you've introduced, Alain."

"If this operation is going to work we must identify all the big questions. Hopefully we'll be able to eliminate them over the course of time. We may get lucky with the take from the tap." Alain looked up at Kurth and, before he could respond, added with a smile, "If we manage to tap the right phone."

Kurth laughed softly and toyed with his snifter. He was less sure of things with each new uncertainty. Alain was perhaps relying too much on the phone tap to produce the information needed. He wondered how Alain felt about it.

"The more engrossed we become with this plan, Alain, the more it depends on what we get out of the tap. It occurs to me that, considering the Iraqis are at war with Iran, Wafiq may be more secure. For instance, what if instead of phoning the Banque Suisse with information on the person making the withdrawal, he uses couriers or DHL to send the information to his contact in the bank?"

Alain scowled at Kurth. "I doubt if either Wafiq or the bank would consider such an arrangement sufficient. The bank would want to confirm everything with their client. Wafiq would want to make sure nothing goes wrong. Look, this is why the tap is essential. As I told you before, if the tap doesn't produce the needed info, we call the whole thing off. The essential first step is for you to try and get Otto on board. There is no way we can mount a tap without his assistance. I will sound out Hashem, but not give him much in the way of specifics. That must await your successful return from Germany. Incidentally, are you going to see Ulla and the kids on this trip?"

"Yes, in fact, I already called her. I'm going to spend a couple of days with them."

Alain had known and liked Ulla. She had finally divorced Kurth because she could not put up with his active pursuit of other women. Ulla was very attractive. Alain mused that she was perhaps one of the most beautiful women he had ever met. She also possessed a distinctively vibrant personality. He wondered if Kurth ever thought seriously of getting back together with her. He knew she had not remarried.

"How are you and Ulla getting along?"

Kurth looked at Alain sharply, a little surprised at the question. "Pretty well. At first we were careful around the kids to not display any undue animosity, but things are pretty relaxed now. We have even gone out to dinner or a concert on occasion. Why do you ask?"

"I always thought it strange that neither of you ever remarried."

"Alain, my friend, women are one thing, marriage is another. I have never thought seriously about another marriage."

"It might be because you never met anyone who could be compared to Ulla."

Kurth almost blushed. "You might be right," he answered, then sat quietly, briefly lost in his own thoughts.

Alain left Kurth alone for a few moments. He decided he had given Kurth enough to chew on for one night. "I think we covered all the ground we can tonight. Why don't you call me when you know your travel plans? We will get together as soon as you get back from Germany. I'll go ahead and have lunch with Hashem and put some more ideas down on paper."

"Good. I'll work on Otto. I have some second thoughts about him."

Alain was immediately alert. "Like what?"

Kurth turned thoughtful, "Suppose Otto reports our approach to the BKA. Alain, I think that given the war between Iran and Iraq, the BKA would consider it natural for the agency to tap the phone of one of Saddam's close associates."

"Yeah, they may and they may not. Suppose they call in the Chief of Station and question him about the tap on Wafiq's private line?"

Kurth frowned. "I assume he would deny it. I suspect the Germans would question the COS in general terms. Otto could only identify me, and I am gainfully employed by a company that does business in Germany. We may be worrying too much. I think that given Otto's impending retirement, he would not want to put the money we are offering him at risk by squealing to the BKA. We could also pay him by the month as long as the tap continues to function. That would give him good reason not to expose the tap."

"You're probably right, Kurth. Paying Otto by the month is also a very good idea. Let's call it a night."

Chapter 4

Washington. May 4, 1982.

AT LUNCH WITH Hashem, Alain explained that the agency had contacted him and proposed an off-line operation. If eventually approved, there would be an operational absolute that there could be no direct involvement of active duty CIA officers. Hashem had been very curious, trying to get answers to specific questions. Despite his questioning Alain like a cross-eyed chicken trying to nab a kernel of corn, Alain had kept him at a verbal arm's length. The lunch was worth the price. From his conversation with Hashem, Alain determined that he was having trouble living on his retirement annuity and making enough money on the side to support his lavish life style consisting primarily of expensive women. In some of his operational accountings, Hashem had demonstrated a great deal of imagination in covering up his private peccadilloes. These accountings, and the use of safe houses for his liaisons, were the cause of his early retirement.

Hashem had convinced some of his important Middle Eastern contacts that his retirement was only a cover. To date, he had been unable to benefit financially from this subterfuge. Hashem told Alain that, unless some lucrative sinecure dropped out of the sky, he was available. Alain kept him in the dark, telling him that he was not authorized to divulge any additional facts until the operation was approved. Alain instructed Hashem that he should only use a pay phone to contact him, adding, "Let's act like we know how to run a secure operation."

Hashem had wanted to know something about the target. Alain told him that, if and when the operation was approved, he would have to relocate to

Europe. Hashem had then fixed him with a steely, suspicious stare and asked where. Alain had smiled enigmatically and told him he would let him know.

→▬◉ ◉▬←

Norbeck. May 12, 1982.

It had been over a week since Kurth had called him from Dulles before departing on a Lufthansa flight to Frankfurt. He wondered why Kurth hadn't called again. He looked at his watch. It was a little after six o'clock. He got up from his chair to fix a martini before grilling a fillet of rockfish he had bought for dinner. The phone rang as he was putting a large olive in his martini. It was Kurth.

"How are things, Alain?"

"They're okay here. I talked to the other player and he is willing, but very curious."

"Who wouldn't be?" Kurth laughed into the phone. "Our German contact is okay within limits."

"Like what?"

"He naturally assumed why I wanted to talk to him. I didn't go into any details, but insisted he keep our conversation to himself."

"What do you think, Kurth, can we count on him?"

"I give that a tentative yes. I will see him again on Friday. I'm going to spend the weekend with Ulla and the kids, then fly home on Monday. I'll call you on Tuesday."

Alain hung up and looked out the window. It had begun to rain. He decided to go for a walk. There was something cleansing about walking in the rain. A walk would also give him time to ponder all of the recent developments. He put on his raincoat, left the townhouse, and walked out to the access road that runs parallel to Georgia Avenue. He turned right and headed south. As if on command, the rain stopped and the sun broke through. A breeze stirred the trees. Sunshine on the wet leaves made them glisten like living jewels. Alain thought that between the cleansing rain and the glistening of the wet leaves he was halfway to a poem, that is, if he was inclined to write poetry.

The sun heating his neck surfaced thoughts of the long, humid summer that lay ahead. Well, maybe he would get the chance to spend it in Hamburg. He hoped Kurth would be more definite when he saw him the following week. Having Otto on board would remove another major variable.

The only other pressing question remaining was Hashem. Could they exert enough control over him to keep him from screwing up the operation? He figured that only he and Kurth needed to know the full details. Otto would know there was a tap on Wafiq's phone. If they could do the tap without Otto and Jack meeting, they would be able to keep the origin of the tapped phone from Blanton. If they had to use Hashem, he would know that it was Wafiq's phone being tapped. Hashem, being Hashem, would speculate on how the tap was put in place unilaterally. Alain thought that he would have to handle his curiosity. He planned to tell him that the BKA was passing the tapes to the German Station under the table. Since Hashem was aware of the previous tap that had been done by the BKA, he probably would not question it being reinstituted. Alain could think of a couple of plausible explanations as to why the BKA would agree to the tap. Given the role allegedly played by the BKA and the need for absolute security, he hoped that Hashem would accept the story.

Alain decided he must arrange things so that Hashem would not accidentally run into any of the others involved in the operation. He would not bring Hashem to Hamburg until after Blanton had installed the tap and left town. Hashem could find a place on the outer fringes of the city. He wanted some distance between the two of them. Under no circumstances would he have Hashem come to his place. They would meet only in restaurants.

He and Hashem would be the only two who would remain in Hamburg. Alain would be the LP (listening post) keeper. He would deliver the tapes for translation to Hashem who would pass them, with the transcript, back to him. Kurth would only be needed, in the first instance, to locate the LP and then to practice imitating Wafiq's voice speaking to his banker in Geneva. While Alain was fluent in German, his accent was definitely American. Kurth would have less trouble imitating Wafiq's accent. If Kurth couldn't come close, they would have to use Hashem. He was good at mimicking voices, but using him for this would complicate the operation. When they deployed to get set up in Hamburg it would just be Alain and Kurth. Blanton would join Alain as soon as he was established in the LP location. Blanton would be finished once the tap was functioning.

Alain had considered a cover for his being in Hamburg. There was a chance his presence might come to the attention of his former colleagues in the agency or the BKA. He had tentatively decided to say he was writing a book on a failed operation that was run out of Hamburg during his final tour in Germany. Stasi, the East German intelligence service, had uncovered the operation and ran it back against them for a few months. Alain planned to write a novel about the operation. Since the BKA was also involved in the operation, if asked by either BKA officers who knew him or by his former colleagues, he could engage them in a detailed conversation about the operation and ask for any suggestions they might wish to make.

When he walked past the Manor Country Club, he decided to return to his townhouse and make some more notes on the book idea. He walked back briskly, feeling confidant that they would eventually go ahead with the operation. He felt invigorated. *After all*, he thought to himself, *how many guys get to rob a Swiss bank?*

By six-thirty the next morning, Alain, an early riser, was downstairs drinking orange juice and patiently waiting for his coffee maker to finish gurgling out the morning dose of caffeine. He went to the front door and picked up the Washington Post. There were no startling international developments on the front page. Alain closed the door, walked to the kitchen, and poured his first cup of coffee. He decided to fix bacon and scrambled eggs. He was frying the bacon when the phone rang. It was Kurth.

"I hope I didn't wake you up," Kurth said before Alain could say hello. "I thought I'd call early and try to line you up for lunch. Can you make it?"

"Sure, shall we meet at the regular place?"

"How about one o'clock? I can't imagine that I'll be tied up at the office, but I will call if there is a problem."

Alain was very curious about the final meeting with Otto. "Everything come out okay in Germany?"

There was a pause at the other end, "I'll talk about it at lunch. See you at one."

Alain didn't want to wait that long. "Come on, Kurth, don't keep me in suspense."

"You know the old agency saw in cable traffic, 'operation a success, details follow'."

Alain smiled in relief as he hung up the phone. He finished his morning chores but could hardly contain himself until one. He was relieved when he finally was able to set out for their luncheon. Kurth beat him to the restaurant.

"Either they change the menu here or we find another restaurant," Kurth said as Alain sat down.

Alain laughed, "Are you suggesting The Cat has lost its enchantment?"

The owner must have heard them and immediately came to their table. "You gentlemen know we change the menu regularly. We also always have specials, and today is more special than usual. We have broiled grouper with a crab sauce."

Kurth answered first, "I'll take it. It's a change."

The owner frowned before writing down his order.

"Likewise for me, Charles," Alain said. Charles rewarded him with a smile, but he frowned at Kurth as he departed.

"Be careful, Kurth, it doesn't pay to upset anyone who is responsible for feeding you," Alain said with a faint smile.

"I wasn't serious. Look on the bright side, maybe the next time we come they will have a different menu."

"Enough with the menus. Let me know about Otto," Alain said. He sat back in his chair and waited for an answer.

Kurth paused. He drank some water before answering.

"Otto is on board. I told him there was a sensitive operation that appeared to be on track. It was going to be run off-line which made it nice for those involved since we would be paid in cash with no records being kept of the payments."

Alain interrupted, "What was Otto's reaction?"

"I could tell from his expression that he was interested. He asked me if the BKA was directly involved."

"Knowing Otto, that's a legitimate concern. What did you tell him?"

"I told him that no one involved has any current connection with our old agency. They are all retired. He seemed impressed with this. I explained to him that the BKA was aware of what was going on, but in no way wanted to be informed officially or unofficially about the operation."

Alain rubbed his chin and pursed his lips, an old habit. "What about his demeanor? Any body language?"

Kurth silently considered Alain's question for a few moments. "I'd say for the most part his expression was one of quiet consideration. I was glad he was concerned about the BKA. I would have been suspicious had he not brought up the subject. He did appear to be satisfied with my explanation. His most noticeable reaction occurred when we discussed money."

"Please explain," Alain interrupted like an interrogator.

"I told him that he would be paid well for what little he had to do. I said we would be running the operation for about three months, but certainly no more than six months. If the operation succeeds, we will all be paid a bonus. In his case, I could guarantee him a bonus of at least forty thousand marks. I emphasized to him that all the money he made would be tax-free which made him grin in appreciation."

"Did he ask for any specifics?"

They were interrupted by the arrival of their lunch. Kurth sampled the wine and the fish before answering Alain's question.

"Of course, Otto is not one to jump before he is sure of where he is going to land. He obviously assumed we needed him for a phone tap. I told him that we would want him to help with a single phone tap. He asked me whose phone we wanted to tap and when we planned to do it. I told him I did not know yet but I could tell him that it would be the phone of a Middle Eastern diplomat. This seemed to satisfy him because he breathed a sigh of relief. He said okay, and suggested I get in touch with him about specifics as soon as possible so that he could find out if there would be a problem with the line we wish to tap."

"That's where you left him?"

Kurth answered, "I told him I would be in touch with him as soon as we got a thumbs up on the operation. He asked me when that might happen and I told him it would probably take a month or so."

"Hmm," Alain murmured more to himself, "It was good you spoke of a time delay. I think it would be a good idea to let this lie dormant for a month or so to see if the BKA questions the agency on the operation. If they do, it will prove we have a problem"

"But if they don't, we still can't be certain Otto has not reported my approach to him to the BKA. Remember, even if the BKA mentions my name, the agency may not question me about such an approach. This is an issue on which we could be permanently in the dark."

"That's true, Kurth, we will just have to rely on your assessment of Otto."

Kurth was less than ecstatic. While Alain was considering all possibilities, the question of Otto's ultimate loyalty already loomed as a critical counter-intelligence question. Despite the potential problem of Otto, Kurth knew that Alain had done a lot of thinking about the operation. He was good at such things, but could at times take an approach that bordered on the irrational.

"I agree that we keep this on the back burner for the time being, then what?"

Alain wondered about Kurth's concern over the operation. In the past, an operation like this one would generate more enthusiasm. Perhaps Kurth was a little too well off in his current job despite its boredom.

"Why don't we let this go until the middle of next month, unless you are planning a trip to Germany sooner?"

"I talked to our district manager this morning and he told me that the only travel to Germany in the near future would be to attend a technical conference which I believe is scheduled for the end of June or the beginning of July."

"That dovetails with what I have in mind, Kurth." Alain polished off the last of his grouper. "In the meantime, I'll see Blanton and go over the technical requirements with him so you will be able to discuss the tap in detail with Otto. I'll also check in with Hashem to make sure he is still available. I'll tell them both that mid-July looks like the start date for the operation."

Kurth's expression displayed concern. "Hashem is known to the Iraqis. How do we handle that problem?"

"I've thought about it and I think we should have him find digs somewhere far from the Iraqi Consulate. That said, the chances of them spotting him are fairly remote. Also, don't forget Hamburg is a free port and, as such, has a large Middle Eastern population. I don't think that what we used to call the active opposition is going to cause us any problems."

Kurth's wry grin displayed no humor. "Don't write the locals off so readily. Your scorn of local police and counter intelligence organizations has gotten you in trouble in the past."

Alain was taken aback by Kurth's comment. His expression telegraphed his displeasure. "Look, Kurth, so far I have been extremely careful about security. I also believe we both have learned from past mistakes. In fact, as you know, in our business you learn more from your failures than your successes."

Kurth laughed just enough to cut any tension. "What about cover?"

"You are okay. You do not have to spend much time on the operation. Any trip you make to Germany will be on your company's account. Blanton is only needed to set things up, so he should be spending just a few days in Germany. Hashem and I are the problems. I believe I have come up with a good cover for my presence. Do you remember operation BLACKROOT?"

"How can I forget? Stasi handed us our asses on a silver platter. What about it?"

"My cover will be that I'm in Hamburg for a couple months to do research on a book I'm writing about BLACKROOT."

Kurth stared at Alain in disbelief. "That will make the agency as happy as steamed clams."

Alain held up his hands to cut off further comment from Kurth. "Well, I certainly would submit anything I wrote to the agency Publications Review Board. This might never come up since I'm only doing research for a book."

Kurth had to admit it might be a usable cover if Alain were ever put in a position where he would be forced to explain why he was spending so much time in Hamburg. The fact that most of BLACKROOT was run out of Hamburg would also fit his cover.

"Okay, Alain, anything else?"

"Yes, but I'll check it out with Blanton first. I assume I will have to get an apartment close to the Iraqi Consulate. When you see Otto, get him to tell you where I will have to live and work. Once you get the information from Otto, you might see if there is anything available in that precise area. I will be talking to Blanton before your next trip to Germany and he can let me know the technical things you must discuss with Otto."

"What about Hashem?"

"I've given the problem of Hashem considerable thought. We don't want him running into any Iraqis, particularly Iraqi officials. He most certainly knows who Wafiq Tikriti is, but I do not know if Tikriti would recognize Hashem if he saw him. It might be a good idea to locate him on the outskirts of Hamburg, but close to the U-Bahn. By the time he arrives, the take from the operation will be time sensitive so I figure on delivering the tapes to him and getting translations every few days. What do you think?"

Kurth wasn't exactly sure what to think. It was clear to him that Alain had pretty much concluded how the operation would be run. "Well yes, Alain, if we have no other choice than to use Hashem, then I have to agree we want distance between the two of you. The fewer meetings you have the better. Locating him on the outskirts of Hamburg is a good idea. Do you think he will buy your comment that the operation is actually agency-sponsored?"

Alain considered Kurth's question. It occurred to him that Kurth seemed to be looking for reasons not to go through with the operation. He had best try and put him at ease.

"I would think so. Remember, my dear Kurth, I will be delivering the tapes to him every few days. He will know almost immediately that the tap is on the Iraqi Consulate. He must assume that the agency is doing this with the cooperation of the BKA. He knows the BKA had a tap on the Consulate before but had to remove it. Since he knows about that, this arrangement would make sense to him. I doubt he will seriously consider the possibility that we have mounted an independent tap operation against the Consulate." Alain paused while he drained his wine glass. "Our problem with Hashem is keeping him out of circulation for the duration of the operation. Given his well earned reputation for womanizing, one can only assume that most of the time his brains are between his legs."

Kurth smiled and responded, "Right you are on the latter issue. I remember he got in some trouble about four or five years ago when a trim young lady in the Near East Division complained to the inspector general about his unwanted advances. Let's hope he can cool it for a couple of months."

"Yeah, it's always the stupid things that screw up an operation, and I don't mean that just figuratively. Well, I don't think we can accomplish anything else today. Let's pay the check and get out of here. I'll call you after I talk to Hashem and Blanton."

"Okay, Alain, I'll call you if, for some reason or other, I have to travel."

Chapter 5

Norbeck. June 4, 1982.

ALAIN CALLED HASHEM Samara'i and had a brief, cryptic conversation with him. Alain told him the deal would be approved and the preliminary work would be done by the second week in July. He told Hashem he would be needed shortly after everything was up and running. Alain also told him that he was calling to make sure he would be available. Samara'i said he would. He asked no questions, but did express concern about how much he was going to get out of his participation. Alain emphasized the size of his bonus if and when the operation went ahead. Samara'i wanted more specifics. Alain promised to buy him lunch and explain everything in detail as soon as they got marching orders. Hashem threatened to walk out if he wasn't satisfied. Alain merely replied knowingly that he didn't think he would back out once he heard the specifics.

After Alain hung up his expression spoke volumes about his feelings for Hashem. He could only wonder if they were making a mistake in counting on him for the most critical part of the operation. He and Kurth were in a bind. They knew of no one else who could take Hashem's place. Alain realized he would have his hands full keeping Hashem from drawing unwanted attention to his lifestyle. Hashem would be a major topic in his next conversation with Kurth. He walked home from the Leisure World Shopping Center where he had made the call. Since there was nothing more to do for the moment, he went out in the kitchen and fixed a martini. While he was stirring the ingredients, it occurred to him that they might locate Samara'i in a town or city some distance from Hamburg.

Alain was very concerned about what Hashem's reaction would be when he learned that the tapes he was to transcribe were from a tap on Wafiq Tikriti's private line. One point in their favor was that Hashem would figure there was no way Alain could have unilaterally put a tap on the line. This would bolster Alain's pitch to him that this was a sanctioned off-line operation. There was a real question of how long the cover story would hold up, but if they were lucky they might get the information they needed after a few weeks and that would allow them to wrap things up quickly. Alain shrugged his shoulders. He was satisfied. While his career with the agency had been modest, it had taught him the need for operational security. Whatever the agency owed him would be paid back when he used his training in operational skills to make himself a rich man. He took his martini into the family room and turned on the television.

⋅→▐▶ ◀▌◀⋅

Tysons Corner. June 7, 1982.

"Jack, I called you and set up this lunch because I want you to ask me questions about the telephone tap part of this operation." Alain made this suggestion to Blanton after they ordered lunch in Blanton's favorite restaurant, Clyde's. Blanton looked at Alain with a bemused expression on his face.

"Well, for starters, where are we doing this phone tap?"

"It will be in Germany."

"If you have the cooperation of the BKA, it will be a snap."

Alain shook his head. "The BKA doesn't want to know about it. It is against their law for the protection of the constitution."

Blanton was concerned. "You're going to do this unilaterally?"

"In a sense yes, let's just say the BKA will close its eyes. The German Station will not even know what is going on. No serving agency staffers are actively involved, but we do have some capabilities."

Blanton hoped he appeared as perturbed as he felt. "Look Dembray, all you have told me is that you plan to tap a telephone in Germany. Can you at least give me some idea where the phone is located? Can we gain access to the phone?"

"Take it easy, Jack. We can't get at the phone in the target installation, but we have the capability of gaining access to the local junction box, or whatever you call it. You know, those street junction boxes that all the phone lines in the immediate area feed into. I assume we need to obtain a listening post in the same area."

Blanton looked at Alain with a blank expression. "For the sake of this discussion, I assume that you can access the local junction box that contains the line you want to tap. Is this the case?"

"Yes," Alain replied immediately.

"Okay, you have two options, but first let me explain. Within your Maryland area code are a very large number of exchanges." Blanton drew a pen out of his shirt pocket. "This is an exchange within the area code." Jack drew a big square on a piece of paper. "Each exchange will have several terminals. Each terminal will handle several thousand pairs, or for your benefit, phone lines." Blanton drew four circles each with lines going back to the square representing the exchange. "Each terminal has a number of local junction boxes that handle a couple hundred pairs." Blanton drew lines from one of the circles representing a terminal to four triangles. "These triangles represent those local junction boxes that you see telephone company personnel working on. It will be important to determine which local junction box services the target. Your first requirement is to have your asset tell us which local junction box services the phone you wish to tap. Is your asset in a position to do this?"

Alain tried to conceal his discomfort as he looked at Blanton. The agency techs had always irked him because they could display technical knowledge beyond his comprehension. "Yes, our asset can do what you say with ease. He is a very experienced phone company employee in the target area."

Blanton rubbed his chin with his left hand. "Then it's pretty simple. Have your asset produce a map of the area serviced by the junction box that contains the target phone line."

"I can't say for sure that he can do that."

"If he can access the junction box, he can get you a map of the area serviced by the junction box. If he can access the junction box, he can also locate where the target pairs are hooked up. I told you there are two options. The first is to rent a listening post in the area served by the target junction box. Be it an apartment or whatever, but a listening post with a live telephone line already in it is the best option. If you can only find a listening post with no telephone, we may have a problem. You will have to have a line run into it. This may take some time, and there may be no unused pairs in the target junction box." Blanton leaned back in his chair and carefully examined Alain's expression. "You might find an LP with a phone line but the service has been cut off for some time. Your man in the telephone company can tell you if there is a problem in reactivating such a line."

If Blanton thought he was presenting Alain with serious problems, it didn't show in the pleased look on Alain's face. Kurth could sort all this out with Otto during his next visit to Germany.

"Let's assume we have an LP with a line into it from the target junction box. What next?"

Blanton looked somewhat incredulous, but answered positively. "If that is the case, and your asset has direct access to the target junction box, it's pretty simple. All he has to do is access the rear of the target junction box and bridge the target pair to the pair coming from your listening post. In effect, your listening post telephone line would then function like an extension of the target telephone line. If your asset is any good, he can conceal the bridge between the two lines. Make a note to bring this up with him. You don't want another lineman reporting something strange he saw while wiring a pair in the box. One last point, once the bridge is made you will not be able to use the telephone in the listening post, but I suppose you know that."

"Yes, it was like that with a tap we had in Vienna. What next?"

"That's where I come in. I would run the line into an actuator that would be wired to a tape recorder. Quick question, will the actuator and tape recorder be concealed?"

"Yes, Jack, they will have to be concealed."

Blanton considered the additional problem of concealment briefly before speaking. "If you can afford it, I would recommend a Kudelski tape recorder. They are the best, absolutely silent running, and you can set it so a tape lasts for two, four or six hours with little degeneration in the sound quality for the increased coverage. You may remember we used the Kudelski in desk drawers when we didn't want the person we were talking with to suspect he was being taped. A new Kudelski tape recorder will set you back a couple thousand marks, but it's worth it. I might be able to find a used one on the cheap." Blanton took a sip of coffee and, when Alain said nothing, he asked, "Any other questions?"

Alain thought for a moment before he answered. "Okay, assume we have successfully tapped the target phone. My only concern is whether the tap could be easily uncovered. We wouldn't want to embarrass both the BKA and the CIA."

Blanton's expression reflected disdain for ops officers who understood little about the fine points of technical operations and could care less. "Look, Alain, a phone line has about forty volts D.C. When you pick up the receiver the line voltage drops to about five volts. I would use an actuator with extremely high impedance. It turns on the tape recorder when the target receiver is lifted. Because of the high impedance, the opening of the listening post line will lower the voltage very little, making the tap difficult to detect."

"Will there be any problems involved in concealing the tape recorder and that other thing, the actuator?" Alain asked. He knew these two items must be concealed, but he hadn't given any thought about how to do it.

Blanton shook his head. "No problem. I'll take care of it when we do the installation. Any other questions?"

"Yes, Jack, some time ago you were involved in procuring alias documents for flash purposes. We will need an Iraqi passport."

Alain succeeded in riveting Jack's attention. "Hold it a minute, Alain, that could be a tall order. Do you need a genuine Iraqi passport or a phony one? First, will this passport be needed to travel, and if so, to where?"

"It will only be needed as bona fides for flash purposes."

Blanton breathed a sigh of relief. "If you just need it for flash purposes maybe we can get a blank counterfeit."

Alain was surprised. "There is a market for blank counterfeit Iraqi passports?"

"There is a large market for all kinds of counterfeit passports. I am not certain if an Iraqi one is obtainable, but there is a guy in Istanbul who deals in counterfeit passports. South American and Lebanese counterfeits are the easiest ones to come by."

Alain considered Blanton's comments. Since the passport would only be used in Switzerland, a counterfeit one was almost as good as a genuine one.

"Well, one of the things you must do is determine if you can buy a counterfeit one. We most certainly will need an Iraqi passport, be it legit or counterfeit."

Blanton was beginning to worry about Alain. "If you're that concerned about the passport, we can always roll an Iraqi for his passport, but that causes other problems such as removing the pictures and replacing them with your guy's picture and matching your guy's physical description with the holder of the genuine passport. I suggest, Alain, that we cross that bridge when we come to it."

"Okay, Jack, relax. I'm just saying we will need an Iraqi passport. A blank counterfeit passport is probably better. Hopefully you can obtain one, then you can put both the physical description and the guy's picture in it."

"Look, Alain, let's not sweat it now. One way or another, I'm sure we can come up with a usable passport. From what you have been telling me we have a couple of months, right?"

"That's right. I suspect we'll have about three months. It could be somewhat less, but again, it could be as much as six months."

"One last question, do you have someone who can make the necessary Arabic entries in the passport?"

"That should be no problem," Alain answered.

Blanton nodded his approval and finished the beer he was drinking. They had little to discuss during the remainder of the lunch, except for a few, actually very few, shared reminiscences. When they had finished and Alain paid the bill, they left the restaurant. Alain told Blanton he would be in touch with him within a couple of weeks.

Chapter 6

Hamburg. June 14, 1982.

"HAITHAM, OLD FRIEND, good to see you. What have you been up to?" Wafiq said as he ushered Haitham Abd al-Nebi into his office.

"*Alhamdulillah* (Praise be to God). I'm fine though a little tired after all the running around I've done since arriving in Europe. It has been a tough couple of months. You must like Hamburg since you've been here a long time," Haitham answered. After he sat down, Wafiq offered him a cigarette from a silver box, which was accepted with practiced grace, something like a cat reaching for a ball of yarn.

"While it's always good to see an old friend, I suspect you have more on your mind than polite conversation."

"You are most correct, Wafiq. Since I last talked to you, I have talked to all our operatives in France and Germany. I did not go to England because it is a special case. What operatives we have at our disposal can adequately cover anti-regime activities mounted by dissident groups," al-Nebi said and paused to enjoy his cigarette.

Wafiq wondered if he was included in the we Haitham used in his comment.

"Wafiq, my problem is with the Iranian opposition groups which are primarily located in France. I don't think they amount to much, particularly after the failure of the coup uncovered by the Iranians about a year ago. I believe the coup, which contained significant military elements, was the only real chance Shapour Bakhtiar had of unseating the Khomeini regime."

"Are there no other possibilities?" Wafiq asked.

"Not of overthrowing the Khomeini regime, but what we must look at now is trying to encourage some of them to cause the regime as much pain as possible. To that end, we must actively consider exiled members of the Iranian military establishment. Senior Iranian officers in Europe, such as General Oviesi, General Aryana and Admiral Madani may be able to stir up some trouble for the Tehran government. Presumably they have some residual support within Iran. Our job is to find out if this is the case, and if so, how best to make use of it."

Haitham paused, obviously wanting some response from Wafiq who was unsure of what he should say. "Haitham, I don't have much faith in exiled Iranian generals doing anything from Europe that could even marginally accomplish something that would cause trouble for the Iranians. They all have highly inflated ideas about what they can do. Because of their self promotion, dealing with them could get very expensive."

Haitham laughed softly, "Well spoken, Wafiq. That is why I have decided that you will deal with these expensive Iranians." Haitham raised his hands to stop the objection that Wafiq was obviously going to raise. "Wafiq, this is something you must do. I have already cleared it with Baghdad. It will not take up much of your time. You will be able to count on our military attaché in Paris. He is not too smart, but I emphasized to him your long and close association with Saddam. Since Baghdad wants us to support these groups, all you can do is limit the amount of money we pass out to these arrogant officers with their hollow capabilities."

Wafiq studied Haitham, a sly, knowing smile played on his lips. "I assume there is a pressing reason why this honor has been bestowed on me?"

Haitham reacted in mock indignation, doing his best not to laugh. "I'm sorry, Wafiq, I had to do it. Don't waste too much time on our senior Iranian contacts. Let our military attaché in Paris hold their hands. By the way, do you know him?"

"Is it still Colonel Qodsi?"

"Yes, let me explain my problem. I hope you can help me, as you know a lot of Iraqi businessmen in Europe. I have a limited number of people to cover two important targets. My main concern is the activities of the Iraqi opposition. My other main concern is what, if anything, the CIA is doing with the Iraqi opposition. I have a limited list of CIA officers that have been known to be involved with opposition persons. We have photographs of some of them. I will show you what we have just in case you pick up something that might bear on this subject. In such a case, it is imperative that you follow up on it. For instance, if you hear something from one of your contacts that sounds like the CIA might be involved with Iraqis here, show him the pictures. If you get a positive identification, I want to know about it as soon as possible."

Finally, the shoe had fallen squarely on Wafiq's foot. His expression could not hide his concern. He didn't mind being paymaster to some opposition Iranian generals. He was sure he could use this as a means of siphoning off a reasonable sum of money, but trying to uncover CIA operatives was something else.

"I suspect you will be giving me a more extensive briefing about exactly how I am to carry out my new responsibilities?"

"Why, you will carry them out with great skill, Wafiq." Haitham smiled and checked his watch. "We can go over the details later. I have an appointment in twenty minutes that I do not want to miss."

⊷▰ ▰⊷

Norbeck. June 15, 1982.

"Hello, Alain, I called you because the conference I mentioned to you is coming up. I am planning to travel on the twenty-first. I wanted to give you enough warning so that we can arrange to sort things out before I leave," Kurth said to Alain after he came on the line.

"I've talked to Jack and now know what we need. Why don't you come to my place this Friday night? That way if anything comes up that we don't understand, I'll have time to get back in touch with Jack and get it straightened out before you leave."

Kurth checked his calendar. "Friday's okay. The usual time?"

"Yeah, except this time bring a bottle of gin."

Kurth laughed as he said goodbye and hung up the receiver, but he made a note to bring a bottle of gin. He called his secretary and asked if there was any trouble with his reservations. She told him that he had confirmed reservations on a Lufthansa flight for June the twenty-first and that, as instructed, she had left the return open.

"Thanks for your trouble, Grace," Kurth answered.

When Alain opened the door that Friday, Kurth handed him the bottle of gin with a grin. "As you commanded, brave leader."

"Well, at least I know you are dependable. I just noticed I'm almost out of gin. Your timing is impeccable," Alain said as he closed the door. "Come in and sit down while I stir up some martinis."

"You mentioned you had seen Jack. What came out of the discussion?"

"Well, Kurth, I decided I had to tell him about the tap. At least where it is to be located, but not whose phone is to be tapped."

Kurth's expression showed a little alarm. He was concerned that Alain may have jumped the gun. "Do you think that was wise before we have everything sorted out?"

"I deemed it necessary," Alain replied, his voice registering mild indignation. "We have the account number. Our remaining key issue is the information we can only get by tapping Wafiq's private line. Further, from my discussion with Blanton, I don't think we must tell him whose line we are tapping."

Kurth almost rose out of his seat. "Really? If that's the case, then only four people will know whose phone is being tapped. Can you imagine that few people being in the know on a sensitive agency operation?"

"I was appalled when I returned to headquarters to brief the chief of the division on operation BLACKROOT. There had to be twenty people in the conference room. In an aside, I asked the division chief if I should go into a detailed explanation before so many people. He looked at me like I had just told him his fly was open. He said that everyone in the room was following the operation with avid interest since they all had an interest in the take from the operation - so much for compartmentalization."

Kurth nodded his agreement, then decided to get the conversation back on track. "Tell me about your discussion with Blanton."

"The key points are as follows. After I told him the tap would be on a phone in Germany, he told me it would be a cinch if we had the cooperation of the BKA. As you know, I have told both Blanton and Samara'i that the agency is funding this as an off-line operation. Blanton immediately assumed that the BKA was involved, pointing out that we would have great difficulty mounting a phone tap in Germany without the cooperation of someone in the PTT. I told him that the BKA was aware we would be mounting a phone tap operation, but that they did not want to know any of the specifics, particularly since it would probably violate their defense of the constitution law. He asked me if we intended to mount the operation on our own. I told him yes, that we had some helpful capabilities in the West German PTT. I did not mention Otto or describe those capabilities in any great detail."

"How did Jack react?"

Alain shrugged his shoulders. "He was all business. He described how the phone system works. He said the local junction box contains a couple hundred pairs. He told me to get a map of the area serviced by the local junction box from our source. We should get an apartment within that same area with an active phone line. If our source is any good, he can then bridge the target pairs with the pairs from the phone line in the rental. Jack's job will be to attach the line in the listening post to a tape recorder and conceal it. Once it's working, Blanton can return to the states."

"Will this bridging of the pairs be detectable by other technicians working on the junction box?"

Alain thought before answering. "Good point. The same possibility came up during my conversation with Blanton. He told me that if our source in the PTT was any good at all he could conceal the bridge."

Kurth nodded his head. "Okay so far. Anything else come up of interest?"

"I told him we would need a passport for flash purposes. He knows a guy in Istanbul who deals in passports, both stolen and counterfeit."

Kurth polished off his martini with a flourish. "You seem to have made some progress. What next?"

Alain beamed a wily smile and said, "Now old friend, it's your turn. If Otto can produce, we have an operation. If he can't, we might as well call it quits. As I see it, you must do two things during your upcoming trip to Germany. See Otto, and tell him that our target is the private line of Wafiq. Get him to identify the local junction box that services Wafiq's private line. Also, ask him to provide you with a map of the area serviced by that junction box."

"Is that all?" Kurth asked sarcastically.

"Of course not," Alain replied just as sarcastically. "You must also use the map of the area to find a suitable LP, preferably one with a functioning phone, or at least one that has been wired for phone service." He leaned back in his chair and polished off his martini. Before Kurth could say anything, he got up and began mixing two more.

"What if Otto is less than cooperative?" Kurth asked as Alain returned with the two new martinis.

"That is where your charm comes in. I suggest that charm and a cash down payment, with the promise of a big bonus if the operation is successful, will be sufficient to woo Otto."

"Well, Alain, we should know one way or the other by the Fourth of July."

"Yes, after dinner I'll show you something I've put on the computer regarding how we will fund this operation. By the way, dinner is a small chicken halved and roasted in a mushroom wine sauce."

"I can hardly wait for the financial details."

Alain told him to be patient, then got up to put dinner together. He put half a chicken on each plate with some rice. "I'm going to start charging you for all these gourmet meals."

"Why do you think I bring booze every time you invite me? I'll pay cash when you open a restaurant."

As always, during dinner they talked about events from their days with the agency. The conversation was laced with anecdotes about people they had known. When they had finished eating, they began drinking coffee and sipping cognac. Alain turned serious.

"Kurth, do you ever wonder if what we did really mattered? Did we change anything? The liberals argue that we may well have done more harm than good."

Kurth was silent for a few moments, considering a problem he had confronted before. Alain was sometimes moody, but Kurth could not recall him questioning the value of the Clandestine Service. He decided on a positive reply.

"I really believe we did make a difference. Both of us were involved in operations that provided the policy makers with excellent intelligence. Hopefully they made good use of it. I think that you're reflecting on the simple fact that it is all behind us. I think it is impossible to come to a judgment now, better to leave that to future historians. Look, Alain, the things we did had relevance to the times in which we did them. You were involved in more covert action than I was and I think some of the things you did must have given the Soviets fits."

Alain gave Kurth a wan but grateful smile. "I don't know, Kurth. We did do some things that worked and, for that matter, worked well."

"And some that didn't," Kurth interjected. "Remember, we were no different than soldiers operating under orders from a higher echelon."

"True, and when we succeeded we were full of self gratification, perhaps more conceit than gratification."

Kurth was not given to philosophical discourse, but it was difficult to escape it with his friend. "Alain, remember Bill Freeman?"

"Yeah, he went blind after he retired."

"Bill once said that ninety percent of what we do turns to shit but, a ten percent return on any investment is great."

Alain looked bemused. "I don't know. Maybe being a spy leads to philosophical speculation."

"Let's not get started down that road."

"Yeah, you're right. Come into the den. I'll boot up the computer and show you what I've done so far."

Kurth followed Alain into the spare bedroom that had been converted into an office. He watched as Alain opened a file on the computer. Kurth saw that it detailed expenses. Alain pointed out amounts he had spent on lunches with Blanton and Hashem Samara'i. No names were included. For all practical purposes the entries looked like part of a budget.

"Look, Kurth, I have listed what I have spent so far. Keep a record of what you spend in your dealings with Otto. I suggest you pay him about fifteen hundred marks as a down payment for his cooperation. I also think that you should remind him that if this operation is a success, he will be well paid in the form of a large tax-free bonus. In the meantime, for every month the tap is in place he will get one thousand marks as a retainer even if he does no work for us. This ought to buy his silence. What do you think?"

Kurth thought briefly. If he agreed with Alain's proposal, it meant that he had begun a trip down a one-way street. He would go along for the time being. He had already decided to drop the whole thing if there was any sign of reticence on Otto's part.

"Okay, I'll pay him the down payment, although I think it might be a little high."

"You might be right, but I don't want Otto to do the wrong thing. Given the amount that we are paying him, he will think twice before biting the hand that feeds him."

Kurth almost laughed out loud. "Well, Alain, I thought I was the one who knew Otto. Your estimate of his character is on the dime. I think the prospect of Otto making tax-free money is the biggest motivating force we can use to buy his cooperation."

Alain ended the evening by saying, "Well then, Kurth, everything is set. Go to it."

Chapter 7

Hamburg. June 22, 1982.

KURTH WAS SITTING at a table inside a classically decorated restaurant that was new to him. It was located on Theaterstrasse near the Binnenalster. He had purposely picked a restaurant where none of the help would recognize him. It was a place that was crowded for lunch but more sparsely populated at night. Since it was only seven o'clock, long before a respectable hour for eating, customers were scarce and, from what Kurth could hear, most were not German. Sitting opposite him was a German male in his early to mid-fifties. With what Kurth had in mind for him and the earlier retirement age in Germany, Otto was going to do very well.

He had a round Santa Claus face, his complexion was ruddy, and he tended to laugh out loud. His blue eyes had retreated noticeably into the pastry of his face. Kurth thought that he was rather overweight. They were both drinking beer. After a healthy swig, the large German spoke.

"Well, Herr von Stiegel, I assume you did not invite me here for my charming company, but for something your employers want from me."

Kurth smiled, thinking, *Good, no beating around the bush.* "You have that right Otto. We would like to retain your excellent services."

Otto laughed out loud. "Well, if this is to be a business dinner, let us get down to business. What do you want me to do?"

"If possible, we want you to tap a specific phone line," Kurth answered.

Otto's reaction was reflected in his quizzical expression. "Why are you talking to me? Operations like this you normally arrange through the BKA."

Kurth had prepared himself for Otto's expected question. "This is an operation that the BKA would just as soon not know about. What we have in mind is not justifiable under the laws for the protection of the constitution."

"Are you sure of that? They have a lot of leeway on that issue."

"Maybe, Otto, but we do not want to make it an issue with them. This is a very sensitive operation. If you agree to do this, it is going to be just between us and will have to remain that way." Otto didn't say anything, so Kurth continued. "We want you to tap a specific telephone and to do it through the local junction box."

Otto's face revealed no change of emotion. "You are not planning to use a transmitter are you? If so, count me out. Transmitters are dangerous."

"I know, Otto, I know. I want you to get me a map of the area serviced by the junction box that has the pairs we wish to tap. That you can do, right?"

Kurth could not tell if he was intriguing Otto. On his part, Otto wondered why the CIA wanted to mount a telephone tap without the knowledge of the BKA. "I can get the map, but you have to give me the number you want tapped. With that I can produce a map of the area served by the local junction box that contains the pair you want to tap. Now will you tell me which line you want to tap?" When Kurth failed to reply immediately, he added, "Look I'm not about to tell anyone that the CIA asked me to tap a phone. You think I'm crazy? I am only a year and a half from retirement."

Kurth thought to himself, *what the hell, win or lose, here goes.*

"We want to tap the private line of the Iraqi consul. The Consulate is in a building on Abteistrasse." Kurth stopped and watched Otto carefully. "You guys had a tap on the Iraqi Consulate a couple of years ago. I know because the BKA passed us the take. Eventually the BKA told us they had to pull it because there was no indication the Iraqi Consulate was engaged in terrorist activities. Now you know why we do not want to raise reinstalling the tap with the BKA through official channels." Kurth drank some beer to give Otto time to digest what he had told him. "Likewise, now you know why the BKA doesn't want to know about it."

Otto thought that so far everything looked plausible, but when dealing with intelligence types you never know. "Okay, Herr von Stiegel, I can get you the map, no problem. What is next?"

"We get a house or apartment within the area of the map, hopefully one with a live phone or one that is at least wired for a phone. You would then bridge the two lines. Incidentally, our expert says that you can conceal the bridge in the back of the junction box. Is that correct?"

Otto decided it was time to be very careful about how he replied to Kurth's questions. "It is possible to a degree. I would have to examine the junction box in question as there are a couple of different types in use."

"How soon can you procure the map I need?"

"That is no problem, a couple of days. I can certainly get it by the weekend. I have a technical question I hope you can answer."

"Shoot, Otto."

"If I put on the tap as you instruct, there will be a larger drop than normal in the voltage on the target phone line once the phone rings and someone picks it up. If the person on the target line has made a note of the voltage drop, the difference will make him suspicious that the line is tapped. I also assume you know you will not be able to use the phone in the apartment you rent?"

"Do not worry. The way the LP will be set up we will not be able to use the phone, even by accident. Our expert says that the actuator he will use has such a high impedance that there will be no significant voltage drop." Kurth noted with pleasure the look of relief on Otto's face.

"Herr von Stiegel, it sounds like you have done your homework. I assume I will be paid for my role in this escapade?"

Kurth grinned in hopes that Otto's question indicated he was on board. "Fifteen hundred marks for your help in putting on the tap and one thousand marks a month as long as the tap is in use. We estimate three to six months."

Otto acted wary. His face screwed up in an expression of contempt. "Forty-five hundred marks is not much for the risks I will be taking."

"You forget, Otto, it is tax-free."

"Still, it is not enough."

"We, including the agency, know that, Otto. This is a sensitive operation. If it is successful, we will all be paid a bonus. Yours will be one hundred thousand marks. And the bonus, Otto, is also tax-free. I cannot guarantee you more than the fifteen hundred marks for the installation and the one thousand per month. The rest depends on success. Now, can we count on your participation?"

Otto briefly reflected on the effect that a bonus of one hundred thousand marks would have on the comfort level of his coming retirement. He decided the reward was worth the risk. "Okay, I am in. You will have the map on Saturday."

"Fine, Otto, let's have some more beer and a nice dinner."

After dinner, Kurth returned to The Prem, his favorite hotel in Hamburg. It was old, a holdover from prewar days, and had a first-rate kitchen. One of the unknown attractions was the night porter. He had been captured on the Western front during World War II and was sent to a prisoner of war camp in Texas. He was proud of the fact that he was an honorary citizen of Texas. Kurth bought him a beer while he had a scotch in the old bar.

Kurth was in a reflective mood. On the one hand he was pleased that Otto had accepted his pitch; however, he could not help wondering about the future. He had gone along with Alain thinking that this was nothing more than a mental exercise on Alain's part. Now he had to face the fact that he may have reached the point of no return. If Otto delivered the required map on Saturday, he would try to locate a suitable listening post. Assuming Otto came through and he found an LP, then they were in business. He shrugged his shoulders as he thought to himself, *well, so be it*. He could well be in a position where he would have to do his best to make sure the plan worked. There was no backing out now. He finished his drink and said good night to the porter. He went to his room, picked up the phone, and called Alain to tell him the good news.

⋅►▬ ◖▬◄⋅

Norbeck.

Alain put the phone down. One more hurdle passed. Blanton had assured him that if they had someone who could access the local junction box, they were half-way home. During the conversation with Kurth, Alain had told him to try and locate an apartment in the area covered by Otto's map. Kurth had said that once he had the map he could pinpoint the target area. In the meantime, he planned a general tour of the target area before meeting with Otto on Saturday to get the map. He would spend part of both Saturday and Sunday looking for rental possibilities in the area. He planned to see Ulla and the kids, then fly home on the twenty-ninth. He promised to call Alain when he returned to Washington.

Alain thought, *so far, so good*. He would meet with Kurth as soon as he returned. He was already anxious to learn what success, if any, Kurth might have finding some suitable real estate. When Kurth returned he would discuss their next step with Blanton. Based on Jack's reactions during their discussion, Alain was confident he would cause few problems. Once Blanton had installed the tap and checked it, he could return to the states. Alain thought to himself that the last hurdle was a piece of real estate in the lovely city of Hamburg.

He left his house thinking about what he would do with his own real estate while he was out of the country. He was going to pick up some groceries at the shopping center. While driving the short distance, he decided to call Hashem. Since they were now going to proceed with the operation, the last thing he wanted was a call from Hashem to his house. One was enough. He parked his car and walked to the nearest pay phone. He dialed Hashem's number and, after two rings, heard Hashem's coarse voice.

"Hi, Hashem, it's Alain."

Hashem did not waste any time on pleasantries. "Look, Alain, what's going on? You told me to stay loose. Do we have a deal or not? If not, let me know now. I do have some other leads I can follow."

"Keep your shirt on, Hashem. I should be able to brief you in detail sometime during the next week. By then I'll have everything settled with the agency's big domes."

"Remember, Alain, this better be worth my while."

Alain held back a derisive laugh. "Glad to hear that you've remained your unspoiled, charming self, Hashem. Unfortunately, our operation, JOINT STRIKE, will not get the final answer and the word on funding until the beginning of July. In the meantime, keep your shirt on."

Hashem mumbled something in Arabic, then questioned Alain. "Can't you give me some idea of how much I can expect? I would just as soon decide right now whether I'm in or not."

"Hashem, I can only tell you that you'll be very busy for a couple of months and will be paid enough to be comfortable where we will be. The kicker in this operation is a big bonus if the operation is successful. In fact, since you will do the most work, you will be the highest paid member of our group."

Hashem was no fool. "Better than whom?"

"All of us involved. What we get prior to the successful completion of the operation is based on our benefactor's decisions. If we are successful, we will all get a very nice bonus. Does that assuage any lingering doubts?" Alain was sure he had assessed Hashem correctly. He was on board, but trying to bargain for the best deal he could make. He would have made a good rug merchant. "And since we now have a go on this operation, do not call me at my house. I will call you using different pay phones. For operational security it is best that there is no apparent connection between us. Okay?"

"Okay, okay, just keep me in touch with what's going on." With that Hashem hung up. To do what, Alain hadn't the faintest idea. Alain thought they might have been wiser to recruit the Iraqi that ran the dry cleaning establishment in the Del Mercado shopping center, although he was probably too well off to buy a recruitment pitch. Alain remained convinced that they would have to close-haul Hashem once they got him to Germany.

⇢▬◉ ◉▬⇠

Hamburg. June 26, 1982.
Kurth stood in a beer hall in Rotherbaum. He was halfway through a beer when Otto walked in. Otto paused after entering and looked around to make sure there was no one in the beer hall he recognized. It was shortly after noon and most of the patrons were sitting in booths drinking beer with their lunch. Otto walked towards Kurth and eased up to the bar like a battleship slipping alongside a pier. Kurth greeted him as if they were old friends, then ordered him a beer. Otto asked Kurth how he was and took a sip of beer.

"I have what you ordered, Herr von Stiegel. Do you have what we agreed to?"

"Yes, I do, Mr. Schmidt. I suggest we enjoy a beer or two then arrange to make the exchange. Agreed?"

"Okay, but just one beer, I made a rash promise to take my wife on a trip outside Hamburg. There are a couple of points I should make while we drink our beers." Otto looked around to make sure no one was within hearing range. "I think you will find the map very detailed as to the precise area served by the same junction box as the target. An important point, I suggest you find an apartment or house with a live pair. The reason is that there are only a couple of unused pairs in the junction box in question. You might not be able to get connected if you rent a place where the service is disconnected, and even if there are unused pairs in the junction box it could take sometime before they make the connection. Second point, I did take a good look at the junction box. I do not think concealment will be a problem."

"Thanks, Otto. It is nice to know that you are still your old, thorough self."

Otto nodded in appreciation, "When you find the house or apartment, all I will need is the telephone number. But, I will not make the connection until you have immobilized the phone and are ready to run the line into the actuator. It would be a disaster if someone besides you picked up the phone after I have wired the two lines and heard someone speaking on the phone. This would be a dead giveaway that the phone was tapped. We would be in deep trouble if that person informed the police or the phone company."

"Understood. We will get our man over here as soon as we find a place. I will give you a call as soon as we are ready."

"Good." Otto finished his beer and said, "Let us go into the men's room and make the exchange."

The men's room was empty. Otto handed Kurth an envelope. "This is the map you must follow, Herr von Stiegel." Kurth thanked him and passed him an envelope containing fifteen hundred marks. They talked about the fine weather as they left the bar. Kurth said goodbye to Otto when they were outside on the sidewalk. He decided to return to his hotel and compare Otto's map with a detailed map of Hamburg he had purchased the previous day. Since it was such a pleasant day, with an almost cloudless sky, a rarity in Hamburg, he decided to walk back to his hotel.

The Prem was located on the eastern side of the Aubenalster. There was a water taxi you could take across the widest part, but given the sunny day, the walk around the Alster was the better choice. As he walked, Kurth thought that he was now in as deep as if he had stepped in quicksand. There is a momentum in things that draws people along. He had gone into this venture with his eyes not entirely open. Initially, he wanted to make sure Alain was not going off half-cocked. He still had serious doubts about the wisdom of robbing a Swiss bank, but so far there were no holes in their planning. Everything they had set out to do had fallen into place. It was now up to the phone tap. If it did not provide the needed information, they would have to scratch the operation. While he had doubts, the success so far had gotten the juices boiling. Since the sun was shining, he passed several attractive young ladies, stripped to the waist, drinking in the sun. It only added to the pleasure of his walk through the park on the banks of the Aubenalster. After lunch at the hotel he would take his map and inquire about vacancies in the neighborhood outlined by Otto's map.

⋅►▮◉ ◉▮◄⋅

Norbeck.

Alain was doing some shopping in the Leisure World Shopping Center. He didn't particularly like shopping there, but it was very close and convenient. It was amazing how rapidly Leisure World had grown since he moved into the area. The local grocery store was full of very old people, some of them remarkably spry. Driving into, and walking, in the parking lot was dangerous since a large number of those coming and going had less than razor sharp reflexes. One morning he had almost been run into by an old lady driving a large, antiquated Cadillac. After he got what he needed and passed through the checkout line, Alain loaded his supplies in his car and drove back home.

He was putting everything away when the phone rang. As soon as he picked up the phone he heard Kurth say, "It's me, Alain. Otto has come through!" With no pause, he continued, "This afternoon, I looked in the neighborhood and found what may be ideal. It is a small second story apartment located in an older house. It has a separate entrance up a short flight of outside stairs. It certainly fits our needs, and I think you will like it. The furniture is adequate. It has a bathroom with a shower, a bedroom, and a large room which doubles as living room and kitchen so you can work your culinary wonders. I told the lady who owns the apartment that I am looking to rent the place for a friend who is an author and is writing a novel that takes place in Hamburg. The rent is reasonable. She wants a deposit and two months rent in advance. If you agree, I will take care of it tomorrow. I am scheduled to see her in the morning. What do you think?"

Alain didn't hesitate. "I'll take your word that it's adequate. Make a deal with her. We'll split the costs when you get back. Does this place have a phone?"

"Yes, it has its own dedicated line."

"Okay Kurth, make the deal. Find out how soon we can occupy the place and I will begin packing whatever I think I'm going to need."

"Since you will be on the lease, I will give her your name, address, and phone number. I will negotiate the rent with her and pay the two months in advance."

"Great, Kurth, that should work out fine. I can be ready to leave immediately. Why don't you call me as soon as you've concluded a rental deal for the apartment? By the way, any chance of your staying so we can get things rolling? I'll see if Blanton can make a quick trip." Alain was anxious to set the operation in motion. He was making a mental note of what he should take with him when Kurth interrupted his thought process.

"I will have no problem staying a few extra days. There are actually a couple of things I can do for my company. I am staying at the Prem."

Alain took the hint. He looked at the calendar. "I'll make reservations to leave on the twenty-ninth. I'll stay at the Intercon. Let's plan to have dinner on the thirtieth at the Black Cat in St. Pauli. I'm sure you remember it."

"Got you, Alain. Your landlady is Anna Baumgartner. She insisted on at least a six-month lease. I agreed. I think you will like the small apartment. She was impressed when I told her you were researching a novel. She seems very pleasant and was surprisingly unsuspicious, unusual in German women. I will ask her to have the lease start on the first of July. I will call as soon as everything is set just in case you have to change your plans."

"I'll get busy on this end. I'll call Blanton and arrange to meet him and get him some money. Hopefully, he can arrive in Hamburg shortly after me. If everything goes well, I'll see you in Hamburg. If we have a problem, I'll call you at your hotel. So long."

It didn't take Alain long to get Blanton on the phone.

"Hello Jack, things are falling into place. I take it you've spent some time in Hamburg?" Alain asked as soon as Blanton picked up the phone

Blanton answered immediately, "Sure, I've been there many times. How soon do I have to be there?"

Alain thought briefly, trying to figure out in his mind how soon they could make all the arrangements. "It would be ideal if you could get there on the thirtieth of this month or the first of July. I suppose the first would be better; it still gives you time to buy everything you need. Do you see any difficulty in getting your supplies?"

Blanton smiled to himself. Ops officers think they are the only ones who know how to function in the real world. "I can get everything I need to take with me on Monday or Tuesday. I'll leave on Tuesday or Wednesday night. Does that fit with your schedule?"

"Sounds good, Jack. Let's have lunch on Monday. We'll sort things out and make some financial arrangements. I want to give you money. Is Clyde's all right with you?"

"Sure, I'll be there at noon."

'Okay good. so long, Jack."

→→■◎ ◎■←←

June 28, 1982.

"Jack, I'm glad you can break away on such short notice. The Company wants this thing up and running as soon as possible. Before I forget it, do you have a favorite hotel in Hamburg?"

Jack thought for a moment. "There are a few. First, tell me how much can I spend?"

Alain smiled. Although Jack was much more relaxed than when they had their first meeting, he still insisted on the details. "Jack, we will pay you three hundred dollars a day starting on the day you arrive and ending on the day you leave. You can stay in a cheap hotel, or whatever. These are unvouchered funds so there will be no accounting. I suspect you will be in Hamburg for about four or five days."

There were a couple of places he knew of that he could stay in that would keep his expenses below a hundred dollars a day. "Tell me the general area of Hamburg where the LP is located."

"It's on the west side of the Alster near the northern end."

"Okay, I know a small, out of the way, businessman's hotel where I can stay. One point, I can carry all the tools I need and the actuator with me. I will have to locate and buy the Kudelski recorder when I get there and also anything else I need to make a concealment device."

"Won't carrying tools focus attention on you?"

Jack frowned, reminding himself that ops types don't understand the tech end of the business. "Alain, you would be surprised how many people fly on planes with tool kits. If asked, I'm flying to Europe to repair a mainframe computer."

"Okay, okay, I just wanted to make sure. I'm giving you a check for twenty-five hundred dollars. We can do an accounting before you leave Hamburg. I'll get you marks to buy what you need in Hamburg. Any questions?" Alain passed Jack a cashier's check for twenty-five hundred dollars.

Jack took the check and put it in his shirt pocket. "Yes Alain, one question. Am I getting any pay besides the three hundred dollars a day I get when I'm working?"

Alain thought briefly before answering. He had to keep Jack on a string. "As I told you, there will be a good bonus if the operation is a success. In addition, you will get five hundred dollars a month as a retainer. How does that sound?"

"Good, but it may take a few days to get everything concealed in the LP."

"That is fine but, I think it best for the security of this operation that you get in and out as soon as possible. Can you arrive in Hamburg on July first?"

"No problem, Alain."

"Make your own hotel reservations. You can tell me where you are staying when we meet. I'm leaving tomorrow. There is a restaurant that overlooks the canal. It's called the Gambas. I'll meet you there for dinner at seven-thirty on July the second. I'll be at the Intercon, but don't call me unless it's an emergency. The less that connects us the better."

"Gotcha, Alain. I know that restaurant. I'll be there at seven-thirty."

"Okay Jack, I'll see you in Hamburg."

After he returned home, Alain began putting together all the things he would need in Germany. Some winter clothes would be necessary as he could be in Hamburg during cold weather. He had made some notes on operation BLACKROOT. He would either rent or buy a used typewriter when he got to Hamburg. He was in the act of mixing a martini when the phone rang.

"Hello, Alain, everything is set. Mrs. Baumgartner signed a receipt for the security deposit and two months rent. She will turn the apartment over on Thursday, the first."

"Good work. If Otto can do his part, we should be up and running in a couple of days. I'm meeting Jack in Hamburg on Friday for dinner. Since I'll have the apartment by then, I plan to take him there the following day so he can do his thing. If you get the chance, line up Otto. I suppose the soonest he can do his part will be on Monday."

Kurth was silent for a minute, making some mental calculations. "Yeah, I suppose that day is our best bet where Otto is concerned. Are we on for dinner this Wednesday?"

Part Two

The Operation

Chapter 8

Hamburg. June 30, 1982.

ALAIN ENTERED THE Black Cat and looked around. The restaurant was relatively small and was divided between two rooms. Kurth had not yet arrived. Alain looked at his watch and noted that he was a few minutes early. The waiter showed him to a table from which he could observe the entrance. He ordered a martini and relaxed. The Black Cat was a place Alain had been to a number of times. Like a lot of older German restaurants, it had stained glass windows. There were timbers stained walnut and the lighting was from both wrought iron lamps on the walls and candles on the tables. Alain had learned to love this atmosphere during his first tour in Germany. He referred to it as German pleasant.

Kurth arrived as the waiter served Alain his martini. Kurth ordered one for himself and sat down. He grinned broadly, "Everything is falling into place on my end. Mrs. Baumgartner expects us sometime tomorrow morning. I also saw Otto briefly today and passed him the telephone number. The bridge connection will be no problem. Otto assured me that he will be able to do it Monday. He wanted me to call him, but I told him it would be better if we met briefly that morning. We agreed to meet at a coffee shop at ten on Monday." Kurth smiled at Alain and asked, "Any questions?"

Alain returned his smile. "Nothing that I can think of at the moment." He sipped his martini and quickly changed his mind. "There is one thing I would like to ask you. All along, through our discussions and planning, I have thought that you were less than convinced about our chances of success. So, how do you feel about the operation now? I mean, do you still have serious misgivings?"

Kurth hesitated before answering. It was not always easy to know what Alain was really asking. He considered the questions carefully. "Look Alain, I always have misgivings about any operation. Did we overlook something that might be key to the operation's success? In this case, I do not think we have any immediate problems. From my dealings with Otto, I am certain that he is looking forward to a bonus, plus the monthly retainer. In my opinion, he isn't a security risk."

"You sound pretty certain," said Alain.

"Well, we must consider the possibility that he may report the tap. The danger to us is between now and Monday. If he is going to report it, he has to do it before the fact. If he decides to report the tap after he has installed it, what will the BKA think of his confession?" Kurth replied. He emphasized his question with an expressive motion of his right hand. "I don't think Otto would take the risk of jail and losing his pension. Suppose he does report the tap to the BKA. I believe they will conclude, given the war between Iran and Iraq, that the CIA has a natural interest in the activities of one of Saddam's close associates."

Alain thought Kurth was mistaken. "That may be stretching things a bit, don't you think?" He was certain that the BKA would raise hell with the CIA Chief of Station in Bonn.

Kurth sipped his martini before he answered. "Not really. The BKA knows the CIA cannot approach them and ask them to tap Tikriti's phone. They would have to refuse on legal grounds. They would probably decide that it was in their best interest to let the CIA go ahead with the tap."

Alain didn't agree, but he decided to change the subject slightly. He gave Kurth a knowing smile and said, "I am not so sure of your conclusion. Who can say what the BKA may or may not do? You do overlook one possibility. Let us suppose that he went to the BKA after your first meeting."

"You're supposing the BKA told Otto to continue to cooperate merely to find out what is going on. I think that unlikely. The BKA would tell him to knock it off because it would create too many problems for them to let him go ahead with the tap. No, I think Otto sees this as his last chance to cash in."

Alain scratched his chin in reflection. "I tend to agree. If Otto goes ahead with the tap, I think we can assume everything is okay. The worst case, which it seems that both of us doubt, would be if the BKA approached the Bonn station and confronted the Chief of Station with evidence of the tap. They certainly wouldn't get much in the way of an answer, only an empty stare. The COS would be concerned that the agency had mounted an operation on his turf without informing him. It has happened before. What I consider crucial is your opinion that Otto is on the up and up with us. My question to you was based on my observation that you now seem more comfortable with the operation. Is that the case?"

Kurth wondered what Alain's main concern was - the operation, or his feelings about it. "I would say yes, because there is a fail-safe element involved. If we do not get the information we need, we have no operation. If we do get what we need, then and only then do we decide whether to go ahead or not. I still believe our real security worry is Hashem. You will be dealing with him and you must use all of your handling skills to keep him focused on what we want him to do." Kurth emphasized you.

"Good point. Hashem is my constant worry. Under no circumstances can he know that anyone other than me is involved in this venture. It is important that I convince him that the tapes he gets from me are from the BKA via an under-the-table arrangement with the agency. I will insist that he preserve the security of the operation because, were the passage of the tapes to surface, it would be a great embarrassment to the BKA."

Kurth silently considered Alain's comments. When he spoke, he sounded doubtful, "You think he'll swallow that story?"

Alain shrugged his shoulders and raised his hands in supplication. "What can he do or say? Tell me he doesn't believe me? I think he will buy the cover story. Look, he only deals with me. It is imperative that he not know that you or Jack are involved. I intend to tell him, once he is involved, that he can't afford to screw up or the agency may move to cut off, or at least limit, his retirement."

Alain stared at Kurth, waiting for a rejoinder, but Kurth remained silent so he continued, "I had a second thought. I will review the tapes, translate all the conversations in German, and then either erase or splice out the German conversations. If Hashem gets curious and questions how the tap was done, I will tell him that the BKA agreed to the tap, but insisted that they erase all the conversations involving German citizens. This should help sell the BKA

involvement. In the final analysis, we have to count on Hashem's greed to moti-
vate him to do the right thing."

Alain thought it best to change the subject and set Hashem aside for the time
being. "Jack is arriving tomorrow and we are having dinner at the Gambas. It's
a pretty good restaurant, and one of their specialties is pretty, young waitresses.
That should appeal to Jack. He thinks he can get everything done in two days at
the most. He is planning to leave as soon as the tap is functioning and we know
we are getting good take. That could be Monday at the earliest, but probably a
few days later. Once everything is up and running, you and I will meet at various places around town. Since you won't be able to call me, I will walk a certain
route for fifteen minutes early in the morning. Sighting each other will trigger a
meeting at an agreed upon place an hour later."

Kurth smiled in agreement. "Yes, let's make the contacts early in the morning. I agree that we get in the habit of walks. When we spot each other, we will
exchange signals and plan to meet. I am not going to be here most of the time.
When I am in Washington, you can call me using the public phone system. We
will set up a regular time for you to call so I can let you know when I'm traveling to Germany on business. Also, who knows what troubles might develop, or
more hopefully, we might get lucky and get the information we need from the
tap in a relatively short time. We'll work out more commo details after the tap is
up and running."

A waiter bringing their dinners interrupted them. Both had ordered
Schwienhaxen, an old favorite of Alain's. After the waiter left, Alain turned the
conversation to Kurth's wife, Ulla, and their two kids. Kurth's face lit up at the
mention of his estranged family. He told Alain that they were all fine and he was
glad to get the opportunity to see them. Kurth then turned so serious that Alain
asked him what was the matter.

"Two nights ago, I took Ulla out to dinner. It was very pleasant. We were
eating outside in the restaurant garden. In candlelight, Ulla has got to be the
world's most beautiful woman. I guess I just couldn't help myself. Being with
her brought home to me how much I miss her. Towards the end of the evening,
I told her that I now deeply regret the divorce."

Alain's face registered considerable surprise. "You really said that?"

Kurth smiled wistfully. "That's not the most surprising statement of the evening. After I spoke, Ulla looked at me with what I was sure were tears in her eyes and said 'not as much as me.'"

Alain had known for some time that Kurth still had strong feelings for Ulla and that the growing kids were an increasing focus of his attention. "You're not thinking of getting back together with her are you?"

"I could do a lot worse, Alain."

They spoke of their past histories together as they ate their dinners. Alain, who had been silent for some time, suddenly pointed his fork at an unseen target. "You know, Kurth, if we pull this off we will each have well over two million dollars. What were our aggregate salaries during our agency careers? I don't think we earned more than three hundred thousand dollars each. I think I'll figure out the exact amount as a pastime." Alain smiled mischievously. "In addition, what we realize will be tax-free."

They finished dinner, had coffee and Asbach, then left the restaurant. Outside, they agreed to meet at ten the following morning near the water taxi mooring. When Alain arrived back at the Intercon and picked up his key, the concierge handed him a message. The note only gave Jack as the name of its author. He was arriving Thursday and would see Alain on Friday night. No hotel reservations were included.

--->===© ©===<---

July 1, 1982.

Mrs. Baumgartner was effusive in explaining the merits of the apartment she was renting to Alain. After exhausting its praises, she asked Alain, "Mr. Schneider tells me you are here to do research on a novel you are writing. Is that not so?"

Alain summoned up the warmest of smiles and answered. "That is correct, Mrs. Baumgartner. The novel is set in Hamburg during the height of the Cold War. I decided to come here to capture more closely the local color and to be sure that I got all of the locales for the novel correct. I will be researching articles that appeared in the press during the mid-sixties." Alain smiled and added, "There is also the value of no one knowing I'm here so I can work uninterrupted."

"Well, Mr. Dembray, I can assure you that you will not be disturbed here. It is a very quiet neighborhood."

"Believe me, Mrs. Baumgartner, that is reassuring in more ways than you might realize."

Alain's comment caused Kurth to raise his eyebrows.

If Mrs. Baumgartner thought Alain's comment in any way odd, she did not show it. "Mr. Dembray, Mr. Schneider has paid the rent for July and August. You are free to take over anytime. I wish you a pleasant stay." She gave Alain a set of keys, explaining which was for the door and which was for the mailbox. Alain thanked her as she left.

After she closed the door, Kurth said, "I'll drive you over to your hotel so you can check out and begin to get set up here."

They drove in silence. On the way back, Alain confirmed their next meeting. "Thanks, Kurth. Let's have dinner Sunday and I'll brief you on what Jack and I accomplish over the weekend. I suppose you are going to see Ulla and the kids?"

"Yes, I am. I'll pick you up in front of the house at seven-thirty for dinner."

"One important point. Have you told Ulla anything about my being in Hamburg?"

"No. Why? Do you see some kind of problem in her knowing you are here?"

"No, but I think it's best that my presence here be known to as few people as possible." Kurth nodded in response to Alain and left.

Alain spent the rest of the day buying things he would need for the apartment. He had noted that the furnishings did include all the necessary kitchen utensils. His first trip was to a market to buy some groceries. After parking his purchases in the apartment, he went to a store that specialized in used office equipment. He bought a typewriter and a couple of reams of paper and a notebook. He then spent the rest of the day in the apartment making notes on the book he was supposedly writing. He also typed a preface to the book and most of the first chapter. As he worked, he thought to himself that a book on operation BLACKROOT would make a good read. He wondered what the reaction of the CIA's Publications Review Board would be if such a book were submitted. He would love to be a fly on the wall during that discussion. Well, they need not worry since what he was writing would never see the light of day.

At seven o'clock he called it quits. He left his work on one end of the table just in case Mrs. Baumgartner got curious and decided to check on the apartment when he wasn't there. He had bought several bottles of wine. He opened a bottle of Plavac, a Yugoslavian red wine very popular in Germany, and thought to himself that he would be drinking Champagne if everything went according to plan. He fried himself a pair of pork chops while he sipped the wine. With luck, everything would go well when he saw Jack the following night. He had considerable experience with technical ops. They were always difficult. If something could go wrong, it usually did. Murphy's law was probably originally propounded by a group of CIA operations officers involved in audio operations. He decided to take a long walk after dinner and made a mental note to buy some gin and vermouth at the first opportunity.

⋗►◉ ◉◄⋖

July 2, 1982.

Alain entered the Gambas and asked the headwaiter if Jack had arrived. The headwaiter answered in the affirmative and directed Alain to a table where Jack was seated drinking a beer. Alain thanked the headwaiter and greeted Jack.

"Glad you got here, Jack. Welcome to Hamburg."

Jack got out of his seat and shook hands with Alain. "Good to see you, Alain. I left the note at your hotel to make sure you were aware that I had arrived."

"I got your note. I moved out of the hotel yesterday. Do you have enough tools to get started tomorrow?"

"I think I have everything we will need. I was able to get a used Kudelski tape deck at a decent price. I brought an actuator with me. I'll give you the bills later. This afternoon, I purchased some telephone wire and a local jack and plug. After I have a good look at the apartment, we may have to go out and buy something so I can conceal the tape deck."

Jack stopped talking when a pretty girl in a peasant dress approached their table. Alain ordered a beer and Jack ordered a second one. They both ordered shrimp dishes, the specialty of the house. After the waitress left, Jack continued. "I'll know better when I see the inside of the apartment." He reached into his shirt pocket and pulled out a card. "Here is where I'm staying. I'm in room 216 if you have to get in touch with me."

"The Oxford? That's a new one on me."

"Actually it's not far from here. It's frequented by German businessmen but it's not used by the agency to put up temporary duty officers."

"Good thinking, Jack. Here is the address of the apartment." Alain passed him a slip of paper. "The entrance is up a short flight of stairs on the right side of the house. Since we don't know what all we'll need or how long it will take you, why don't you come by at about nine tomorrow morning?"

"I'll be there."

The waitress arrived with their dinners. Alain ordered another beer, but Jack passed. They ate in silence. Jack was one of those persons who like to do one thing at a time. Alain interrupted Jack's focus on his dinner with a question.

"Jack, is a used tapedeck a good idea?"

Unable to fully conceal his disdain at such a dumb question, Jack responded, "Alain, the Kudelski is the best damn tape deck ever made. I went over this one carefully and tested it for a full weekend before I was willing to buy it. Don't worry, it will do the job. The important thing is to rig your apartment so nothing can go wrong. Once I get things set up, you can ask me all the questions you want."

Alain was somewhat taken aback until he remembered that tech officers did not respond fondly to questions on any technical decision they had made. He raised both hands in a kind of supplication. "Okay Jack, I was only asking a legitimate question."

"Well, limit them to operational concerns. Let me worry about the technical aspects of this operation."

"Agreed," was the only answer that came to Alain's mind. "Okay, then it's all settled. I'll expect to see you at about nine o'clock tomorrow morning. I'll have coffee and beer on hand, anything else?"

"Yeah, I hope there is no chance of our being disturbed while I am making the installation. At some point the apartment could look like it is undergoing major repairs."

"No problem, Jack, as long as we can clean up the mess."

"No worry, just keep in mind that it might take most of tomorrow and the next day to get everything set up. The concealment device for the recorder will also take some thought and a day of work."

"Yeah, I remember some of the tech ops I was involved in. The problem was not with the equipment, but how to conceal it."

Jack smiled a very crooked smile as if he was laughing out of the side of his mouth. "You got that right, case officer."

Alain ignored Jack's deprecating tone. "Any other problems you can think of?"

"Well, I think it's good tomorrow is Saturday. Once I look at the concealment possibilities in your digs, we might have to go out to buy something and, as you know, doing anything in Germany on a Sunday is difficult."

"Agreed, Jack. Let's both get a good night's sleep. I will expect you around nine tomorrow morning."

Jack reached across the table to shake hands. "I'll be there."

→—◉ ◉—←

July 3, 1982.

Alain was on his second cup of coffee when there was a knock on his front door at two minutes after nine. He smiled briefly. Time, particularly being on time, was a critical aspect of operations in the clandestine service. It was something you never forgot. He rose from his seat and opened the door.

"Come in, Jack, and fix yourself a cup of coffee. Have you had breakfast? If not, I can fix you some bacon and eggs."

Jack looked at him, "No. I had something at the hotel. Coffee will be fine."

"How do like your coffee?"

"Black as my soul."

Alain noted that Jack was already looking over the apartment. He opened the closets, then looked at where the phone jack was on the outside wall.

"I see the Germans, in their usual efficiency, have run the phone line into the outside wall and positioned the phone jack receptacle immediately inside the spot where the phone line runs into the apartment. This might make our job very simple."

Alain had always thought it better to humor techs. "How so, Jack?"

"See the receptacle the phone is plugged into? I plan to make it a dummy receptacle. I will then channel the live wire to a place where we can run the hot line into the actuator and, of course, the recorder."

"Okay, fine, Jack, but why the need for a dummy receptacle?"

Jack looked at Alain with the most condescending expression he could muster. "Look Alain, if someone plugs the phone into the dummy jack, which is really the bypassed jack, the line will be dead and they will not be able to fuck up the tap. When the operation is finished, I will simply reconnect the now dead jack and it will be live once again. Very simple."

"Why not leave the phone in the dead jack?" Alain responded.

Again Jack looked at Alain with the expression he usually reserved for junior case officers. "Well, Alain, I thought if you pulled the phone out of the jack you could say you removed it because you didn't want to be disturbed. Put the damn thing in one of the closets. Once the tap is hot, there is no circumstance under which you can use the phone without alerting the target that his phone is tapped. If anyone wants to make a call, they will have to ask you where the phone is. I assume you might have a *putzfrau* in here once in a while to clean up. It is customary for Germans to hide the phones so someone can't make a call on their bill without asking permission."

Alain was impressed. "So if someone does try to use the phone in the usual jack the line will be dead?"

"Precisely, my dear Watson," Jack responded. "They will probably assume you haven't paid the bill, so the PTT cut off your phone service. Disconnecting the live jack is the easy part, now we must decide on where we will run the live phone wire into the actuator and how we conceal it and the Kudelski tape deck." Jack began looking at the outside wall and several places within the same room. After some time, he turned to Alain and said, "We might have to go on a shopping expedition."

"For what, Jack?"

"Well look, Alain, what I'm going to do is remove the incoming line from the present phone jack. I will then splice the extra phone wire I brought with me onto the live phone wire and conceal it behind the baseboard. The live phone line has to run behind the baseboard to the house current outlet where we can connect it directly to the actuator and the actuator to the Kudelski. What we need is something big to set against the wall that will conceal the connection. We could buy something like a stereo or a stand up TV that has room inside for me to connect and conceal the Kudelski. If we can go out and find something usable, I'll have your tap up and running by tonight or tomorrow at the latest."

"One question, Jack. You mentioned you are going to run the phone line behind the baseboard. Can you do this without it being obvious that there is something wrong with the baseboard?"

"I think I can channel it behind the baseboard and then bring it back out underneath whatever we can find as a concealment device."

Alain's expression was filled with doubt. "Isn't that a lot of work?"

Jack's irritation was beginning to show. "Look Alain, I brought all the tools I will need with me. In the name of God, we have the whole damn weekend to get it right."

"Okay, okay, I didn't mean to ruffle your feathers. Whenever you're ready we can go out and look for whatever you think might fill the bill."

Jack was amused. "You speak better German than me. Look in the phone book yellow pages for shops that advertise repair of televisions, radios, and stereos. We might be able to pick up a serviceable stereo or an old stand up radio. The older stereos and radios had large spaces for housing the speakers. The Kudelski is fairly small, so we don't need a hell of a lot of room to conceal it. While we are at it, we'll pick up a used tape deck and some ear phones so you can listen to the take."

"I'll look in the phone book and come up with some addresses. We can leave anytime you're ready."

⇥⟩▬◯ ◯▬⟨⇤

"Wafiq, I think we are making some progress," Haitham Abd al-Nebi said as he entered Wafiq's office unannounced.

"In what way?" Wafiq got up from his desk to greet al-Nebi.

Haitham massaged his mustache before replying. "I think, no, I believe, we have recruited sufficient nets of loyal Iraqis in the major cities in Germany that can report accurately, and in some detail, on the efforts of opposition types in Germany. I am not very concerned about the ability of these groups to do anything meaningful. Our real worry is whether they are in contact with and receiving support or direction from the CIA. Such an arrangement could cause us real problems. On their own these organizations are nothing more than discussion groups."

Wafiq was amused. "If that is your estimate of their capabilities, I would suspect that the CIA views these opposition groups in much the same light."

It was Haitham's turn to smile. "Politics, my dear Wafiq, politics. It is no worry of yours except for the possible CIA involvement. I am arranging a briefing for you and your trusted aide, Ahmad. One of my men will brief you and Ahmad on the identities of CIA officers who have experience working in Iraq and could presumably be expected to be working against us given the current circumstances. We have identified about twenty of their officers and we have pictures of ten of them."

Wafiq was amazed at al-Nebi's request. "Haitham, old friend, is it not highly unlikely that Ahmad or I will ever be in a position to see one of these CIA agents?"

Haitham sighed audibly. "You are no doubt correct, but you and Ahmad represent two additional pairs of eyeballs and we need all of the help we can get."

"As you wish, Haitham. I will await the briefing from your officer."

"I, and one of my men, will brief you and Ahmad during the next few days. We will do it after hours when all the other Consulate employees have left."

"We can do it upstairs in my quarters."

"Excellent. Do you have a safe where you can keep descriptions and pictures of the CIA agents?"

"Yes, I have one upstairs."

"Good," Haitham grinned in satisfaction. "A slight change of subject, Wafiq."

Wafiq smiled wanly. "Why do I have the feeling I'm not going to like the change of subject?"

"I have talked to Col. Qodsi in Paris. He is anxiously awaiting your arrival in Paris. He is in over his head dealing with some of the more sophisticated Iranian opposition leaders. He plans to introduce you to some of them who are willing to talk to us. The most important is Shapour Bakhtiar. He gets special consideration from the French because he is a French citizen and his son is an officer in the French Police. Qodsi will introduce you as the man who controls the funds. I think you will get along well with Bakhtiar."

Wafiq was thoughtful. "I take it the man we are most concerned with is Bakhtiar?"

"Not entirely. We are also talking to Gen. Oviesi and have provided him with some support. Admiral Madani is a different case. The Arabs in Khuzistan despise him because he dealt with them harshly when he was the Governor of Khuzistan. He also makes some pretty grandiose claims about his ability to manipulate things in Iran. There you have it."

Wafiq's looked bewildered. He posed a question to al-Nebi. "My understanding is that the Americans are also mucking around with these people. Don't you find it odd that we are apparently allied with the Americans?"

Haitham had half expected Wafiq's question. "We are at war, which in itself is a strange endeavor. The primary importance of war is to give future historians something to do. Don't try to make rational sense out of something as irrational as war."

"Okay, Haitham, but I conclude that you do not expect much from any of the three you mentioned. If we are providing the most support to Bakhtiar, what is the rationale?"

"Good point. Since he was the last Prime Minister appointed by the Shah, he at least has some legitimate claim to the leadership of the Iranian government."

Wafiq laughed, which startled al-Nebi, and then said, "I don't think that is a consideration that worries Khomieni."

"There is something else. We in the General Directorate of Intelligence believe that the Nozheh coup two years ago was a blow to any hope of success for Bakhtiar. I remember Qodsi reporting how upbeat Bakhtiar was before the coup. He told Qodsi in early 1980 that he would be back in Iran in a matter of months. Since the failure of the coup, which apparently relied heavily on air force officers, Bakhtiar appears to be more circumspect."

"He doesn't sound like a horse I would bet on to win a race."

"That, Wafiq, is an assumption that I and others believe to be the real case. This is one reason I want you to go to Paris as soon as possible, have a couple of long talks with Bakhtiar, and come to some conclusions about him. We desperately need your help, old friend."

Although he was mentally reluctant to go along with Haitham's proposals, Wafiq knew he would have to make the effort. Paris was not a bad place to spend some time. "Okay, Haitham, I'll call Qodsi tomorrow and make arrangements to travel to Paris. I assume Bakhtiar is the only person you want me to see?"

"Yes, he is the most important. There are some other more minor players, but my colleagues and I can handle them. Fortunately, Gen. Oviesi is willing to travel to Baghdad, so our business with him is pretty much handled out of Baghdad."

Wafiq merely nodded his head in agreement since he had nothing else to say. Haitham got up, said goodbye, and left after warning Wafiq to keep their relationship confidential.

⇥⇤ ⇥⇤

Alain and Jack Blanton returned from their shopping trip late in the afternoon. Jack was ecstatic about finding a large, used Telefunken radio. It was in surprisingly good working order. While in the second hand shop, he had unscrewed the thin plywood back cover telling the owner of the shop he wanted to check on the speaker. He decided he could easily conceal the Kudelski tape deck inside the back of the radio.

"Well, Alain, it's no stereo, but you got yourself a damn fine radio for next to nothing, and I have everything I need to do the installation."

Alain was surprised at Jack's conduct. He was as happy as a kid who had just traded for a prized baseball card. *What the hell*, Alain thought to himself, *some people are just as goofy about cars*. Alain opened up two bottles of beer.

"Good, Jack, let's hope we don't run into any problems."

"If it's okay with you, I'd like to do the major work tomorrow, just in case we run into a problem. In the meantime, let me open the back and make sure we can fit the tape deck in it." Jack took out a Swiss knife as he spoke. He prized out the knife's screwdriver and opened the back of the radio. "Bring me that package I brought with me. It has the tape deck and actuator in it."

Alain went to a closet and retrieved the package. With the radio on the kitchen table, Jack carefully placed the tape deck in the bottom of the radio. He was forced to position it lengthwise, parallel to the width of the radio with the controls facing outwards. He attached the actuator to the tape deck input. When he was satisfied with the installation, he replaced the back of the radio, then sat down to drink the beer Alain handed him.

"We have some options you can think about between now and tomorrow morning. The phone line is pretty easy. As I told you before, I will leave the input socket where it is. It will just be dead. I will then splice some telephone wire I purchased today onto the live wire and channel it behind the baseboard to wherever you want to locate the radio. I suggest placing it against the wall in front of that house current receptacle." Jack pointed to a house current receptacle on the outer wall that was not far from the phone input socket. "If we use that receptacle to plug in the radio, it will not take me long to channel the phone line behind the baseboard."

"You're the technician, Jack. Do what you think best."

Jack nodded his head in agreement. "Since the Kudelski runs on batteries, we do not need to mess with the house current. I intend to drill a hole in the bottom of the radio, run the phone line through it, and connect it to the actuator. I will conceal the phone line under the baseboard and quarter round, then under the rug. The line will be threaded through a small hole in the rug and into the hole in the bottom of the radio. As a precaution, I'll attach a phone input socket on the baseboard across the room with a piece of phone line attached to it. I'll run the wire under the rug. If anyone happens to spot the live phone line that leads into the radio they will assume it is the same wire attached to the phone input socket on the opposite baseboard. In short, the setup should pass any inspection except one done by professionals."

Alain was impressed. Whatever faults Jack had, he was a thorough technician. "Well, Jack, let's hope that we don't give any professionals cause to come snooping."

Jack screwed the piece of plywood back on the radio and placed the radio where he intended it to be after he finished the installation the following day.

"I've finished with everything I can do today."

"Good, Jack, let's go get something to eat."

→⊫● ●⊧←

July 4, 1982.

Alain was finishing his second cup of coffee when Jack knocked at the door. Alain had gotten up early and gone for a walk before returning to the apartment and fixing himself a simple breakfast. He opened the door and said, "Jack, Happy Fourth of July! Come on in and have a cup of coffee."

"Fine, I take it black," Jack said as he entered the apartment lugging a heavy suitcase. "This suitcase has practically everything you need for an audio operation except for a paint matching kit, but I was never any good at paint matching anyway."

"Really?" Alain responded.

"Yeah, paint matching is an art," Jack said, toying with his coffee. He took a long drink, then got up from his seat. "I'll get started. If there are no problems, I should be finished early in the afternoon."

Jack opened the suitcase he had brought with him, selected a small screwdriver, and proceeded to unfasten the phone input socket from the baseboard. Next, he unfastened the telephone line from the phone input jack. He paused momentarily to drink some coffee and then took a three by six piece of plywood from his suitcase. He wrapped the piece of plywood in a couple sheets of newspaper. Alain was fascinated as he watched Jack take a small prying iron from his suitcase and, with the plywood as a base against the wall, carefully pry the baseboard out from the wall. It was out far enough for him to reach behind the baseboard and pull the disconnected telephone wire back through the hole where it had been attached to the telephone input socket. With a small soldering iron, he spliced a length of new telephone line to the one he had removed from the receptacle. He then attached a short piece of telephone wire to the input jack, pushed the fake wire through the hole from which he had just pulled the live phone wire, and reattached the dummy phone socket to its place on the baseboard.

"You can keep the telephone plugged into this jack if you want, Alain, but frankly I'd keep it in the closet. Then, if anyone does try to make a call with it, they will assume you have canceled the service."

"Suppose someone dials this number, what will happen?"

"They will hear a ring or, in some cases, a busy signal. That will happen when the impulses from the number dialing this number hit the exchange which services your phone line."

"Is there any chance it will ring in the target?"

"No, because the exchange is causing this number to ring, not the target's number. Look at it this way, your line is the same number as the target's line, but the exchange doesn't know this. When this number is dialed, the exchange relays the dialed pulses to your local junction box. In most cases, whoever is dialing the number hears a ring."

Alain wondered why he hadn't thought to ask these questions when he was involved in other operations. Maybe it was because he had more at stake in this operation. Jack interrupted his train of thought to make another observation. "This is why you can't use the phone. In effect it will be an extension of the target's phone. If he, or anyone else, picks up the target phone while you are making a call from here, whoever is on the target end will hear everything you say and will know that something is radically wrong."

"Gotcha, Jack. I just never focused on the problem before."

"Few ops officers ever do."

Jack finished his coffee, smiling inwardly at the technical ignorance of case officers in general, and went back to work. He carefully pried the baseboard out until he had run the wire to the location of the house current receptacle. He next cut off the wire at a length more than he needed. He attached a six-inch piece of thin wire to the end of the telephone wire. Next, he pried out the quarter round at the base of the baseboard and drilled a small hole in the bottom of the baseboard close to the house current receptacle. He used a small rasp to form a small arch in the bottom of the quarter round. Using long nosed pliers, he fished the wire he had attached to the telephone wire through the hole in the baseboard and the arch in the quarter round. He was then able to pull the telephone wire through the hole and under the quarter round. Using the rasp again, he worked on the aperture in the quarter round until he was satisfied that it fit snugly over the telephone wire. He finished this part of the installation by carefully tapping the base board and quarter round back into place. This operation took well over an hour.

"Any more coffee left?" Jack asked Alain.

"Yeah, let me get you some." Alain took a fresh cup from the cupboard and poured him another cup of coffee.

"Well, the main job's finished. It should not take much longer to finish the rest. Thanks for the coffee. I believe techs drink more coffee and beer on the job than anyone in the agency."

"Jack, I always thought you were one of best techs I ever worked with," Alain said in an attempt to express some gratitude for Jack's efforts.

"Thanks."

Jack was not given to excesses of conversation, except when he was discussing his arcane profession. He got up from his chair and put the radio back up on the table. He unscrewed the back cover and removed the Kudelski tape deck and actuator. He studied the interior for a moment, particularly the position the actuator would be in when the installation was finished.

"I'll leave excess telephone wire inside the radio. I am also only going to replace two of the screws so you can get the back off easily. The excess wire will allow you to move the radio so you can get at the tape deck. I'll make the hole big enough so that the wire slides in and out easily. Now, I want you to hold the radio at an angle so I can drill a hole in the bottom."

Alain grabbed hold of the radio and asked, "What now, Jack?"

"Just lean it towards you," Jack answered.

Alain slowly lowered the radio towards himself. Jack motioned him to stop and said, "That's good." He drilled a hole with a three quarter inch bit and measured from the hole to the back edge of radio with a small tape measure. Next he used the tape measure to locate a point on the rug that would be under the hole in the bottom of the radio. He made a hole in the rug with a scratch awl.

"Alain, give me a hand with this rug. I'm going to run the phone wire under the rug to the hole and pull it through."

They both fiddled with the rug and the wire until they were able to pull the wire through the hole. Jack put the radio on the floor near the power receptacle. Next he checked the position of the tape deck and the actuator in the bottom of the radio. Jack removed a phone jack from his suitcase and soldered it to the end of the phone line. He pushed the wire through the hole in the bottom of the radio and fitted the phone jack into its receptacle on the actuator.

"Well, Alain, the installation is complete," Jack said, as he plugged the radio into the house current receptacle and placed it as close to the wall as it would go. The phone line was totally concealed. To see it, the radio had to be moved.

Alain frowned, "Why go to so much trouble to conceal the phone line under the rug?"

Blanton gave Alain a curious look. "As I explained yesterday, I'm going to put a telephone input jack on the baseboard on the opposite wall." As he spoke Jack took a four-foot length of phone wire and soldered an input jack onto it. He then screwed the input receptacle onto the baseboard on the far wall and plugged the phone jack into it. "Help me lift the rug and run the phone line under it." When he was done he put a small table by the input jack. "Now if anyone gets curious they will think someone just ran a telephone line under the rug so they could have the phone on this table on the opposite side of the room."

It seemed like a lot of bother to Alain, but he nodded his head in agreement. "I'll remember your explanation. I was thinking of other things yesterday. Now that you are finished, how about a beer?"

"I thought you'd never ask."

Alain smiled as he took two bottles of beer out of the refrigerator. "Well, I guess we should know Monday afternoon if everything works or if Murphy's Law has jabbed us in the ass."

It was Jack's turn to laugh. "Don't worry, Alain, I'll stick around until everything works. I'm pretty certain at the moment that everything on our end is okay. What time is this supposed to go live?"

"If everything goes all right it should be live by noon on Monday. Why don't you go ahead and make reservations to leave on Tuesday morning? Also, plan on coming by here around four in the afternoon on Monday. If everything seems okay you can leave on Tuesday."

"Will do." Jack answered as he polished off his beer and got up to leave. "I guess it's best we don't see each other until Monday. I'll be here at four."

Alain nodded his agreement. "Yes, a well-known European Division operations officer seen in the company of a well-traveled tech could raise some eyebrows. Let's hope everything works on Monday."

⇥▆ ▆⇤

Kurth had picked up Alain and driven him to a restaurant on the road heading south from Hamburg towards Luneburg. They stopped at The Staghorn, a restaurant famous for venison and wild boar. Kurth was obviously pleased when Alain explained in some detail the installation that Jack had made.

"Yes, it would seem that the only thing left is for Otto to work his magic in the junction box," Alain said with a note of hope in his voice.

A waiter arrived with a platter of venison and two fresh beers. He also brought roasted potatoes and a bowl of beans. Alain and Kurth served themselves. After sampling the venison, Alain remarked that it was quite tasty.

"It's because they sew suet through the meat. The melting fat is what renders the meat tender," Kurth responded. He had been to the restaurant several times. His ex-wife, Ulla, had introduced him to it. "I'm having coffee with Otto tomorrow morning. He says he has written up his work schedule to give him plenty of time to do the bridge before noon. I told him I'd buy lunch. If everything is okay, I'll meet you at the Bierstube on the Alster right near where you are staying. I should be able to make it by one-thirty."

"Good, Jack is coming by in the late afternoon. I don't want him to see you. If everything is okay, I will begin listening to the tapes. Once we have a backlog, I'll send for Hashem. I suspect that what will interest us most will be in German."

"Yeah, make sure you erase all the conversations involving Germans before you pass the tapes to Hashem. It's imperative that we build up the cover with Hashem that this is an agency-sanctioned operation, and most importantly, that the BKA has erased all the conversations involving Germans."

"Agreed, but I don't intend to erase the German conversations. I am going to cut them out of the tape and then splice the tape together. We are going to need the conversations Wafiq Tikriti has with Germans so you can practice imitating his accent. On Monday morning, I'm going back to the store where Jack and I purchased the needed supplies. They sell tape splicers. I thought Jack might ask too many questions if I bought one while we were at the store." Kurth nodded his agreement and Alain continued, "I just hope there is enough intelligence on the tapes to convince Hashem that the tap is worthwhile. Hashem is a suspicious bastard and the last thing I want him to do is to begin questioning why the agency is so interested in tapping this particular telephone."

Kurth grimaced. "It would be great if we could get the information we need in a very short time."

"Don't count on it. Incidentally, when are you planning to return to Washington?"

"If there are no problems, I'll probably leave on Wednesday."

"Okay we'll review our commo plan when we see each other tomorrow afternoon."

Kurth raised his beer. "Good, then let's enjoy the venison.

⇥⬤ ⬤⇤

July 5, 1982.

It was raining outside. There were several people in the coffee shop who looked like they had stopped in to escape the rain. Kurth and Otto were drinking coffee. Kurth was careful to dress like a German businessman. All his clothes were European made. His one problem was that his striking good looks made him unforgettable if the police were ever inclined to ask potential witnesses if they had seen him in such and such a place at such and such a time. Kurth had just told Otto that everything was in place on his end.

"Good. I can be finished with the job before lunch," Otto said as he looked at his watch and made some mental calculations.

"Very good, Otto. Let's meet for lunch. Name a place that would be convenient for you and where you are not known."

Otto thought for a few moments. "I can be at the Belgrade Restaurant on Werderstrasse by twelve. It is not far from where I will be doing your work. Do you know how to get there? It is not far from the intersection of Parkallee and Werderstrasse."

"No problem, Otto. I'll be there at twelve o'clock on the dot."

Otto rubbed his chin and looked away. "What about my promised pay?"

Kurth answered, "No worry, Otto. If everything is working, I'll call you either tonight or tomorrow night and arrange to meet you. Okay?"

"Sounds fine. I do have a couple of questions for you. I want whoever is in the listening post to never use the phone. I do not want an investigation. Also, if anything does go wrong, or someone starts getting curious about the listening post, warn me immediately. I will remove the bridge and any other evidence in that junction box. Agreed?"

Kurth was pleased. Otto was not a good enough actor to feign such concern, it was genuine. "Agreed, Otto, and the same goes for you, the last thing we want is to end up with egg on our faces."

Otto got up from his chair and extended his hand. After they shook hands, Otto said, "Then we have a deal. I'm off to do the dirty work. I will see you at lunch."

Kurth arrived at the Belgrade Restaurant on time. Considering it was lunchtime, there were few patrons. An older man with Germanic features greeted him and ushered him to a booth in the back. When he asked Kurth what he would like to drink, his accent gave him away as being from the Balkans. Kurth ordered a beer and said he would order lunch when his friend arrived.

The Belgrade was a rather small establishment. There was a bar along one wall just inside the entrance. They also had two booths on the front wall with windows that gave a good view of the street if one was interested in watching passing traffic. The back wall, opposite the bar, had three booths and there were four tables in the center of the room. Two middle-aged men were sitting at the bar and, from their conversation, it was obvious they were also from the Balkans. Kurth knew there were many Yugoslavian restaurants throughout Germany that were run by Croats. They had allied with the Germans during World War Two and fled from Yugoslavia when the Communists took over.

Otto arrived and nodded to the waiter. He ordered a beer before he sat down opposite Kurth. They shook hands across the table. Otto watched as a rather ample young lady drew his beer.

"I'll explain things after we order," Otto said, adding something about the rain.

"The weather is pretty bad, even by Hamburg standards," Kurth said. The waiter arrived and they ordered a Balkan grill platter for two. Kurth observed that the restaurant was beginning to fill up, which he considered a promising sign. When the waiter left, Kurth turned his attention to Otto.

"Well, Otto, how did it go?"

"Everything should be fine. The tap is on the private line that does not go through the Consulate switchboard. If, for some reason, there is the need for a PTT serviceman to open the back of the junction box, I do not think he will notice anything wrong."

"Good work, Otto. I'll probably call you tonight. We'll meet at the Koenig at the time I give you on the phone. Is there any specific time you will not be able to make a meeting in the next couple of days?"

"Lunch time would be best for me. We could grab a couple of beers at the Koenig."

"Good, we will do the pass in the men's room, like we did before."

The waiter arrived with a large platter of assorted grilled meats. When they began eating, Kurth was pleasantly surprised at how well the meats were prepared. "This is not bad, Otto. You obviously have been here before."

"Not recently, it's been close to a year since I was last here. It's out of the usual area where I work. My wife doesn't care for these Balkan grills so, when we go out, we go to other restaurants."

"Well, it was a good choice," Kurth said as he raised his glass. "Let's drink to a successful business venture."

⇥▬◉ ◉▬⇤

Alain had spent the morning writing copious, but by and large fictional, notes about the operation code named BLACKROOT. He smirked as he made his notes. It was a failed operation in East Germany which the Stasi successfully penetrated shortly after it was launched. He had done an outline of the book he was supposed to be writing and was now trying to think of things that would bring the outline to life. He glanced at his watch. It was almost one o'clock and still no word from Kurth. He was getting edgy.

He had proposed the bank operation to Kurth based on his analysis that it was workable and the risks would be outweighed by the potential return. As he considered their involvement, it occurred to him that they had pretty much reached the point where the operation had taken on an existence of its own. If they were to abort, it must be soon. For the first time, he was having doubts about why he had pursued the operation in the first place. He was not rich, but he was comfortable. He was pretty much able to do whatever he pleased. He had argued to himself that he was not doing it for the money, but for the challenge and the accomplishment - like the man who climbed the mountain because it was there. In this case, he had to admit that he was not climbing a mountain - he was robbing a bank. He had to ask himself if people really robbed banks simply because of the challenge.

He could see himself a year from now, sitting in the evening, watching the light fade on the Rockies, smirking to himself that he had been the brains behind the robbery of a Swiss bank - a robbery he hoped would never be solved. He dismissed the image from his imagination and wondered if he was robbing a bank merely to prove that the agency was wrong about him and his capabilities. No, he thought, he was trying to prove to himself that he was a superb operations officer who had not been appreciated by his superiors in the operations directorate. *"Who are you kidding?* Alain questioned himself. He had to admit to a certain amount of bitterness over being forced into early retirement from the agency.

Face it, he said to himself, *a couple million dollars will make life very comfortable indeed.* It would also be his way of proving to himself that he was an effective planner. The irony was that if everything went as planned, no one would know what he had accomplished, a kind of Hobson's choice. It did occur to him that if his primary reason for mounting the operation were money, he would have a good reason. But the truth was, he had to admit that the additional money would probably not bring any major changes in his life style. He would certainly upgrade his cabin in Wyoming, but that was all that crossed his mind at the moment. Neither of his two wives understood why he had a cabin in Wyoming. He wondered how many times people put themselves in similar positions without fully understanding why.

He looked at his watch and his face knotted in concern over Kurth's whereabouts. If Otto had gotten cold feet then it was all over. He returned to making notes about the phantom book he was writing. In a relatively short time, the doorbell rang. He quickly went to the door and opened it. Kurth brushed by him, carrying a brown bag. When he got to the kitchen table he reached into the bag, withdrew a bottle of Henkell Sekt, and set it down.

"Alain," he said, "let's drink to our success. The initial crucial step in our little operation has been successfully negotiated. I have just come from lunch with one of the key members of our enterprise and he informed me that everything is in place." Kurth was effusive, "Do we have anything resembling wine glasses to drink to this milestone in our enterprise?"

"Yes, we do. There are a several of those glasses with green tinted stems that Germans use for white wine. I'll get a couple from the cabinet." Alain went to the cabinet, extracted two wine glasses, and put them on the table next to the bottle of Henkell. "They are not champagne flutes, but they will do."

Kurth poured the wine. "I think that we should drink to this auspicious beginning, but maybe we should make sure that the tap is functioning."

"Good thinking," Alain said with a smirk. "I'll take the back off the radio and we can watch to see if there is any action on the target's line." Alain used an old Swiss Army knife to remove the two screws holding the flimsy back of the radio. He set the plywood back of the radio aside. Both he and Kurth watched the Kudelski tape for several minutes before Alain announced that there appeared to be no calls on Wafiq's private line.

"Maybe he's out to a late lunch," Kurth offered as an explanation.

"Wait a minute," Alain exclaimed. "Jack showed me the counter. It measures how much tape is used. He told me to always make sure it was set on zero when

I put a new tape on the deck. This would make it easy to edit the tape. He specifically showed me that the counter was on zero before he replaced the back of the radio. If there have been any calls since Otto rigged the bridge, they should be registered on the counter." Alain looked at the counter. "Great! The counter registers eighty-three which means we probably have a couple of calls taped."

"What now, Alain? How soon before you call Hashem?" Kurth answered.

Alain thought for a moment. "The key information will probably be in German which I will pick up by reviewing the tapes. I don't think it's necessary to call for Hashem until we have several weeks of tapes. When he gets here, I want to keep him busy. His real function comes when we actually rob the bank."

"That's good thinking. Let's hope we get everything we need quickly."

"Agreed, my real worry is that our own people will find out I'm here, or the BKA will find out and ask why I am here."

Kurth smiled sympathetically. "How long do we run the tap before we must conclude that this isn't going to work?"

"I think if we don't get the information we need within six months, we call it quits."

"Agreed. Well, I'm planning to leave the day after tomorrow. When is Jack coming by to check everything out?"

"He should be here in a little over an hour. Why don't we meet tomorrow at your convenience? If everything is all right with the tape, you can go ahead and leave the day after tomorrow."

"Let's make it relatively early. If everything is okay, I can check out of my hotel. All I must do before leaving is pay off Otto. What about commo? I can't call you here."

"Let's meet tomorrow morning at ten at the cafe opposite the Four Seasons Hotel. With regards to commo, I'll call you at your office every Monday and Thursday. You can brief me on any upcoming travels to Germany. If there is anything unusual, I'll call immediately to let you know what is wrong, particularly if there is a need for you to come here and contact Otto."

"Monday and Thursday are okay for keeping me posted fairly regularly. If my secretary answers the phone, speak to her with a German accent. I'll tell her you're one of my many German relatives. If there's an emergency, you can even call after business hours and leave a message for me. Use the name Siegfried and just say that our cousin has died. I will leave as soon as possible and come here to see what the problem is."

"Okay, let's hope we are in the homestretch." They shook hands and Kurth left.

Alain cleaned the two wine glasses and put them back in the cabinet. He put the bottle of wine in the refrigerator. He did not want to have to explain to Blanton that he was drinking with someone. He went back to making notes on his fictitious interpretation of operation BLACKROOT. As he made an increasing number of notes, the thought occurred to him that maybe he could write something worth publishing. He certainly had the time now that he was retired, and since what he was writing was basically fiction, he should not have much trouble getting the Publications Review Board to pass on it. He was thinking about including a romantic interest between one of the CIA case officers involved in the operation and a German girl who was actually a Stasi plant. He was writing a description of the girl when the doorbell rang. Alain opened the door and Blanton entered carrying a bag and a large box. They exchanged greetings and Blanton set his packages down on the table.

Alain smiled at him and said, "Jack, it appears that everything is working. When I checked, the counter seems to be working well."

"Good, Alain. I've brought a tape recorder for you. Let's get it set up." Blanton took the tape recorder out of its box and plugged it into an outlet near the table. He took a set of headphones and four new tapes out of the bag. "Let's review everything. Alain, stop the tape deck, remove the tape, and put this new tape in its place."

Alain did as he was told. Blanton took the tape Alain had removed and put it on the tape recorder. He plugged the headphones into the tape recorder and gave them to Alain. "Have a listen to see how good the quality is."

Alain put on the headphones, turned the tape recorder on, and pushed start. He listened for a couple of minutes, then pushed the stop button. "There are three conversations on the tape. Two of them are in Arabic and one in German. The German one is obviously a call to a German girl friend, lots of flirting. His

German is pretty good. One of the conversations in Arabic is with a woman, maybe a wife."

Blanton nodded his head. "How is the quality?"

"Very good. I had no trouble getting all of the conversation in German."

"Well, you are up and running. Here is a list of how I spent the money you gave me. You owe me exactly two hundred and twenty-seven dollars."

"Good, Jack, I figured I owed you something. Let me get it for you. Remember, the more we save from the advance, the more we will have to divide when the operation is over." Alain got some cash from his bedroom and counted it out for Blanton. "How about a drink to celebrate?"

"I have yet to turn down a drink."

"Beer or wine?"

"I'll stick with beer."

Alain got two beers from the refrigerator and gave one to Blanton. After they toasted the success of the installation, Blanton said, "Since everything seems okay, I'll leave tomorrow as planned. How long is this tap supposed to go on?"

Alain shrugged his shoulders. "They told me six months at the most. I think they are trying to determine if the guy whose phone is tapped is involved in anything interesting."

"Okay, don't forget to keep fresh batteries in the Kudelski. You can pick up additional tapes anywhere. If anything goes wrong, give me a call and I'll come right over."

"Good, Jack. Thanks for all you have done."

⇀▰ ▰↽

July 6, 1982.

It was an unusually bright morning for Hamburg. Alain had walked to the coffee shop. There were several people there who looked like they had just come from daily mass. They were drinking coffee and eating pastries. Kurth arrived minutes after Alain. He ordered some coffee and joined Alain at his table. Alain had ordered a couple of the pastries. They were quite good so he told Kurth to help himself.

After he drank some coffee, Kurth questioned Alain, "Well, was there anything else on the tape?"

"Yes, there was an additional call in German. Wafiq is going to Paris for a week. He leaves tomorrow and plans to return on the thirteenth."

This bit of news caused Kurth to raise his eyebrows. "Any indication why he is going to Paris."

"No, the conversation was with Lufthansa."

"Well, if he is in Paris, there shouldn't be much for you to do for a week."

Alain ate some more of a pastry, his face in a familiar frown. It was always difficult to tell what Alain's frowns indicated. "I've decided to look at the German conversations every night and make notes on anything pertinent to our operation. I'll buy the tape splicer tomorrow morning. I hope one of us is able to mimic Wafiq by using the tapes of him speaking German. That is a very crucial step in this operation. You and I can both practice imitating his voice. I will erase the rest of the German conversations."

"Good thinking. I'm paying off Otto tonight. From my talks with him, I'm pretty sure he is on the up and up with us."

"What makes you so sure?"

"He asks the right questions and expresses the proper concerns. For instance, he insisted that I contact him immediately if there is any problem so that he can remove the bridge."

Alain nodded his appreciation. Otto was the only outsider involved in the operation and, as such, was potentially the weak link. Fortunately, he didn't have any inclination as to why they needed the tap.

"Good. I can now worry less about Otto. Let's review our commo. I've come up with some minor changes to our previous planning. I will just call you to check in every Thursday. If something comes up that needs your immediate presence in Germany, I will call and, if you are not in the office, will leave a message in German identifying myself as Siegfried and saying our cousin has died. I will also take a long walk every morning, leaving the house at precisely nine local time. I will walk to this coffee shop and have a cup of coffee. This should cover us if you come to Germany unexpectedly. You can wait for me in the coffee shop."

Kurth thought briefly before replying. "That should work. It's always best to dumb things down as much as possible. What about Hashem?"

"I want to wait as long as possible. It would be ideal if we could get something from the tapes indicating that we might have an operation before bringing Hashem over. I intend to call him toward the end of the month. I'll tell him that if all goes well I will need him sometime in mid-August."

As usual Kurth grimaced at the mention of Hashem's name. "I agree. The less time Hashem spends in Hamburg the better."

"Okay, Kurth, that's about it. I'll get back to working on my book. Have a pleasant trip back to Washington." Alain got up, shook Kurth's hand, and left the coffee shop.

Chapter 9

Hamburg. July 14, 1982.

"WELL WAFIQ, HOW was Paris?" Haitham Abd al-Nebi asked as he entered Wafiq's office. Wafiq grimaced and raised his hands, palms up, indicating that he didn't know exactly what to make of what had transpired in Paris.

"Difficult to say. My talks with Shapour Bakhtiar were interesting. We talked alone. If he is telling the truth, he has done a lot of planning but, as a realist, I must caution you that his plans seem very airy. In the first place, he requires an enormous amount of logistical support, things like helicopters and specialized weapons. I asked if he had enough people versed in the use of the various weapons he mentioned. He said he did, but I have my doubts. He is also obviously underestimating the financial backing he will need to carry out his plans. He asked for a relatively modest increase in the monthly payments we make to him. He said we could help by urging the Saudis to provide more in the way of financial assistance."

Haitham was immediately interested. "Did he give you any idea of how much the Saudis are currently providing him?"

"Yes and no, he mentioned no specific figures. He did tell me that Saudi financial aid to him to date has been limited. He said that they have promised him more in the future. He did tell me something I thought you would find very interesting. He told me that the Americans urged the Saudis to provide him with financial assistance."

Haitham raised his elegantly trimmed pair of eyebrows. "That is interesting, and it also makes sense. I wonder if the Americans are aware of our financial assistance to Bakhtiar. Did you get any inkling from him?"

Wafiq nodded his head with vigor. "I think you can consider that a certainty. Incidentally, they are also aware of our assistance to General Oviesi. Col. Qodsi told me that Oviesi said the Americans were aware of his trips to Baghdad and of our financial assistance to him. Qodsi is very concerned about how the Americans found out."

That's an easy one, thought Haitham to himself. Oviesi obviously thought it was in his best interest to tell the Americans. If they found out about his Iraqi funding without Oviesi having told them about it, they might have cut him off. "Oviesi has made several trips to Baghdad. The Americans are certainly aware of his travels and properly concluded these trips were for the purpose of dunning us for money."

"Haitham, I am just a simple businessman. This makes no sense to me. We are curiously allied with the Americans in this enterprise. We could probably save a lot of money by conferring with them and agreeing on how much the two of us should fund Bakhtiar and Oviesi."

As he laughed out loud, Haitham responded, "Your suggestion is not as off beat as you think. I, however, do not want to be the one to suggest it to Saddam."

⊷▭◉ ◉▭⊷

July 16, 1982.

Alain sipped a beer as he listened to tape from the period of Wafiq Tikriti's return on the thirteenth until two that afternoon. There were several conversations in German. Two of them involved a girl named Gerta with whom Wafiq was having a torrid affair. He had called her the day after he returned and arranged to meet her at seven in the evening on the fifteenth at the usual place. She had called him in the morning to talk about what a great time last night had been and proceeded to describe their exploits in graphic detail. On his part, Wafiq complimented her on her passion, telling her how anxious he was to see her soon. Alain noted the facts from these calls in a brief paragraph.

There was also a conversation late in the evening of the thirteenth, the day Wafiq returned from Paris. He called a female whom he referred to as Ingrid.

He asked her if the letter he was expecting had arrived. She told him it had and that it was in the office. He told her he would dictate an answer the following morning. Alain made a brief note that Ingrid must be a local hire working in Wafiq's office.

There was a very interesting call, made earlier in the day, that Alain was listening to for the second time. Wafiq had called the Banque Suisse in Geneva. When his call was answered, he asked for a Mr. Schlagel. The switchboard operator connected him and someone said, "Hello."

Wafiq answered, "Hello, Irwin, how are you?"

They obviously knew each other well. After some small talk, Wafiq asked if any deposits had been made in the account since his last call. Schlagel had asked him to wait a minute, then came back on the line to say that fourteen million dollars had been deposited the day before. Wafiq thanked him, saying that he had several checks to write and wanted to make sure the deposit had been made. Alain thought to himself, *At least we now know the name of the person he deals with in the Banque Suisse.* Alain made some notes and then listened to the beginning of the call several times, counting the number of clicks when Wafiq dialed the number. He then added the phone number to his notes. He would call his reconstruction of the number in the next few days to make sure he had correctly deciphered the number of the Banque Suisse Branch where Wafiq did business.

There were two calls from persons who obviously had dealings with Wafiq. Both calls dealt with shipments of unidentified goods to Iraq. One of the calls dealt with a shipment that had been scheduled to arrive in Amman on the twelfth of July. Wafiq had promised payment as soon as he received confirmation that the shipment had arrived in Baghdad. Both of the calls were in German.

Since Alain had decided to save some of the German conversations, he took the tape splicer out of the closet and set it up on the kitchen table. Using the splicer, he carefully cut out all the conversations he had of Wafiq speaking German. He then spliced these segments together on a spare tape reel, eliminating the ones with the girlfriend. He planned to practice trying to imitate Wafiq's German. The next time Kurth was in Germany, he would give him part of the tape and let him also practice imitating Wafiq. The success of the operation depended on one of them being able to at least come close to imitating Wafiq's German.

Alain was surprised at the very limited number of conversations on the tape. He took the notes he made from the tapes, which at the moment were only one sheet of paper, and concealed the paper by removing the bottom drawer of the dresser in his bedroom and placing the notes on the plywood bottom of the dresser. He then replaced the drawer. He was stumped briefly on what to do with the tape. Finally, he decided to conceal it in the back of the radio. The tape deck did not take up much space. There was room for several tape reels. When he had everything back in place, he opened another beer and decided he was going to have a lot of time on his hands to write his book.

→─● ●─←

July 27, 1982.

"I am glad I caught you in the office," Col. Qodsi said to Wafiq over the phone. "I saw Bakhtiar last night and he wants to see you as soon as possible."

Wafiq didn't like the sound of Qodsi's voice. "Why so soon? I was just there at the beginning of the month."

There was a long pause at the other end of the line. Wafiq thought that Qodsi probably didn't know the answer to his question. Finally, Qodsi responded, "I prefer not to discuss the matter on the telephone. One point you should bear in mind. He thinks you are an important person, one who looks right up the ass of the camel. I think it best that you come here and we can talk before you see Bakhtiar. He suggested this weekend. He will keep Saturday open."

"Okay, I will fly over on Friday," Wafiq replied, with little enthusiasm. "I will call you later in the week to tell you where I am staying. If you are free, let us have dinner Friday night."

"It will be my pleasure. *Illa liqah* (until we meet)."

After he hung up, Wafiq considered his very brief conversation with Colonel Qodsi. The brevity was unusual. Normally, there would be considerable time devoted to mutual flattery. Since this was absent, Wafiq assumed that Qodsi was upset by his appearance on the scene. Wafiq thought for a few moments on what he should do about it, but in the end, he decided it was best to let Qodsi do the worrying. He had his own worries. He was concerned about how much Saddam really expected from the likes of Shapour Bakhtiar. Sooner or later, Baghdad would ask for his views on Bakhtiar's capabilities. They were spending enviable sums on Bakhtiar's potential ability to affect the progress of the war. Wafiq, being a survivor, would append his analysis to Col. Qodsi's and Haitham Abd al-Nebi's estimates of what Bakhtiar was capable or not capable of doing.

There were some attractive side benefits to visiting Paris. On his last trip, he had met an attractive Syrian lady currently at loose ends. Thinking of his new interest aroused him so he placed a call to Gerta. Gerta was always available and almost within walking distance, not a two-hour flight away.

⇢▸▪◉ ◉▪◂⇠

"You are traveling on Saturday, the thirty-first? Good. There are some developments we can discuss that you will find interesting. When can you be in Hamburg?" Alain was talking to Kurth from an international phone booth at the Hamburg Airport. He sometimes called from the railroad station, or anywhere he could use one of the red PTT calling cards.

"I first plan to see Ulla and the kids, then I have some business to attend to in Hanover next Monday. I'll get a train to Hamburg late Monday and see you Tuesday morning."

They had agreed to keep phone conversations short, so Alain confirmed the Tuesday morning meeting and hung up.

⇢▸▪◉ ◉▪◂⇠

Paris. July 30, 1982.
"You mean to say that he wants the use of several helicopters to move people?" Wafiq asked incredulously. Col. Qodsi shrugged his shoulders and turned his palms towards the heavens to indicate that he had no explanation.

"Yes, and he added that he had asked the Americans but they turned him down."

Wafiq's laugh was more like a smirk. "Well, at least the Americans are showing good sense. Did he say anything to back up his request?"

"He claims that he has recruited a group of military officers, or rather ex-military officers, among whom are several Bakhtiari clansmen who have assured our friend Shapour Bakhtiar that they can cause much disruption behind the Iranian lines. They claim they can cut communications, which aren't particularly good to begin with, and also disrupt the production of oil from the fields within and near the Bakhtiari tribal areas."

Wafiq wondered what the DGI in Baghdad thought about Bakhtiar's claims. Qodsi interrupted his thought process. "He insists that this is something he is doing primarily to help us in the war. He apparently has bigger plans he will probably want to discuss with you." Col. Qodsi stopped, offered a cigarette from a silver case, took one himself and then lit both. "One other point you should be aware of."

"Yes, what is it?" Wafiq was still mulling over the request for helicopters.

"As you know, Bakhtiar has French citizenship due to his marriage with a French woman. The French provide him with around the clock protection. A key figure in the protection is his son, who is an officer in the French Police. I suggest to you that we must assume the French authorities are fully briefed on our conversations with Bakhtiar."

"How nice," Wafiq replied, wondering what support the French Government was giving Bakhtiar. In a more serious voice, he asked, "What does Baghdad have to say on this point?"

Qodsi was taken aback by Wafiq's question. He assumed that Wafiq was better informed than he was. "I cannot give you a full briefing because I do not know. I would assume from the fact of your involvement that they are not overly concerned on this point. This is something you might raise with them."

Touché, thought Wafiq. Qodsi had put the ball in his court. Never underestimate someone's intelligence. He decided to flatter Qodsi, something he was very good at. "Well done, Colonel. What time do we see Mr. Bakhtiar?"

"He has asked us to stop by tomorrow afternoon at three o'clock. His son will probably be there. I will point him out to you."

Wafiq remained silent for a short time. They were in a Lebanese restaurant justly famous for its cuisine. They had finished eating and were having Turkish coffee. He thought that it was one thing for the French to know they were seeing Bakhtiar on a regular basis but, he did not want to expand the numbers of those in the know. He decided to make his thinking clear to Qodsi. "Why don't you pick me up at my hotel tomorrow at about two-thirty? I think it best that we take the Metro. His apartment is not far from the Nouilly Station. It will be better than showing up in an Embassy car."

Qodsi agreed, paid the bill, and left after wishing Wafiq a good night. While walking back to his hotel, Wafiq thought of calling his new Syrian acquaintance, Muna, but decided she could wait until he finished with Bakhtiar the following day. Since it was early, he went to the hotel bar and ordered a Cognac. He was very concerned about his new assignment, Shapour Bakhtiar. He suspected that Saddam did not fully trust Col. Qodsi, but then Saddam didn't fully trust anyone. He would have to be very careful since Saddam would be receiving reports both from him and from unidentified others, including Colonel Qodsi and Haitham Abd al-Nebi. Wafiq sipped his Cognac thoughtfully, hoping perhaps for some inspiration, but had to be satisfied with a warm feeling in his stomach.

->=== (===<-

Goslar. August 1,1982.

"I meant what I said, Ulla. I have long regretted our divorce. The regret grows with each passing year. I was not much at regretting things in the past, but I now know what a burden regret can be." He smiled wryly at Ulla and saw that her eyes glistened with moisture. He leaned forward and said, "I keep thinking of the old saw, time heals all wounds." Ulla didn't answer at once. She averted her eyes from Kurth and looked at the Harz Mountains in the distance. They were seated at a small table outside a cafe. Both were drinking beer. Ulla drank some before answering him.

"Our divorce has not been an event I look back on with any pleasure. Perhaps we have both matured. I thought you would remarry and am still surprised that you haven't." She was seated facing the setting sun and its rays seemed caught in her hair. Her eyes were pale blue, full of expression. He remembered he was enamored of her the first time he looked into those eyes. She looked intently at him and said, "I never seriously considered remarrying."

Kurth smiled, but it was one of those painful ones in which no pleasure resides. "I was certain you would marry immediately and was worried it would cause me some difficulties in seeing the kids."

"How do you mean?"

"Well, I would be very uncomfortable coming to see them and having to face you and your new husband."

Ulla's face registered amusement. "You know it might have been worth it for me to marry just to see how you would have reacted to meeting my new husband for the first time."

They both laughed and Kurth reached across the table to take her hand. They were still holding hands sometime later.

→■◯ ◯■←

Hamburg. August 3, 1982.

Kurth arrived at their designated meeting spot, the coffee shop opposite the Four Seasons Hotel, before Alain. He ordered coffee and some pastries and waited impatiently for Alain to arrive. He had walked to the coffee shop from the Prem Hotel. His watch read six minutes after nine and there was no sign of Alain. He wondered if anything was wrong. He was still uneasy about their enterprise. There were numerous ways in which things could go wrong but nothing that would likely deter Alain from pursuing the operation like a modern Galahad in search of the Holy Grail. Just thinking of Alain's operation made him frown. In fact, frowning came easily when he considered some of Alain's past operational ideas. He hoped it was just a good exercise. Alain finally showed up at ten past nine. He ordered coffee, sat down with Kurth, and began eating a pastry.

"Well?" Kurth asked.

Alain smiled, put down the remains of the pastry, and drank some coffee before answering Kurth. "Well, I think we have a possible window for mounting the operation. As we speak, Wafiq is in Paris. At least, he was there yesterday."

"So what? His being in Paris could be a one-time thing. Do you have any idea why he is there?"

"I don't think this is a one-time thing. He has been there twice since we last met. I found out about both trips because he had his German secretary make the plane reservations. Early last week, he called a female in Paris named Muna. He apparently called her at her work place because he had to speak English to the person who answered the phone. He asked for Muna Derasi. I'm not sure about the last name."

Kurth interrupted, "Obviously, he has a new involvement."

"No, while he was out of his office here, he got a call from Paris that was answered by his German Secretary. It was Col. Qodsi calling from Paris. Fortunately, the conversation was in English. The secretary instructed Qodsi to call back in an hour. I suspect that the two trips to Paris are official and Muna is after-hours amusement."

Kurth thought Alain was reading a lot into two trips to Paris. He smiled halfheartedly at Alain. "I suspect you are saying that the ideal time to pull off the operation would be during one of Wafiq's absences in Paris?"

"Well, we are on the same page. I think that the only way we can chance the operation is when Wafiq is out of town. I want you to give some thought as to how you think the operation can be mounted if we get lucky and our tap produces the crucial information we need." Alain paused ever so briefly, "Let's review what we know. First, Wafiq travels. On the current trip to Paris he departed last Friday and, as of yesterday, he was still in Paris. That means that when he goes to Paris we can count on him being there for several days. Second, we know the name of his contact in the Banque Suisse." Alain smiled, relishing Kurth's expression of surprise. "Wafiq called him last week, his name is Irwin Schlagel."

Kurth pursed his lips, his expression stating clearly that progress was being made. "That's fine, Alain, but we need a lot more before we can think of mounting the operation."

Alain was somewhat irritated with his friend, "Look, Kurth, you know what I know. Give some thought about the minimum additional information we need to mount our operation and how we would go about it. I will do the same thing and we can compare notes before you return to Washington."

"That's a good idea. What about Hashem?"

"I think the less time he spends here the better. We can wait a while before we bring him over. I suspect that the information we need may come from phone conversations between Schlagel and Wafiq."

Kurth wasn't so sure, "The Arabic conversations might give us definite information about potential trips out of town long before he makes plane reservations. Hashem is the only way we can get that information. One other thing we desperately need to know is how he arranges for a third party to withdraw from the account. Advance word of any such transaction may only be in Arabic."

Alain had to admit that Kurth had a valid point. "Good point. I think the timing for bringing Hashem over should be right after the tap produces a conversation between Wafiq and his banker, Irwin Schlagel. Such a conversation should give us the mechanics of the transaction."

"There is a time problem. It will take us a while to get our ducks in line."

"That, Kurth, is why I want your ideas on how to mount the operation when the time comes. We must be pretty well prepared when we get a window to pull it off."

"Agreed. I'll be tied up until the weekend."

Alain toyed with his coffee cup. When he was thinking, he liked to toy with anything at hand such as cutlery, pens or pencils. "I want you to come to the apartment after dark. That way Mrs. Baumgartner won't get a good look at you. There is something I want to show you."

"Okay, I'll come by late Friday night. Mrs. Baumgartner and I have talked a couple of times. I don't want her to see me so expect me after nine."

With all their business concluded, Alain asked him about Ulla and the kids. Alain's question brought a smile to Kurth's face. "They are all fine. Ulla is one fine mother. Living in the shadow of the Harz Mountains is great for the kids. Ulla's parents are still alive so the kids are well cared for."

"I find it hard to believe that a sophisticate like Ulla would be happy living in an isolated village with the closest town of any size being Goslar."

"An unusual woman, Alain, she loves the place and is devoted to the kids." Kurth's expression told more than his words. "You know, Alain, I said something to her this trip that I thought I would never say. I told her the divorce was the worst thing that ever happened to me. She laughed and said the divorce was hardly something she recalled fondly." Kurth sat silently for a moment pondering something. "I thought I'd have a ball after the divorce, going from one attractive woman to another, enjoying life to the fullest. I was surprised at how soon it all got old."

Alain laughed. "Maybe it's true, wisdom only comes with age."

--->===) (===<---

Hamburg. August 6, 1982.

Kurth arrived at Alain's apartment shortly after nine in the evening. Alain fixed drinks of scotch and water and turned on the radio Blanton had purchased to conceal the tape recorder. Kurth had given serious thought to the key pieces of information they must acquire if they were even going to consider mounting the operation. In some complex operations, the more information you gather in support of the operation, the more questions you have to answer. Kurth wasn't at all sure the tap would provide all the answers. Too often technical operations that appear promising before the fact do not produce intelligence worth the effort to mount them.

Alain busied himself with dinner in between sips of scotch. He was pan grilling two thick pork chops. He put a salad he had made on the table, then checked on a pot in which he was cooking string beans. Alain gestured to Kurth with his stirring spoon.

"The tap seems to be working well. Let's hope it produces the key items we need."

"I'm told that patience is always rewarded," Kurth answered him.

"Well, let's eat. We can review things after we finish."

Alain brought two plates with a pork chop and some string beans on each to the table. They ate quickly, discussing how beautiful a city Hamburg could be on the rare occasions that the sun appeared. After dinner, Alain poured coffee and a glass of Asbach for himself. Kurth declined the Asbach and, instead, fixed himself a scotch and soda. After a couple of healthy pulls on his scotch, Kurth broke the silence.

"Per your instructions, I have given this caper a lot of thought. So far we haven't learned a lot. We do know that a Mr. Schlagel is the officer in the Banque Suisse with whom Wafiq deals on matters concerning the account. I did some checking through my company and learned that Mr. Schlagel is a fairly senior officer in the Banque Suisse. This means the account is a large one. The Swiss do not go this far out of their way unless it is a large account. First, and most critical, we must obtain from the tap at least one withdrawal arranged by Wafiq. It may take more than one. All we have to go on at the moment is your recollections from the take on the previous tap. Have you picked up any indication about a possible withdrawal in the near future?"

Alain rubbed his chin before answering. He had hoped the tap would have produced more information on the bank account and the arrangements for third person withdrawals. "So far there is nothing on any withdrawals. There was a conversation yesterday in which Wafiq asked Schlagel about the account. Per Schlagel, as of the fourth there were at least eighteen million dollars in the account."

Alain's comments made Kurth breath deeply. "At least we know there is enough money in the account to guarantee a comfortable retirement. Anything else turn up?"

"Yes, as you mentioned before, the first indication of a third party withdrawal will probably be in one of the Arabic conversations on the tap. For instance, Wafiq's call to Schlagel came after two calls from Baghdad which I can't understand. I think it is possible that the call to his banker was a natural follow up to the two calls."

"All the more reason for Hashem's presence here," Kurth interjected.

"I think we can wait a while, Kurth. Remember the key information for us may not be in Arabic. It will probably be a conversation between Wafiq and Schlagel," Alain responded. "Look, let's set Hashem aside for the moment. The less time he spends here the better. What do you have to add?"

Kurth hoped he wasn't leading himself into a trap set by Alain. "If we get the needed information on third person withdrawals then, of course, Hashem's big role comes into play. I am assuming all the persons making these withdrawals are Iraqis. It would be nice if this were not the case, but I think we can be pretty sure they will be Iraqis. This means we must provide Hashem with Iraqi documentation. This could be a problem. But then, knowing you, I assume you have a solution to this problem."

"Blanton claims to have a contact who can provide a counterfeit Iraqi passport that will be good enough for flash purposes and identification. Hashem will also need a light disguise. As soon as we obtain the information on the withdrawal, I'll get Blanton back over here to get the passport. I will tell Hashem to get the disguise himself. He has used them before and I'll tell him to keep it simple."

Kurth nodded his agreement, "I don't think we can do much more planning until we have more information."

Alain frowned and furrowed his brow in thought. "There is one other thing we must think about. One of us must imitate Wafiq when he speaks in German with Schlagel. I think I mentioned it to you before. I have cut out all the German conversations to date to fit with our cover story that the BKA deleted all conversations involving Germans. I have saved the conversations between Wafiq and Schlagel. I want you to practice imitating Wafiq speaking German. When we do the operation, I want to be in Geneva to make sure Hashem turns over the bearer bonds." Alain got up from his chair and went into the bedroom. He returned holding a spool with a small amount of tape on it. He smiled and handed it to Kurth. "Here, Kurth, this will give you something to do in your plush office back in Washington."

Kurth smiled. "I would like to only travel here on legitimate company business so I am well covered. Since I average a trip to Germany every four or five weeks this should work out okay. If there is an emergency, just signal me. When you call, use the death in the family ploy we discussed at the last meeting. In getting leave, I can also tell the company that attending the funeral will give me a chance to see Ulla and kids."

Alain nodded his approval and accompanied Kurth to the door. "Okay, Kurth, let's hope the tap gives us a breakthrough in the near future."

⇥ ⇤

August 9, 1982.

"Haitham, old friend, I must confess to you that I am concerned about our dealings with Bakhtiar. I feel like I am encased in glass in Paris. The French know we are dealing with him and Bakhtiar has told the Americans he is seeing us. Maybe we should arrive at a tripartite agreement on what to do with Bakhtiar."

Haitham laughed, "It's enough to drive a man to the opium pipe. I suspect Saddam involved you to make some sense out of it. I know for a fact that he is convinced that these opposition groups can do something to help our war effort."

Wafiq was far from reassured. "Haitham, you are an intelligence officer. According to what Qodsi told me in Paris, and what I heard directly from Bakhtiar last week, the Americans have refused to provide any material support. He specifically asked for helicopters and, by his own admission, was turned down flat. He says he gets all the money he needs from several sources. His problem is that he has no way of getting the material and logistic support he claims he needs to be successful. What do you think?"

Haitham stroked his mustache with the thumb and forefinger of his left hand. "I suppose the Americans provide him funds for the same reason we do. They, like us, hope he can do something to frustrate and cause problems for the Iranians. I think you should see him a few more times. Get a feel for what he may be able to do, but more importantly, what he can't do. Send your findings to Baghdad, carefully worded of course. You might want to ask Qodsi's opinions to flatter him and also involve him in the conclusions you make in your report."

"You are right. Sooner or later I must provide Baghdad with my views. In addition, I get to go to Paris, and that I enjoy. Several trips to Paris in the next couple of months will be relaxing. Tell me, Haitham, have you and your people picked up any worthwhile information on Iranian opposition groups?"

Initially, Haitham didn't want to get involved with Iranian opposition groups. Wafiq was not privy to the fact that Zaki Sa'duni had charged him to determine not only the potential of Iraqi opposition groups in Europe, but also to develop information on Iranian attempts to manipulate Iraqi opposition groups. Friendships count heavily among Arabs. Haitham decided to brief Wafiq on Sa'duni's interest in Iranian attempts to manipulate Iraqi opposition groups, since this would be a natural subject for Wafiq to bring up with Bakhtiar.

"In truth, old friend, since we are not targeted against Iranian Opposition groups, what information we do get is a by-product of our basic interests. I can tell you that we assess the Iranian opposition groups as being unable to directly influence events in Iran. On the other hand, Iran can use the Da'wa Party to mount disruption operations in Southern Iraq. They assassinated several Iraqi senior officials in Southern Iraq during the early days of the war. I think it might be worthwhile for you to ask Bakhtiar if he knows anything about Iranian dealings with Iraqi opposition groups. On my part, I will see what information I can get on the potential of Iranian opposition groups. Baghdad is very much interested in just what kind of an organization the young Shah has."

A smile of satisfaction lit up Wafiq's face. "Thanks, Haitham, I need all the help I can get. The young Shah has come up in my discussions in Paris. At the moment I can make no definitive conclusion, but I suspect Bakhtiar is well disposed towards the young man."

Wafiq's comment brought an expression of interest to Haitham's face. "I think we should both try to develop more information on the young Shah's activities. I am sure Baghdad would prefer the Shah in power over the mullahs."

Wafiq laughed. "That goes without saying, Haitham."

⋯⊱━⊰ ⊱━⊰⋯

August 12, 1982.

Alain was a little concerned. A week had passed since Wafiq returned from Paris. There had been no indication of a pending withdrawal from the Banque Swiss account nor had there been any calls between Wafiq and Schlagel, the bank manager. Since his return, Wafiq had spent two nights with his German girl friend,

Gerta. Yesterday he had called Muna in Paris, but Alain got nothing from their conversation since it was in Arabic.

He had been out most of the day getting some exercise and shopping for food and drink. It was late in the afternoon when he returned to the apartment. He decided to check the tape deck before he prepared his dinner of bratwurst, beer, and a salad. He opened the back of the radio, took the tape off the deck, and replaced it with a new one. He put the tape on his tape recorder and, using the earphones, began to listen to the tape. There was a call from Gerta in which she and Wafiq explained what they would do to each other when they met the following day. Wafiq had proposed meeting her for dinner at his favorite restaurant but Gerta insisted that he come to her place first.

There were several calls in Arabic. A call towards the end of the tape caught Alain's attention. It was from Wafiq to the Banque Suisse. He asked to speak to Mr. Irwin Schlagel. When Schlagel came on the line, Wafiq told him there was someone coming from Baghdad to make a withdrawal. Schlagel asked if the arrangements would be the same as before. Wafiq told him they would. He was assuming that the person to make the withdrawal would arrive in Hamburg at the beginning of next week, but was uncertain because of the disruption of travel due to the war. Schlagel told Wafiq to call him with the details as soon as the person making the withdrawal arrived in Hamburg. Wafiq thanked Schlagel profusely and hung up.

There was nothing else of any significance on the tape, but Alain was euphoric. Hopefully, he was close to gaining the critical information on how Wafiq and Schlagel made the arrangements for a third party to make a withdrawal from the bank. Alain spent several minutes in deep thought, nurturing his bottle of beer. He considered getting Hashem Samara'i to Hamburg as soon as possible so they could get a reading on the various conversations in Arabic. Those conversations would possibly be the only way they could get advance notification of Wafiq's pending travel. In the end, he thought it best to take no precipitous action until he had the critical piece of information in hand. It was possible that any arrangements made between Schlagel and Wafiq would complete all the information he needed to plan the actual operation.

He put down the earphones and busied himself with his solitary dinner. He wondered what Jane was doing. He missed their now regular dates. She was a lively dinner companion who was able to get more out of an evening with Alain than most people.

→▶ ◀←

Washington. August 12, 1982.

Kurth sat in his office, a worried look on his face. The lack of any word from Alain was disconcerting. He considered all sorts of possibilities. Had the tap been accidentally uncovered? He dismissed this as unlikely. He thought that the most likely possibility was that Wafiq had devised a new system for arranging third party withdrawals from the account. Such a development would make their proposed operation even more difficult.

He wished Alain would call with some kind of development that would need his presence in Germany. He was thinking more about Ulla than the operation. Since saying goodbye, Ulla had been constantly in his thoughts. He found he could think of nothing but his growing desire for them to take up where they had left off. He came close to proposing a second chance to her during his last visit to Germany, but sensed she would have rejected the idea. He wondered if she ached for him the way he ached for her. His thoughts were interrupted by the ring of his telephone.

→▶ ◀←

Hamburg. August 14, 1982.

Haitham Abd al-Nebi entered Wafiq's office unannounced. "Wafiq, old friend, I thought I'd stop by to mull some things over with you, then take you to lunch."

"*Ahlan wa-sahlan.* You are most welcome, Haitham. I must go to Paris in the near future and need your counsel before I meet with Shapour Bakhtiar and some of his advisors." Wafiq smiled at Haitham and motioned him to a chair. Actually, the reason Wafiq was planning a trip to Paris concerned Muna more than Bakhtiar. He had called her the previous evening and promised to be with her in Paris within the week. Wafiq mentally set Muna aside and focused his attention on Haitham.

"What news do you have for me and how can I be of service?"

"There are several questions I want to bring up with you. First, and most important to us at the moment, is determining what the CIA is doing with dissident Iraqis. One of my officers is running a double agent against the CIA. This agent has met twice recently with CIA case officers, once in Cyprus and once in Switzerland. The most interesting fact to come out of these meetings is the agent's claim that the CIA is very actively seeking out dissident Iraqis all over Europe."

Wafiq was incredulous. He respected people like Haitham and Zaki Sa'duni whom he knew. But, besides a few talented individuals, the Iraqi intelligence services were not noted for competence. "You believe the agent?"

"Yes, because the CIA case officers asked his opinion about various Iraqi opposition groups and also asked the agent to speculate on whether the CIA could approach certain individuals."

Wafiq was still uncertain. "Haitham, I just cannot see the CIA asking some agent such questions after one or two meetings."

Haitham was a little irritated at Wafiq. Professional intelligence officers do not like their competence questioned. "I can understand your questions. The two meetings I mentioned are only the most recent and the first time the CIA case officers have asked the agent such sensitive questions. They have been meeting with this agent for the better part of a year. They gave him a polygraph examination about six months ago."

"Did he pass?"

Haitham shrugged, "Who knows? They didn't tell him if he passed or flunked. Since they have continued to run him as a case for six months after the test, we assume he passed. The significance of these last two meetings is that we can expect the CIA to be very active among the Iraqi community in Europe. In the past, the CIA has used Arab-American citizens to approach Iraqis in Europe. I have given you pictures of those we have identified. You also have information on non-Arab CIA case officers who have been active against Iraqi officials trying to recruit them as intelligence agents. Given their experience against us, we assume they are also seeking to recruit dissident Iraqis. I suppose they intend to use them to engage in disruption activities back in Iraq."

"Would you consider this Consulate a target?"

"I doubt it. You are off the beaten track, but you never know. What I have been doing in the past month is briefing all of my people. I have them study photographs of known CIA officers. We have been encouraging all loyal Iraqis living in Europe to report any suspicious contacts between dissident Iraqis and Americans in Europe. In fact, Wafiq, I want you to study the photographs that I gave you of CIA agents. All of those men have operated against us in the past."

Wafiq found it difficult to accept Haitham's deep concern about the CIA and dissident Iraqis. Hamburg was hardly swarming with Iraqis. He had not come across any activities by Iraqis that could be considered hostile to Saddam's regime. On the other hand, he had never really taken it upon himself to determine if there were any Iraqi dissidents lurking about Hamburg.

"Haitham, I must confess to you that it never occurred to me that there may be dissident Iraqis in Hamburg who are involved in some kind of anti-regime activity. There are some Shias here who frequent the Iranian mosque, but they are mostly businessmen and a few students. Ahmad goes to the mosque on occasion. He is very loyal to the regime and I am sure that he would report anything he deemed suspicious. I have given you the names of several Iraqi businessmen resident in Hamburg. Is there anything more specific you want me to do?"

Haitham considered Wafiq's question. More to the point, he considered Wafiq. He had known Wafiq for some time and respected his intelligence, but his personal assessment led him to believe that Wafiq would avoid engaging in intelligence activities. He decided to ask Wafiq to do things that would not unduly burden him. "Do you have a listing of all the Iraqi students studying in the area?"

"We can put one together. I can get you a list of all those on government scholarships immediately, since we are directly involved in funding their education."

"That would be very helpful. I will have one of my younger officers go over the list and target some individuals for recruitment. We may be able to make one or two of them of interest to one of the opposition groups, and perhaps the CIA. Anything else?"

"Well, from time to time we get non-scholarship students coming in to have their passports renewed, or for various other reasons. We always make a note of their visits and we have their addresses on record. It will take us some time to go through all our files. As you can see, Ahmad and I are the only Iraqi officials here. All the others are German citizens."

"I can lend you one of my men. He can work after hours or on the weekends if you wish. I don't want one of your local employees alerting the local police about anything they view as suspicious."

Wafiq knew full well that he was in a position where he had to cooperate. "Look, I can say he is someone who has come from Baghdad to look into the Consulate's activities. In fact, he can stay with me. I have plenty of room upstairs."

"Excellent, Wafiq, excellent."

⇥▬ ▬⇤

August 16, 1982.

Alain ate a sandwich for lunch and washed it down with a beer. He thought to himself that sitting on a telephone tap had to be one of the most boring jobs in the world. The only break in the boredom was when Wafiq called his Swiss banker on Thursday about someone making a withdrawal. Now, he was worried. Four days had passed with nothing further on the tap. He wondered if Wafiq had changed the system. There was a possibility the Banque Suisse may have insisted on some changes. If this was the case, they were out of business. He told himself not to panic.

He decided to occupy himself by working on the book he was writing as a cover. He made some notes about his characters. At six o'clock, he took a break to fix a drink. He would listen to the day's take while enjoying his martini. He put aside his notes. After preparing stew ingredients for his dinner, he fixed his martini. With the stew on simmer, he retrieved the tape from the back of the radio. He listened to several conversations in Arabic. One involved Wafiq with a very excited Muna. He didn't need to understand Arabic to figure out the gist of their conversation. She was blowing him kisses interspersed with long, low moans. Alain smiled. War or no war, Wafiq was taking good care of his personal needs.

Two calls later, Alain sat bolt upright in his chair. A woman had answered Wafiq's call. Alain was certain it was the receptionist in the Banque Suisse. He was right. Wafiq asked to speak to Mr. Schlagel. When Schlagel came on the line, they exchanged greetings. Alain surmised from their phone conversation that the two had done a lot of business together. Alain replayed the exchange several times.

"Irwin, an Iraqi gentleman will call at your bank at eleven o'clock the day after tomorrow, the eighteenth. His name is Sa'id Basrawi, his father's name is Isma'il. Today, I will DHL a photocopy of his passport, one half of a ten-mark note and a piece of paper containing three signatures executed by Basrawi in my presence. The amount he is to withdraw is three million, two hundred and fifty thousand dollars. The three million should be in bearer bonds and the two hundred and fifty thousand in cash." There was a slight pause at the other end of line. Alain assumed that Schlagel was writing down the facts.

"I will take care of everything as in the past, Mr. Tikriti. If there is any problem, I will call you immediately." There was a slight pause, then Schlagel spoke again, "Do you want me to call you to confirm that the withdrawal has been made?"

"That is not necessary, Irwin. I will be tied up the day after tomorrow. I am leaving for Paris that evening. Oh, I have one question. What will the account balance be after the withdrawal?"

There was a pause while Irwin called up the account. Finally, Irwin told him that the account had just received a substantial deposit. He told Wafiq that, after the withdrawal, there would be twenty-one million dollars left in the account. What intrigued Alain the most was that, less than two minutes after Wafiq hung up, Schlagel called back and confirmed everything Wafiq had told him in the previous conversation.

Alain picked up his martini, sipped it thoughtfully, and smiled. He wondered how much of the withdrawal would be transferred to private accounts. Well, hopefully, that is what he would be doing with the account. He decided it was time to pull the troops together. He would first call Kurth to see how soon he could be in

Hamburg. They needed to get their heads together and do some serious planning. It was already obvious to Alain that the best time to mount the operation would be during one of Wafiq's now fairly frequent visits to Paris. He would call Blanton and ask him how long it would take him to get an Iraqi passport. He decided to wait a few days before calling Hashem. The less time he spent in Hamburg, the better. Hashem was the type of person who cut a wide swath wherever he went. Alain picked up his martini, leaned back in his chair, and considered where he would go to dinner to celebrate. The stew would keep until tomorrow.

-->|==) (==|<--

Paris. August 18, 1982.

Wafiq and Muna ate dinner at a small restaurant near Muna's apartment. Afterwards, they walked the short distance to her apartment. As soon as she closed the door behind them, she began kissing Wafiq passionately. They literally tore each other's clothes off as they made their way to the bedroom. Their mutual desires overwhelmed them both in a very brief, passionate encounter. Shortly thereafter, they lay side by side talking. Wafiq, gazing at Muna's nude body, concluded that she worked hard at keeping her figure. He wondered why she had never married. Muna smiled at him and told him to get some sleep since she would wake him in a couple of hours. Wafiq said he could hardly wait. He lay quietly, thinking about the incredible passion that Muna put into sex. He had never experienced anything to match it in any other woman. The most attractive aspect of the affair was that she was in Paris and he was in Hamburg. It was a very nice arrangement, no complications. He grinned, enjoying his predicament - Muna in Paris, Gerta in Hamburg, and his wife in Baghdad. Well, one must enjoy the pleasures of life while one can, thought Wafiq. He must build up the importance of his contact with Bakhtiar in Paris as something of value to the Iraqi war effort so that he could continue to make frequent trips to Paris. He had no sooner dozed off than Muna woke him up by blowing into his ear.

-->|==) (==|<--

Hamburg. August 19, 1982.

Kurth had listened to the conversation between Wafiq and Schlagel three times. Finally, he turned off the tape recorder and said to Alain. "It's incredible. This system they are using now resembles the system they were using when we had the tap on a couple of years ago. I was certain that, by this time, they would have devised another system and that would put an end to our operation. Well, old friend, let's put our heads together and see if we can devise a workable plan. I suggest that we start with the robbery and work backwards. Any thoughts?" Kurth asked, a pleased grin on his face.

Alain was surprised, but also upbeat. This was the first time Kurth was so positive. This was an opportunity. He had expected Kurth to remain at least a little reticent.

"Well, the only worry I have at the moment is that Hashem has to be the one to go into the Banque Suisse and make the withdrawal. On the plus side, he will have no difficulty impersonating an Iraqi. Our problem is how do we get Hashem into the Banque Suisse?" Alain questioned Kurth.

Kurth looked at Alain, a little surprised at the question. "What the hell, Alain, he will be impersonating an Iraqi official. This is something he has done in the past. Let's not create problems where none exist."

"If we have no alternative but Hashem, we must devise some effective controls over him and a very good cover story about the money."

"I agree that we have no other option than to have Hashem make the withdrawal. My first serious consideration is whether we can document Hashem as an Iraqi official."

Alain smiled his most enthusiastic smile of the evening. "Blanton is on his way here. He is certain he can obtain an Iraqi passport in Istanbul. He claims it will be adequate for flash purposes."

Kurth's face expressed both surprise and disbelief. "You are sure Blanton can do this? This is a pivotal concern. The conversation between Wafiq and Schlagel, when they discussed the passport, gave all the details. Whatever these details, they must reflect the current appearance and numeration of Iraqi passports."

"A point well taken, but remember, the documentation will only be for flash purposes."

"Right so far, but how do we handle the call to Schlagel and his return call?"

"That's up to you and Otto."

Kurth frowned. "What the hell are you getting at, Otto and me?"

Alain smiled like he was about to explain something to a teenager. "Otto is the key now. In fact, our success depends on his ability to do certain things for us."

The point Alain was trying to make was less than obvious to Kurth, who wondered where exactly their discussion would lead. "I gather you have something in mind you wish me to take up with our dear Otto?" Kurth questioned Alain with a smirk.

"First, let me brief you on some developments. For some reason, Baghdad has apparently involved Wafiq in the expatriate Iranian opposition organizations. Wafiq has made at least three trips to Paris in the last two months. I am uncertain as to what role, if any, he is playing with the Iranian exile groups. All I have to go on is that I heard the name Bakhtiar mentioned on the tapes. As you know, he is the leader of one of the more prominent Iranian opposition organizations." Alain paused for effect before continuing, "When in Paris, Wafiq also spends some time with a Middle Eastern woman named Muna with whom he is having a rather tempestuous affair. We will get additional details on precisely what Wafiq is doing in Paris once Hashem is in place in Hamburg and can review the Arabic conversations on the tapes. The liaison with Muna may explain the frequency of Wafiq's trips to Paris rather than official business. It's difficult to know, since the conversations are in Arabic. The panting, oohing, and cooing are the same in any language."

Kurth held back a smile. "Didn't you mention to me before that he may be having an affair with a local German girl?"

Alain's face broke into a wide grin. "Yeah, and a very hot one at that. She is a local girl named Gerta. Their German conversations are very explicit. In fact, Gerta is pretty demanding of Wafiq's services."

"It would seem that our friend Wafiq has a good thing going, two girls, each in a different country. Reminds me of that Alec Guinness movie where he had two wives." Kurth got up from the table and went to the refrigerator. "I'm going to have a beer. Should I open one for you?"

"Sure, why not. Let's get down to business. First, have you practiced imitating Wafiq's voice? I'm really counting on you. German isn't my native tongue, so I'm having a difficult time trying to imitate Wafiq's accent."

"I have practiced in my apartment. I think I'm fairly close on the accent, but probably not on the tone."

Alain was thoughtful. Fooling Schlagel was possibly the most critical part of the operation. "We'll run a couple of tests later before we go to dinner. If you are reasonably close, we can always say you have a cold or are suffering from allergies."

They drank the beers in silence for a short time, both considering their problem. On his part, Alain thought the best course of action was to decide on the timing of the operation first. He pointed the index finger of his right hand towards the ceiling, Alain's way of indicating he had an inspiration.

"The only time we can pull off this operation is when Wafiq is in Paris. We will have advance notice of this through the tap, particularly when Hashem gets his fat ass here. The way I see it, you will call Schlagel. Using your best imitation of Wafiq you will give him the details of the withdrawal. Based on what we now know you will tell Schlagel that the transaction will take place in two days. We already have an example of the information that Wafiq supplies Schlagel."

Alain stopped long enough to take a deep pull on his bottle of beer. He pointed his index finger at Kurth. "Now comes the hard part. Can you convince Otto to rig the tap so it rings here and not in Wafiq's office for one hour?"

Given the drift of Alain's comments, Kurth had already assumed the question.

"Yeah, okay, but what happens if someone in the Consulate tries to use Wafiq's private line?"

Alain frowned, "As far as I can recall, no one used the private line when he was in Paris. I will go over the tapes and make double sure."

"Even so, Alain, it's something we must consider. It may not be a problem at all. If someone picks up the phone and the line is dead, hopefully, they may not think that anything is amiss, especially if they pick it up a short time later and it functions."

"Otto might have some suggestions, particularly for what we are paying him. I think he should be able to dismantle Wafiq's line for an hour, but let's consider Otto when we have a window for the operation. The line only needs to be activated for a short period of time. The important thing for our planning now is that we must have that phone line active in this apartment for about an hour. I suspect we can get Otto's cooperation."

Kurth considered the point and decided he could obtain Otto's cooperation. The offer of a bonus might help. He was more concerned about the actual mechanics, once the window appeared. "Okay, Alain, for the moment let's assume we have Otto's cooperation, who does what?"

"Wait a minute, there is one small additional consideration. When Wafiq called about the withdrawal for an Iraqi named Basrawi, Schlagel asked him if he should call him to confirm that the withdrawal had been made."

"What then?"

"Wafiq told Schlagel that a confirmation call was not necessary because he was leaving for Paris."

"So what's our problem? I can say the same thing since Wafiq will actually be in Paris anyway."

"That's not the point. The pattern is the point. Does Schlagel usually phone Wafiq to confirm a transaction? Well, it's not worth worrying about. I suspect it would be asking too much of Otto to have him arrange to have the line switched to this apartment on two separate days."

Kurth nodded his agreement. Given the way they handled the transactions, he didn't think Schlagel's suspicions would be aroused if he was told that a confirmation of the transaction was not necessary. Otto was under the impression that the BKA was a silent partner in this operation, so he should not be overly worried about some changes, especially if it meant additional payoffs. There was another point he thought could be of some importance.

"Alain, how long does Wafiq spend in Paris on these visits?"

Alain's face lit up. "Good point. I can only respond based on what I know from the tapes. I always have the day of departure because his German secretary makes his travel arrangements. I then listen for when he returns. The first trip he made to Paris was only three days, but that was pre-Muna. The last trip was at least 6 days. That gives us a good window."

"And last, but most important of all, our major problem, Hashem. Any new thoughts?"

Alain wished he had studied Arabic instead of German. When he and Kurth planned an operation for the agency, they always came back to the weak link. In the current planning, the weak link was an unappealing Iraqi with an overweight body and an underweight brain, more given to wine and women than disciplined action.

"We have no alternative but to use him. I am hoping that once he gets here, we get a window pretty soon after his arrival. Hashem could become a pain in the ass in a very short time." Alain paused as if trying to put together some string of words that would put Kurth at ease. "Let's hope we pull this off before Hashem attracts too much attention. It would be a disaster if the BKA became aware of his presence in Hamburg and questioned the station about what he is doing in Germany."

"I'm sure the station would also be more than a little curious about Hashem."

"You're right about that. I intend to tell him he must lay low until we wind things up. It would be very embarrassing to the agency if the BKA questioned Hashem's presence in Germany. When we go to Geneva to pull off the operation, I will be in Geneva with him. I am sure that when I tell him why he is really here he won't turn down the hundred thousand dollars. I know he can't live on his retirement. One hundred thousand tax-free dollars should be sufficient inducement."

Kurth was not fully reassured. "I never trusted the son-of-a-bitch."

"You don't have to. He has no way of knowing of your involvement. I will be the only one he knows about in the operation. I am also the only one who knows about your involvement. I am assuming that Otto is not going to tell anyone what he has done for you. Blanton, who is now on his way here, knows about the apartment and, of course, knows I'm running an off-line operation for the agency. That's it."

Kurth was reassured, although he still had some doubts. He intended to keep those doubts until he was certain the operation would work. "Okay, Alain, let's go for a walk and get a good dinner together."

→──⊙ ⊙──←

August 21, 1982.

Hashem Samara'i had arrived in Hamburg late in the morning. Per Alain's instructions, he had found a small flat in Stellingen that he could rent for a month. He had walked four blocks from his flat and then taken two taxis to a Bierstube that was about five blocks from the wharf where he was to meet Alain. He drank a beer, noted that no one had entered the Bierstube after him, finished the beer quickly, and left. As he walked along, he mentally reviewed his curiosity about Alain's operation. This was going to be a very interesting meeting.

Hashem knew Hamburg well, better than most agency officers were aware of, including Alain. He had probably made more unofficial trips than official ones. He was attracted to the tall, beautiful blondes that were abundant in Hamburg. He walked along at a leisurely pace enjoying the scenery, mostly the females, that he passed on his way to his meeting with Alain. They were meeting at one of the floating restaurants along the Alster. He found the one Alain had recommended and walked out on the gangway to the restaurant. It looked like it had been built on a barge. After he entered the restaurant, he spotted Alain seated at a small table by a window. Alain saw him as he walked to the table.

"Glad you could make it, Hashem. Sit down and have a beer, then we'll have a very late lunch or an early dinner."

Hashem was not about to be patronized by Alain. "This better be worth the trouble, Alain."

All he got in return was a wry smile from Alain. "I'm surprised, Hashem, I thought you would be pleased with a free trip to your favorite hunting grounds."

Hashem grumbled by way of a reply. He was in his usual dire straits. He was anxious to find out about the operation, but even more anxious to hear the financial terms. When the beer came, they ordered fish. The waiter left and Hashem wasted no time.

"Okay, Alain, what's the deal?"

Alain drank some beer and leaned back in his chair. He lowered his voice in answer to Hashem's question. "This operation is off-line. The BKA has stretched their law for the protection of the constitution and are providing us tapes from a specific phone line. The officer who gets the tapes from the BKA is a declared officer. I get the tapes from an undeclared station officer. I am the only one in contact with the station. I am also the only one the station is aware of in the operation."

Hashem thought this a little odd, "Why all the secrecy?"

Alain shrugged his shoulders, "Now that you are here, we may be able to answer that Hashem."

Hashem's expression was that of a bazaar merchant, but internally he was uncertain about what Alain was doing and just what comprised the operation. Alain was never one of his favorite persons, but money was involved and feelings don't enter into business deals.

He questioned Alain with a simple, "How so?"

"The briefcase at my side contains the initial take from a tap arranged for us by the BKA. The tap is on the private line of Wafiq Tikriti, an old friend of yours."

Hashem's curiosity was aroused. A couple of years ago the agency was interested in Wafiq because he was one of Saddam Hussein's close companions. He was dropped as a target because the agency concluded he couldn't be recruited.

"I thought we wrote him off as a target."

"That's right, but the Iran/Iraq war and Wafiq's role in it are apparently of some concern to Langley. Wafiq is handling at least one large Iraqi government account. He also travels a lot, most recently on several trips to Paris. Why does the Iraqi Consul in Hamburg control a government account and why the trips to Paris?"

Hashem chuckled, "Given his reputation, the trips to Paris may be due to an itch between his legs."

It was Alain's turn to laugh. "My station contact tells me he goes to meet with Shapour Bakhtiar, the Iranian exile leader. The station doesn't understand this because the Iraqi Military Attaché in Paris is already in regular contact with Bakhtiar. I waited to call you until we had a fair sized batch of tapes for you to translate. Listen to them and make legible translations for me. The tapes are numbered and dated, please indicate on your translations which tape the translation refers to. The agency is particularly interested in any arms deals he may be doing illegally. They are also interested in any financial discussions, particularly anything concerning the bank account in Switzerland. Don't bother with conversations of no interest. Given your experience, I will trust your judgment on what is of interest. Please pay close attention to his travels. I have left a note for you in with the tapes. It gives directions to our next meeting site which will be next Tuesday."

"What about money? I rented a small flat for a month for about nine hundred bucks. Also, what do I get paid for this job?"

Alain had expected this from Hashem. "For the time being you are on a per diem of forty-five dollars a day. Even you can eat well on that. You will find an envelope in the briefcase containing fifteen hundred dollars. You can account with me at our next meeting that is noted for you in the brief case. Our big pay-out will come from a successful operation."

"About which I know nothing."

Alain smiled like a man who knew everything. "Patience, Hashem. All in good time, all in good time." Before Hashem could complain, Alain held up his hand and said, "One last thing, disguise yourself slightly. I want you to grow a scruffy beard. Let your mustache grow bushy. Next Tuesday morning, use an eyebrow pencil to fill in your beard and comb your hair differently. I want you to get a couple of passport photos taken and pass them to me at our Tuesday meeting."

Hashem looked at Alain with deep suspicion. "What the hell is going on? Why do you need passport photos of me?"

"Keep your shorts on Hashem. I may be able to explain more at our next meeting."

"You want a lot in a short time without any explanation of exactly what the fuck it is we are doing."

Hashem was very agitated, but it had little effect on Alain. He figured once Hashem showed up, they had him. Alain looked at him with a far away smile.

"Patience, Hashem. I think you will get the gist of what we are up to when you translate those tapes. We may not have much time."

⇥▬◉ ◉▬⇤

August 24, 1982.

Alain was reviewing the translations that Hashem had passed him at their noon meeting. They now had a plan in place to meet every few days to pass tapes and translations to each other. The conversations between Wafiq and Colonel Qodsi in Paris would be of some interest to the agency. He wondered if they or the DST, the French Internal Service, had tapped the line. It was quite clear to Colonel Qodsi and Wafiq that Baghdad had decided Qodsi was beyond his means in dealing with Bakhtiar, the preeminent Iranian opposition figure in Europe. Alain concluded that Wafiq had handled his role very well, as Qodsi actually appeared to be relieved. Alain made some notes about Muna in Paris. Apparently, it was Wafiq that had pursued her. Hashem, in translating the tapes, made some side notes stating that Muna was either obsessed with Wafiq or she was a candidate for an Oscar.

What caught Alain's attention was a call, apparently from Baghdad, stating that a Mr. Basrawi would be arriving in Hamburg and that Wafiq should make the arrangements for him to withdraw funds from the official account. Whoever made the call said that Basrawi would be carrying a personal letter from Mustafa Naghshabandi that would contain the exact amount of the withdrawal. *Bingo*, Alain said to himself. Not only did this confirm what he had learned from the German call between Wafiq and Schlagel about the withdrawal, but he was pleased to conclude that they would definitely get advance notice. There was nothing else in the translations of interest to Alain, so he decided to listen to the German conversations from the past two days.

After listening to two calls from Gerta to Wafiq, in which she described a couple of their past assignations and added what she intended for their next meeting, Alain set aside the earphones and turned off the tape recorder. He decided to think about operational considerations. He expected Blanton in an hour or so. He must not indicate to Blanton anything about their planning. He suspected Blanton would not be a problem. What he didn't know was what concerned him. He tried to recall if there was any past operation involving Hashem where Blanton might have also been involved and thus gotten to know Hashem. He would handle that issue when and if Blanton recognized Hashem from the passport photos. The scruffy beard might protect Hashem's identity from Blanton. If Blanton were to recognize Hashem from the pictures it could complicate the operation.

→→● ●←←

August 25, 1982.

Alain was nursing a beer when Blanton knocked at the door. He let him in.

"Come on in and have a beer, Jack."

"I've made reservations to fly to Istanbul tomorrow afternoon, if that's okay with you," Jack said. He sat down and accepted a beer from Alain.

The same old Jack, Alain thought, *not much on small talk*.

"That should be okay. Here is the picture I want in the Iraqi passport," Alain replied, handing the picture to Blanton. "Can your contact in Istanbul put it in the passport, or do you plan to do it?"

"I think it would be best for the picture to be in the passport before I leave Istanbul. A blank passport without a picture, and no description of the owner, would attract the attention of airport officials just in case they inspected my brief case. I can come up with a good story on why I have the passport."

"Good, here is the name and the description I want to appear in the passport." Alain handed a piece of paper to Blanton.

"Thanks. How is the tap working?"

"No problems. The sound is quite good. I have already passed some of the take to the agency. They seemed pleased."

Alain himself was especially pleased that Blanton did not seem to recognize Hashem from the photograph. He wondered about that, because their paths almost certainly had crossed at some point in the past. But then, ten years ago Hashem looked a lot better than now.

"I'll check it out before I leave. Any idea on how long they plan to run this op?"

"Nothing specific. From what I have listened to on the tape, I suspect it's a fishing expedition based on some collateral information. I can only understand the German conversations. Most of the conversations are in Arabic. I'm sure there will be no feedback to me."

"Okay, I should be back with your Iraqi passport in three or four days. Let me check on the tap, then I'll be on my way." Jack looked over the equipment, then thought of something, "Remember, Alain, it is important that we remove the tap as soon as it becomes irrelevant. Call me and I'll get here as soon as possible."

Alain nodded his head in agreement and Jack left.

-→■◎ ◎■◄-

August 26, 1982.

Wafiq was late getting to his office. Ingrid brought him a cup of coffee. He had barely taken a sip of coffee when his phone rang. It was Gerta who called to thank him for the most pleasant moments they had shared during the course of the previous evening. She told him she was still tingling. Wafiq's tingling had, by then, subsided to pleasant exhaustion. He had never run a marathon but, for exhilaration and exhaustion, it must compare to a night with Gerta. She pressed him on when they would see each other again. They finally agreed to meet for dinner on Saturday. Wafiq figured he would need until then to regain his strength.

He began going through the morning mail, but was interrupted a short time later when Haitham Abd al-Nebi walked into his office. He ordered a coffee for Haitham, then asked him, "Well Haitham, as always it is a pleasure to see you. What brings you to my humble office? Is there anything I can do for you?" The latter question was rhetorical. The only reason Haitham saw anybody was to tell them what they could do for him. Wafiq waited impatiently for Haitham to tell him what efforts were expected of him.

"Nothing really, everything is going fine."

Wafiq was pleasantly surprised, "That's good to hear. From the news reports, I gather the war is not going too well for us at the moment."

Haitham frowned and toyed with his coffee cup before replying. "You are right about that, Wafiq. Incidentally, your reports to Baghdad on your conversations with Bakhtiar have been received with great interest." Haitham rubbed his chin, as if carrying on some kind of internal debate, before questioning Wafiq. "What do you think, Wafiq, is there really any benefit in our funding Bakhtiar?"

Wafiq shrugged, "I don't know. I find it difficult to believe that Bakhtiar can do anything in Iran at the moment when the Iranians are engaged in a life and death struggle with us. On the plus side, he must be a constant worry to the Iranian government. I would think that Iran's main concern must be what kind of aid Bakhtiar is getting and from whom. Someone is concerned about Bakhtiar since there has already been one attempt on his life that came close to being a successful assassination."

Haitham pursed his lips, doubt written on his face. "Yes, it was a close call. The assassin shot the guard outside Bakhtiar's door, then shot the lock off the door. The police, led by Bakhtiar's son, overpowered the intruder just as he broke into the apartment. I suppose you could conclude that Bakhtiar is of some concern to the Iranians, but as far as I can tell, the Iranians don't appear to be overly anxious about what he may or may not do. It's my view that Bakhtiar will not pan out as an investment, but given our lack of other alternatives, we must support him."

"True, Haitham. Bakhtiar talks to me like he has all kinds of internal assets, but with a war on we have no way of confirming his claims."

"Or denying them," Haitham interjected. "There may be another problem."

"Such as?" Wafiq did not like the serious expression on Haitham's face.

"Have you ever heard of Hashem Samara'i?"

"I know a few of the Samara'i clan. It is a very large clan, but I do not recall ever meeting a Hashem. Is there any reason I should?"

"He is a CIA operative who has been a thorn in our side in the past. One of my men thinks he spotted him on the Reeperbahn last night. I am very curious as to why the CIA has assigned such a man to Hamburg. Hamburg is not exactly a hotbed of anti-Saddam activity."

Wafiq's curiosity got the better of him. "You are way beyond me, Haitham. I know virtually nothing about CIA activity in Hamburg except for rare rumors one picks up at the Mosque or at diplomatic functions. If this man is really Hashem Samara'i, could he not be here for reasons other than Iraq?"

"That's a possibility, Wafiq, but I doubt it. He has been pretty much targeted against us throughout his career. Keep your ears open and please report to me anything you hear on the diplomatic circuit. Last night he was with a woman who may or may not be a prostitute. My man followed them to the woman's flat. It became apparent that Hashem was there for the night. I've told my man to keep a watch on the woman's comings and goings. I've brought a couple of photos of Hashem. Let your man, Ahmad, see them, and tell him to keep his eyes open. I'm very curious as to why such a high profile CIA operative is in Hamburg. I want a positive identification before I report anything to Baghdad."

⋯→▬ ▬←⋯

Alain had made his usual Thursday call to Kurth. He let him know that Blanton had stopped in, checked the equipment, and was on his way east. Hashem had checked in and was producing some stuff of interest. The most important thing derived from Hashem's first translations was that the home office gave the local office advance notice before a deal was closed. He told Kurth that he would call him immediately if and when the home office notified the local office of an impending deal. He asked Kurth if he could leave on a moment's notice. Kurth answered in the affirmative, saying he could always cite family reasons requiring his presence in Germany.

Kurth hung up, and sat back in his comfortable executive chair. He continued to wonder if his friend was not leading them both down a dead end. He had to confess to himself that the excitement engendered by his participation in Alain's operation was exhilarating, but he could not help thinking that this was a last shot by the over-the-hill gang. Alain seemed oblivious to the fact that stealing five million dollars from a Swiss bank would spark an international investigation.

Kurth did a quick mental run through of the operation. The only persons aware of his participation were Alain and Otto. The only danger Otto faced was the possibility that someone would discover the tap. Kurth was uncertain if the mere discovery of the tap would lead to Otto. Probably not, but, if the tap were discovered, the numbers of the target line and the listening post would be uncovered and that fact would lead to Alain. Kurth had told Otto that he would call him as soon as he could remove the tap. It would seem that the only technical weakness in their planning was the possibility that the tap would be discovered. He was also still concerned about their major human problem, Hashem.

Kurth had not mentioned to Alain the possibility that he would be traveling to Germany at the beginning of September. He decided he would do a little lobbying for the trip. It would involve talking to several German clients. He could keep to his schedule. The only problem would be if the company wanted to send someone with him. He was sure he could convince his bosses that the trip was worthwhile. He would argue that he wanted to get more involved and thus learn more about the company's German business. When in Germany, he planned to argue with Alain not to stretch their luck. So far everything had gone well, but then they had, as yet, taken no undue risks. This indicated to Kurth that if they decided the operation was a go, they should mount it as soon as a window presented itself. Their luck couldn't hold out forever.

⊷▰ ▰⊶

Hamburg. August 27, 1982.
"But Muna, I just can't fly to Paris without having a reason. You know I love you and can't stand to be without you, but there is a war on and, at the moment, we are not doing too well."

"Well, if you can't come here, why don't I fly over there so we can be together? Maybe I can get away next Friday, fly over there, and spend the weekend with you?" Muna purred at him over the phone. Wafiq thought he was glad he wasn't married to her. His immediate problem was to keep her from coming to Hamburg. He would be exhausted running between her and Gerta over the course of a weekend.

"Beloved, I would love to have you here, but I live on the upper floor of the Consulate. My life is an open book and I have several visitors coming from Iraq next week. I don't know what it's all about. I must fly to Paris around the end of the first week in September. I promise to spend a lot of time with you. Maybe we can go to the countryside outside of Paris somewhere for a couple of days. Why don't you pick a nice place where we could spend a long weekend? I will call you as soon as I make my travel arrangements. You have no idea how much I miss not being able to see you every day."

"Give me as much advance notice as you can, and when you will be free while here. I know a nice inn out in the country. I just can't wait to undress you. I will wait for you, but it won't be easy. Good bye, my love."

Wafiq hung up the telephone and looked at his desk calendar. He had tentatively planned to go to Paris on or about the seventh or eighth of September. He decided to call Colonel Qodsi to make arrangements. He daydreamed briefly as the phone rang, picturing Gerta in his thoughts, happy that he was seeing her Saturday night. Between Gerta and Muna, he was beginning to feel like a teenager - a tired teenager.

August 29, 1982.

Alain was a little late for his meeting with Hashem Samara'i. Hashem had suggested a restaurant that Alain did not know at their meeting the previous evening to exchange materials. It was an Indian restaurant named The Star. It took some time for Alain to locate it. Hashem spotted him as soon as he entered the restaurant. He stood up and motioned Alain to the table.

"Hello, Alain, sit down and have a drink. I already ordered for us. I also have the latest readout."

Alain looked around the restaurant before answering, "Anything interesting?"

"Yeah, two days ago, Muna, the broad in Paris, called Wafiq and begged him to come see her. She said how much she missed him and even said she had thought of flying to Hamburg to see him. This made our boy nervous. He calmed her down by telling her he would be in Paris at the end of the first week in September. He also told her he would take time off and go some place with her for a couple of days."

"Well, at least he leads an entertaining sex life. Anything else?"

"He also called Col. Qodsi in Paris and told him that he would be there next week. He asked Qodsi to alert Bakhtiar. Qodsi told Wafiq he was seeing one of Bakhtiar's so-called military experts on Monday. He asked Wafiq to let him know as soon as he had firm reservations." Hashem drank some beer and, when Alain had nothing to say, continued, "I find it curious that Wafiq is dealing with Bakhtiar. He knows nothing about Iran and I would think that the Iraqis must have someone who could deal more intelligently with Bakhtiar."

Alain shrugged and said, "I suspect Wafiq is doing what he is doing because he has the trust of Saddam."

"Maybe so, but you would think someone with first hand knowledge of Iran would also be involved."

"The Iraqis are no different than we are. Since when do our politicians rely on someone with first hand knowledge of any subject?"

Hashem laughed out loud, a laugh that rent the silence like the rutting of a wild boar, turning heads in their direction. "One other thing, on Saturday, there was a call from Baghdad saying that a deposit had been made in the bank in the amount of twenty-two million dollars. You said you were interested in any financial information."

Alain tried not to look too interested, but did comment that that was a pretty substantial sum for a small Consulate. Hashem was not satisfied. "It would seem that whatever Wafiq is doing with this account might be what interests our late employers. Also, I have a question. Why are there no calls in German?"

Alain felt relieved. Hashem had asked the question he had hoped for. He gestured with his hand as he answered, "That, my friend, is because the BKA deletes all calls involving German citizens. I asked my agency contact the same question. It has to do with their law, The Protection of the Constitution. I suspect items might appear on a tap of Wafiq's telephone which could well contain indications of German aid to Iraq that the BKA would just as soon keep from us."

"How long do you think this operation will go on?"

"I would assume as long as our former employers think it is worthwhile. Incidentally, why the Indian restaurant?"

Hashem laughed, this time more subdued. "This is one restaurant where we won't run into any Iraqis or, for that matter, any agency officers we know."

"Good thinking, Hashem. The fewer explanations we have to volunteer, the better. The food is even quite decent. Since Wafiq is planning a trip to Paris, let's meet next Saturday. We'll meet at the same time and place. If something comes up and we must meet sooner, I'll give you a call."

"Okay, I'll go along with this, even though I'm only getting expenses."

"Come on Hashem, you are getting more than the government per diem. Don't forget, the attraction for both of us is the bonus we'll get once the operation is over."

Hashem stared at Alain for over a minute. He was about to question Alain about the bonus they were to eventually get, hopefully in the not too distant future, but thought better of it. "Okay, until next Saturday."

Alain could hardly wait for his next regular commo call to Kurth.

>━━○ ○━━<

September 2, 1982.

Alain waited patiently as the phone rang in Kurth's office. He was calling from the train station. When Kurth answered, Alain identified himself as his cousin and spoke in German.

"We have a family problem that requires your presence here as soon as possible. How soon can you come?"

Kurth wondered what the problem was or whether enough had fallen into place that Alain had decided they could go through with the operation. "How soon is as soon as possible? I and my bosses had been planning for me to travel next week."

Alain broke in, "I would like you to get here this weekend as some of the problems are quite urgent. Jack dropped by yesterday with the one item we need for our other colleague. If this business deal is to go through, it will have to be within the next ten days."

"I think I might be able to leave tomorrow night or Saturday afternoon at the latest. My company wants me to spend some time in Europe working on several business deals with our German partners. I'll meet you at the usual place either Saturday morning or Sunday morning for coffee."

"Very good. We have a lot of family business to discuss and we must take care of a few pressing financial problems. It will be good to see you. Good bye."

→═◉ ◉═←

September 4, 1982.

Alain had spent half an hour drinking coffee at the coffee shop opposite the Four Seasons Hotel, but Kurth had not shown up. He had spent the rest of the day going over plans for the operation and concluded that some of the things he had added made it look like a plausible operation, at least to him. He was certain it would work. He thought he could bring Kurth to accept it, but was worried about Hashem. After mulling over everything for the umpteenth time, he left the apartment and walked to his meeting with Hashem. When he arrived, Hashem was already seated at the bar. He was having a beer and flirting with the barmaid, who feigned interest pretty well. Hashem greeted Alain like an old friend.

"Hi, Alain, order a beer and let's retire to a table."

With the order placed, Hashem guided Alain to a table where no one was within hearing range. There was little small talk. Hashem had apparently outgrown Middle Eastern politeness years ago.

"Your friend is leaving for Paris early on the eighth. He had a couple of conversations with Col. Qodsi in Paris and arrangements have been made for them to meet with Bakhtiar for dinner that night. He also called Muna who is going to make arrangements for them to drive out to the countryside on Friday. Muna told him she would make reservations for them at a lovely inn about sixty kilometers outside Paris. They plan to return to the city on Monday. Wafiq has reservations to return to Hamburg the following day."

"That would be the fourteenth, right?" Alain interjected.

"That's what my calendar says."

"Anything else, Hashem?"

Hashem looked at Alain carefully. The news of Wafiq's travel obviously interested him. He couldn't figure out why. Wafiq's affair with some Syrian woman in Paris was of no great moment. The fact that Wafiq was seeing Bakhtiar was nothing special. Bakhtiar saw a lot of people, but with no apparent results to date. There had to be something else about Wafiq's travels, something that was of great interest to Alain. He decided not to question Alain in this regard.

"Our friend, Wafiq, has some very well placed friends in Baghdad. He had a call from Mustafa Naghshabandi. I couldn't get much out of it. Naghshabandi had him copy down some figures from previous correspondence saying there was an urgent need for them. I've got it all written down for you."

Hashem reached inside his jacket and passed Alain a small sheaf of papers. Alain told him there were two tapes in the small tote bag he placed on the table. Their dinners arrived, three kinds of veal that they both sampled. When another pair of beers arrived on order, Alain relaxed.

"My agency contact tells me that they intend to act in the very near future and from what they have told me, there are roles for both of us."

Hashem was visibly upset, "You told them I am involved?"

"No, Hashem, but someone with brains might have figured out that you are involved. Remember this is an off-line operation, no questions asked. What is attractive to me is that there will be no record of how much we get for our role. They have only hinted that it will be substantial."

"They are very short on details don't you think?"

"Hashem, I was told that everything will be explained to me at the next meeting with my agency contact."

"Just who the hell is your agency contact? Don't give me any crap about not knowing him or that he is someone you never saw before and is dealing with you in alias. You just ain't that dumb, Alain."

"Look, Hashem, I'm the guy in the middle. No one in the agency knows I am dealing with you. They may guess it's you, but they haven't heard it from me. I think they don't want to know who is involved just in case something goes wrong and they are questioned by the BKA. As you indicated, I obviously know with whom I'm meeting. Incidentally, he is someone I trust, but being the man in the middle, I am not going to tell you his name. Okay?"

"Okay, okay, don't get so excited. Look, Alain, I have reason for concern. I don't know if I'm in danger or even if I am unwittingly participating in a scam."

Alain was inwardly amused. *When in the hell would Hashem not participate in a scam if he knew he was going to make money?* He decided to try and calm him down.

"We obviously are not engaged in anything on the up and up. It is an unsanctioned operation. There are minimal risks. One thing I can tell you now is that one way or the other the whole thing will be over by the end of the month."

"That's reassuring. The major point is when and how will we get paid?"

"You will be paid on the day the operation ends. It will be in cash, and there will be no record of the payment."

The mention of pay and a specific date he would be paid had a noticeable calming effect on Hashem. On his part, he decided to get to the point that interested him the most.

"That's great but you forgot to mention the amount of compensation we will get."

Alain smiled with satisfaction. "I will let you know that the next time I see you. I'll call when I want to see you. This place is as good as any. We'll meet here for lunch. There is nothing more I can say at the moment."

Their waiter had brought the bill while they were talking. Alain put enough notes to cover it on the tray holding the bill, got up from his chair, and said goodbye to Hashem. Without further delay, Alain headed towards the door.

->—◉ ◉—<-

September 5, 1982.

Alain and Kurth had been involved in intense conversation since Kurth had shown up at the coffee shop. Kurth had been alarmed when Alain said that most of the pieces had fallen into place and that they had a window during which they could run the operation. It would have to be on Thursday or Friday, the ninth or the tenth, while Wafiq was in Paris. It was certain that he would be away on those two days. Kurth toyed with the spoon in his coffee. He looked at his old friend for a while before questioning him.

"Okay, Alain, this is kind of sudden. Explain to me how and when everything fell into place."

"I got the key information from Hashem last night. Wafiq is leaving for Paris early on the eighth and not returning until the fourteenth. I told you on the phone that Blanton stopped by on the first with the Iraqi passport. I asked him to stay in Hamburg for the time being as we might need him in the next few days."

"It sounds like you got it all figured out. That's fine, but there are a lot of things we don't have."

Alain responded, "Not really. As you say, I've got it all figured out." Alain stopped, drank some coffee, and waited for a response from Kurth.

"From your confidence, I guess you do. Okay, let me in on your planning."

Alain favored Kurth with one of his smirks. "We make a call to the banker, Schlagel, on the eighth and give him the information. We tell him that we have sent him a photocopy of the passport, the half of a ten-mark note, three signatures for comparison with the signature on the passport, and the amount to be withdrawn. In the phone conversation we tell him the name on the passport, the number on the ten-mark note and the amount to be withdrawn."

Kurth looked alarmed. "As I recall, Schlagel always calls right back to confirm that Wafiq actually made the call. How do we handle that?"

"That, my friend, is where you come in. I want you to come by tonight for supper. I'll fix something worth your presence. I want you to practice the previous conversation that Wafiq had with Schlagel. If you are close enough to a reasonable resemblance of Wafiq's German accent, we have it made. You can always tell him you have a cold. I presume you have done some practicing?"

Kurth grew a little impatient. "You haven't answered my question and it is a key one. Schlagel calls back immediately and I assume we will be calling him from a pay phone. I don't think I can tell him not to bother calling me back. He would be immediately suspicious, call the Consulate, and be told that Wafiq is in Paris"

"Again my friend, that is where you come in. You must get Otto to reroute any calls to Wafiq to my number. Since Wafiq is away, if anyone tries to use his phone, they will probably not be alarmed if it is back up quickly. It would be needed for an hour or less. Once Schlagel calls back, Otto can take out the bridge and put everything back in order. You can also tell Schlagel that you are off to Paris and he needn't call back once the withdrawal is made. I assume that eventually there may be an investigation by the Iraqis. If Wafiq's line is checked for a tap, there will be no evidence. Blanton will come and put everything back in order. We will pay him off with our ill-gotten gains and he can return home to enjoy his retirement."

Kurth was impressed. It could work. He was fairly confident of his ability to imitate Wafiq's voice. "Let me think about this. Wafiq is certainly going to be in a fair amount of hot water once the Iraqis learn that some of their funds have been hijacked. Incidentally, how much are we planning to heist?"

"A nice round sum. Five million, one hundred thousand dollars."

"Well, Alain, you certainly have my attention. Why the odd sum?"

"We are going to take five million in bearer bonds. The one hundred thousand will be Hashem's bonus. This sum mimics past withdrawals that were almost always three to seven million in bearer bonds and a much smaller amount in cash. These amounts should not give rise to suspicion on the part of Schlagel."

Kurth's expression was that of a man who had just bitten into a bad oyster. "Do you really think Hashem will buy into this? Knowing his suspicious nature, he is certainly going to be curious about the five million in bearer bonds."

"I think I can put your mind at ease about that subject. But we can review everything over dinner tonight. In the meantime, you get in touch with Otto. You think he might present a problem?"

"I don't think so. He will be glad it is coming to an end and he will get his cut. I'll bring the wine. What will it be, red or white?"

"White will do fine."

Alain spent the rest of the day preparing a remarkable dinner. By the time Kurth got there, white wine in hand, the meal was cooked to perfection. They ate right away.

"That was a very tasty veal rib. But then, I would expect that from you. Maybe you can write a cook book after all this is over," Kurth said as he finished eating.

"Hopefully, as a very rich man," Alain smiled. "Any problems with Otto?"

"He was very glad that this is ending. I suspect he has concluded that the tap probably does not have the silent approval of the BKA, but then he is already hooked. He would have a hard time explaining what he did after the fact. I think the promise of a sizable reward is sufficient to calm his fears. I am going to meet him on Tuesday, just in case there are any last minute changes in our plans. What I'll need is the exact time we want him to rewire the junction box so that Wafiq's private number only rings in your apartment. I told him the rewiring must be in place for no more than an hour. What he plans to do is to make the change and then go somewhere for lunch or coffee depending on the time. He will give me the contact number for the place when we meet for lunch on Tuesday."

"Very good, Kurth, I'm relieved there were no serious issues with him."

"No, he just wanted to know how much his bonus would be."

Alain broke out in a laugh. "Good old Otto. What did you tell him?"

"I told him that the tax-free value of his bonus would be worth much more than his annual salary. That seemed to satisfy him."

Alain got up from the table, went to the kitchen cabinet, and brought out the bottle of Asbach with two small brandy glasses he had purchased for the occasion. He poured some of the brandy in each glass with a flourish and said, "Let's drink to success."

"Gladly, but with one reservation."

Alain was immediately alert. Kurth, at times, had certainly been less than enthusiastic about the operation. "What's your reservation?"

"Alain, we are professional intelligence officers. We are very security conscious, but there are persons who are just as careful as we are and among them are bankers."

"Okay, Kurth, what the hell are you getting at?"

Kurth smiled and gestured emphatically with his hand. "Look, when we trained an agent in secret writing, we gave him signals to indicate if he was under control. There were other signals, but the important one was the question of control. I suggest to you that maybe Wafiq and Schlagel have devised a set of signals for use in their phone conversations as an additional check. It is plausible that Iraqi opposition elements could force Wafiq to make arrangements for one of them to make a withdrawal. I'm only speculating, but I think we should listen carefully to the conversation between Wafiq and Schlagel that resulted in the last withdrawal. What do you think?"

Alain considered Kurth's concerns. "I appreciate your point, Kurth, but I do think that Schlagel's call back to Wafiq's private number would be all the confirmation Schlagel would need to be assured he was dealing with Wafiq. Your concern is certainly valid. Let's not overlook anything at this late date. I'll set up the tape recorder. We'll do a careful examination of everything on the tape. After all, we don't want our old buddy, Hashem, walking into a trap."

He went into the bedroom, came out with the tape recorder, and set it up on the kitchen table. It took him several minutes to retrieve the tape in question from inside the radio. He put the tape on the tape recorder and turned it on. After a few seconds, he stopped the tape recorder.

"Okay, Kurth, this is where the crucial conversation begins. I will let it run through. I suggest we both take notes."

The tape began with a female voice telling the caller he had reached the Banque Suisse. Wafiq's voice came on the line in German, "Mr. Schlagel, please."

"Whom shall I say is calling?"

"Wafiq Tikriti."

"Sorry, Mr. Tikriti, I did not recognize your voice. I will connect you immediately."

There was a brief pause before Schlagel came on the line. "So good to hear from you, Mr. Tikriti. How are you?"

"I'm fine, Irwin. How are you and your beautiful wife?"

"Excellent. We are looking forward to the skiing season. How can I be of service?"

"Irwin, an Iraqi gentleman will call at your bank at eleven o'clock the day after tomorrow, the eighteenth. His name is Sa'id Basrawi, his father's name is Isma'il. Today, I will DHL a photocopy of his passport, one half of a ten mark note and a piece of paper containing three signatures executed by Basrawi in my presence. The amount he is to withdraw is three million, two hundred and fifty thousand dollars. The three million should be in bearer bonds and the two hundred and fifty thousand in cash."

"I will take care of everything as in the past, Mr. Tikriti. If there is a problem, I will call you immediately." There was a ten second pause on the tape. "Do you want me to call you to confirm that the withdrawal has been made?"

"That is not necessary, Irwin. I will be tied up the day after tomorrow. I am leaving for Paris that evening. Oh, I have one question. What will the account balance be after the withdrawal?" There was a pause and Schlagel could be heard on another line calling up the account balance. He came back on the line.

"There will be twenty-one million dollars in the account, Mr. Tikriti."

"Thank you, Irwin."

Alain stopped the tape recorder. "Okay, Kurth, here is the punch line. This call came a little over a minute after Wafiq hung up." Alain started the tape again.

"Hello," Wafiq said, answering the phone.

"How are you, Mr. Tikriti? It is Schlagel calling to confirm your earlier call."

"Thank you very much, Mr. Schlagel. Good bye."

"You are most welcome and goodbye, Mr. Tikriti."

Alain turned off the tape recorder. "Well, Kurth, any thoughts?"

"Our difficulty is that we don't have a similar call for comparison. Wafiq said the withdrawal would take place on the day after tomorrow, the eighteenth."

"At eleven o'clock," Alain added.

"Could be a signal in the time and date. When did Wafiq make the call?"

Alain checked his notes. "It was on the sixteenth. Also, the bit about Paris is accurate. So we can use it again."

"What about eleven o'clock? It could mean the transaction would take place maybe an hour later or an hour earlier."

Alain shrugged his shoulders. "I doubt it. It could lead to confusion very easily. If there is any signal it has something to do with things said in the first conversation and how that conversation relates to the second conversation. I found it curious that Schlagel's secretary did not recognize Wafiq's voice."

"Could be that she was new," Kurth speculated.

"Maybe, but how many Arabs call Schlagel and ask for him in highly accented German? There is nothing we can do but hope there was some reason the secretary didn't recognize Wafiq's voice."

Kurth nodded agreement. "One thing we should bear in mind is that Wafiq said he would DHL the passport and other items today. I better bear that in mind when I make the call. But there has to be something else. Play the damned tape again."

They both listened intently as Alain played both conversations again. Kurth frowned and drank some Asbach, then his face lightened up. "There is something inconsistent, a change in the second conversation. Play the first conversation again, then stop." Kurth listened intently to the first conversation. Alain stopped the tape at the end of the first conversation. Kurth pointed at the tape recorder. "Please note, Alain, when Wafiq calls the bank he gets Schlagel's secretary. He identifies himself and asks to speak with Mr. Schlagel. Now play that first conversation again. Please note that during his conversation with Schlagel, Wafiq always refers to him as Irwin." They listened to the first conversation, then looked at each other. Kurth smiled and said, "Play the second conversation."

They both listened to the short conversation. "Wafiq referred to Schlagel as Mr. Schlagel. It could be a signal," Alain said.

Kurth toyed with his nose before answering. "Unfortunately, we do not have another exchange between the two for comparison. Even if it isn't a signal, I will be careful to refer to him as Irwin in my initial conversation and as Mr. Schlagel when he makes the confirming call. One other possibility is whether there is any correlation between the time of Wafiq's call to Schlagel and eleven o'clock, the time Basrawi was to show up for the withdrawal?"

Alain looked at his notes. "The call was made at about ten after eleven, but he was held up by a passionate conversation with Muna, in Paris."

Kurth laughed, but without humor. "That's something else to keep in mind. One good thing is that Wafiq will actually be in Paris, so I can say I'm traveling to Paris late in the day and will not be in Hamburg when the withdrawal is made."

"Kurth, I want you to do a script based on the conversation between Schlagel and Wafiq. Practice it and keep trying to perfect the accent. We will plan on calling Schlagel this Wednesday. You will instruct him that the withdrawal will be made on Friday, the tenth. You will give him the name, the father's name, and the passport number of the person making the withdrawal. You will say that he will have one half of a ten-mark note, adding the note's serial number. Via DHL, you will send him a photocopy of the passport, three exemplar signatures and the other one half of the ten-mark note." Alain continued, fixing Kurth with a supercilious smile, "The ball is in your court. We must take advantage of this window of opportunity. We cannot wait for someone to make another withdrawal so we can compare conversations." Alain finished, "Also, Wafiq might not be conveniently traveling to Paris again. No, it's now or never."

Kurth, like many others, did not appreciate Alain's special smile, by which he was well known. One young lady had remarked that when Alain favored her with that peculiar smile she felt like Eve being conned by the serpent in the Garden of Eden. "Fine, Alain, all the ducks seem to be in line, but there is one very important item. What is the name of the Iraqi who is supposed to make the withdrawal?"

"Wait, I have it written down. I'll bring the passport. That should allay your fears." Alain got up from the table, went into the bedroom, and brought out the passport. He handed it to Kurth, who opened the passport and found a very scruffy Hashem Samara'i staring at him. He chuckled, then noted no entries in the passport. "You think this will pass muster?"

"Why not? He is not going to travel on it. It is only going to be used for flash purposes. He might not even have to show it to Schlagel, since we are sending Schlagel a photocopy of the passport via DHL."

Kurth frowned. "Look, Alain, it's what you don't think of that kills you. Suppose Schlagel looks at the passport and asks why there are no entries in it. Hashem better have a good explanation."

"Such a stickler for detail. Your German ancestry is showing, Kurth. I don't like explanations any more than you do, but in this case there happens to be one. Hashem can simply tell Schlagel that, given the war with Iran, this passport is only being used to establish bona fides."

"Okay, but where did you come up with the name, Tarek Shammar?"

"I didn't. Blanton found it in the local Hamburg phone book. Who cares? I suspect that Schlagel is not an expert on Iraqi names."

From Kurth's expression, Alain could only surmise that he was unconvinced. Kurth rubbed his chin thoughtfully. "You better get that passport from him when he passes the bearer bonds. Just make sure it gets destroyed."

"Good idea, Kurth. When you see Otto on Tuesday, tell him to have the tap rearranged by a quarter to eleven on Wednesday morning. You can tell him that you will probably call him by eleven-thirty, then he can make sure everything is back to normal. I'll contact Blanton and have him fix up the apartment after the calls are made." Kurth nodded hesitantly before Alain went on, "I think we should drive. Five million bucks takes up a lot of room. I called Rentke and hinted that I might see him in a couple of days with some business. The other moneychangers we used were the Frenchman, Drouget, and the old Arab, Fuad. I think, in this case, we had best skip Fuad and just use Rentke and Drouget. I'll rent a car with a Carnet. We both have international driver's licenses. I plan to stay at the Bristol. What about you?"

"I'll stay at the Intercon. I'll also get marks when doing the bearer bond exchange. You don't suspect any problem in changing such large sums, do you?"

"No, in fact we can ask for a little premium as there are a lot of people who would like to get their hands on bearer bonds."

"Right, Alain, as I recall you did a lot of money laundering in the past."

Alain smiled, "One learns a lot of useful trades in our business. Okay, that about wraps it up for the time being. Why don't you come by here around five in the afternoon tomorrow? I will have seen Blanton by then and worked out things with him. I'm also having lunch with Hashem tomorrow and will explain his role as a bank robber to him. I am assuming he will try to get more money from us, but I can't see him turning down such a large tax-free sum."

Kurth was dubious. "There may be some trouble with Hashem."

"I will take a transcript of the critical tape and let him read it to show him how easy it will be to pull this off."

Kurth remained skeptical, "Maybe Alain, but you're also letting him know he is the key to the operation's success."

"If he declines, I'll tell him that is okay by me. I'll say that I will just have to tell my agency contact that if they want to go through with it they will have to find someone to take Hashem's place. Then I will get up to leave. I'm willing to bet Hashem will chase after me faster than a racehorse. In any case, I'll let you know Monday afternoon."

"I'll come up with a script and practice it," Kurth said. He shook hands and left.

Kurth decided to walk back to the Intercontinental Hotel where he was staying. He wanted time to reflect on what had transpired since his initial involvement in Alain's planning. At first, he had considered Alain's scheme as nothing more than an attempt to logically pursue an irrational concept. He had felt a responsibility to dissuade Alain from turning his conceptual thinking into an operational reality. He thought that the best way to do this was to point out inconsistencies in his planning, but as things progressed he found himself more and more drawn into Alain's plans. He smirked as he recalled the times Alain had been able to convince him on the way the operation should be run, no matter how great his initial doubts.

He had never seriously considered doing anything criminal, although as a CIA operations officer he had certainly broken laws frequently. He now had to confront his feelings because, within days, they would either win or lose. He was amused at the fact that they would be robbing a tyrant like Saddam Hussein. *Talk about just deserts, he thought to himself.* He concluded that his real problem was his lingering doubts about the wisdom of robbing a Swiss bank. He had to confess to himself that there was a real possibility they could actually carry it off.

He did have an advantage in that Alain was the only one in the group who was aware of his involvement. This he considered a definite plus. He was not worried about Otto. Once the tap, in the form of the bridge, was removed, no one could trace anything to Otto. There would be no evidence that the tap had actually been made. He knew that Otto would make sure that no trace of the bridge remained in the junction box. The only person who could lead the authorities to him was Alain. Kurth, being a gambler, concluded that the odds were worth the bet. He and Alain had invested about twenty thousand dollars each in the operation and, if everything went well, they should each net well over two million dollars. *Not bad for a small investment,* he reflected. Having reviewed the odds on success, he relaxed and continued his walk to the hotel at a brisker pace.

Kurth had delayed calling Ulla. He decided to call and tell her that he had just arrived in Germany unexpectedly. He planned to tell her he would be tied up with business for several days and would take some time off when he was finished. He looked at his watch. If he called immediately, he might even be able to say good night to the kids.

Chapter 10

Hamburg. September 6, 1982.

ALAIN AND HASHEM had eaten a leisurely lunch at the Indian restaurant. Alain found it quite good. The duck was well prepared and the garlic shrimp had been excellent. Although Alain had kept him in suspense, Hashem did not show it. Alain thought it must have been a struggle for Hashem. Despite this, the conversation had been easy. They had dwelt on old shared experiences in the agency.

Finally, Hashem blurted out, "Okay, Alain, let's have it. You didn't bring me here to reminisce on old times. What's going on?"

Alain proffered Hashem the blandest smile he could muster. "Quite right, Hashem, with a little luck, by next Friday night you will be a lot better off financially than you are now."

"How much better off?"

Alain decided to let him wait. He purposely drank some tea before answering Hashem. "If all goes well, and there is no reason it shouldn't, you will be well paid."

Hashem brightened at the money reference. "You mentioned my role. What is it?"

"Why Hashem, old friend, you are going to rob a bank - a Swiss bank at that."

Hashem remain silent, staring incredulously at Alain.

"What? Rob a bank? You aren't serious, are you?"

"While it will be a robbery, in point of fact, it will all be arranged beforehand. The banker will graciously turn the money over to you."

"I don't know what the hell you've been smoking, Alain, but you better change brands."

Alain reached into his inside coat pocket and pulled out some papers.

"To set the record straight, Hashem, I don't smoke. I saw my local agency contact on Saturday. He explained what it is we are to do. He told me that he would have the critical information for the job in the next couple of days. You recall there are no calls in German on the tapes we got from my agency contact."

"That's right. You told me the BKA had deleted all the calls involving German citizens."

"Read this transcription, and then I will explain things, hopefully to your satisfaction."

Hashem's expression changed rapidly as he read the transcript. When he had finished reading it, he read it over again before looking at Alain.

"When and how did you get this? You told me that the BKA had deleted all the calls in German."

"Now you know why the agency was so interested in the tap. When I have explained things to you, you will know why they wanted this operation to be off-line. When I got that transcript, I was as surprised as you, Hashem, my old friend. As to the when, I got the transcript this morning. As to the how, it was handed to me when I met my agency contact this morning."

Hashem seemed less than satisfied. He chewed on air for a few moments, considering both the transcript and how it fit into Alain's confidence in their ability to rob a Swiss bank. He considered Alain's poker face as he spoke.

"Okay, for the moment, let's assume that what you told me is the gospel truth. From the beginning, I suspected there was something hidden under a rock because the tapes I have transcribed are in no way descriptive enough to warrant a sensitive off-line operation. What did your agency contact tell you and what do you make of it?"

Alain let Hashem stew in his own questions before he answered. He decided to be as dramatic as possible.

"Next Friday - you, Hashem - are going to rob the Banque Suisse."

Hashem laughed incredulously, "Are you out of your fucking mind, Alain? This is crazy. Why, in the name of God, would the agency stoop to bank robbery? You better have some good answers."

"Listen carefully, Hashem. My agency contact told me that on Wednesday, at eleven o'clock in the morning, the Mr. Schlagel on the tape would receive a telephone call. In this conversation, Mr. Schlagel will be told that an Iraqi gentleman will arrive at the bank on Friday morning at eleven o'clock. He will have one half of a ten mark note with a specific serial number together with the account number. Mr. Schlagel will also be told the exact amount this gentleman is to withdraw. He will then be informed that a photocopy of the gentleman's passport and the other half of the ten-mark note are being sent to him by DHL along with three samples of the gentleman's signature."

Hashem interrupted Alain's explanation, his voice as sarcastic as he could muster, "Now I know you are nuts. You expect me to walk into a Swiss bank and calmly make a withdrawal. Oh, by the way, how much am I supposed to withdraw?"

"You will withdraw exactly five million, one hundred thousand dollars. Five million will be in bearer bonds and the one hundred thousand dollars will be in cash."

"Wait one fucking second, Alain." Hashem waved the transcript in front of him. "According to this transcript, this Mr. Schlagel calls Wafiq back immediately, obviously to confirm he was actually talking to Wafiq. This could be a pretty dicey problem."

Alain was thoughtful. At least Hashem was asking the right questions. "Good question, Hashem. My agency contact assured me that Schlagel's call is no problem. It will all be taken care off. He did hint that the techs would do their magic for that brief period and no one will be the wiser. As you know, Wafiq will be in Paris."

"If I am dumb enough to do this, what do I get?"

"The one hundred thousand dollars are yours. I haggled with my agency contact for some time, and he finally agreed to the one hundred thousand."

"What do you get? I'll bet a lot more. One other point, what about the passport?"

Alain felt more secure. He was sure Hashem would do the deed. He would never pass up one hundred thousand dollars in tax-free cash. "I have been promised twenty-five thousand dollars in cash and a three year consulting contract." Alain reached into his coat pocket, removed the Iraqi passport, and passed it to

Hashem. "A gift from the agency. My contact warned me that it is only suitable for flash purposes. It is a photocopy of this passport that will be sent to Mr. Schlagel in Geneva."

Hashem examined the passport carefully. He was impressed, it would certainly hold up for flash purposes. The techs had even made his beard appear a little heavier. It matched his now heavier beard pretty well.

"How about some more operational details?" Hashem said as he returned the passport.

This brought a smile from Alain. He drank some tea, then said, "My agency contact will set up shop in Geneva tomorrow with five other agency officers. From my talks with him, they urgently need the bearer bonds next weekend. For what, I do not know. But now you know the reason for the secrecy. They need bearer bonds that, from all appearances, were issued to an Iraqi official. One member of this team will actually be in the bank when you arrive. I suspect he is one of those guys that move money for the agency. Three of the agency men are a surveillance team. They will be on the street"

"Okay, suppose I agree, what's the go no-go deadline?"

"I will call you on Wednesday morning at nine o'clock. Be sure to be by your phone. If you are going to do it, you have to make up your mind now."

Hashem scratched his chin. "I keep the one hundred big ones? As a curiosity, what happens if I say no?"

"I suppose they will find someone else. They might even call the whole thing off, but I think they will bring in someone else. They seem very anxious to get their hands on the bearer bonds and, I assume, picked this timing because Wafiq will be away."

"Whose account is it?"

This was not a question Alain wanted to hear from Hashem, but he knew it was one Hashem was bound to ask. Whatever else Hashem was, he was also an experienced operations officer.

"It's an Iraqi Government account controlled by Wafiq. According to my agency contact, Wafiq uses the account to pay for purchases he makes on the gray arms market. The account is one of several that Saddam Hussein uses to siphon off money into his personal accounts." In response to a raised eyebrow from Hashem, he added, "The plural is correct."

Hashem thought for a couple of minutes before speaking. Then, in a very serious tone, he said, "Okay, I'll do it. You know damn well I can use the money. Tell me exactly how the operation will be run, then I may have some questions." Hashem sat back in his seat and lit a cigar.

"I will call you at nine on Wednesday morning and tell you we're on for tomorrow if it's a go. If something is wrong, I will tell you I can't make it tomorrow. You get yourself to Geneva. I have reservations for Thursday at the Bristol Hotel. I want you to come to the hotel at six o'clock on Thursday evening. Call me on the house phone and come up to the room. We will do a quick review of what will transpire on Friday. I want you out of the hotel in about half an hour as I'm tentatively meeting with the agency contact at seven."

"You can fully brief me in a half an hour?"

"I think so. We can go over last minute plans when I pick you up the next morning. Get a hotel some distance from the Bristol. At our meeting Thursday evening, I will brief you on the final arrangements to pick you up and drive you to the bank. I will drop you off as close to eleven o'clock as possible. I will be back in front of the bank in ten minutes. If you have a briefcase, bring it. If you don't have one, get one. You will put the one hundred thousand that is yours in the briefcase. Schlagel will probably put the bearer bonds in an envelope. When you come out of the bank, get in the car, and give me both the bearer bonds and the Iraqi passport. I'll drop you off wherever you want. Then you are on your own, one hundred thousand dollars richer." Alain took a folded sheet of paper out of his pocket and handed it to Hashem. "Sign Tarek Shammar three times for me."

Hashem wrote the three signatures. "Okay, but what if something goes wrong?"

"Good point. Check out of your hotel before I pick you up. According to my contact, there is about twenty million in the account. The only thing that could go wrong would be Schlagel insisting on checking with Wafiq. Stay calm. Do not raise any objections. Tell him that Wafiq will be back in Hamburg next week. You will have him call Schlagel to confirm the withdrawal. Leave the bank and get in my car," Alain was dead serious. "We will do a surveillance detection route and I will drive you to the airport. Take the first plane you can to get out of Geneva. Since Schlagel doesn't know your true name, you should have no trouble. If Schlagel picks up the phone as you leave, it means we will have to move fast. You better check on what flights there are around noon. Even if everything goes down all right, I think that you should leave Geneva as soon as possible."

Hashem appeared to be reassured. He looked like he was trying to frame more questions, but gave up. "Okay, I'll wait for your call Wednesday morning. I wish I knew what the agency was planning to do with the bearer bonds."

"So do I, Hashem, so do I."

Later in the day, Alain was able to reach Blanton. He told Blanton to come to the apartment Wednesday afternoon at two o'clock. He would be waiting for him. Blanton said he would be there. After hanging up, he rushed back to his apartment to get there before Kurth arrived. Fifteen minutes later, they greeted each other and Kurth immediately asked the key question.

"How did it go with Hashem?"

Alain grinned. "He came around pretty much like I thought he would. He was very curious about what the agency intended to do with the bearer bonds."

Kurth laughed. "What did you tell him?"

"Nothing."

"I would have told him it was part of some kind of sting operation. Hashem has reason to despise the Iraqis. It might have made him even more willing to get involved."

"Believe me, Kurth, he's willing enough, but you have a point. I will mention something along those lines to him when I see him Thursday night. Right now, let's review the operation to see if we overlooked anything. First, I think that we should not see each other outside of this apartment at all, except as an operational necessity. Why don't you come by for dinner tomorrow night?"

"As I have always told you, Alain, I would never turn down a dinner invitation from you. How about a review of where we stand?"

"Right. At my meeting with Hashem today, I told him I would call him at nine o'clock Wednesday morning to indicate if the operation was a go or a no-go. I gave him the name of my hotel in Geneva and told him to come to the hotel at six in the evening on Thursday. He is to get my room number by calling me on the house phone. I told him he had to be out of the room by six-thirty because

I have to meet with my agency contact at about seven. That will give us enough time to review everything. I explained that the next morning I would pick him up at his hotel, drive him to the bank, and then pick him up after he had made the withdrawal. I included details about the agency personnel watching over things, including a man in the bank and a three-man surveillance team on the street outside the bank."

Kurth asked, "What was Hashem's reaction to all this?"

"In the end, he accepted that it looked very good. He did ask me what planning had been done in case something goes wrong."

"So, what did you tell him?"

"I explained to him that the only snag would be if Schlagel insisted that he call Wafiq to confirm the withdrawal. This would mean that the jig is up and we are out five million dollars. I told him that he should agree with Schlagel. Since Wafiq would be in Paris until next Tuesday, Hashem would return to Hamburg and have Wafiq call Schlagel as soon as he returned. Hashem should then bid Schlagel a fond goodbye and leave. Since no laws have been broken and Schlagel has acted in the best interests of his client, Wafiq, I doubt that any further action would be taken."

Kurth was somewhat skeptical, but decided to agree with Alain. "What you say is logical. At the moment I can't think of anything else to question with regard to Schlagel."

"The only thing I can think of is the possibility that Wafiq has given Schlagel Col. Qodsi's office number in Paris. In this case, it might take Qodsi some time to locate Wafiq. If, for some reason, Schlagel wants to confirm the transaction with Wafiq, Hashem can leave the bank saying he will take care of some business and return in the afternoon. By afternoon, he should be out of the country. In short, a delay of any kind by Schlagel would force us to terminate the operation and get the hell out of Switzerland."

Kurth's expression suddenly changed. He spoke rapidly, "What if Hashem gets greedy and decides he might as well take a chance and make off with everything?"

"The same thought occurred to me, Kurth. That is why I told Hashem that six agency personnel would be in Geneva to provide surveillance. The agency knows that the person we have picked to make the withdrawal is Hashem. I told him there would be someone in the bank when he arrived. There will also be a three-man surveillance team in the street. I plan to tell him that my agency contact will also be in the vicinity and will be well-armed. All this is to make sure we can make a getaway if required. I think Hashem will settle for the one hundred thousand."

Alain stopped talking and waited for some comment from Kurth. When none was forthcoming, he continued, "Okay, I've arranged for Blanton to come by at two o'clock Wednesday afternoon. He will do what is needed to put the phone lines back to normal. As I said before, my next meeting with Hashem will be at my hotel in Geneva at six this Thursday. We will go over any last minute instructions, presumably from the agency. I have a rented car parked out front. I will leave here as soon as Blanton arrives and pick you up at the Intercon. We can take turns driving. I'm taking my large suitcase. It should hold two million in hundreds. You'll need something big. Given the fact that you can get marks in denominations of five hundred, you should be able to fit the equivalent of three million dollars into a large brief case."

Kurth nodded his approval. "I have a large sports bag. We best plan that we might not get the whole sum in the largest notes."

"True, Kurth. I'll also take my brief case. One last question, does Hashem know you have retired?"

"I don't think so. We don't exactly travel in the same circles."

"Good. Do your best to keep him from spotting you. If he does spot you, hopefully he will assume you are one of the agency officers deployed to Geneva for the operation. In the meantime, if you think of anything, we can discuss it at dinner tomorrow night."

It had been a long evening for the two old friends. They had spent a great deal of time going over every possible scenario. Both agreed that the first order of business in Geneva would be a casing of the bank. If there was more than one exit they could be in trouble. They decided that they would case the bank separately, then compare notes when they met Thursday evening. They set their meeting for seven-thirty.

Finally, Kurth got up to go. "I can't think of anything else. I don't think I should come here tomorrow night." He added, "It will save you the trouble of cooking a gourmet meal."

"You're right, it's best we take no more chances than we have to. Make your arrangements with Otto. What time can I call you at the hotel tomorrow to confirm that Otto will do the job?"

"I will be in my room from four until I hear from you." Kurth replied.

Alain nodded his agreement, "If everything is okay, I will expect you here no later than ten-thirty Wednesday morning."

⇥ ⇤

Wafiq was working late in his office clearing up some business before his departure for Paris the following morning. Ingrid had called to confirm his reservation and made a reservation for his return on Tuesday, the fourteenth. Wafiq was half working and half daydreaming about his upcoming long weekend with Muna. He was also concerned about why Haitham Abd al-Nebi was coming to see him. Haitham had called early to make sure he would be there. Wafiq looked at his watch and wondered what was keeping him. He didn't have to wait long. He heard the outer door to the office open and close. Ingrid led Haitham into his office. She asked if they would like her to make coffee. Both men shook their heads and Ingrid left the office, closing the door behind her.

"I won't take up much of your time, Wafiq. I just wanted to apprise you of my concerns."

Wafiq wondered what so concerned his old friend, he looked very disturbed indeed. "You look like you have offended Saddam himself, old friend. What's the trouble?"

Haitham wrung his hands nervously. "You remember I told you how one of my men spotted Hashem Samara'i. As you know, we have had him under surveillance on and off, usually by following his girlfriend. One thing troubles me."

"What's that?"

"He has grown a closely cropped beard. When someone like Hashem grows a beard, it is for some operational purpose. In Hashem's case, it probably has something to do with us. He has been more trouble than a mad dog in the past. I wanted to warn you that it could well have something to do with you."

This worried Wafiq, but he did his best not to show it. "Haitham, I will be back from Paris next Tuesday. Why don't you come by that evening? We can discuss what to do about your old friend over dinner."

Haitham scowled. "He's no friend of mine. I'll drop by late Tuesday afternoon. In the meantime, I'll try to find out more about him. *Illa liqah.*"

⇢⊨◉ ◉⊨⇠

Hamburg. September 7, 1982.
Alain had left his apartment a little before four in the afternoon and walked about half a mile before stopping to use a pay phone. He put a couple of pfennig coins in the telephone. When the hotel operator answered the phone, he gave her Kurth's room number. There was a short pause before Kurth's voice came on the line.

"Hello."

"I just called to see if our business deal is in play," Alain answered.

"I had lunch with my German business contact and he assured me he would take care of everything. In fact, he seemed relieved that we can conclude our business deal. He is expecting my call sometime between eleven-thirty and noon tomorrow."

"Excellent, I'll see you tomorrow." Alain hung up the phone as an excited smile animated his face.

⇢⊨◉ ◉⊨⇠

Hamburg. September 8, 1982.
Alain walked around the Alster until he came to a pay phone he had not yet used. He took a piece of paper with Hashem's phone number written on it out of

his pocket. He looked at the number as he dialed. Alain had never been good at remembering phone numbers. He listened to the ringing until Hashem's disembodied voice came on the line.

"Hello."

"It's me, we are on for tomorrow. It's a go. I'll see you tomorrow night. Any problems?"

"No, I'm all set. I'll see you tomorrow night. Goodbye."

"Goodbye." *So far so good,* Alain thought as he walked away from the pay phone. He looked at his watch. He had plenty of time before Kurth's scheduled arrival at his apartment at ten-thirty. He took his time. He always thought he got his best ideas when walking alone. When he was back in the apartment, he made a pot of coffee. He was about finished with a cup when Kurth arrived. As soon as Kurth had a cup of coffee in front of him, he pulled out some notes and showed them to Alain. Kurth had drawn up a script with his usual Germanic thoroughness.

"Excellent, Kurth, I think you have covered everything. I sent a photocopy of the Iraqi passport, the signature exemplars and the one half of a ten-mark note to Schlagel this morning. I was told it would be delivered this afternoon. Here is the other half. Since Wafiq did not mention a serial number in his last conversation with Schlagel, you should do the same." After some banter, Alain said, "It's time for the curtain to go up. Let's hope that Otto has done his part."

Alain got up and brought the phone out of the closet. He had taken the input jack out of the actuator. He plugged the input jack into the phone and handed it and a slip of paper with the phone number to his partner. Kurth picked up the receiver and gave the okay sign with his right hand thumb and forefinger. Alain watched intently as Kurth dialed Schlagel's number.

"Mr. Schlagel, please." Pause. "Wafiq Tikriti." Pause. "I am fine, Irwin. Has the skiing season begun yet?" Pause. "Irwin, an Iraqi gentleman will call at your bank at eleven o'clock the day after tomorrow, the tenth. I sent you this morning a photocopy of his passport, signature exemplars, and one half of a ten-mark note. The name on the passport is Tarek Shammar, father's name Kamel. The amount he is to withdraw is five million, one hundred thousand dollars. The five million should be in bearer bonds and the one hundred thousand dollars in cash." Pause. "Not necessary, Irwin. I am leaving for Paris this afternoon and will not be back until next week. I am expecting a deposit. What will the balance be after the withdrawal?" Pause. "Thank you, Irwin." Kurth hung up the phone.

Turning to Alain, he said, "The secretary did not sound like the one in the recording. Most promising was the fact that Schlagel did not question my accent."

"My friend, you were magnificent. I was shocked at how close you were to Wafiq's accent and tone of voice."

They were interrupted by Schlagel's return call. Kurth picked up the phone and said, "Hello." Pause. "Thank you very much, Mr. Schlagel. Goodbye." After a brief pause, Kurth hung up the phone. "So far, so good. I'll take off and get in touch with Otto. What time will you come by the hotel to pick me up?"

Alain thought for a moment. "I told Blanton to come by at two this afternoon. I can leave as soon as he gets here. He will lock up. It's only minutes to your hotel from here."

"I've already checked out. The concierge has my bags. I was able to fold up the sports bag and put it in my suitcase. I had to put my underwear and shirts in my brief case in order to fit the sports bag in my suitcase. I'm going to grab a bite, but I'll be back in the hotel lobby by two o'clock."

"Okay then, I'll pick you up shortly after two. How long do you think it will take us to get to the Swiss border?"

"That depends on how much we press and how many stops we make."

"We'll stay somewhere near the Swiss border to get a good night's sleep."

After Kurth left, Alain tried to relax before his meeting with Jack. Things were going remarkably well. It wasn't long before there was a knock on the door.

"You are right on time, Jack. Look, I've got to run. There's beer in the refrigerator. Put everything back the way it was. You can have the Kudelski tape recorder concealed in the radio if you want it."

"Thanks. I will take the Kudelski if you don't want it." Jack was already opening a small briefcase that contained his tools.

"Be my guest. I plan to leave the radio for the landlady. Incidentally, the phone now works, and supposedly all evidence that there was a tap has been removed."

Jack responded, "Good to know."

"When you finish, just close the door after you. Make sure it is locked. I'll probably call you sometime Sunday. You can make reservations to fly out on Monday if you want."

"Okay, Alain, goodbye."

Alain left the apartment, curious as to why Jack had not asked him about his payment. He got into the rented Mercedes, started the engine, eased the car away from the curb, and headed for the Intercon hotel. A few minutes later, Kurth saw him as he pulled into the hotel driveway. Alain got out and opened the trunk for Kurth's suitcase and briefcase. Alain closed the trunk and they got in the car.

"Splurging on a Mercedes, Alain! This operation better work."

"Well, we've done everything we could to make it work. While I find Hashem somewhat odious, he is a professional, so everything should go smoothly. We can talk on the way and decide what we have to do tomorrow after we get to Geneva. I think we should drive until about eight o'clock tonight, then find a place to stay and have a good dinner."

Kurth joked, "Those about to die had a fine dinner."

"None of your low brow humor," Alain said as he guided the car out of the hotel driveway.

Kurth turned serious, "Look old friend. It's nearly five hundred miles to the Swiss border crossing at Basel. I suggest we see how much time it takes to get to Karlsruhe. If we get to Karlsruhe and decide to stay there, we can easily make Geneva sometime in the middle of the afternoon at the latest. Don't forget that the evening rush hour is going to slow us down a little. If we do make great time and are up to it, we can push on to Baden, or even Offenburg. As far as I am concerned, I'll be happy if we get to Karlsruhe before nine o'clock."

"Sounds fair enough, Kurth, let's see how far we can get by eight or eight-thirty. I want to get to Geneva tomorrow in time to take a quick look at the Banque Suisse and check out the time it takes me to drop someone off, then circle around to pick him up. If Schlagel is the efficient Swiss banker that I think he is, he will have the bearer bonds and cash ready."

They drove in silence for about fifteen minutes before Kurth asked Alain, "You said you had called Rentke, right?"

"Yes, I called him and told him I would have some business for him. Why? What's on your mind?"

"Well, I think it best that you go see Rentke tomorrow afternoon and I will see Drouget. You certainly want the two million in one hundred dollar notes. I will try to get as many five hundred mark notes as possible. If Drouget can't come up with a lot of large notes, I'll take one million in dollars. Did you, by any chance, open up a bank account in Hamburg?"

"I had to. I drew on it for expenses and also for the expenses of Hashem and Blanton," Alain answered.

"Look, I don't mind driving back to Hamburg with a million or so, but don't you think we could have Drouget and Rentke provide us with some kind of financial instrument so we don't have to take everything in cash?"

"Come on, dummy. We can't have them transfer money to our accounts. They don't know us by our true names," Alain said sarcastically.

"Yes, that's true, Alain, but they don't know that the names on the accounts are our true names. Knowing those guys, the five million dollars in bearer bonds are a commodity they can sell at a large markup to any number of customers. They will have them less than twenty-four hours. Those bonds will have changed hands several times before they are eventually returned to the Banque Suisse. We have no worry about anyone trying to trace them since no Swiss laws have been broken."

Alain considered what Kurth had said while he barreled down the Autobahn at high speed. "Let's give this some thought. If Drouget can come up with two million dollars in five hundred mark notes, that would be good. We better work on a couple of alternatives, then check in with those two as soon as possible. Suppose Drouget can supply you the five hundred mark notes. I can get half a million dollars from Rentke in cash and ask him to wire the balance to an account in Hamburg. That still creates a paper trail. Even if it is highly unlikely there will ever be an investigation, I was a case officer too long to leave a paper trail. Let's think on it for a while. There has to be a better way."

At five-thirty, they pulled into one of the rest stops on the Autobahn to stretch their legs, make a pit stop, and fill the gas tank. Kurth took the wheel when they left and within two minutes he was doing over eighty miles an hour, much to Alain's chagrin.

"Look, Kurth, in two days we will both be millionaires. There is a condition."

"What's that, Alain?"

"We must get there alive."

Kurth laughed and slowed down to an even eighty. "How's that, captain caution?"

"Just keep your eyes on the road."

Kurth concentrated on driving. After a little over two hours had gone by, he said, "It's eight o'clock and we should be in Karlsruhe in twenty minutes or so. I know a pretty good place we can stay on the outskirts of town. They serve a great breakfast. We can be on the road tomorrow morning at eight. What do you say?"

"Yes, let's stop, eat dinner, and get a good night's sleep."

Kurth looked at him quizzically, "For a skinny guy, you sure like to eat."

→▭◑ ◐▭←

Geneva. September 9, 1982.

Dinner the night before had been surprisingly good. They also had a pleasant evening revisiting past associations. After a full night's sleep, they ate a filling breakfast. Alain commented that the meals would have satisfied a starving truck driver. Kurth was again at the wheel as they left the hotel and pulled onto the Autobahn. It was seven-thirty. Kurth figured they should be in Geneva by the early afternoon.

"Alain, I think we should deal with our money changing friends first. What do you say? Any final ideas on how we should handle the bearer bonds?"

Alain had given the matter considerable thought. "Yes, I think it would be a mistake to leave any kind of paper trail. As you said, the bonds will be hard to trace after they are returned to the Banque Suisse. You can bet the financial institution that redeems them will be above reproach. Second, the moneychangers are never going to be questioned about the bonds. As you said, they will only have them a short time. Even if asked, they do not know our true names."

While Kurth kept his eyes on the road, Alain paused for effect, "The problem with any kind of transfer is that it would have to be to my true name account in Hamburg. It is still a risk, even if it is unlikely. What I plan to do is to go see Rentke when we get there and tell him I want two packages of a million dollars each. If I need to, I can give him bearer bonds to cover the first million and tell him I'll be back after I get rid of that package. As I recall, there is an alley behind his establishment. I'll ask him today if I can park there while I pick up the packages. If I can park there, I will pick up both packages at the same time. You can be in the car. I'll put the packages in the trunk. That's why I rented a Mercedes, plenty of trunk space." Alain took a break to see if Kurth was following his logic. Alain continued, "Drouget's place of business overlooks the central bus station and there is plenty of parking. I'll drive you there, get as close as possible, and wait in the car while you pick up the money. Then we hit the road. With any luck, we should be on our way in an hour or so. We'll do a surveillance detection route to make sure no one has gotten curious. What do you think?"

Kurth was silent for a few minutes trying to think of holes he could punch in Alain's statements. "I have to say, doing it your way we leave no trails, but we are going to have four or five large bundles. If we happen to get in a wreck, the countryside is going to look like it is growing money."

Alain laughed, "Okay, when we get to Geneva, we will park in that central parking lot just opposite Drouget's cash emporium. I can walk to Rentke's place. Once I finish my business with Rentke, I'll walk back and meet you in the McDonald's just up the street from the parking lot. Don't forget to ask Drouget to throw in a couple of extra bucks so you can enjoy yourself in Geneva."

"Okay, once we make the arrangements with Drouget and Rentke, we can check out the bank and spot some places where I can watch Hashem enter and leave the bank. If that son of a bitch tries to pull a fast one, I swear I'll kill the swine."

Alain smiled, "You certainly have strong feelings about Hashem. I don't think he'll try anything. After all, he knows there are going to be several agency officers around, including one in the bank. I just hope I can find a place where I can keep the entrance to the bank in sight so I can pick him up as soon as he leaves the bank."

"Well, one thing is on our side."

"What's that?"

Kurth scowled at Alain, "I can run faster than he can."

They drove on in relative silence, enjoying the scenery. The trees were just beginning to turn. They made Lausanne in good time and decided to grab lunch before continuing on to Geneva.

They entered Geneva on Rue de Lausanne. As they passed the botanical gardens on the right, Alain said to Kurth, "When you get to Rue du Mont-Blanc, turn left and go down to the international bus station. There is usually parking there. Kurth followed Alain's instructions and parked the Mercedes in the parking lot.

"Okay, Alain, I'll see you in the McDonald's. Incidentally, the Cafe de Paris is right near McDonald's. They have that very good pepper steak."

Alain nodded his agreement as they both got out of the car. Alain said goodbye and walked down Rue du Mont-Blanc to the bridge that crossed over the Rhône River as it emptied into Lake Geneva. He noticed that the Jet D'eau was not working. Rentke maintained his offices in a building on Rue de la Madeleine. It would be a nice walk. Alain had done business with him on several occasions. One transaction involved exchanging a million dollars for Iraqi dinars. It took Rentke two days to scrounge up that many dinars. What was interesting was that Rentke never batted an eye, nor did he ask any questions.

It took Alain a good fifteen minutes to get to Rentke's place of business. When he entered the office, a young woman greeted him in French and asked him what she could do for him. He answered her in German, asking for Herr Rentke, and gave her the name he had used with Rentke in arranging transactions for the agency. She buzzed Rentke and he came out of his office. He seemed shorter and heavier than the last time Alain had seen him. He had the face of a cherub adorned with a Hitler mustache and heavy jowls. He had a warm smile for Alain.

"So good to see you, Mr. Rogers. It has been a long time. Come into my office."

Rentke only handled large, special transactions. He had three kiosks around the city that handled the tourist trade. After they were seated and had exchanged pleasantries, Alain asked Rentke if he could come up with two million in one hundred dollar bills the following day.

"No problem. As I recall, you always brought bearer bonds, right?" Rentke asked as he started doing some figuring on his calculator.

"Correct. I would like to pick up the money before noon tomorrow. Is it possible to park in the alley behind this building?"

Rentke continued punching numbers into his calculator for a few seconds. "Yes, I can arrange that. Is it possible to have someone sitting in the car in case you are blocking a truck or the police come along?"

"No problem, you know we always travel with a bodyguard. I would like the money in two packages of one million dollars each."

"I will have my receptionist waiting for you at the back door. It has my name on it. The money will be in a safe in a vault in the adjoining room. I will come down and get it for you. Just in case you or your principals decide not to make the deal, I need three hundred dollars from you to cover my expenses in raising that much money. I will return it to you tomorrow."

"Will five hundred marks do?"

"Yes, that's fine. Then I will see you tomorrow. There is a buzzer beside the door."

"One other point, Mr. Rentke. Those bonds will bring a premium when you transact them. How about a cut for me so I can enjoy myself for the weekend in Switzerland?"

Rentke responded with a smile. "Yes, Mr. Rogers, I think I can spare something. Should I include it in one of the packages?"

Alain feigned alarm. "No, just put it in a separate envelope with the marks."

Rentke thought to himself, *so Mr. Rogers is making money off of his CIA employers. So be it. It's no concern of mine.* "I will do that Mr. Rogers. Goodbye until tomorrow."

Alain was amused as he left Rentke's place of business. He assumed Rentke thought that Mr. Rogers had gone the way of all flesh. On his part, Rentke picked up the phone as soon as Alain left. He dialed and waited.

"I think I can obtain two of the securities you need, at the usual commission, if you are still interested." There was an answer in the affirmative. "Excellent, I'll call you tomorrow afternoon."

Alain walked briskly back across the bridge over the Rhône and, a few minutes later, greeted Kurth in the McDonald's. Kurth was nursing a cup of coffee. Alan bought a cup and sat down with Kurth.

"How did it go with Drouget?"

"What's nice about dealing with people like Drouget and Rentke is that they are only interested in the deal at hand, they ask no other questions."

"Can Drouget come up with many large bills?"

"I was pleasantly surprised. He said that he thought he could get at least one and a half million dollars in five hundred mark notes and maybe more. I told him to try to bring the total up to two million dollars in marks. I told him to put the marks in one package and the other million dollars in a separate package. Just the way we had them do it in the old days."

Alain was elated that everything was going well. "Finish your coffee so we can go case the bank."

Alain swallowed his last gulp of coffee, got up from his seat, and said, "The Banque Suisse branch we are concerned with is located on the North side of Rue de Rive between Rue du Prince and Rue de la Tour-Maîtresse. First, let's drive by it and get a look at it. I want to see if there is somewhere I can park or stand while waiting for Hashem. I will let you out and you can check for rear exits from the Bank and look for a place where you can observe the front of the bank."

Kurth's expression turned grim, "Yeah, I want to find a place where I can watch him enter the bank, then a second place where I can watch him exit the bank. I forgot to tell you. I will be carrying tomorrow."

Alain was not surprised. Hashem had better not try to pull a fast one - Kurth could be ruthless when necessary. "I thought you would be," Alain answered. "We will also have to work out some signals." They arrived at the rented Mercedes. Alain got in the driver's seat and Kurth sat down beside him.

Alain started the car and eased into traffic. "I'm going to cross over the Pont du Mont-Blanc then proceed straight to the intersection where Rue de la Croix-d'Or becomes Rue de Rive. As soon as possible after I cross the intersection, I'll stop and let you out. I don't think we should be seen together any more than necessary. You can then take a good look at possible vantage points along Rue de Rive. I'll double back and make some runs from the bank circling around. I intend to time the shortest run possible then choose one circle that takes about ten minutes to complete. I figure it won't take long for Hashem to make the transaction. I hope to spot a place where I can wait in the car and see him as he comes out of the bank. One of the most important things for you to determine is if there is another exit from the bank. While I may not be as animated about it, I don't trust Hashem any more than you do."

Kurth nodded his head in agreement, but was still concerned about Hashem. Stealing the money was one thing, but he hoped he wouldn't have to kill Hashem to get it from him. "Alain. I'm glad I brought my Browning automatic. My only hope is that, if Hashem tries any funny business, flashing it at him will be enough. Shooting could raise some serious complications."

"That's an understatement, Kurth," Alain replied with a half smile on his lips.

Kurth returned Alain's smile with a serious frown, then got back to the problem at hand. "Okay, I'll check everything. There may not be another entrance to the bank proper, but there may be an entrance to the bank's offices. I'll walk completely around the block."

"Good, Kurth." Alain suddenly thought of something, "Schlagel will probably handle this transaction in his office. If there is another entrance, we will have to make plans to cover it."

As they drove along Place de Longemalle, Kurth spoke. "Okay, where do we meet after the casing?"

"When you are finished, grab a cab and meet me at McDonald's. We can compare notes over a cup of coffee."

"Okay, see you later," was Kurth's parting shot as he got out of the car.

Alain continued on and took the appropriate turns until he got to the Rond-Point de Rive. He then drove west until he drew parallel to the Banque Suisse. He looked at his watch and took the first right onto Rue du Prince. He stayed on Rue du Prince until he reached Rue du Rhône, turned right on Rue du Rhône, then proceeded east until he made another right onto Rue Pierre-Fatio. He checked the traffic as he made a right turn which took him into the Rond-Point de Rive. He made the first turn out of the circle onto Rue de Rive. He then drove west until he reached the Banque Suisse. He checked his watch. It had taken about nine minutes. He figured he could make the route a minute longer by going slower. He thought he could stand for a short time about fifty meters from the bank. He decided to time just going around the block, then stand for a minute or so at the spot he had picked about fifty meters from the bank. He timed the run around the block and it was right about ten minutes. He stopped the car for about a minute and, with the exception of a few angry glances, nothing happened.

He thought he had learned all that he could so he drove the car to its parking place, walked to McDonald's, brought a cup of coffee, and waited for Kurth. His wait took a little longer than expected. When Kurth finally arrived, Alain had finished his coffee and was in the process of getting a second one. Kurth paid for his and sat down with Alain. He took a long drink of coffee before saying anything.

"I checked out every office building on the block," Kurth said.

"And?" Alain questioned.

"As far as I could determine, there is only one entrance to the bank and that is on Rue de Rive. I suspect that all the offices are in the rear. I walked around the bank twice and noticed two doors in the rear of the bank. Also, there is a glass door to your immediate left as you enter the bank. This leads to a stairway. There is a second door on the street which has several names printed on it. All of them are non-bank businesses. I used the street door and went up the steps. There are two floors above the bank and neither floor has any bank offices on it."

"Good work. It would appear that Hashem must exit the same way he goes in."

"That would seem to be the case. Also, there is a bookshop named Artou across the street from the bank. I plan to position myself on the Southeast corner of Rue Verdaine where it runs into Rue de Rive. From there I can observe your arrival at the bank. After a couple of minutes, I intend to go to the Artou book shop where I can observe Hashem's exit from the bank. If he makes one false move, I'll be on him like a cat."

Alain smiled, "Good work, Kurth. I think I've come up with a gimmick which will give Hashem second thoughts if he has any plans about making off with the bearer bonds."

Kurth was intrigued, "Well, mastermind, what have you come up with?"

"When I drive him to the bank tomorrow morning, I intend to tell him that if I don't signal that I have the bonds, the agency monetary officer who deals with the Banque Suisse will tell them there is a scam involving bearer bonds issued by the bank. The bank will withhold payment of the bonds until they can determine if this is indeed the case. I also intend to take his wallet, his U.S. passport, and his airline ticket before he leaves the car. When he comes by tonight, I plan to remind him to check out of the hotel before I pick him up. He will then be unable to say he has left stuff in the hotel."

"I think we have pretty much covered all the bases. I forget, what time is Hashem coming to your hotel?" Kurth asked.

"He is to be there at six tonight."

"Do you know where he is staying?"

"He called me before we left and told me he had reservations at the Hotel Suisse."

Kurth was alarmed, "That's not far from here."

Alain looked at his watch. "Relax. His plane is due at three o'clock, ten minutes from now. Look, why don't you drop me off at my hotel? Everything I need is in my briefcase. I'll leave the big suitcase in the car trunk. You can take the car to your hotel. Why don't we drive out towards Versoix later and have a good dinner at that restaurant overlooking the lake? The one that specializes in lake perch."

"Good. I'll drop you off now and come by at seven-thirty tonight to pick you up. Is that okay with you?"

"Fine by me. My instructions to Hashem are going to be simple and direct. I don't think it will take me more than fifteen or twenty minutes. He thinks that I will be meeting with my contact at seven but I will make sure he hasn't followed me when I leave. If I'm sure I'm clean, I'll start walking along the quay. I'll walk north since that's the road we'll take to Versoix." Kurth nodded his head in agreement.

After checking in to his hotel, Alain had taken a brief nap. He was sitting in the easy chair in his room reading one of his favorite books, a collection of Robert A. Heinlein's earlier works, *Expanded Universe*, when the phone rang. Alain looked at his watch, relieved that Hashem was right on time.

"Hello."

"It's your six o'clock appointment." Hashem's voice was unmistakable.

Alain gave him the room number and within minutes there was a knock on the door. When he opened it, Hashem walked in and sat down in the easy chair.

"Have a seat, Hashem."

"Okay, Alain, let's have it."

"It's very simple. I will pick you up in front of your hotel at quarter to eleven. Be sure to check out before I pick you up. I will give you the Iraqi passport and one half of the ten-mark note. You will need both with Schlagel. It should be around eleven when I let you out. Given Swiss efficiency, the transaction shouldn't take long. I'll circle around and be waiting for you at fifteen minutes after eleven. If for some reason there is a delay, I'll circle the block, which only takes a few minutes. Important point, did you make any plane reservations?"

"Yes, I did. One is for twelve forty-five and another at two. I have a question. Does the agency know it's me that's impersonating the Iraqi?"

Alain smiled. Hashem was a worrier. "Probably, but if they do my contact has not brought it up. Look at it this way Hashem, how many agency staffers or retirees could pull this off? You have to admit, Hashem, that you are one of a very small group of candidates. In fact, I couldn't come up with anyone but you. Consider yourself lucky, you're going to get a lot of money tax-free."

"Okay, you pick me up at my hotel tomorrow morning at ten forty-five. You drop me off at about eleven. I enter the bank and ask for Mr. Schlagel. I show Schlagel the Iraqi passport and the half of a ten-mark note. He gives me one hundred thousand in cash and five million in bearer bonds. I leave the bank and you pick me up. I keep the one hundred thousand and give you the bearer bonds. What next?"

"My first scheduled contact to turn over the bonds is exactly twenty-five minutes after I pick you up when you exit the bank. I will drop you off at the cabstand at Place du Port. You should be able to make the twelve forty-five flight with ease."

Hashem's expression turned grim as he asked, "From your explanation, I assume that the agency will have us under surveillance, right?"

"I have been told there will be two three-man teams. One of the teams is made up of Fosdicks. I was told they would be armed."

Hashem's laugh was humorless, "I assume their main mission is not to protect us. Not very trusting are they?" The question was rhetorical.

"I was told that the bearer bonds are critical to some kind of deception operation they are running. They have to do something with the bonds tomorrow afternoon."

"That explains the tight schedule," Hashem interrupted. "In Hamburg you told me the agency will also have someone in the bank."

"Yes, my contact told me he would be a member of the other three-man team. Once you enter the bank and are escorted into Schlagel's office, their man in the bank will exit the bank and signal that you are with Schlagel."

"Why did they tell you all these details?" Hashem asked, while rubbing his chin in a thoughtful gesture. "That's out of character for our old employers."

"They explained these details for the purpose of convincing me that the two of us had better not make any foolish plans where the bearer bonds are concerned. Once I pick you up after you exit the bank, the time of the pick-up will be relayed to my agency contact. He will expect me within twenty-five minutes. If I do not make the drop of the bearer bonds within the twenty-five minutes, the man who was in the bank will go back in the bank and tell Schlagel there has been a scam and he should suspend payment on the bonds. He will advise Schlagel to check with the owner of the account on which they were drawn. In effect the bonds are then useless to us. My contact emphasized that under no circumstances should we alter the precise amounts of the withdrawal. Schlagel will not deliver if we change anything."

"Don't worry, Alain, I have that part down pat. Anything else?"

"No, I'll see you tomorrow morning. I suggest you exit through the bar. It has a separate exit. Walk to your hotel. The exercise will do you good."

"To keep you happy, I'll use the stairs." Hashem got out of his chair, shook hands with Alain, and left the room.

After Hashem closed the door, Alain looked at this watch. It was twenty-two minutes after six. He decided to wait fifteen minutes before leaving the hotel. He intended to do a surveillance detection route to make sure Hashem did not follow him. He also wanted to make sure that no one else had developed an interest in him.

After an elaborate route to determine if Hashem, out of curiosity, had decided to follow him, Alain decided he was clean. He walked to the Quai du Mont-Blanc to walk north along the water. He had covered less than two hundred yards when Kurth pulled up to the curb and Alain got in the car. As soon as he was seated, Kurth asked, "How did it go with Hashem?"

Alain explained the conversation with Hashem in great detail. When he finished, Kurth was laughing quietly. "That was a great ploy about the bonds not being worth anything to you and Hashem. Do you think he bought it?" Kurth asked.

"He doesn't have much in the way of options. Why risk an easy one hundred thousand dollars?"

"Yeah, you are right. Go over tomorrow again, please," Kurth said, turning serious.

"I will drop Hashem off at the Place du Port. There is a cabstand there. He has a reservation on a plane leaving at twelve forty-five so he should be able to make it with ease. After I drop him off, I will double back and pick you up on the north side of the Rue du Rhône. You should be walking west and be well west of the bank by that time. We will go to Drouget's office first. I will wait for you in the parking lot opposite his office. Once we have loaded the cash in the trunk, you will drive me to the alley behind Rentke's office. He said to ring the bell and his secretary will open the door. He told me that he would have the money in two open boxes. Once I have confirmed it contains the money, I'll bring it to the car and we can be off. We will drive straight to my apartment in Hamburg where we can keep the money until Monday. I have a large safe deposit box in the Dresdener Bank. I hope I can cram most of the money into it. I intend to pay off Blanton on Saturday. He is leaving either Sunday or Monday. What about you?"

Kurth looked pleased with himself. "If this comes off, I intend to resign from the company I work for. I have two safe deposit boxes, one in Hamburg and one in Goslar. When we get to Hamburg, I'll take enough to pay off Otto and enough to spend lavishly on Ulla and the kids plus another hundred thousand in marks for the safe deposit box. I intend to remarry Ulla, that is, if she will agree."

"I always thought divorcing Ulla was the dumbest thing you ever did. Well, if this comes off we can certainly live comfortably enough. Call me Saturday afternoon. We can square up any accountings and then go have a dinner celebration."

"Or failure. Let's be sure to have a good dinner tonight."

Chapter II

Geneva. Sept.10, 1982.

ALAIN PULLED UP in front of the Hotel Suisse exactly on time. He was pleased that Hashem was already outside. He was carrying a briefcase and a small suit bag. He spotted Alain as soon as the car stopped. He got into the front seat beside Alain after putting the suit bag on the back seat. He kept the briefcase with him.

"Good morning, Alain, I hope you slept well. I slept very well. You know, for some reason, I always sleep well before going on an operation."

"Glad to hear that, Hashem. Okay, you know the drill. Put everything with your name on it in this envelope." Alain handed him a large manila envelope.

"What's the deal, Alain? I'm only going to be in the bank a few minutes."

"I don't want anything to go wrong. Put your passport, air ticket, wallet and anything else in your brief case that may indicate your true identity in this envelope. You are within minutes of earning yourself a hundred thousand dollars. Don't do anything to fuck it up."

Hashem glared at Alain, but opened up his briefcase and put his passport and airline ticket in the envelope. He sorted through some things in his briefcase, took out some papers, and put them in the envelope. He reached into his inside jacket pocket, pulled out his wallet, and put it in the envelope. When he finished, he handed the envelope to Alain.

"Just slide it under your seat, Hashem." Alain handed him the Iraqi passport. "The half ten-mark note is in the passport."

Hashem opened the passport and found the note. "Check," he said as he put the passport in his inside coat pocket. Traffic was light. They pulled up in front of the bank with three minutes to spare.

"Use a good, gruff Iraqi accent, Hashem," Alain said as he got out of the car.

"*Shukran, ya akh*," Hashem thanked him sarcastically, and gruffly, as he closed the car door.

Alain watched until he entered the bank. He pulled away from the curb and executed the large circle route he had practiced the previous day. He said a silent prayer that everything would go well. As he made the last turn onto Rue de Rive, he slowed the car down to a crawl. He stopped the car about fifty yards before the bank's front door. He spotted Hashem as he left the bank. It was exactly sixteen minutes after eleven. *Thank God for Swiss efficiency*, Alain said to himself as he stopped the car for Hashem. He drove forward immediately.

"It was all very businesslike," Hashem beamed as he opened his briefcase. Alain could see the bundles of one hundred dollar bills arranged neatly inside. He took out a large envelope.

"Here are the bearer bonds."

"Open the envelope, Hashem."

"What, old friend, you question my integrity? I'm deeply hurt." Hashem's smile showed no indication of great pain.

"Can the horse shit, Hashem. Show me the bonds."

Hashem had already pulled the bonds out of the envelope. He carefully displayed ten bearer bonds each in the sum of five hundred thousand dollars. Alain took the bonds, put them back into the envelope, and placed it under his seat.

"I'm letting you out at the taxi stand at the Place du Port. You can grab a taxi and be at the airport before twelve. Incidentally, how long are you staying in Hamburg?"

"I intend to do a little celebrating." From Hashem's expression, the celebrating included women. "What about yourself?"

"I have to do all our accountings. I'll probably leave next Wednesday. Incidentally, you can keep what remains of the advance I got for you. They don't want receipts. As my contact told me, there can be no official record, so all I have to do is certify that I spent all the money for operational purposes."

As he pulled into the taxi stand, Alain handed Hashem the envelope with his belongings. "Here you are, Hashem. Give me the Iraqi passport."

Hashem complied and Alain gave him a final send off. "Thanks for your help. If by chance we run into each other before I leave Hamburg, act like we don't know each other. One thing that might interest you, my inside contact wanted me to know that the bonds were needed for some kind of scam operation the agency is running."

Hashem smiled, "It's nice to know we are engaged in something worth while. *Illa liqa*." He got out of the car and headed for a waiting taxi. Alain watched briefly, then headed back to pick up Kurth.

He was elated. They had actually pulled it off. Kurth would be able to live like a king in a small German town. He turned onto the Rue du Rhône and, after a bit, spotted Kurth walking on the sidewalk a considerable distance from the bank. He stopped the car a short distance ahead of Kurth.

As Kurth entered the car, Alain smiled broadly and said, "We may not have been the most successful CIA operations officers, but we sure are successful bank robbers." He handed the envelope with bonds in it to Kurth. "Take out six for Drouget. I'll park where we parked yesterday and wait for you."

"I only hope Drouget was able to get a large quantity of five hundred mark notes. If not, I don't think I can fit all the cash in the large sports bag I brought. One thing for sure is that it's going to weigh a lot."

Alan laughed and said, "All those trips to the health spa will finally pay off."

Both stopped talking as they pulled into the parking lot. Kurth got out of the car and headed towards the building where Drouget had a suite of offices. Alain watched him until he disappeared through the door. Alain took a cigar out of his coat pocket and lit it with the car lighter. He would have to remember to buy some good cigars now that he could afford them.

He felt pleasantly at ease which surprised him. He thought he would be on a larger high, maybe the enormity of what they had accomplished had not yet sunk in. After about twenty minutes, he spotted Kurth exiting the building. As Kurth approached the car, he got out and opened the trunk. When Kurth got close to Alain, he said, "This bag is really heavy. Drouget threw in an extra ten thousand marks for the bearer bonds."

"Good, you take over as driver," Alain said as they both got in the car.

Kurth drove to the back alley behind Rentke's office. Alain got out of the car and rang the bell. A young woman opened the door and waved Alain in. Rentke had already come down, opened the vault in the adjoining room, and was opening his safe. He took out two boxes and turned to Alain.

"There are one hundred bundles of hundred dollar bills in each box. Please count them."

It took Alain close to fifteen minutes to count the bundles. He gave Rentke the four bearer bonds and Rentke sealed the boxes. Rentke then opened his desk drawer and took out an envelope.

"Here is a bonus of four thousand dollars."

Alain put the envelope in his inside coat pocket. "Thank you."

"Let me help you," Rentke said as he picked up one of the boxes and headed to the door. They put the two boxes in the back seat of the Mercedes. Alain thanked Rentke and got into the car. As they pulled away, he looked at his watch and said to Kurth, "It's just about twelve-thirty. How long will it take us to get to Hamburg?"

"If we only stop for gas, have no problems, and we keep up a steady pace, we should get there in the wee hours of tomorrow morning."

"I have a good bottle of Champagne chilling in Hamburg," Alain said to Kurth. "When we get out of town, pull off the road somewhere and we'll put the two boxes in the trunk."

"Okay," Kurth answered. Slowly, he began to laugh, "You know, if it somehow got out that the two of us heisted over five million dollars, every crook in Europe would be out hunting for us."

"That's far from reassuring. Thanks for bringing it up," Alain replied sarcastically.

When they were well outside of Geneva, Kurth turned the car into a church parking lot. They jammed the two boxes of dollars into the trunk and made a hurried departure from the parking lot. Kurth kept the car within the speed limit. This was one time in his life that he did not want to chance being stopped by the police. He explained to Alain why he was driving under the speed limit. Alain nodded his head in agreement. They drove on in silence, Kurth concentrating on his driving.

"Once we cross the border into Germany, we can stop to get gas and something to eat. Considering the circumstances, we should be able to hold on without food for a couple of hours."

"I'm too elated to be hungry. We should be singing," Kurth answered. He laughed and added, "I would like to see Wafiq's face when he learns that someone has lightened his account to the tune of five million, one hundred thousand dollars."

They drove on in silence, each figuring out the best way to handle the money. Kurth broke the silence. "Hashem has his payoff, so we don't have to worry about him. You are going to pay off Blanton Saturday morning. When we get to your apartment I'll take one hundred thousand marks and arrange to pay off Otto before I drop by your apartment tomorrow afternoon. Since you now have a working phone, I'll call before I come to your apartment."

"How much are you going to pay Otto?" Alain thought that one hundred thousand marks was a lot for what little Otto had done.

"I'm paying him the one hundred thousand marks as a bonus because that's the amount I promised him." Kurth was a little perturbed. "Alain, you're tighter than a sideways fart. Remember, we couldn't have done this operation without good old Otto."

"Okay, okay. I'll call Blanton as soon as I get up tomorrow morning. Forty thousand tax-free dollars should make him a happy man."

"Blanton is a pretty matter of fact guy. I was surprised you didn't have more trouble with Hashem." Kurth commented to Alain.

"I think he weighed what I explained to him, particularly the fact that the bearer bonds were worthless to him. I am sure he had some doubts about what I told him, but decided it would probably be best to just take the hundred thousand and run."

Kurth frowned, his concern over Hashem showed on his face. "I'm really relieved that his role is over. As you know, I considered him to be the weak, but necessary, link in our planning. Did he say what he was going to do?"

"Unfortunately, he is going to hang around Hamburg for a week or so. He apparently has hooked up with some woman. He told me he plans to do some celebrating. He claims he rents the place he is staying in by the month, so he may hang around until the end of the current month. My one worry is that, given his new found wealth, he may be pretty high profile in Hamburg."

Kurth was suddenly less than reassured. "Alain, my friend, I think it behooves us to spend as little time in Hamburg as possible. Hopefully, we can take care of all our business on Monday, then get the hell out of town."

"My sentiments exactly," Alain responded. "We will figure out our accounts and divide up the swag. I intend to make a couple of trips to the bank. I have rented a very large safe deposit box. In fact, I had never seen one so big. When the bank clerk asked me why I needed such a big box, I explained to him that I do business in Hamburg but do not have a local office. Since I have a lot of paper work that I need when I am here, I thought of using a safe deposit box for storage. That seemed to satisfy him."

"Good thinking," Kurth said. "I will fill the box I have with as many marks as possible and take the rest of the money to Goslar. I opened an account the last time I was there. Well, we are close to the German border."

The crossing was uneventful. They stopped at the first rest stop. Kurth sat in the car while Alain went into the small restaurant. He returned with sandwiches and several bottles of soda. Once Alain was in the car, Kurth went into the restaurant for a pit stop while Alain filled the gas tank. As soon as Kurth returned, Alain drove out onto the Autobahn. He drove for four uneventful hours, interrupted only by Kurth's constant nagging about not driving too fast. They made a second pit stop. Kurth took over the wheel after they had gassed up. Alain watched the speedometer with trepidation as it rapidly climbed now that Kurth was driving.

"Don't worry, you'll get a chance to spend that money," Kurth looked at Alain and laughed.

"I wonder," Alain answered.

It was dark when Kurth stopped the car in front of Alain's apartment. They quickly lugged the two boxes of money and Kurth's huge sports bag into the apartment. As he closed the door, Alain asked Kurth if he would like some Champagne.

"I don't think so, Alain. Let's save it for tomorrow afternoon."

"Good idea. I'm going to set the alarm for eight and go to bed. Hopefully, I'll have taken care of Blanton by noon. Give me a call around two."

"Will do," Kurth answered as he unzipped the sports bag and took out two neat bundles of five hundred mark notes. "This should open Otto's eyes when I pass it to him tomorrow morning. Give me a bag or something for this money."

Alain looked in the kitchen cabinets until he found a suitable small paper bag. "Here, will this do?"

"Yes, let me borrow your brief case. I'll bring it with me tomorrow." Kurth put the money in the paper bag and the bag into the briefcase. "I'll see you to-morrow," Kurth said as he opened the door.

Alain smiled at him and replied, "Don't worry, I'll be here."

→►══◎ ◎══◄←

Hamburg. Sept. 11, 1982.

Alain had called Blanton as soon as the alarm woke him up. He told Blanton to come to the apartment around ten, and added that he should bring his briefcase. Blanton was on time. Alain asked him if he wanted a beer or coffee. Blanton smiled at him.

"I always drink coffee until noon. I start lunch with a beer." Blanton motioned to his handiwork, "I was able to put everything back in place pretty easily. I don't think the landlady will notice anything different."

"Yes, you did. I looked it over myself. The coffee's ready." Alain poured him a cup of coffee and set it down in front of him. He opened one of the cupboard doors and took out four bundles of one hundred dollar bills. He set the bundles down in front of Blanton and said, "Here's your bonus as agreed upon, Jack, forty thousand dollars."

"Thanks," Blanton said, obviously pleased by the look on his face.

"And, it's tax-free." Alain watched as the look of quiet appreciation etched in waves across Blanton's face.

"You know, Alain, all this time I was not exactly sure everything would turn out all right. I'm grateful to you for being on the up and up with me," Blanton said as he put the money in his briefcase. "If you no longer need me, I'll go ahead and confirm my reservations for tomorrow."

"Nothing else, Jack, we're all finished. I don't know what, if anything, the agency got out of this, but they seemed pleased and made no bones about passing me the money. One last thing, I assume you are not out of pocket on expenses are you? I did my accountings with them on the expenses and, in your case, I wrote off what I gave you as having been expensed."

"First rate. I figured that I owed you about three hundred dollars."

"Keep it with my thanks," Alain told Blanton as he escorted him to the door. "Don't spend it all in one place, Jack."

Blanton's answer was an evil smile on his face as he left the apartment.

Alain had another cup of coffee. He planned to stay in the apartment until Monday. His first business would be to get most of the money into his safe deposit boxes. He wondered how Otto had reacted when Kurth paid him the money. Alain assumed that Otto was now looking forward to retirement. He decided to calculate his expenses.

At the kitchen table, he picked up a pen and began figuring how much he had paid Blanton. He had made two round trips and had spent a total of about two weeks in a hotel. Alain had given him twenty-one hundred dollars for living expenses, based on a generous calculation of one hundred and fifty dollars a day. He had also given him seven hundred dollars to cover his purchases. His two round trips came to about two thousand, six hundred dollars. The trip to Istanbul was an additional fifteen hundred dollars. Blanton's total expenses came to six thousand, nine hundred dollars.

Hashem's expenses were somewhat less; thirteen hundred dollars for an air ticket, nine hundred for a month's rent, plus eighteen hundred for one month's expenses at sixty dollars a day. Hashem could not complain that they had put a crimp in his life style. He had received a total of four thousand dollars from Alain. Hashem's expenses together with the six thousand, nine hundred dollars he had shelled out to Blanton came to ten thousand, nine hundred dollars.

He busied himself going over the copious notes he had made on the BLACKROOT operation. He broke for lunch, then continued perusing his notes. He had always wanted to do some writing and he thought he could put together a readable book from the notes he had made. Now that he was wealthy, he could embark on a second career. When he got back to Washington, he planned to call his ex-wife, Jane Brophy. She was a first rate editor and knew some people in the publishing business. He laughed to himself, thinking maybe he could hire her to edit his book.

He was interrupted when Kurth arrived and rang the doorbell. He looked at his watch and saw that it was a little past two. He let Kurth in and, with a flourish, took the bottle of champagne out of the refrigerator. He set the two champagne glasses he had brought for the occasion on the table. After he filled the two glasses, he handed one to Kurth.

Alain raised his glass and, in the most stentorian tone he could muster, said, "Let us toast our most revered benefactor, Saddam Hussein."

Kurth, in mock seriousness, raised his glass and said, "I'll second that."

After they each drank some champagne, Kurth added, "Maybe we should send Saddam a thank you note." They both laughed as they sat down at the kitchen table.

Kurth's expression changed as he opened the serious conversation, "I saw Otto and gave him the one hundred thousand marks."

"Any problems?" Alain asked.

"Far from it. That, and the rest of the money we gave him, is an enormous amount when you consider it's all tax-free. Did you settle with Blanton?"

"Yes, I gave him forty thousand dollars and he was most appreciative, especially when I let him keep the three hundred odd dollars in expense money he had not spent."

Kurth still couldn't believe they had pulled it off. "Well, I guess the only thing left is to sort out expenses and divide the loot. How much did you give to Jack and Hashem to cover expenses?"

"Ten thousand, nine hundred dollars all told. You gave me five thousand dollars as your share. So, on their accounts, you owe me four hundred and fifty dollars."

"Wait a minute Alain, what about your expenses? All of my travel expenses have been paid by my company. You've paid three months rent on this apartment and may have to cough up more. Also, this operation was your idea. You did most of the work and took most of the risks. Keep the four thousand dollars that Rentke gave you and I'll give you the ten thousand marks that Drouget gave me. Is that okay with you?"

"Fine by me. Let's get it all out and figure each other's share," Alain said. They got up and went into the bedroom, lugged the money into the kitchen, and piled it on the table.

Kurth surveyed the piles. "Drouget gave me four million, eight hundred thousand marks and one million dollars. I gave Otto one hundred thousand marks which leaves us with four million, seven hundred thousand marks. I assume you want mostly dollars, right?"

"Yes, but I will need some marks. I will have to make numerous trips to Europe to smuggle money back into the States. Since you plan to stay here, Kurth, give me one hundred thousand marks and you take the rest. That will leave me with one hundred and ten thousand marks which should pay for my travel." Alain fiddled with his pocket calculator. "Okay, you should now have one million, nine hundred and sixteen thousand, six hundred and sixty-six dollars in marks."

"Make it easy on yourself, Alain, round it out to one million, nine hundred and seventeen thousand dollars." Kurth said as he took the one million dollars from his sports bag and carefully counted out two piles of five hundred thousand dollars each. He pushed one of the piles across the table to Alain. "As far as I'm concerned, we are square. I end up with a split of two million, four hundred and nineteen thousand dollars and you get the rest. You have a problem I don't have. I'm leaving all of my share in Germany, you are going to have to do a lot of traveling to get the larger part of your share safely to the states."

"Actually, I plan to leave most of it in two safe deposit boxes I have rented in two different banks. I rented the second safe deposit box in case the first one could not hold all the loot. I have accounts in both banks. I intend to spend a lot of time in Europe in the future. I plan to fly to Washington on Wednesday. I think it would be best if I stay there until around the end of this month."

"Any specific reason for flying off so soon?"

"Yeah, Hashem must have found a willing female. He told me he was going to stay in Hamburg for a week or two. Since he has paid the rent on his apartment through the end of this month, I assume that he will stay until the month's end. I don't want to take the chance of running into him, however remote. In the meantime, we have to keep this loot safe until Monday when we can do our banking business." Alain noted the expression of concern on Kurth's face when he mentioned concealing the large pile of cash on the kitchen table. Alain smiled at Kurth's concern. "Don't worry, I think I've solved the storage problem."

Kurth showed immediate interest. "How so?"

"Come into the bed room. I was very curious about the construction of this house. As you know, there are steps leading up to the door of this apartment. It is clear that this apartment was added on to the side of the house long after the original house was built. When I saw that the roof on the apartment had a steeper pitch than the old roof, I concluded that there had to be storage space above the ceiling of the apartment. There is a removable panel in the ceiling of the large bedroom closet. Bring that chair over."

Kurth handed the chair to Alain, who set it down inside the closet. He stood on the chair and, after some jiggling, removed the panel in the closet ceiling. He stepped down from the chair, went into the kitchen, and returned with a flashlight. He smiled at Kurth and, holding the flashlight, said, "This is one of my additional expenses."

Kurth took the flashlight, stepped on the chair, and examined the space. On the far side was the original wall. There was no other way to get into the space. Kurth was satisfied.

"I'll put my share in the sports bag. Put as much as you can in those two boxes. You might have to use a couple of bags." Kurth poured his share from the kitchen table into the sports bag and took it into the bedroom. "We better make as little noise as possible. I don't want Mrs. Baumgartner to wonder what we are doing. Bring your boxes in and then let's make some plans for a spectacular dinner."

--->==◉ ◉==<---

Sept. 13, 1982.

Alain and Kurth had spent a busy morning and afternoon. They had gone to their respective banks and made arrangements. In Kurth's case, this was easy. He put his five hundred thousand dollars in the safety deposit box along with two hundred thousand marks in five hundred mark notes. He deposited ten thousand marks in his account in the bank. He planned to divide the remaining money between the account and the safety deposit box he had opened in a local bank in Goslar. In fact, he was anxious to get to Goslar to see his ex-wife and children.

Safely sequestering his gains was somewhat more difficult for Alain. He had opened accounts some time ago in two different banks. He was able to stash one million, seven hundred thousand dollars split between the two very large safe deposit boxes he had rented. After the morning deposits, each bank account now held almost sixty thousand marks. He still had a sizable amount left. He figured he could smuggle about forty thousand dollars into the United States when he arrived there next Wednesday. In the future, he planned to spend a lot of time in Europe since that was where most of his wealth was. He had first class bookings on a Wednesday flight from Hamburg to the United States. When he made the reservations, he asked for a round trip ticket with the return open.

It might be necessary to negotiate as much as a year's lease with Mrs. Baumgartner before he left. Thinking through all the details, he decided to only take twenty-five thousand dollars with him on his trip to Washington. He could do this openly since it would be under the amount he had to declare. He would have the money in his brief case. If the brief case were opened for inspection by a customs official, he would ask to declare it. The remainder that he could not fit into the safe deposit boxes would remain in the attic until he returned. Mrs. Baumgartner might nose around his apartment, but he doubted she would investigate the attic.

He decided to fix himself a drink while he waited for Kurth. Once he had obtained a year's lease from Mrs. Baumgartner, he would get some things to brighten up the flat. He would also bring some things from the house in Maryland. He thought to himself, as he sipped his martini, that being wealthy was certainly relaxing to one's sense of personal well-being.

Alain looked at his watch and at his empty martini glass. He wondered what was keeping Kurth. It was six-thirty and Kurth said he would show up around six or so. Alain decided that the situation called for another martini which he rapidly constructed. It was near seven when Kurth finally appeared. Kurth was all apologies for being so late but he said he had been busy buying presents for Ulla and the kids. He planned to drive to Goslar after he checked out of the Intercontinental the following morning.

"So you have everything arranged?" Alain asked.

Kurth smiled warmly. "Yes, I called Ulla last night. We had a long conversation. I am going to take up permanent residence in Goslar if Ulla will agree to remarry me."

"Since she hasn't remarried and has appeared to warm up to you over the past few years, I think there is a good chance of that." Alain was pretty sure that Ulla would welcome Kurth back. He had known them both well over the years and was far more sympathetic to Ulla when the split occurred. "I have made reservations to leave here Wednesday morning. I will come back in two or three weeks. When I get back, I will call Goslar and we'll get together. Anything else I should know?"

"No, I think we have covered everything. Why don't we go to dinner?"

→➤◉ ◉◄←

Goslar. September 14, 1982.

Kurth looked at Ulla across the table. He thought she had never looked so beautiful. He had arrived in Goslar late in the afternoon and checked into the local inn. He had called her and invited her to dinner. She told him she would walk to her favorite restaurant, The Blind Owl, and meet him there. They talked about the kids. Ulla had the usual complaint about how they were far too independent for their ages. Kurth smiled, but was pleased that their kids showed an independent streak. When they finished eating, Kurth took her to where he had parked a brand new Mercedes and ushered her into the car. She was impressed.

"Your company lets you rent a Mercedes?"

Kurth just smiled. "The bean counters will argue about it."

It took little time to drive the mile from the restaurant to her house. Ulla invited him in for coffee. In the kitchen, as Ulla started making the coffee, Kurth stopped her.

"Ulla, I hope I don't make a fool of myself. I now know that every day that has passed since we divorced, I have fallen more in love with you. If you will have me, I want to marry you." He paused and looked at her. When she didn't answer him he said, "Will you marry me?"

She looked at him but said nothing. To him, it seemed that her expression had softened. She took his hand and led him into her bedroom. Kurth held her hands still as she began to take off her blouse.

"Does this mean that you agree to my proposal?"

"Yes, my darling. I have been dreaming of this moment for years." She then kissed him passionately.

Kurth smiled at her and said," Let's do this soon."

"What do you mean?" Ulla asked.

"Let's get married tomorrow. I think the kids will approve."

Ulla smiled and, as an answer, kissed him again.

Denouement

Chapter 12

Baghdad. Sept. 21, 1982.

"Mustafa, I am calling you since you are the closest to Saddam. There is an apparent irregularity in one of the Swiss accounts that I must bring to your attention."

"What is the problem?" Mustafa Naghshabandi wondered why Ghassan Mraithi was calling. His immediate concern was Ghassan's secretive tone, disconcerting coming from the Chief of Government Accounts.

"I think I should explain in person. There is a fairly considerable sum involved. A mutual friend of ours could be in serious trouble if we can not clear up this irregularity."

Mustafa sensed from Ghassan's voice that it was something urgent. "Okay, calm down and come see me. We will discuss your concerns over tea."

"Thank you, Mustafa. I will be there shortly. I have something to show you."

Mustafa picked up the newspaper. He took pleasure in comparing newspaper reports on the war with the dispatches his office received from the front. He was curious about Ghassan's concern since he could not recall any instance where there had been an irregularity that could not be explained. He did not have long to wait. When Ghassan was shown in, he looked like he had run from his office. Mustafa told him to sit down and ordered tea which arrived almost as soon as he put down the phone. While they both sipped tea, Mustafa asked Ghassan what was bothering him.

"There is an unusual withdrawal from the government account in the Banque Suisse in Geneva. This is the account controlled by our mutual friend, Wafiq Tikriti."

"Ghassan, I assume it is a withdrawal for which you have no explanation." Since the problem concerned an account Wafiq controlled, it could probably be cleared up quickly.

Ghassan withdrew an envelope from his inside coat pocket. "There are basically four types of activity in this account. We deposit funds in the account by electronic transfer. Wafiq writes checks on the account to pay invoices for transactions he makes on our behalf. He provides us with copies of the invoices. Wafiq also personally withdraws funds from this account. He reports these withdrawals to us along with an explanation. From time to time, officials travel to Europe from Baghdad who must draw on this account. These withdrawals are special because they are used to pay arms dealers for deals negotiated by the person making the withdrawal." Ghassan paused briefly and continued, "These are cases where the legality of the deal could be questioned. The arms dealer involved, for his own protection, usually demands payment in cash by the man with whom he negotiated the deal. All receipts of withdrawals and canceled checks are sent to me by the bank and I match them up against copies of the invoices sent to me either by Wafiq or the person who withdrew the funds from the bank. Wafiq accounts for both the funds he personally withdraws and funds withdrawn by other officials. Wafiq makes the arrangements for any official to withdraw a specific amount from the bank. The bank sends me a notification of the withdrawal with the monthly account statement."

Mustafa was beginning to wonder if Ghassan, who seemed to be repeating himself, would ever get to the point. "I am aware of how the account is handled, Ghassan, so what has you so agitated?"

"Please look at this withdrawal statement. It is signed by someone named Tarek Shammar. I do not know any Tarek Shammar and I never sent any message to Wafiq Tikriti to arrange for this Shammar to withdraw funds from the bank."

Ghassan now had Mustafa's interest. "How much was the withdrawal?"

"Five million, one hundred thousand dollars."

Mustafa looked intently at Ghassan, "You know absolutely nothing about this and Wafiq has sent you nothing on the withdrawal?"

"That is correct. Five million dollars were taken in bearer bonds and the one hundred thousand dollars in cash. I assume the bearer bonds have already been cashed and been returned to the bank for a rectification of accounts."

Mustafa thought about what to do. He took the envelope with the various statements from the bank, thanked Ghassan for bringing the matter to his attention before taking any action, then dismissed him with a final command to do nothing until he received further instructions. As soon as Ghassan left, he picked up the phone and dialed Lt. Col. Zaki Sa'duni, a key official in the General Intelligence Directorate and longtime friend of Mustafa. They exchanged pleasantries before Mustafa said, "Zaki, can you come over to see me? There is something I need to discuss with you before I bring it up with the boss."

After a brief pause, Zaki answered, "Am I correct in thinking this is something you are reluctant to discuss over the phone?"

"Yes, Zaki, I need your sage advice before we bring this up with Saddam."

Zaki privately hoped the subject wasn't bad news. Saddam did not like to hear bad news, especially since the only news he was getting from the war front did not augur well for the immediate future. He reluctantly answered, "I can be there in half an hour."

"*Shukran ya sadiqi,*" Mustafa thanked him and hung up the phone.

Zaki Sa'duni appeared on time. At Mustafa's urging, he shoehorned his considerable bulk into a chair built for someone of more modest frame. "What has got you so worked up, Mustafa?" As an answer, Mustafa handed the withdrawal statement to Zaki.

"Mustafa, who is this Shammar person? Is he someone from the Shammar tribe?"

"I have no idea, Zaki. All I can tell you is that this is not an authorized withdrawal."

"Have you contacted Wafiq Tikriti?"

"No, Zaki, I thought it better to talk to you first. I also suspect that we should leave that up to Saddam."

"Good thinking. Our first step is to find out how Wafiq is involved."

"Or not involved," Mustafa added.

"How soon can we see Saddam?"

"He is meeting with a few generals, probably lecturing them on their lack of military capabilities. I have already told him there is something that needs his urgent attention."

"Good," Zaki thought for a few seconds. "You know, Mustafa, I find it hard to believe that Wafiq would involve himself in such a theft, if it is a theft. I think we should suggest to Saddam that we get Wafiq to Baghdad as soon as possible and find out what, if anything, he knows about this."

The door to Saddam's office opened and three very sheepish looking generals emerged. When Saddam saw Mustafa and Zaki, he motioned them into his office. From his expression, it was clear that he was not in a good mood.

Zaki preferred not to deal with Saddam when he was in bad spirits. They had been close friends for years, starting out as young thugs in their hometown of Tikrit. Zaki was also related to Saddam by marriage. He knew from experience that Saddam dealt as harshly with friends as he did with unknowns. This session was not going to be pleasant.

"Well, Mustafa, what is it that needs my urgent attention?" Saddam demanded.

Mustafa glanced at Zaki. Zaki nodded to him. Mustafa handed Saddam the withdrawal statement as he spoke. "Ghassan Mraithi gave this to me a short time ago. He says that he has no idea who this Shammar person is, nor has he received any communication from Wafiq regarding this withdrawal."

Saddam studied the bank statement before commenting. "Has Wafiq ever done anything like this in the past?"

"Never," Mustafa answered him unequivocally. "I talked to him right after he returned from Paris and he did not mention the withdrawal. I also called him two days ago and again he didn't mention the withdrawal."

Saddam looked confused. "I have known Wafiq since we were both very young. He is a true friend. I can't imagine him being involved in a scam to rob us. What do you think, Zaki? You are the smartest man I know in a military uniform."

Zaki pulled his thoughts together before answering Saddam. "I suggest to you that we start at the beginning. If the withdrawal is in any way legitimate, Wafiq must know something about it. Let us first establish whether he does. I think you should tell him his presence is urgently required in Baghdad."

Saddam was uncertain about Zaki's suggestion. He asked pointedly, "Okay, Zaki, then what?"

"If, after interrogation and suitable incentives to talk, we conclude that Wafiq knows nothing about the withdrawal, then we backtrack by going to the bank to see what we can find out about the person or persons who actually made the withdrawal. Somebody has gotten their hands on a large amount of our money. Fortunately, Haitham Abd al-Nebi, one of our best operatives, is in Hamburg. He can help with the investigation."

By way of answering, Saddam picked up the telephone and told the operator to get Wafiq in Hamburg. Zaki and Mustafa waited while the call was put through.

Finally, Saddam said, "Wafiq, I need you here as soon as possible. Fly to Amman tomorrow. I am instructing the Embassy in Amman to give you a car and a driver. Call Mustafa as soon as you get to Baghdad." Saddam hung up the phone before Wafiq could say anything. He then looked at Zaki and asked, "What if he does not come?"

Zaki smiled maliciously, "That would be tantamount to an admission of guilt and we would hunt him down."

"Okay," Saddam said as he dismissed them with a wave of his arm towards the door. "When he gets here, Mustafa, call me."

The two men bowed their way out of Saddam's office.

Once outside, Mustafa said to Zaki, "I am certain that, if this is a scam or robbery, Wafiq had nothing to do with it."

"Let us hope so," Zaki said as he left Mustafa's office.

⌖

Norbeck. Sept. 22, 1982.

Alain and his former wife, Jane Brophy, had finished dinner but were still in the kitchen. Alain excused himself and went to the bedroom he had outfitted as a den. He returned with a file folder from which he withdrew some cards.

"Jane, I am returning to Hamburg tomorrow. I want you to sign these instruments which I will take with me."

"What are they?" Jane asked, always apprehensive of requests to sign anything.

Alain handed her four cards. He pointed to two of them, "These two are signature cards which give you access to two bank accounts I have in Hamburg. I have already executed documents at the two banks making the accounts joint. I will take the signature cards with me and give them to the banks. The other ones are for safe deposit boxes. Please sign each of the cards." He reached into his pocket and withdrew two small plastic envelopes. "Here are your keys to the safe deposit boxes."

Jane was mystified by the whole process and seemed reluctant to sign. "I don't understand. Why do you have two accounts in Hamburg? I'm confused by this."

"Jane, while I didn't make the grade as a husband, I do love you, and while we didn't make it as husband and wife, we are still good friends. You are, dear heart, the only family I have. If anything happens to me, I want you to go to Hamburg and do what you want with the bank accounts and the contents of the safe deposit boxes."

Jane smiled, "I always thought you were a little crazy. It is one of the odd things that makes you attractive." She signed the cards. "Would it be impertinent if I asked whether it would be worth my while to check out these accounts?"

Alain laughed, "Yes it would, but I admire impertinence. I can assure you the trip will be well worth the trouble." Alain handed her two business cards, one for each of the banks, and said, "If you are planning a trip to Europe anytime in the near future, feel free to make a withdrawal. These two banks have branches all over Europe. There will always be a few thousand marks in each account."

"You still haven't explained why you need two bank accounts and two safe deposit boxes in Europe."

Alain thought to himself, *make this good.* He said, "I opened the account in one bank first. When I needed a safe deposit box, they didn't have one as large as I needed. I finally found a bank that had huge safe deposit boxes. I had to open an account in that bank to be able to rent the box. The results of all my research are in those two boxes." *Good thinking,* Alain said to himself.

Jane frowned at him before smiling, "A crazy arrangement, but then it's you, Alain."

-→-■-◉ ◉-■-←-

Baghdad. Sept. 23, 1982.

Wafiq Tikriti had flown to Amman the previous day and taken a cab to the Iraqi Embassy. He spent the night as a guest in the Ambassador's house. The following morning, he left for Baghdad immediately after breakfast. The driver of the Embassy car was a Jordanian who had served in the Jordanian Army. He drove fast, but with care. They didn't stop until they reached Rutba Wells, where clearing customs took a few minutes. Wafiq assumed customs had been alerted to his arrival. In Baghdad by early afternoon, he directed the driver to his sister's house. He freshened up, had something to eat, and called Mustafa Naghshabandi who told him to wait there. He would come by the house to pick him up.

Wafiq was drinking a cup of tea when Mustafa arrived. He must have left his office immediately after the phone call. Wafiq anxiously wondered why he had been called back so suddenly for no apparent reason. He ushered Mustafa into his sister's house and offered him tea.

"Mustafa, what is going on?"

Mustafa did not answer him immediately but peered into his teacup. Finally, he said, "We must leave. We have a problem that you may be able to solve."

With that, Mustafa stood up and the two men left the house. When they were in the back seat of the Mercedes, Mustafa ordered the car to go to Zaki Sa'duni's office.

"Why are we going to Zaki's office?" Wafiq asked in an uneasy tone.

"It is better that Zaki explains things to you. He thinks you can help him resolve a serious problem."

"With pleasure, but given my background, I can not think of how I could help someone like Zaki. He is one the smartest persons I know."

Mustafa smiled deceptively, "I suspect this is a case where you can be of immense help to Zaki."

"So be it," Wafiq said.

Both men remained silent, each with his own thoughts, until they reached the GID (General Intelligence Directorate), referred to by Baghdadis as the *Mukhabarat*. The office building housing the GID was rather large. Once inside, they were confronted by a barricade manned by two junior officers who recognized Mustafa immediately. One of them, the more senior of the two, told the other to call Sa'duni's office. He then turned to the two men, "*Ahlan wa sahlan*, please follow me." He led them to an elevator which they rode to the fifth floor. From the elevator, he directed them to a suite of offices, ushered them in, and left.

Zaki emerged from an office to the right and greeted them. "Please gentlemen, come into my office." He signaled to a servant to bring tea, led them to one side of the office, and motioned to seats around a coffee table. From where he sat, Wafiq had a good view of the Tigris snaking its way through Baghdad. He thought that maybe tonight he would go to one of the cafes along the Tigris and have some grilled *masgoof.* There was a brief period of conversation about the war while they drank tea. After some polite conversation, Mustafa got up, said he had some urgent business, and left.

Once Mustafa was gone, Zaki focused his eyes on his visitor, and said, "Wafiq, I have known you for a long time. I know you are one of Saddam's closest associates."

Wafiq began to wonder what this was all about. He was uncertain whether he should say something or not. He decided to sit tight. Zaki got up from his chair and walked over to his desk.

"There is a problem with the bank account you control in Geneva. Who is Tarek Shammar?"

"I don't know any Tarek Shammar," Wafiq replied.

Zaki decided not to waste time. He handed Wafiq the withdrawal statement.

"Then, perhaps you can explain this?"

Wafiq took the statement, looked at it, and replied, "I know nothing about this, Zaki. Who is Tarek Shammar?"

"My understanding, Wafiq, is that you control the account. If someone withdraws money from the account, you make all the arrangements. Is that not so?" Zaki asked in a voice with an edge to it.

"That is right. There must be some mistake. I did not make any arrangements for a Tarek Shammar to make a withdrawal from the account." Wafiq paused, trying to gather his thoughts. Sweat was running down his back. He hoped his face was not flushed.

"Please, let me see that statement again." Wafiq looked at the statement Zaki handed back to him. "Zaki, this statement is dated the tenth of September. I was in Paris."

"You could have made the arrangements before you departed for Paris."

"You can check with the Consulate employees. They will confirm no such person came to the Consulate."

"To get your hands on five million dollars might be a great temptation." Sa'duni smiled as he took the withdrawal statement from Wafiq and put it in his coat pocket.

"According to the withdrawal statement it was five million, one hundred thousand dollars." Wafiq answered, trying to put on as brave a front as possible while a wave of cold fear took hold of him. He knew he could be in for a rough time. "One other thing, Zaki. When I returned from Paris, no one in the Consulate mentioned anyone coming from Baghdad to make a withdrawal. This is a set practice. Whoever is to make such a withdrawal must first come to Hamburg. I then make the necessary arrangements with a manager in the Banque Suisse named Irwin Schlagel." Wafiq paused, then added hastily, "That is it, Zaki. We can ask Schlagel about the withdrawal."

"That is a possibility, Wafiq. Eventually we will get to the bottom of this. I don't have to tell you that Saddam is very upset about someone stealing from him."

They were interrupted by a knock on the office door. Zaki immediately said, "Come in." Two young men entered the office. One of them was a young lieutenant in uniform. He had an athletic build. He was about five foot nine and obviously someone who worked at keeping in shape. It was the second man who caught Wafiq's attention. He was in civilian clothes that didn't fit. They were ill-fitting because of his seemingly expanding girth. He had a swarthy complexion with a mustache that mimicked Saddam's. His eyes were dark and set back in his puffy countenance. Wafiq had little doubt about what duties he performed for the GID.

"Wafiq," Zaki said, "I must leave. Will you please answer all the questions my men put to you? If you can think of anything to add to what you have already said, please feel free to tell them. I will see you later."

Wafiq assumed that it wouldn't be long before he would tell them anything they wanted to hear. The younger man's voice cut through his growing fear.

"Mr. Tikriti, I am Lt. Rashid Walidi. My colleague is named Mohammad. Will you please come with us?"

Wafiq got up from his chair and followed his new friends to the elevator. They entered the elevator and went all the way to the basement. Lt. Walidi led him to a door that he opened with a key. The room was sparsely furnished. Walidi led Wafiq to a backless bench on one side of the table. After Wafiq was seated on the bench, Walidi took a seat across the table from him. Mohammad took up a position standing behind Wafiq. Lt. Walidi smiled grimly at Wafiq. He withdrew a copy of the withdrawal statement from his shirt pocket and, with an abrupt flourish, placed it in front of Wafiq.

"And now, Mr. Tikriti, please tell us everything you know about this withdrawal, together with details about how someone other than you can withdraw from this account."

Back in Mustapha's office, Zaki and he continued speculating, "What do you think, Zaki, is Wafiq in any way involved in this withdrawal?"

"I am not sure at the moment. I have sent word to Haitham Abd al-Nebi to question the staff about any visitors to the Consulate during the week of September sixth through the tenth. Since Wafiq was in Paris, Haitham should be able to determine if anyone generated anything from the Consulate."

"Wafiq could have traveled to Geneva from Paris," Mustafa interjected.

"I have already sent word to Qodsi to give me a day by day account of Wafiq's stay in Paris. If Wafiq did go to Geneva to make the withdrawal, the banker in Geneva could be in on the scam." Zaki scowled at nothing in particular.

"Or maybe he could have used an Arab accomplice. What do you intend to do?" Mustafa asked, thinking it would not be in anybody's interest to be on Zaki's bad side.

"Once my men decide if Wafiq is telling the truth or not, we will proceed. The more I consider the circumstances, the more I suspect Wafiq is telling the truth. I do not think he has the skills to pull off such a professional robbery. Think about it, Mustafa, he would have needed a lot of help to pull this off, including the cooperation of the Swiss banker."

"I hope they are not doing too much damage to Wafiq, Zaki."

"Do not worry, Mustafa. Nothing will show, he will just have some discomfort for a few days. When they are certain he is telling the truth, Lt. Walidi will bring him to me."

Mustafa nodded his head. "Okay, I will inform Saddam that the case is being actively investigated."

Zaki smiled. Mustafa had such a way with words. "Good bye, Mustafa. Do not worry about Wafiq. We will know in a very short time if he is telling the truth." Zaki got up from his chair and left Mustafa's office.

Lt. Walidi's interrogation had become increasingly uncomfortable for Wafiq. When the polite questioning ended, each answer to Walidi's questions had gotten him a harsh slap or a jab in the solar plexus from the sidekick, Mohammed. Walidi paused to light a cigarette. Mohammed went to a cabinet and returned with something that was flat and wide with a handle. To Wafiq, it looked like the tail of a platypus he had seen in a zoo. Walidi finished the cigarette, stamped out the butt in an ashtray, and began going over the same ground with Wafiq. This time, each answer from Wafiq was met with a swat from the ominous platypus tail. This unique instrument allowed the pain to be distributed over a wider expanse of Wafiq's now suffering body. His physical pain was compounded by the mental anxiety he was suffering because he could not sort out what had happened.

On his part, Walidi was beginning to think that Wafiq was telling the truth. Wafiq continued to insist that he knew nothing about a man named Tarek Shammar, the man who allegedly withdrew the money from the bank. Wafiq repeated that he had neither made arrangements from Paris nor had he gone to Switzerland for the withdrawal.

Finally, Walidi left the room and came back with a glass of water for Wafiq who drank it like he hadn't had water in a couple of days. He was glad for the respite. After a few swats of the platypus tail, he was willing to admit to anything. What held him back was his inability to come up with a credible story of how he had pulled off the scam. After he finished the water, Walidi spoke to him.

"Okay, Mr. Tikriti, I am inclined to believe you. For your sake, I hope you are telling the truth. I can assure you that we will not be so pleasant if you return for a second time." Walidi's burly assistant emphasized the comment with a sneering laugh. "Pull yourself together, Mr. Tikriti, I am going to take you to Col. Sa'duni's office."

Wafiq's attempt to get up resulted in his collapse back on the bench. In his lifetime, he had never experienced such pain before. Walidi left the room and returned with a second glass of water and two aspirins. He handed the water and aspirins to Wafiq.

"Take these, they will ease your pain."

Wafiq swallowed the aspirin. Walidi came to his side, grasped his left arm, and helped him up from the bench. The two of them walked slowly to the elevator. They took it to the fifth floor. The walk to Zaki's office was excruciating for Wafiq. When they entered, Wafiq was greeted like a long lost friend. Zaki made no mention of what had happened. Wafiq was absolutely astounded. He realized he should know better.

"I want you to know, Wafiq, that I have every confidence in you and I will report the same to Saddam." Zaki motioned Wafiq to a chair. This did not sit well with Wafiq who would have preferred to stand. He decided to say nothing. Obviously, there was a next step, so he decided it was best to remain quiet.

The phone rang. Zaki picked it up and heard Mustapha urgently say, "Get over here as soon as you can. Saddam is more than a little irritated about some unknown party stealing his money. He very obviously intends to take some kind of drastic action," Mustafa said emphatically.

"I will be there as soon as possible," Zaki responded. He instructed Wafiq to stay seated and wait for him.

Once there, Mustapha immediately directed Zaki to Saddam's office. After very brief greetings, Zaki said, "We are certain he is telling the truth."

Saddam listened intently to Zaki's description of Wafiq's state of mind before speaking. He was more than irritated. "I was sure Wafiq would not do such a thing. He has always been loyal. How is he?"

"No serious damage. He should be feeling better in the morning." Zaki answered, omitting which morning that might be.

"What additional steps have you taken to determine if Wafiq is innocent?" Saddam said, as he walked to a large window with a good view of Baghdad.

Mustafa nodded to Zaki, who answered, "I have sent a message to Qodsi in Paris. Wafiq was in Paris when the theft was made. I told Qodsi to give me a full report on Wafiq's activities in Paris. I have also sent word to Haitham Abd al-Nebi asking him for a report on all activities within the Hamburg Consulate during the week when the illicit withdrawal was made."

Saddam turned from the window, his brow knit in thought like an animal deciding the best way to get his prey. He motioned to Zaki and, in a cold, hard voice, said to him, "I want you to take charge of the investigation. I want whoever made off with our money to pay dearly. What I want now is for you to tell me what you intend to do first."

Zaki thought that a trip out of Baghdad in the throes of war would be a pleasant break. "We will start at the bank where the robbery occurred and go on from there. When Wafiq made arrangements for someone to withdraw from the account, he always sent a copy of the person's passport to the Swiss banker a couple of days in advance of the withdrawal. Also, one or more of the bank's surveillance cameras should have a picture of the person who made the withdrawal."

Saddam questioned, "You think you can identify the person who robbed the account from surveillance pictures?"

"I think it is a good possibility that whoever pulled this off will be recognizable from the surveillance photos." Zaki was more than a little uneasy because of Saddam's famous temper tantrums. "There is one thing for certain, the person who made the withdrawal could not have carried out the robbery on his own. It took a team of highly competent people to pull off this robbery. The only alternative would be for Wafiq to do it with a cooperating Arab, or with the cooperation of the Swiss banker."

Saddam's initial response was to slam his fist on the windowsill. As he spoke, his face was livid, "Are you certain that Wafiq was not involved? How else can you explain someone finding out how Wafiq made the arrangements for a withdrawal?"

Zaki tried to be as patient as possible. He envied Mustafa, who was sitting quietly, listening to the exchange. "We will start with the Swiss banker. Do not worry. We will identify those who planned and executed this robbery."

"What are your specific plans?" Saddam voice boomed, "I want this cleaned up as soon as possible."

"I am taking Wafiq with me to Amman. We will fly to Geneva from Amman. I have already talked to Haitham Abd al-Nebi. He will meet us in Geneva. I plan to have Haitham and Wafiq meet with the Swiss banker. Haitham is as smooth as a pebble in a mountain stream. He looks like a successful businessman. I have learned from past experience that my appearance is somewhat frightening. I will send you a report as soon as Haitham and Wafiq have talked to the Swiss banker."

"Very good, now get out of here. I must solve some problems that surpass the abilities of my generals." Saddam returned to his desk, signaling the end of the meeting.

Mustafa nodded to Zaki and they rose in unison, wished Saddam their best, then left his presence. Once outside the office, Mustafa asked Zaki about the chances of catching the person or persons involved in the unauthorized withdrawal from the Banque Suisse. Zaki was forthright in his answer.

"We start our investigation at the beginning. For us, that is the withdrawal on September tenth. Hopefully, we will get some information from Wafiq's Swiss banker friend that will give us a clue as to who was involved. If we draw a blank in Geneva, it could be a very difficult investigation."

"Zaki, in Saddam's office you mentioned surveillance cameras. Even if there are some pictures, the robber would probably be wearing a disguise."

"That is possible. Mustafa. At close quarters there are limits to how well you can disguise yourself without raising the suspicions of those with whom you are dealing. Wearing a mustache or a nice hairpiece is good, as is growing a beard. I am going now to pay a call on Wafiq, have him call his banker friend, and ask that they save the passport photographs used by this Tarek Shammar."

Mustafa did not think this a very good idea. "Zaki, you said there was a possibility that Wafiq and the banker rigged this robbery themselves. If you have Wafiq call the banker, the banker could take it as a signal and destroy the photographs of the passport and the surveillance camera film."

"Very true, Mustafa, but we must be good poker players and make our play based on the odds. If Wafiq and the banker are in cahoots, I can guarantee you that no surveillance film of the robber exists, nor are there any photographs of the robber's passport, if they ever existed. I am proceeding on the assumption that Wafiq and his banker friend are innocent. I want Wafiq to tell the banker to preserve such evidence before he destroys it as part of his routine. If the banker says that he has already destroyed these pieces of evidence, then my suspicions of Wafiq will be rekindled."

Mustafa smiled, "You are a very devious man, my friend, very devious indeed."

"In a devious business, Mustafa, you must be more devious than your enemies."

Zaki quickly followed through on his plan to have Wafiq call Irwin Schlagel. He sat quietly, on an extension, listening carefully to the exchange between the two. Wafiq had begun the conversation by telling Schlagel that there was some confusion over a withdrawal, made on September tenth, by a Tarek Shammar. Schlagel replied that he had followed Wafiq's instructions in the usual manner. Zaki's ears picked up when Schlagel said that he had made a note of Wafiq's call on the eighth. Zaki held his breath when Wafiq asked if Schlagel still had the papers that were sent to him by DHL. Schlagel said that he did. Wafiq asked him not to destroy them and to also check the surveillance cameras for pictures of the Mr. Shammar who made the withdrawal. Schlagel expressed some alarm at this question and asked, "Is there something wrong, Mr. Tikriti?"

Wafiq looked at Zaki who nodded at him to answer Schlagel's question. "I am not sure, Irwin. I will be in Geneva two or three days from now and will call on you. I suspect that between us and Baghdad we can sort this all out."

"I am at your service, Mr. Tikriti. I shall await your call." Wafiq thanked him and hung up. Zaki noted the strange expression on Wafiq's face. He had planned to interrogate Wafiq about the September eighth telephone call but decided to hold off for the moment.

"What is the matter, Wafiq?" Zaki asked.

"I did not call Schlagel on the eighth, Zaki. I was in Paris."

"You could have called from Paris."

"Not possible. On withdrawals, I call Schlagel using my private line. He confirms my call by calling me back on my private line. We came up with this arrangement to insure we would not be victimized by some scam. I find it difficult to believe that someone tried to imitate me on my own phone. He would have had to call from my office and be there when Schlagel called back. This is very confusing."

Zaki noted Wafiq's expression of confusion. It seemed genuine. He decided to allay Wafiq's fears. "There are many possibilities. Let us assume that you are as innocent as you say you are. It is possible someone may have been trained to imitate your voice," Zaki said, speculating on a possible answer to the genesis of the telephone call.

"Yes, but what about the call back from Schlagel? As I told you, that call was always to the private line in my office."

"That, Wafiq, is something we must investigate."

Wafiq was obviously mystified. He looked at Zaki, concern showing in his eyes, and asked, "What are we going to do?"

"We will drive to Amman tomorrow and fly to Geneva the day after tomorrow. We will find out everything we can in Geneva, then go to Hamburg, unless our findings in Geneva lead us to some other place. I have instructed my driver to take you home," Zaki said, his expression displaying concern for Wafiq's well being. "Get some rest, some good food, and drink. I will be in touch with you tomorrow. Walidi will escort you to my car."

--》■◎ ◎■《--

September 24,1982.

They had departed Baghdad early in the morning. Zaki and Wafiq were sitting in the back seat of a Mercedes that was being driven by one of Zaki's minions. Wafiq could not comprehend how someone, or some group, could generate the information necessary to pull off such a robbery. He decided to see if the whole thing was as mystifying to Zaki.

"Zaki, you are one of the smartest persons I know. Considering the meticulous planning and the personnel requirements involved, I just do not understand how someone could get the information needed to successfully pull off the robbery. How could they do it?"

Zaki smiled by way of an answer. "Look, Wafiq, we know that it is possible because somebody did it. Look at it this way. What did they need? First, they needed someone to imitate your voice well enough to fool Schlagel. This is difficult but not impossible. The information they needed could have come from someone working in your office. We will take a hard look at everyone who had access to your office."

"Ahmad is the only one who has that kind of information," Wafiq answered with all the certainty he could muster. "I was very careful to keep these transactions from my German secretary."

"What role did Ahmad play?"

"He would get photocopies of the passports and also deliver everything to DHL for shipment to Schlagel."

Zaki became quite interested, "Then Ahmad knows how you work this type of withdrawal."

"Pretty much so, yes."

"Please be more precise, Wafiq."

Wafiq considered Zaki's request carefully. He was certain that Ahmad had played no role in the robbery. He tried to recall precisely what Ahmad knew about the various transactions made over the past couple of years.

"Ahmad may be innocent. All he did was photocopy the passport to be used by the person making the withdrawal. I put the photocopy in a DHL envelope together with half of a ten-mark note. The person making the withdrawal signed his name three times on a piece of paper and I also added that to the envelope. I would then call DHL and tell them Ahmad was on his way with a package to be sent to Geneva. To the best of my recollection, Ahmad never knew the total contents of the package."

"Wafiq, he could have taken the envelope to an accomplice who opened it."

"That may be the case, but there is the issue of the telephone calls. I always used my private line. It does not go through the Consulate switchboard. Ahmad was not privy to any of my conversations with Schlagel."

Zaki had to concede that Ahmad's involvement would have needed accomplices. "Does anyone besides you live in the building?"

Wafiq replied, "No, originally it was two apartments, one on each floor. The larger one on the first floor houses the offices. The second floor is my quarters. Why do you ask?"

"Is the private line in your office the same as the line in your quarters?" Before Wafiq could answer, Zaki added another question. "When you made your calls to Schlagel, did you do so in your office or in your quarters?"

Wafiq thought that Zaki was trying to solve the crime before they got to Amman. "In answer to your first question, the number is different. It is a private line that does not go through the consulate switchboard. I always called Schlagel using the private line in my quarters. The important point is that Schlagel always confirmed my call to him about the withdrawal by calling me back at my private number ten minutes after we hung up. This way nobody knew about my arrangements with Schlagel."

Unless your private line was tapped, thought Zaki. He decided to keep this possibility to himself for the time being. "You are beginning to sound like a lawyer, Wafiq," Zaki said with a lop-sided grin. "Since you had to be in your quarters to make and answer the call, and you can prove you were in Paris on September 8, I would have to admit it looks like you have an air-tight alibi."

"Thanks," Wafiq replied without conviction.

⇥═◑ ◐═⇤

Geneva. September 25, 1982.

Zaki and Wafiq had spent the previous night in Amman as the ambassador's guest. They left early in the morning and, after changing planes in Frankfurt, arrived in Geneva where they were met by Haitham Abd al-Nebi. He took them to a luxurious apartment in Versoix. The apartment belonged to an Iraqi arms dealer with very close ties to Saddam.

Haitham began, "There was nothing unusual in the Consulate during Wafiq's absence in Paris. I was there everyday. No one called on Wafiq's private phone and there were no incoming calls of any significance."

Zaki nodded his head as he spoke, "That is about what I expected, Haitham. I think we have been taken in by some very skillful and capable people."

"Since you used the plural, I gather you believe we are dealing with a professional gang."

"At the moment, I see no other conclusion. Wafiq is in the next room talking to his banker friend. I told him to get an early appointment tomorrow. I want you to go with Wafiq to meet with the banker. I think it best I not tag along. You have a distinguished appearance, Haitham. I am told I have an appearance that inspires fear."

Haitham almost laughed, but thought better of it. "If you still believe there is a chance the banker is involved, scaring him a bit might not be a bad idea."

"I am beginning to think that possibility is remote. I think it would be best not to frighten the banker, at least for the time being."

They were interrupted by Wafiq entering from an adjoining room saying, "I called Schlagel and he agreed to meet with us Monday morning at ten o'clock."

"Shit!" Zaki exclaimed. "I always forget that Sunday is a holiday in Europe. Anything else from your Swiss banker, Wafiq?"

Wafiq shrugged his shoulders, and rolled his eyes dramatically. "He is very much concerned about the withdrawal. I could tell he wanted to discuss it sooner rather than later. I told him I would explain everything to him Monday morning."

"Did you tell him you would bring someone else with you?" Zaki asked.

"No, because I was unsure how you wanted this meeting handled."

"Good work, Wafiq." Zaki then posed another question. "Haitham, have you gotten a report from Qodsi in Paris?" Zaki asked this while sneaking a glance at Wafiq. He noted that Wafiq suddenly became much more alert.

"Not yet, Zaki." Haitham answered, looking at his watch. "I'll call him at home and see if he has come up with anything." Haitham got up and went into an adjoining room. Wafiq wondered if this had been staged for his benefit. Zaki looked at him and laughed quietly. "Relax, Wafiq. I am doing my best to clear you of all suspicion. Saddam wants to be absolutely certain of your innocence."

Haitham returned while Zaki and Wafiq were talking. He nodded to Zaki, "Qodsi said that, as far as he knows, Wafiq never left Paris. He is doing a little more looking around and will give me a call if he comes up with anything."

Wafiq breathed a sigh of relief. He was glad to know that Qodsi did not know about Muna or their trip to the countryside.

"Well gentlemen, we may as well enjoy our day off. Our host insists that we join him for dinner. He plans to take us to his favorite restaurant. He also has planned a trip to Montreux for us tomorrow." Haitham made his announcement with the air of a headwaiter.

⇥▬▬◗ ◖▬▬⇤

Geneva. September 27, 1982.

Haitham and Wafiq arrived at the Banque Suisse at ten o'clock. They were ushered into Schlagel's office by a very prim secretary. Schlagel stood and invited them to sit in twin chairs facing him. After Haitham was introduced, Schlagel asked if there was anything wrong regarding the recent withdrawal.

"We really do not know," Haitham answered. "If we see the passport photograph, or any frames from your surveillance cameras, we might be able to clear everything up. One question, how was the withdrawal made?"

"The gentleman withdrawing the money took five million dollars in bearer bonds and one hundred thousand dollars in cash." Schlagel opened a drawer in his desk and retrieved a file. He opened it and passed the photocopy of the passport across the desk to Haitham and Wafiq. While they were looking at the photocopy of the passport, he passed some stills from the surveillance camera. "There is only one still that shows most of the gentleman's face." Schlagel's tone reflected some anxiety. Swiss banks were rarely robbed.

Haitham studied the photographs briefly. His face suddenly changed expression, he smiled at Schlagel, and said, "The photographs clear it all up, Mr. Schlagel. It is merely a question of the right hand not knowing what the left hand is doing." Haitham passed everything back to Schlagel except the one clear surveillance camera photo. "If you do not mind, Mr. Schlagel, I would like to keep this photo."

This all caught Schlagel by surprise. He was now more confused than before. He told Haitham to keep the photo. Haitham read Schlagel's facial expression and decided to reassure him.

"Mr. Schlagel, the man who withdrew the money was using an alias. Given who he is, he could not take the risk of traveling in his true name. The war, and the disruption caused by it, has forced us to take unusual measures. Would you be so kind as to allow me to use your telephone? I will call our Consulate in Hamburg and tell them we have resolved the matter of the withdrawal."

"Please do so, sir," Schlagel said as he pushed the telephone across the desk to Haitham. "I am glad the matter is cleared up. I was concerned that there had been a serious mistake."

Schlagel had talked about the withdrawal in two phone conversations with Mr. Tikriti, so he could not understand how Wafiq was seemingly unaware of what was going on. His confusion was compounded by the fact that Mr. Tikriti had sent him photocopies of the passport and a half of the ten-mark note. Being a true Swiss gentleman, he decided to say nothing.

"You can relax now, Mr. Schlagel. Apparently, Baghdad was unaware that the gentleman making the withdrawal was in alias. That is why they questioned the withdrawal," said Haitham as he began dialing a number on the phone.

While things may have been cleared up for Schlagel, Wafiq was more confused than ever. He wondered what in the hell was going on. He listened carefully to Haitham's end of the conversation in Arabic. It was clear he was giving orders, although he made his comments as brief as possible. As best Wafiq could discern, Haitham ordered the person on the other end of the line to keep watch on someone in Hamburg and said that he would be back there the following day. When Haitham was satisfied his instructions would be carried out, he hung up the phone, and slid it back across the desk to Schlagel.

"Thank you so much for seeing us today, Mr. Schlagel. Everything has been cleared up. With your permission, we will take our leave."

"I am glad that you are satisfied, Mr. Nebi. Our bank values its clients very much." Schlagel said this with sincerity, although he was still confused over how someone had not checked everything out in Baghdad. He assumed that the man who made the withdrawal was unknown to Mr. Tikriti. If they were satisfied, the bank was satisfied.

Haitham wished Schlagel the best and he left the bank with Wafiq. When they were outside, Wafiq asked what was going on. Haitham turned to him, his expression had changed immediately after they left the bank. It had been a long time since he had seen Haitham so grim.

"Wafiq, believe it or not, we may have been robbed by the CIA."

Wafiq was stunned, "You can't be serious."

"Dead serious, old friend. Despite the short-cropped beard, I think the man in the picture was the man I told you about in Hamburg, Hashem Samara'i. I'll get the surveillance team to look at the picture for confirmation. The bank photo is not very good and the passport photo shows a man with a scruffy beard, but I'm certain it is Samara'i. Wait until Zaki hears this. As soon as we get back to Hamburg, I want you to call Schlagel and tell him to send that file to you for safe keeping. You can make up any story you think he will buy. We have a very serious problem. Now we must go and confer with Zaki."

Haitham and Wafiq briefed Zaki on the meeting with Schlagel. He sat in stunned disbelief. He held his huge head in his hands as if in meditation. Finally, he slapped both knees with his hands and spoke.

"Haitham, do you really think this was a CIA operation? I find it hard to believe. You have sent me reports about Samara'i's presence in Hamburg. Is it possible that our old enemy acted on his own?"

Zaki's question wasn't as innocent as it sounded. He was one of the few who were aware that the CIA was supplying Iraq with intelligence on Iranian military operations. He found it hard to believe that the CIA would provide needed intelligence information with one hand and then rob an official Iraqi account with the other hand.

Haitham considered Zaki's questions. Both had occurred to him when he saw the picture of Hashem Samara'i. "I have been thinking along the same lines as you, Zaki. I also find it hard to believe that the CIA is behind this operation. We have a problem we must resolve and the only one who can do it is Samara'i himself. As soon as I saw the passport photo, I was pretty sure that Tarek Shammar is none other than our old nemesis, Samara'i. I called Hamburg and talked to one of my men. Samara'i is still in Hamburg, or was last night since he spent the night with his German girlfriend. I told them to keep him under surveillance. If he attempts to leave, they have my instructions to pick him up and keep him in one of our safe houses."

Zaki thought about Haitham's comments. Finally, he nodded at Wafiq, "This pretty well clears you, Wafiq. Samara'i is the only clue we have. Haitham, are you returning to Hamburg tomorrow?" Haitham nodded in the affirmative and Zaki continued, "I want you to have your people pick him up and work him over until he talks."

Haitham was surprised that Zaki would issue such an order without first clearing it with Baghdad. Zaki read Haitham's expression and smiled grimly, "Haitham, our first priority is to find out if this is a rogue operation or if the CIA is really involved. There is only one way to find out and that is from the lips of Hashem Samara'i. Go to Hamburg and get on with it."

"And when we have gotten everything possible out of Samara'i, what do we do with the body?"

"We will send a message to whoever did this," Zaki replied. "Drop his body in a public place. Put a sign around his neck with a single word in Arabic, *'Qisas* (retaliation).'"

Hamburg. September 28, 1982.

Zaki was on his way to Jordan and would probably drive on to Baghdad the next day. He planned to see Saddam as soon as he arrived to brief him on the details of what they had learned. Haitham and Wafiq arrived back in Hamburg around noon. Ahmad, Wafiq's loyal employee, met them at the airport.

After they arrived at the Consulate and were served coffee by Ingrid, Haitham used the phone to call someone. Once the party he called was on the line, he issued some peremptory commands and hung up. He turned to Wafiq and said, "I am being picked up in about ten minutes. I will not return until after we have dealt with Samara'i. I am not going to tell you anything about where we will hold him, or what we plan to do with him. It will be best that you are innocent and unable to answer questions if and when you are questioned by the police."

Haitham walked to the door to leave the office. At the door, he turned and said. "Be careful. The police will most certainly make inquiries about Samara'i since our old enemy was and, to the best of my knowledge, is still an Iraqi citizen."

–>–>⊨◉ ◉⊨<–<–

Alain had arrived back in Hamburg on Sunday, the twenty-sixth. He spent the next two days tying up all the loose ends. There was no money left in the attic of the apartment. He paid for his airline tickets in cash and was planning to return home early on Friday, the first of October. Since everything was going so well, he was planning to take forty thousand dollars in cash with him on his return trip.

He was also thankful that he had not run into Hashem. He wondered idly if Hashem was still in Hamburg. Hashem had said that he planned to stay for a few days before returning to Washington. He decided to go out, make a call to Kurth, and then have a good dinner. He was surprised, but pleased, that Kurth and Ulla were back together. He would pay them a visit on the occasion of his next business trip to Hamburg. He smiled as he thought how ironic the whole business was. It was their agency training and skills that were responsible for their success in robbing the bank.

–>–>⊨◉ ◉⊨<–<–

Somewhere south of Hamburg. September 29, 1982. 2100 hours.

Hashem knew he was in a precarious position. He had gone to the apartment of his German girlfriend at seven o'clock that evening. He planned to take her to dinner before spending the night with her. As he approached her apartment building on foot, a car pulled up to the curb parallel to the direction he was walking. Two men came up behind him, grabbed him by the arms, and hustled him into the car. He had been blindfolded but thought they may have driven for the better part of an hour. He did not know if the length of the drive was to confuse him, or whether they had driven directly to the place they were holding him.

Once inside the building, they tied him to a very sturdy chair and removed his blindfold. He was able to count three other men in the room. He was sure he recognized the tall, distinguished one, but could not place him. They started with simple questions. His answer to the most recent question was rewarded with a resounding slap from the tall man.

"You, Hashem, son of a thousand whores, are in deep trouble. We want some answers and we want them fast. Now tell me about this bank job you were involved in."

"I don't know what you're talking about," Hashem answered. He was rewarded with another slap from the elegant gentleman who then turned to one of the other two men and said, "He is all yours, Mahmud." Mahmud introduced himself by slamming his foot into Hashem's right instep. Hashem could not help screaming in pain.

"This is not going to get any more pleasant, Hashem," Haitham said. He asked Hashem if he would like a cigarette. Hashem nodded. Haitham motioned to Mahmud who lit a cigarette and put it in Hashem's mouth. "Enjoy that cigarette. The next one will not be so enjoyable," Haitham warned.

Hashem was left to his thoughts while the three men conferred in a corner of the room. Hashem figured he must be outside the city in a house in an isolated area since they did not seem to be worried about noise. He concentrated on smoking the cigarette he held by his lips alone. The thought occurred to him that it could well be his last cigarette. At about eleven, they untied him from the chair, handcuffed one arm to the head of a solid bedstand in an adjoining room, and tied his one foot to the foot of the bed. He was allowed to sleep.

--→●→ ●→←-

September 30, 1982. 1830 hours.

Alain had been busy during his short stay in Hamburg. He was a meticulous person and was now satisfied that everything was in order. The two bank accounts were now joint accounts. Jane could also access the two safe deposit boxes. Arrangements had been made with the two banks so that they could debit his accounts to pay the rent on the two boxes. All the money from the attic above the bedroom of the apartment had been removed. He toyed with the idea of opening an account in the Bahamas, but decided against it.

His airline ticket had him flying to London the following morning, then on Pan Am to Washington. He would have liked to spend a couple of days in London but, since he was carrying over forty thousand dollars back with him this time, he had decided a stopover was questionable. He went to the refrigerator and pulled out the last beer. He would drink it, get cleaned up, and go out to have a celebratory dinner.

Earlier that day, Alain had spent an hour talking to Mrs. Baumgartner who seemed genuinely sorry to see him go. Fortunately, he would not have to extend his lease. Since he was leaving early in the morning, he told her he would leave the keys to the apartment in her mailbox. He opened the beer, sat down, and began planning the rest of his life.

⇥▅ ▅⇤

Time had not passed pleasantly for Hashem. They had woken him up at six o'clock that morning and given him some tea and bread to eat. The questioning continued all day, the only break was for a simple lunch. Hashem's face was beginning to look disfigured and he was certain Mahmud had done serious damage to his left eye. He had some bad burns on his right arm that had been administered with Mahmud's cigarette. Hashem figured it was about eight o'clock in the evening. He was surprised that he was still alive. He could not understand why they had let him sleep the previous night. The torture he had suffered through was very painful, but not life threatening. They seemed to be limited in how far they could go in torturing him. Their instructions must have included keeping him alive, at least until they could get to the bottom of how they were robbed with such apparent ease.

Hashem had not revealed much to them. What surprised him was the fact that they had asked him no questions about agency operations in Iraq. They stuck to the robbery and kept repeating questions over and over. Mahmud was smoking a cigarette while waiting to resume his work. During this pause, the well-dressed Iraqi, who had disappeared sometime earlier, suddenly walked into the room. He spoke to Hashem.

"Hashem, my colleague is going to give you a demonstration of what you are in for if you do not cooperate."

"I doubt if I can expect anything, even if I cooperate fully." Hashem managed his reply despite badly swollen lips.

"Oh, I think we can come to some sort of mutually acceptable agreement, Hashem," Haitham replied. He then said to Mahmud, "Leave his mouth alone. I want him to be able to talk after you convince him he has no other choice."

Mahmud began by taking off Hashem's shoes and socks. He tied Hashem's right foot to the chair and began pressing a lighted cigarette to the sole of Hashem's left foot, which was resting on and tied to a second chair. Hashem's cries of pain had no effect on either Mahmud or the other men watching. When the cigarette burned out, Mahmud took a pair of large pliers from a box at his side, and began crushing Hashem's big toe.

"Hashem, old adversary, as you know, the big toe is most sensitive." Haitham said as he motioned to Mahmud who selected a second pair of pliers like a doctor picking an instrument for an operation. Mahmud grasped Hashem's mangled big toe with the one pair of pliers, and with the other pair pulled on the toenail until it finally came out. Hashem's screams were incredibly loud. Tears of anguish mixed with the sweat on his blood red face.

"I think it is about time you tell us all you know."

Hashem was having trouble catching his breath. The pain from his toe almost made him faint. Finally, he said, "What's the difference? Even if I talk, you will kill me."

Haitham smiled, "Well, I think we may have the basis for a bargain."

"What kind of bargain?"

"I will be honest with you, Hashem. You are right, you are going to die. The question is how you die. That is in your hands."

Hashem wished he could think clearly. The pain was making cogent thought difficult. He finally managed to say, "I don't understand."

"I received my orders from Baghdad. I am to kill you. How I do it is up to me. If you cooperate, I will make it as painless as possible." Haitham produced a Browning 9mm automatic with a silencer. Holding it up in front of Hashem, he said, "I give my solemn promise that I will administer a coup de grace after we have talked. Now, I will have my colleagues produce a nice dinner. Isma'il is a very good cook. And, by the way, I brought some scotch and vodka. Which would you prefer?"

"Scotch, and plenty of it."

"I take it we have an agreement?"

Hashem looked at Haitham, resigned to the fact that he was going to die. "I'll adhere to my part of the bargain. I don't see why I should protect the person who got me into this mess. Now, can I have the scotch with ice?"

Haitham smiled triumphantly, then told Mahmud to bring in ice, scotch, soda and two glasses. "Good, Hashem, I will let you start where you want."

Mahmud arrived with everything on a tray. Haitham asked Hashem how he wanted his scotch. Hashem answered, "On the rocks, about half scotch and half soda." Mahmud loosened the bindings on his hands but left his feet tied to the chair. Hashem rubbed his wrists to get some circulation back in hands. He accepted the drink from Haitham and took a sip. It burned his split lip, but felt good on his stomach.

Haitham raised his glass to Hashem, "You may be an enemy, Hashem, but I salute your bravery."

They both drank. Hashem took in his surroundings in a different light. He knew that the room they were in was in the back of a house somewhere out in an isolated area, but he had no idea how big the house was. There were two small windows in an exterior wall through which only dense woods were visible. Hashem decided he had no choice but to begin commenting on what he knew about the robbery. He knew he would not be able to bear a repetition of the ordeal he had been put through by Mahmud.

"I was contacted last spring by a retired officer whom I knew fairly well. He told me the agency wanted to run an operation, but there were some issues involved which led the agency to decide that the operation had to be run off-line."

Haitham interjected, "What do you mean by off-line?"

"It means that there was to be no official involvement by the United States government." It occurred to Hashem that no one knew about his current whereabouts. Alain was the only one he had dealt with and, as far as he knew, Alain had already left Hamburg and returned to the States. He was alone and would die alone.

"And what was the name of this retired officer?"

Hashem hesitated. He was not particularly interested in protecting Alain. He considered him to be a supercilious son-of-a-bitch, but he thought the pause might make them accept his answer. He was interrupted by Haitham who asked, "Why the hesitation, Hashem? You have already told us you were dealing with an agency officer."

"That's not quite accurate. I was dealing with a retired officer. He was the only one I dealt with during the course of this operation."

"Since I don't think you want Mahmud to resume working on your remaining toenails and fingernails, I assume you are prepared to answer all of our questions. Now please, who is the retired officer?"

Hashem figured that Alain was relatively safe and, probably, no longer in Europe. Alain would likely take steps to protect himself when he learned of Hashem's death. He took a long drink of scotch.

"Alain Dembray."

"Would you spell that name for me?"

Hashem spelled out Alain's full name, then added, "He retired a couple of years ago."

"He was involved in the Middle East?" Haitham asked.

"Not exactly, but he was involved in a couple of operations that involved monitoring the actions of various Middle East factions who had supporters in Europe."

"You were involved in the same operations?"

"Yes." Hashem decided it was best to keep his answers as brief as possible.

Haitham decided this line of questioning was leading nowhere. "Tell me when this Dembray first contacted you about the operation, as you call it."

Hashem sipped some scotch and tried to recall when Alain had first contacted him. "As best as I can remember, it was early last May. He invited me to lunch. At the lunch he had little to say except that the agency was considering an off-line operation. If it was approved, and I agreed to participate, we would have to move to Europe to set up shop."

"That is all that he said?"

"That's it. He wanted to know if I would be free to spend some time in Europe. He did hint that I would be well paid for my participation."

Haitham was incredulous. "He made it clear this was a CIA operation?"

Hashem gave Haitham a lopsided smile. "Yes, except he emphasized that the agency wanted virtual deniability."

"What happened next?"

"I didn't hear from Dembray for several weeks, well into June. I called him to see if the operation was a go since I had other offers to consider. He told me to keep my shirt on. Everything was approved and he would get back to me."

"Mr. Dembray appears to be very secretive. Tell us when you were ordered to go to Hamburg and what you were told about the operation."

Hashem pulled his thoughts together, finished the scotch, and motioned for a refill. Mahmud took his glass but, from his expression, it was clear that he would have preferred to work on Hashem's other big toe.

"In early August, Dembray called me and told me to come to Hamburg. We agreed on a date and he told me to meet him for lunch in a restaurant we both knew. I was waiting for him in the restaurant when he arrived. We had a couple of beers and then had lunch. I asked Dembray what the deal was." Hashem paused to take his refill from Mahmud. "Dembray explained that the agency had gotten the cooperation of the BKA. He explained that the BKA had agreed to put a tap on Tikriti's private line. The BKA also agreed to provide the CIA with the take from this tap on a non-attributable basis."

Haitham felt some inner satisfaction. Hashem had confirmed his belief that the information needed to access the account and make the withdrawal was obtained from a tap on Wafiq's phone. He did wonder about Hashem's claim that the BKA was providing the take from the tap.

"Why are you so sure the BKA provided the tap? Is it not within the realm of possibility that Dembray lied to you to cover the direct involvement of the

CIA? Could it not have been done by the CIA without the knowledge of the BKA?" Haitham asked.

"That would be very difficult. In the first case, the quality of the tapes was excellent, which indicates that the tap was done by arranging for a direct tap on the line through the telephone company central junction box. For the agency to mount a unilateral operation to tap the target line would require some well-placed assets in the local phone company. Such an operation would be a major effort with the very real possibility that the tap could have been discovered." Hashem took a drink of his second scotch. It was beginning to put a dull edge on his pain. "One other point. All the tapes I received from Dembray had the conversations with German citizens removed. This is something the BKA would have done as a matter of course to give them some cover if the tap was ever publicly exposed."

Haitham, after rubbing his jaw in thought, responded quite suddenly, "You are telling me that the CIA and the BKA mounted a joint operation against Iraq, the goal of which was to rob one of our accounts of five million, one hundred thousand dollars?"

"That's about the sum of it," Hashem answered.

Haitham shifted gears, "You stayed in Hamburg from the time you arrived in early August. Is that correct?"

"Yeah, except for the overnight trip to Geneva to make the withdrawal from the Banque Suisse."

"I would hardly call it a withdrawal," Haitham's face, and voice, expressed anger. "Was Dembray staying in Hamburg the whole time?"

"I don't know. I only saw him when we met in restaurants."

"Where did he stay when in Hamburg?"

"I don't know. He was very careful. We would meet only in restaurants. At each meeting he would give me the time and place of the next meeting. We rarely met in a restaurant more than once, except for a Chinese restaurant called The Star. Dembray figured it unlikely that we would run into anyone we knew there."

"Hashem, I find it difficult to believe that the take from a tap on Wafiq's private telephone could produce information of any great interest to the United States."

Hashem smiled wanly. "You're right. The crap I was translating bore no real importance, although Wafiq does have some rather athletic lovers. The real jolt came on September sixth."

Haitham replied with one word, "Explain."

"That was the day the real operation was first broached to me. Dembray showed me a transcript of a conversation between Wafiq Tikriti and his Swiss banker, Irwin Schlagel. In this conversation, Tikriti told Schlagel that a certain individual would be making a withdrawal from the bank at a specific time on a specific day. He gave the man's name and said that he would send Schlagel photocopies of the man's passport and one half of a ten-mark note plus samples of his signature. He gave the serial number of the ten-mark note, together with the specific amount the person would be withdrawing." Hashem paused and took a long drink of scotch. He was really beginning to feel the effects of the rather good scotch Haitham had supplied.

Haitham immediately thought of several questions. "Did Dembray tell you how he obtained the magical transcript which told you everything you needed to know?"

"Yes, he told me that his German station contact provided it to him. But I think there was one piece of information which was the key to such arrangements for withdrawals."

"I am not sure what you mean."

Hashem smiled. None of these guys were as smart as they acted. "Ten minutes after Wafiq hung up, Schlagel called back to confirm his call. It was quite clear this was a confirmation process agreed upon by Wafiq and Schlagel. Dembray said that we now had all the information we needed to pull off the robbery."

"What did you think?"

"Something like I had just driven over a cliff. For the first time, I realized this whole operation was designed to rob an Iraqi account in a Swiss bank. My initial reaction was to tell Dembray I thought he was nuts. He told me to calm down and look at the two transcripts. The withdrawal mentioned in the transcripts went off without a hitch."

Haitham was in a dilemma. He was now certain the CIA had actually been the ones who pulled off the heist of the account. He still found it difficult to comprehend how successful they were. He was briefly at a loss for words. "If, as you say, this was a CIA operation, why would they rob an Iraqi account? Is the CIA that short of funds?"

Hashem couldn't help laughing. "I don't think it was because they are short of funds. I suspected that they used the bearer bonds to embarrass someone in the Iraqi Government and create some dissension among the ranks. But I really don't know. One thing is certain. They put a lot into it. They got the BKA to co-operate. They got someone who could imitate Wafiq Tikriti's voice well enough to fool Schlagel and had our technical people produce an Iraqi passport that was good enough for flash purposes."

"Do you think that Dembray could have managed it himself by recruiting enough people to pull off the operation?"

"It's not impossible, but think of what he would have to do on his own, first, the phone tap. As I told you, the tapes I got from Dembray were of a very high quality. Tapping Tikriti's phone directly from the line would be impossible without the cooperation of the BKA. The agency would need well-placed assets in the phone company to do it unilaterally. That would leave only two choices. One would involve tapping into the line at some point and running a wire to a listening post. This would not produce the voice quality I heard on the tapes I translated." Hashem sipped from his drink. "The only other way to tap Tikriti's phone would be to access the local junction box that contains the pairs from the Iraqi Consulate. That creates serious problems because the only way to do such a tap is to install a bridge between Tikriti's private line and another line in the junction box, in effect creating another extension on Tikriti's line. But to do this you must have access to the phone to which Tikriti's line is bridged. Dembray would have needed assets in the phone company and he would have had to rent an apartment or house that had a phone serviced by the same junction box as Tikriti's private line. He would also have needed a trusted technician to make all the connections in the listening post. That is a pretty tall order for one man to do in a couple of months."

Haitham's eyes were beginning to glaze over. He took a time out to refresh their drinks while he considered what to ask Hashem next. "Imagine for the moment that Dembray was able to do all this. Did you ever have any indication from him that someone else was involved?"

"Only his station contact, whose name he never mentioned."

"That would be the local station in Hamburg?"

"No, the station in Bonn."

"If the station was involved, could they have engineered the tap for Dembray?"

"You mean mount the tap unilaterally?" Although he doubted the possibility, he considered Haitham's question before answering. "That, I doubt. On something like this they would certainly discuss things with the BKA. It is possible that the BKA turned its back and let the CIA mount the tap. The BKA would not have done so if they knew the purpose of the tap was to pull off a bank robbery."

"But you said that Dembray told you the CIA was getting the tapes from the BKA unofficially. If what you just said is true, then the CIA misled the BKA."

"I think you've got it right. For some reason the CIA desperately needed five million dollars in bearer bonds. Under no circumstances could they be traced back to the CIA or the U.S. Government. Most important, the account to be robbed had to be an official Iraqi Government account. Look, if you consider the way this operation was mounted, I think you could speculate on any number of uses for five million dollars in bearer bonds. I know I could." Hashem allowed himself a smile of satisfaction. "One thing I forgot. There was a note of urgency about pulling off the robbery. At least that is the impression Dembray gave me. I concluded that the CIA needed those bonds in a hurry for some operation. Dembray told me he had to pass them to a station officer within hours of getting them."

Haitham's interest was again piqued. "Did he tell you who the officer was?"

"No, but I assume it was his contact who supplied him with the tapes."

"When you traveled to Geneva to pull off the robbery, was it just you and Dembray?" Haitham was finding it difficult to believe that the whole operation could have been pulled off with only two men involved.

"That's true except Dembray did say that several officers from CIA Headquarters were in Geneva to mount a counter surveillance. One was supposedly in the bank when I went in."

"Did you notice anyone you knew?"

"I did not go out of my way to detect surveillance. There were a fair number of customers in the bank when I went in. If the agency had a man in the bank it could have been one of any number of persons."

They were interrupted when Mahmud and another man whom Hashem assumed was the cook, Isma'il, entered the room. They brought in a table and began to bring in some food. Since Hashem was still attached to the chair, Mahmud and the other man lifted him in the chair and carried him to the table. Haitham joined him. There was tabouli, pita with hummous, and several kinds of kabobs.

Haitham motioned for Hashem to eat. "Please, I hope Isma'il has done well."

On his part, Hashem hoped that his teeth had not been loosened too much by Mahmud's ministrations. He decided it prudent to test first by having some tabouli and pita with hummous. The scotch had dimmed his pain. He asked for, and received, another scotch which he downed in a few minutes. With classic Arab fatalism, he decided that since he would be dead in a matter of an hour or so, he would enjoy his last meal with as much scotch as he could consume. He motioned toward Mahmud with his glass. Mahmud looked at Haitham who nodded. Mahmud put ice and scotch in Hashem's glass and passed it back to him.

Haitham was enjoying the meal. Interrogating someone always made him hungry. He decided to make a final effort with Hashem before he became too drunk to answer coherently. "As I understand you, Hashem, the only other person you were involved with during the entire course of the operation was this Dembray, is that not the case?"

"Yes, I met with no one else during the course of the operation. I saw no one else that I recognized."

"But there could have been someone else."

Hashem gulped down a hefty swallow of scotch before answering, "As I told you, the only other person referred to was his inside contact. Incidentally, I didn't mention it before, but the fact that Dembray was getting the tapes from an inside officer in Bonn is another indication that the telephone tap was not a unilateral one mounted by the agency. They would never try such an operation in Germany. You would almost have to go to God to get it approved."

Haitham laughed, "Okay, Hashem, just you and Dembray were involved. Dembray got the tapes from the inside officer and passed them to you. Do you have any idea who the inside officer is?"

"Sorry, the last business I had with the Bonn station was two or three years before I retired. I'm sure there is no one I know there now."

Haitham wondered how much more he could get out of Hashem. He was not sure if Hashem was telling him everything he knew. He figured that the only follow up was with this person Dembray. He decided to question Hashem further.

"Tell me more about Dembray. Where does he live? Is he married? Any children?" Haitham waited for Hashem's answer.

"I've never been to his house but I know he lives in Maryland, somewhere in Montgomery County."

"How do you know for sure?"

"His phone number has a Maryland area code."

"Do you have his number?"

"Not here, I left it at home."

Haitham digested what he had just heard. With a name and an area code, they should be able to find this Dembray.

"What about family?"

"He was married twice. I know nothing about his first wife, except that he divorced her long ago. His second wife, from whom he is also divorced, works for the agency."

"What is her name?"

"Jane Brophy."

Hashem wondered why Haitham was asking about Jane. Was he actually planning on pursuing Dembray and Jane Brophy? Well, he figured there was a sizable piece of change involved and that Saddam must be smarting about being relieved of over five million dollars. He decided to add a little to what he had said.

"I'm not sure, but I would guess that Dembray divorced his first wife more than twenty-five years ago. I met him a couple of years after he joined the agency. He was divorced at the time and was playing the field."

Haitham frowned and asked, "What does this mean, playing the field?"

Hashem laughed and was sorry immediately. Laughing was not what his battered face needed. The pain was sharp, despite the generous doses of scotch. "It means that he was seeing a substantial number of women. He married Jane about ten years ago. The marriage didn't last long."

Haitham half muttered to himself, "This Dembray fellow did not take very well to marriage."

"Apparently not," Hashem answered and watched as Haitham poured him another generous glass of scotch. Hashem accepted the gesture as a clear indication that his end was near. He thought to himself that his demise was probably within minutes. In summing up his current existence, he really didn't have a lot to live for. The only thing he regretted was not being able to spend all of his hundred thousand dollars. He was lost in thought and a bit woozy from drinking far too much scotch.

"Precisely what did you and Dembray get out of this?"

Hashem thought briefly before answering. He knew from his experience as a case officer that anytime anyone delayed in answering a question it was a clear indication they were considering what to answer. "Dembray told me his pay would be a three-year contract with the agency that would bring him about thirty thousand dollars a year. All his expenses were covered and he was given about twenty-five thousand dollars to cover his work on the operation. At least, that's what he told me."

"What about you?" Haitham asked.

Hashem lied, "I was given part of the one hundred thousand dollars cash we got from the robbery, fifteen thousand dollars to be exact, with a bonus of another fifty thousand dollars to be paid to me in the States. This is so I would not have to declare bringing such a sum into the United States."

"One more question, Hashem. Does this Jane woman know much about Dembray's activities?"

"I couldn't answer that. Divorced people don't tend to socialize much."

Haitham replenished Hashem's half emptied glass with another couple of ounces. "In sum, Hashem, as far as you know the only other persons involved in this operation were this man Dembray and a CIA officer from the agency's contingent in Bonn. Is that correct?"

"That's about it," Hashem slurred. He gulped down the last of his scotch. He was very woozy, but the thought of what was about to happen sobered him like a hand reaching through his mind's fog. His head began to sag from the effect of the scotch. Haitham stood behind him. He withdrew a Browning 9mm automatic from a shoulder holster, adjusted the silencer, and moved to Hashem's right side. He placed the automatic at Hashem's right temple, said *Allah hu Akbar,* and fired. The 9mm bullet tore through Hashem's skull, scrambled Hashem's brain as it exploded inside his skull, and then tore a large hole as it exited the left side of his head. Hashem neither saw nor felt anything. His lights were turned out permanently. There was no fuzzy feeling, no bright light to accompany his passage from life, only an empty blackness.

Haitham turned to Mahmud who was standing by the door to the kitchen. "Take him somewhere and dump him. My only concern is that you dump him in a place where he is sure to be found tomorrow morning. I want our adversaries to know that we are after them. Leave all his identifying documents on him and don't touch the money. We are not thieves."

Mahmud nodded his understanding before leaving the room. He returned with Isma'il. The two of them lugged Hashem's limp, heavy body to the trunk of the Mercedes.

Chapter 13

SECRET

CITE: BONN 14221
TO: DIRECTOR
  EYES ONLY CHIEF/CIC
  1.YESTERDAY AFTERNOON, OCTOBER 1, I WAS CALLED TO A MEETING WITH THE CHIEF, BKA. HE TOLD ME THAT EARLY IN THE MORNING THE HAMBURG POLICE RECOVERED A BODY FROM A PARKING LOT IN HAMBURG. THE POLICE REPORT OUTLINED ALL THE DOCUMENTS ON THE BODY TOGETHER WITH THE ODD FACT THAT HE WAS CARRYING SEVERAL THOUSAND MARKS. THESE DOCUMENTS IDENTIFIED THE BODY AS THAT OF HASHEM SAMARA'I. SINCE THE BKA KNEW OF SAMARA'I'S PAST ASSOCIATION WITH THE AGENCY, I WAS CONTACTED IMMEDIATELY. CHIEF, BKA, SHOWED ME SEVERAL PICTURES TAKEN BY FORENSICS. DESPITE SOME FACIAL DISFIGUREMENT, I RECOGNIZED SAMARA'I. HE HAD OBVIOUSLY SUFFERED SOME SERIOUS TORTURE. HIS RIGHT BIG TOE WAS GROTESQUELY DISFIGURED AND WAS MISSING THE NAIL. HIS DEATH WAS CAUSED BY A PISTOL BEING FIRED INTO THE TEMPLE ON THE RIGHT SIDE OF HIS HEAD. A LARGE PORTION OF THE LEFT SIDE OF HIS HEAD IS NO LONGER THERE. AT THIS TIME, THE BKA HAS NO INFOR-

MATION ON WHO MIGHT HAVE BEEN RESPONSIBLE. THEY HAVE NATURALLY RULED OUT ROBBERY.

2. CHIEF, BKA, PROMISED ME A COPY OF THE FORENSIC REPORT AND AUTOPSY REPORT AS SOON AS HE GETS THEM. HE BLUNTLY ASKED ME WHAT SAMARA'I WAS DOING IN GERMANY. HE DIDN'T APPEAR TO BELIEVE ME WHEN I TOLD HIM I HADN'T THE SLIGHTEST IDEA OF WHAT SAMARA'I WAS DOING IN GERMANY. HE ASKED IF WE COULD COME UP WITH ANY POSSIBILITIES REGARDING WHO MIGHT HAVE A REASON TO TORTURE ONE OF OUR OFFICERS, THEN ADMINISTER WHAT LOOKS TO CHIEF, BKA, LIKE A COUP DE GRACE. CHIEF, BKA, SAID THAT ALTHOUGH THE INVESTIGATION WILL BE CARRIED OUT BY THE LOCALS IN HAMBURG, THE BKA WILL ALSO PLAY A ROLE BECAUSE OF WHO SAMARA'I WAS. I PROMISED OUR COOPERATION IN THE INVESTIGATION. NO ONE HERE OR IN HAMBURG WAS AWARE OF SAMARA'I'S PRESENCE IN GERMANY. MAYBE SOME OF HIS AGENCY ASSOCIATES BOTH RETIRED AND STILL WORKING CAN SHED SOME LIGHT ON WHAT SAMARA'I WAS DOING IN GERMANY.

3. FILE: DEFER.

SECRET

--》═◎ ◎═《--

CIA HQS. October 2, 1982.

THE CHIEF, COUNTER Intelligence, Reginald Smythe, was a small, intense man who his detractors would say suffered from a Mickey Rooney complex. No one had ever doubted his brilliance. He had the eyes of a ferret and the tenacity to go along with the eyes. He paced nervously around his office at CIA Headquarters in Langley, Virginia. The Chief of the Near East Division, Sam Clauson, and the

Chief of the European Division, Everett O'Brien, had just entered the office. They had both received info copies of the cable so they were aware of what was bugging Smythe on this beautiful Saturday afternoon.

"Did we have any contractual relationship with Samara'i, Sam?" Smythe started the conversation.

"Absolutely not. He retired a little over two years ago and although he would have liked a contract, we were not inclined to hire him on that basis," Clauson answered.

Smythe turned to Chief/EUR and asked, "What about you, Everett? He was in Germany when he was killed."

"Same as Sam, we did not know he was in Germany." O'Brien replied while he considered the various possibilities on who had done in Samara'i.

"Okay, here is what we do. I damn sure want to find out who knocked off Samara'i, even if he was retired. Everett, send a cable to Chief, Bonn, and instruct him to tell the BKA that they will have our full cooperation in the investigation into the death of Samara'i." Smythe thought for a moment, then added, "Also instruct him to tell Chief, BKA, that the Director has taken an immediate interest in this case. It goes without saying that the Chief, BKA, should be given the assurances of the Director that Samara'i was in no way in Germany on our behalf. Get the exact date of his retirement and add that to the cable. Also, add that he had no contractual arrangement with any component of the agency."

"I'll check with everyone in the division who knew Samara'i and see if I can come up with anything. Samara'i knew a lot of people in the European Division, one of them may know something," Clauson said, turning to O'Brien.

Smythe nodded his agreement to Clauson, "We are going to put out an agency-wide announcement of Samara'i's untimely demise and ask anyone who has any information on what he was doing in Germany to contact Chief/CIC immediately. I want both of you to canvas your divisions for the names of retirees who may have been in contact with Samara'i. There is a chance one of them may have some information. I've already asked the FBI to get Samara'i's phone records. That's all for now."

Clauson and O'Brien left the office together. "Wasn't there a female reports officer in the European division that Samara'i was living with?" Clauson asked O'Brien.

"Yeah, I think you're right. It was Betty Swingle. She retired at about the same time that Samara'i did. She may know something, but as I recall, she expected to marry Samara'i, so there may have been a falling out."

Clauson nodded his agreement, "Yeah, you're probably right, but you better ask someone who knew her to give her a call on the chance she may have heard something."

→■● ●■←

Norbeck. October 3, 1982. 1730 hours.

Alain fixed himself a martini, turned on the television, and tuned it to the evening news. He was enormously pleased with himself. After all, everything had gone well. With over fifty thousand dollars in his local safe deposit box, he planned to live well. After a few sips of his martini, his phone rang. He answered the phone and heard Jane Brophy's voice.

"Alain, have you heard the news? Samara'i has been murdered."

"Murdered? By whom, one of his many jilted girl friends?" Alain answered.

"Sorry, Alain, this was by somebody who really didn't like him. He was obviously subjected to pretty intense torture then killed. The German police found his body in a parking lot in Hamburg. You didn't know about this? You were in Hamburg, weren't you?"

"I left early morning two days ago. When was he killed?" Alain decided to add a question to cover himself, "What was he doing in Hamburg?"

"I called you on the chance you might know. The agency is very interested in finding out what he was doing in Hamburg. One of the reasons they are so anxious is that the BKA is also interested in finding out what Samara'i was doing in Hamburg. Did you run into him while you were there?"

"No. I can think of several people who would like to do him in based on some of the German operations in which he was involved. I would be interested in how and why he was killed. Look, let's have dinner. How about tomorrow night?"

"Okay," Jane said, "but not tomorrow, the day after is better for me. Are you coming over here?"

"I'll be there at about six-thirty."

"I'll have the martinis chilled."

Alain hung up the phone. His face showed concern that, in Alain's case, meant worry. He wondered how the Iraqis could have determined that Hashem was the man who actually withdrew the money from the bank. Hashem's beard was pretty heavy and thick by the time the robbery actually took place. The only way he could have been recognized is from the photographs of his Iraqi passport or the bank surveillance camera. It seemed highly unlikely that they could have recognized him from the photographs on the passport because they lacked contrast and were not very clear. The surveillance camera seemed the only logical choice, and that meant that someone was investigating the robbery. Given the condition of Hashem's body, the Iraqi General Intelligence Directorate was probably involved in the investigation.

He decided to call Kurth. He dialed the number in Germany and waited. Ulla came on the line. Alain exchanged pleasantries with her. She excitedly told Alain that she and Kurth were going to remarry. Alain offered his congratulations, telling Ulla that he thought Kurth had been a fool to divorce her. When Kurth came on the line, Alain asked, "Have you heard the news?"

Kurth said that he had, adding, "It has been well covered in the German newspapers, especially the torture angle."

"It could have been one of his old girl friends or, for that matter, a whole cabal of them." Alain made this comment just in case the phone conversation came to the notice of the National Security Agency.

Kurth caught on, "I wonder what he was doing in Hamburg? I'm sure our previous employers have not rehired him, but then I could be wrong."

"Well, maybe we will never know the full story. Jane tells me that both our former employers and their German counterparts seem to be very interested in what Hashem was doing in Hamburg."

"As the old saw goes, dead men tell no tales."

This brought a smirk from Alain. "Well, so much for Hashem. Ulla told me about your plans to remarry. Congratulations. I'm glad you finally came to your senses."

"We plan to invite you to the wedding. Stay in touch, we plan to marry sometime next month."

They said their goodbyes and hung up. Alain became very thoughtful. If the Iraqi GID had tortured Hashem, then they knew of his involvement. He wondered what they thought about the CIA robbing an Iraqi government account.

--⊷⊙⊙⊶--

Baghdad. October 5, 1982. 1000 hours.

Saddam Hussein was angry to the point of being incensed. His anger was a product of his confusion at what he had been told. He barked at the three men seated in his office, "You mean to tell me that it was the CIA that robbed the account of five million, one hundred thousand dollars? I do not believe that the CIA just walked into a Swiss bank and calmly walked out with all that money." Saddam folded his arms and sat back in his chair, threatening any one of them to explain to him how all this had happened.

Zaki Sa'duni nodded to Haitham Abd al-Nebi, who answered Saddam's question somewhat reluctantly. "We worked Samara'i over pretty well and that was his story. He did not seem to have any reason to lie. He made it clear that he did not like the only person with whom he worked. He is the other person named in our report, Alain Dembray."

From Saddam's expression, he was less than satisfied. "What do you think, Zaki?"

Zaki fidgeted in his chair. It was something like an elephant hunkering down in a comfortable clump of grass. Having established a comfort zone, he gave his explanation. "Wafiq's telephone was tapped by the CIA. This is the only way to explain how Dembray got the information needed to access the account. Even if Dembray was somehow able to tap Wafiq's private line on his own, how did he get the account number? There is also the phone call to the Swiss banker who handles the account. The voice was so close to Wafiq's that it fooled both the banker and his secretary. If he did manage all this, Mr. Dembray is quite an operator. But I agree with you, why on earth would the CIA rob one of our accounts now? They are actively engaged in providing us intelligence on Iranian troop movements."

Mustafa Naghshabandi had not said a word during the course of the meeting. He had merely followed all the comments closely. He would make notes of everything that had transpired after the meeting was over. He could tell by Saddam's expression that he was going to give orders on precisely what was to be done. Saddam had paid careful attention to Zaki's explanation and made up his mind quickly.

"Since this Dembray is the only lead we have, I want you to get him. If at all possible, get him alive. We must get to the bottom of this. I will personally confront the CIA officer we are dealing with here. Zaki, pick some of your best men who are also fluent in English. I want you and Haitham to make plans to go to the United States and get your hands on Dembray. Once you have put a small team together, get back to me and we will go over your plans."

Saddam picked up some papers and began reading, a certain sign they were to leave. Mustafa accompanied them through the door. He was obviously upset. He turned to Haitham and Zaki, "Please, come to my office for some coffee."

The three retired to his office. Naghshabandi told his personal servant to bring coffee as he motioned Zaki and Haitham to chairs. Once they were seated, he said to them, "How, old friends, do you intend to kidnap this Mr. Dembray and bring him to Baghdad?"

Zaki smiled. "With great difficulty. I am not very enthusiastic about going to America, locating this man, then forcibly bringing him to Baghdad."

Naghshabandi smiled. He had anticipated Zaki's reply. "I can tell you this, old friend, whatever you want, or whoever you need, just let me know. I know Saddam and he wants this Mr. Dembray no matter what it takes to get him. Now, tell me how you intend to proceed initially. I know you well, Zaki. You think faster and more accurately than any man I have ever met. Do you have any ideas on what initial steps you might take?"

Zaki had obviously given some serious thought to the problem. He pounded his fist in his left hand and said, "We can not use any of our officials in the United States. The FBI has them pretty well covered. If any of our officials inquire about Dembray, I think we can assume the FBI would find out about it. I am also concerned about the CIA. We have assassinated one of their officers who participated in a sanctioned operation. This means we must take great care in putting together an operational team. They will have to be chosen from the best we have since we will have to operate under the CIA's nose." Zaki thought for a minute, "But, most of all, they must be clean. We should also be certain that they have never come to the attention of the CIA. This will make our use of alias documents more effective."

Naghshabandi's smile contained no humor. "Okay, you have told us some things we cannot do. I would like your ideas on what we can do."

"I have not finished relating all the things we cannot do," Zaki replied with humor. "Once we start, there can be no communications between the operational team and Baghdad. I do not trust the security of our communications, at least not where the National Security Agency is concerned." Zaki paused to assess the effect of his words, then continued, "I am going to send Haitham to Ottawa. He will be our link if we need something. He will be in charge of all communications with Baghdad. We have a unique asset that I have used in Europe. His father was Spanish and his mother was the daughter of a senior Iraqi diplomat. The daughter met her Spanish husband when her father was assigned to our Embassy in Madrid. I knew the Iraqi parents well and was of some help to the daughter and her Spanish husband in calming down the crisis created when she married a non-Muslim foreigner."

Zaki paused briefly to take a sip of coffee. "Her son's name is Ramon Santos. He is a naturalized U.S. citizen and also has a Spanish passport. He has a degree in business administration that he got at UCLA. He is in international banking and has been very valuable to me. Given his position in the banking community, I will have him find out everything he can about Mr. Dembray. He is a very good investigator. He should be able to provide us with detailed information about Mr. Dembray's financial status, address, car make and license number."

Mustafa seemed less than satisfied. "America is an open society. I could probably get the same information on my own."

"Not without some difficulty and a lot of wasted effort," Zaki rejoined immediately. "Once we have the basic information we need, we will hold a session to create a plan for capturing Dembray alive and somehow moving him to Baghdad. This is the only part of the whole operation that bothers me. This Dembray obviously knows that we have tortured and executed Samara'i. It will not be easy to take him alive. Since this was a sanctioned operation, the CIA may have arranged FBI protection for him. Mustafa, you must convince Saddam that while we will exert every effort to take him alive, in all probability he will be killed either by our hands or his own."

Mustafa looked at Zaki through the eerie silence that gripped everyone in the room. "I do not look forward to telling Saddam that you, Zaki, may not be able to carry out his wishes. I do concede that you have a point." Mustafa rose from his seat, signaling that the meeting over, "We will meet at about four in the afternoon the day after tomorrow. That gives you and Haitham time to plan and take some initial steps. *Illa liqa.*"

Zaki and Haitham left Mustafa's office and went to Zaki's office. They spent a lot of time going over their plan. They decided that Haitham would leave Baghdad after their next meeting with Mustafa. Zaki would alert Santos, currently in Los Angeles, that he should expect to hear from Haitham in the next few days and be prepared to go to Canada to meet with him. Haitham would instruct him on what to do. They spent hours going over possible needs and selecting personnel. They came up with a dozen names, all well trained men with near fluent English.

Finally, Zaki yawned and said, "That is enough for one day. We will meet Mustafa on Thursday. You can drive to Amman early Friday morning. Go ahead and make arrangements to get to Ottawa as soon as possible. We will have Mustafa arrange for your interim assignment to Canada as special assistant to the Ambassador. As I recall, he is an old friend of Mustafa's and will ask no questions. We should sleep on things and meet tomorrow morning."

Reston. October 5, 1982. 1900 hours.

Jane greeted him at her front door. "I see you were as good as your promise," Alain said, nodding to the pitcher of martinis in her hand, as he kissed her on the cheek.

"Alain, my dear, a love of martinis was one of the few things we had in common." Jane smiled as she poured him one. Alain returned her smile. He wanted to find out all he could about Hashem's death, but didn't want to appear overly concerned. He decided to approach the question of Hashem's death obliquely.

"So how is the agency functioning without my deft presence?"

"We'll manage. There is great concern in the Near East division about Sharon's invasion of Lebanon, what's left is the usual problems. Sometimes when I read cables I can't help saying to myself that it's the same shit I read twenty years ago, only the names have changed," Jane answered. "Let me check on dinner."

Alain followed her into the kitchen. It was in the back of her townhouse which was surprisingly bright and airy. There were large windows with a view of one of Reston's lakes or ponds. Alain was unsure at what size a pond becomes a lake. There was a sliding door that led to a small deck. Alain decided it was as good a time as any to bring up Hashem.

"Tell me Jane, does this business about Hashem have people upset?"

"I should say so. They are most concerned because his murder is being investigated by the BKA. Chief/CI, Reggie Smythe is in charge of our investigation. He has sent out an administrative notice asking for information from anybody who has any knowledge of why Hashem was in Germany. He has also sent out one of those cables that go everywhere asking for replies from anyone who might know something." Jane turned to check something in the oven, then added, "It is odd that you and Hashem were in Hamburg at the same time and didn't see each other. Incidentally, what in the hell were you actually doing in Hamburg?"

Alain's antennae were immediately deployed. "In answer to your question, let me point out that Hashem and I were not exactly bosom buddies. If Hashem was in Germany, I'm sure it must have been on some kind of business. I can't imagine the agency hiring him back as a contractor since they had forced him into retirement in the first place. As for me, I went to Germany to do research on a book about a very interesting operation that we ran against East Germany. There is no reason you would have ever heard of it. The crypt was BLACKROOT. I came back with a lot of notes on things I had forgotten. Hashem was unaware of the operation so I would have had no reason to consult him. What has the agency learned about Hashem's untimely, but not long regretted, demise?"

Jane's expression indicated it was all a mystery to her. "The word being put out in the agency is that he most definitely was not under contract. If he was in Germany on business, he was dealing with some pretty unsavory characters."

"I agree with you, Jane. I suspect that, in the end, they will find out it was one of the Near Eastern intelligence services he worked against in the past," Alain suggested.

Jane was not so sure. "I doubt one of those services would have tortured him, blown out his brains, then dumped him in a public parking lot to be found. Such an arrangement fits the Mafia or some other criminal organization that knocks off people who don't do as they are told."

Alain digested Jane's comments before saying anything further. "I never credited Hashem with any great wisdom, but I find it hard to believe he would get involved in criminal activity. I do agree with you that I doubt it was a hostile service, unless Hashem did something we don't know about and they exacted their revenge. What has the agency been able to learn?"

"How the hell do I know? I am an intelligence analyst. I told you Reggie Smythe is handling the agency's investigation and you can't pry information out of him with a crowbar. Come on, everything is ready. The hell with Hashem, let's eat."

"I'm with you, girl of my dreams. By the way, have you heard that Kurth and Ulla are going to be remarried?"

"I liked Ulla. I hope this means that Kurth has come to his senses and changed his attitude toward women."

--⊷ ⊶--

Baghdad. October 7, 1982. 1600 hours.

"Have you put together a team?" Mustafa asked as Zaki and Haitham entered his office.

"Yes, we have," Zaki responded. "Haitham leaves tomorrow. He will drive to Amman and make arrangements to fly to Ottawa. He will handle all communications and procurement. One of his first assignments will be to obtain a safe site for the team. The Intelligence Directorate has good contacts with loyal Iraqi businessmen in Canada who should be able to provide such a site. Ramon Santos was supposed to arrive in Washington last night. He will develop all the basic information on our target, fly to Ottawa, and report to Haitham. Santos told me to give him three or four days to check Dembray out. When he has developed enough information on the target, our team will depart from Baghdad. I have selected four very good men. They all know English and I am sure the Central Intelligence Agency has not identified any of them as belonging to my unit. We are providing them with alias documents and putting together cover legends for them. They will be documented as Jordanians. Since we must travel through Amman, we will pick up pocket litter there. I will be traveling in alias using a genuine Turkish passport." Zaki stopped to give Mustafa a chance to digest the comments.

Mustafa smiled, "It is reassuring to know that you are as efficient as ever. According to my counting, you have a team of seven men."

"That is true, but Santos' role will be limited to developing information on Dembray. I do not want him to do anything that might bring him to the attention of the FBI. He is too valuable an asset. I cannot afford to lose him." Zaki recalled for Mustafa the operation where Santos had disposed of the potential leader of an anti-regime movement. It was a classic operation. If he was forced to use Santos he would, but this was a decision that could be put off until much later.

"What do the other four men know?" Mustafa asked Zaki.

"At the moment nothing except that they have been chosen for a special mission that will require all their skills. I have cautioned them to tell no one in or outside the GID about their assignment. I added that if they are successful, they will be well rewarded."

"Anything else I should know?" Mustafa asked.

"There is one other point. Lt. Walidi is one of the four I am taking with me. He was involved in the interrogation of Wafiq Tikriti. This will keep the knowledge of this little operation within our small group."

The meeting ended with Mustafa giving some final instructions. "Goodbye and good luck, Haitham. All your communications will come directly to me. I will do my best to get you anything you need. The sooner we can deal with this Dembray, the better."

Zaki and Haitham left Mustafa's office. They walked to the elevator. Before it arrived, Zaki said to Haitham, "Send me word of your arrival. Keep all of your communications short and make them as cryptic as possible. I do not trust the security of our communications. I am certain the National Security Agency may be reading at least some of them." Zaki reached into his inside coat pocket, pulled out a small notebook, and handed it to Haitham. "This notebook contains several hundred words and their code equivalent. Use it when you are writing messages. Super encipherment will make the work of the NSA's analysts a little more difficult and possibly buy us enough time to complete this operation." The two men shook hands. Haitham entered the elevator and disappeared behind the closing doors.

⟶▬◉ ◉▬◀

Norbeck. October 8, 1982.

Alain had a problem. Given Hashem's condition when he was found, there was a good possibility that he had implicated Alain in the robbery. The more he thought about it, the more he considered this a possibility, the more certain he was that the Iraqis knew of his participation. He would have to be careful. He calculated that the Iraqis must have some rudimentary investigative capability in the United States. Given his name and what other details the Iraqis might have gotten from Hashem, it would not take them too long to determine where he lived and come after him. He decided that he had to do something fast. He couldn't afford to sit tight. He decided that the best move would be to hit the road, but to do it in a way that would make tracking him down very difficult. He began making some notes on a yellow pad. As he wrote, he thought of the many times he had outlined operational proposals on similar pads when he was in the Directorate of Operations.

His first note was to leave no paper trails. That meant doing everything in cash and traveling in a way that left no record. He thought he would disappear by taking a bus to a small town in Maryland. He would pay for the ticket in cash and stay in a motel under a false name. He would buy a good used car. This would be the only time he would leave any kind of paper trail since he would have to license the car in his true name. He thought about this plan for a few minutes then scratched out his notes. Maybe he was being too paranoid. Why not just leave in his current car? It was highly unlikely the Iraqis could locate him if he kept moving and paid for all his expenses in cash. America is a big place. He considered calling Jane first thing in the morning and telling her that he was going to visit some relatives in Tennessee. He actually had an old aunt there that she knew about. He would simply tell her he would be gone for some time and would call her when he got back.

He figured he could hole up in his cabin in Wyoming. He picked up his pen again and began writing what he should take with him. He smiled. Staying in his cabin in the dead of winter in Wyoming, he would need some good survival equipment. What he didn't have, he would buy. He looked in the yellow pages and noted down the addresses of military surplus stores and others that specialized in camping equipment. He checked the calendar. He would try to leave on Monday the eleventh. He looked at his watch and realized he had time to get some shopping done. He would buy the weapons he needed first. He had a Browning automatic. He would buy a couple of boxes of ammunition for it. He decided to buy a pump shotgun and a model 70 Winchester. He wanted to be prepared just in case.

-->=◉ ◉=<-

Ottawa. October 12, 1982.

Haitham sat in a comfortable office in the Iraqi Embassy in Ottawa. Mustafa had worked his magic with the Iraqi Ambassador. Santos had just left the office and Haitham was reading the long report he had left with him. Haitham was absolutely amazed at how much information had been amassed in such a short time. Santos had told him it was easy if you knew which buttons to push. He asked Haitham to read the report and suggested they meet the next day. He had insisted on not meeting in the Embassy anymore, and had given him the address of a restaurant some distance from the Embassy. Haitham thought to himself that Santos was a very careful and skilled operator. He wished his service had more people like him.

The report started out with some basic information on Alain Dembray. It included his date and place of birth, and the names of his parents. There were also the dates of his two marriages and the subsequent divorces. Haitham noted that Dembray had been divorced from Jane Brophy for almost three years. The report gave details on Dembray's house in Norbeck, Maryland together with details on the mortgage and the name of the bank that held the mortgage. The report also listed Dembray's car make and license number. There was some financial information that was contained in a credit report. Santos told Haitham that he had been able to obtain three different financial reports. They all contained similar information.

Santos noted that one of the reports had a paragraph that detailed the purchase of a cabin and land in Wyoming. The date of the purchase was in the summer of 1976. There was no indication of a mortgage. The address was vague, so many miles northeast of Pine Springs. Haitham noted that Dembray was well off, but certainly not rich. There was no indication of any unusual activity in his bank account or investment account. In short, there was nothing to indicate that he had just come into a lot of money. He planned to ask Santos to spend a day or two in the Norbeck area to obtain details about Dembray's house and the surrounding neighborhood. They would need more detailed information to help plan the kidnapping of Dembray. He looked at his watch. He decided that he had time to go brief Lt. Walidi and make sure that the team was settled. He had some instructions he wanted to pass on to Walidi, and the sooner the better.

October 13, 1982.

The meal had been very good and very expensive. Santos had learned to live well. The restaurant was old, strangely named The Cattlemen's Fountain. The motif reflected Canada's frontier days.

"Let me review our conversation, Haitham. You want me to find out as much as I can about this Dembray's life patterns, right?"

Haitham smiled, "That is right. I must plan a kidnapping and I need as much information about Dembray as possible."

Santos thought for a few moments before answering, "Okay, Haitham, I assume this is, as usual, of the utmost urgency. I'll leave immediately, but it might take me some time. I'll try to get back here within a week. If we assume that Dembray is aware of the untimely demise of his friend, he might reasonably conclude that he is next on our list. We might be dealing with a man who is making himself hard to find."

"Just find out all you can and get back to me as soon as possible."

--→≡◎ ◎≡←--

Pine Springs. October 16, 1982.

Alain drove his rented Jeep down the main street of Pine Springs. He had driven to Cheyenne, leased a Jeep for six months, and stored his car with the dealer. He had paid cash for the lease and told the dealer, only half jokingly, that he was leaving his car as collateral in case he didn't survive the winter. In answer to a question from the dealer, he said that he had a cabin near Boulder. He left Cheyenne early on the fourteenth. He drove on Interstate 80 West until he reached Rock Springs and spent the night there. He got up before dawn, ate breakfast, and headed North on U.S. 191. From there, it was just a while east on a local road until he got to Pine Springs. He drove through Pine Springs, and after three miles, turned off on a dirt road.

Driving through some of the best scenery in the West, Alain saw that the Wind River Range was already heavily covered with new snow. Wind River Peak, at 13,192 feet, was beautiful in the afternoon sun. Fortunately, there had been no heavy snows so far, and the road was easily passable. A few miles along the dirt road, he turned off onto a dirt track and in a rugged half mile reached his cabin. It was located not far from the Bridger-Teton National Forest.

He parked the jeep in the lea of the woodshed. After he walked around the cabin to check things out, he unlocked the front door of the cabin and spent some time stowing his gear. He was pleased with the condition of the cabin. He hadn't been there in over a year, but Ed Satterly and his wife, Emma, had taken good care of it. He had called them before he left Maryland and asked them to make sure he had enough wood since he planned to stay for a couple of months and work on a book. He stopped by their place late in the morning as he made his way to town. They lived in a small cabin on the main road leading to Pine Springs, right near the dirt road to Alain's place. He paid them off, adding fifty bucks more than they asked. Ed was so pleased that he insisted Alain sample some of his special whiskey. He went outside and fetched a gallon ceramic jug from his woodshed. He poured three generous drinks, raised his glass and, with Emma, welcomed Alain back to God's country.

The drive to Pine Springs to pick up needed provisions went quickly. Alain was finished his shopping and back home by the middle of the afternoon. It was not far from the town to his remote retreat. The cabin was set in the middle of four acres that Alain's father had bought for a song. Alain built the cabin while he was married to Jane. It was very comfortable, consisting of a large living room with a huge fireplace. There was a big, open kitchen that had a window looking back up the mountains. The sole bedroom was very comfortable. The bathroom had cost him almost as much as the rest of the cabin. There was a generator in the woodshed that provided electricity to the house. It also operated the pump that supplied water to a tank on the rise to the left of the cabin.

He had only been able to get Jane to the cabin on two occasions. She had readily conceded that the scenery was spectacular. She even liked the daily glimpses of wildlife, except for a bad experience with a nosy bear. In the end, she confessed to Alain that she just couldn't take the isolation for more than a couple of days. His last addition was a porch that faced west. He fixed himself a martini and took a seat on the porch. It was pretty chilly, especially drinking a martini, but the view of the setting sun was breathtaking. He relaxed with his drink until the Salt River Range of mountains obscured the sun.

Inside, he gave some thought to dinner. Instead, he spent some time distracted by the guns he had brought with him. He fitted a scope to the rifle and planned to sight it in the following morning. He opened his briefcase and took out the now rather voluminous notes on operation BLACKROOT. He smiled at the thought that he would have a lot of time to work on his book. Dinner could wait.

Norbeck. October 18, 1982. 1800 hours.

Santos sat in a coffee shop located in the Leisure World Shopping Center. He had spent the weekend checking out Dembray's house. He called several times, but there was no answer. If Dembray had an answering machine it was turned off, which could mean he was out of town. He drove by the house twice Saturday evening, twice Sunday evening, and on all occasions no light emanated from Dembray's house. He had called early this morning with no answer and, then again, a half an hour later with no answer. After looking at his watch, he decided to make a run on the street in front of Dembray's house.

Santos found his car and left the shopping center using the Leisure World access road. He stopped at the light and, when it changed, crossed Georgia Avenue and turned right onto the road that ran alongside the Manor Country Club. He turned into Dembray's townhouse development and made a right on the street that ran in front of his house. As he approached, he noted a car pulling into the driveway of the adjacent house. A man got out of the car and walked towards the house next to Dembray's. Since the lights were on, he assumed the man had a wife or a companion. Santos drove away, a plan forming in his mind.

Norbeck. October 19, 1982.

Santos was in his car in the shopping center parking lot. He had called Dembray's number twice during the day with no answer. He decided to go ahead with the plan he had formulated the previous evening. He would arrive at Dembray's house at about the same time as he had the previous evening, hoping to be there when the man he had observed the previous evening returned home from work. He checked his watch and noted that it was about the same time he had left the shopping center the previous evening. He turned the key in the ignition and eased his car out of the parking lot. In a matter of minutes, he was driving by Dembray's house. It was just about the time he had made a pass the previous evening. The man he spotted the previous evening had apparently not yet arrived home since there was no car in the driveway. He decided to drive around the block and then park his car in Dembray's driveway. When he again approached Dembray's house, he pulled into the driveway. He got out of the car, went to the front door, and rang the doorbell. He waited several seconds and pressed the doorbell again. He walked across the lawn to a window and began peering into the house. While he was so occupied, the man he had spotted the previous evening pulled into his driveway. He parked his car and got out, wearing an expression of curiosity as he watched Santos. Finally, he said to Santos, "He's not there."

Santos acted startled, then started walking towards the neighbor. He decided that the best way to put the man at ease would be to immediately introduce himself as an old friend of Dembray's. He needed to get some information, otherwise they would have an impossible time finding Dembray.

"I'm sorry. I hope I haven't startled you," Santos said, walking rapidly towards the neighbor. "My name is Ricardo Boldini. I'm an old friend of Alain's. Do you know if, by any chance, he will return soon?"

The neighbor accepted Santos' outstretched hand. "Glad to meet a friend of Alain's. I'm his next-door neighbor, Jack McGee. I think he will be gone for a long time. He left about a week ago."

Santos feigned despair, "I'm sorry to hear that. I haven't seen him in some time." Santos thought to himself, *what the hell, my best bet is to use the information I have on Dembray*. With great care, he did his best to frame his face in an expression of sudden inspiration. "You say he will be gone for a long time. You don't suppose he is going to that crazy cabin he has in Wyoming?"

McGee mulled over Santos' question. "He said goodbye to me the night before he left. He didn't specify where he was going, but you might be right.

I assume that he is going to do some hunting. He was loaded down with cold weather gear. I also saw him load a rifle and shotgun into his car trunk."

"Thanks a lot, Mr. McGee. I'm sure sorry I missed him." Santos started to walk towards his car, stopped, and asked, "Did he leave a forwarding address?"

"Not with us, but I assume he made arrangements at the local post office with regard to his mail."

"Again, thank you, Mr. McGee. I'll check with the post office." He waved as he moved towards his car. "Have a good evening."

⊷▬◉ ◉▬⊶

Ottawa. October 21, 1982.

Santos had arrived in Ottawa midmorning on a direct flight from Washington. He had called Haitham and arranged to meet him in a restaurant he knew of that was not too far from the Iraqi Embassy. When Haitham arrived, Santos gave him a full briefing of what he had done. He watched as Haitham considered his report.

"So, you are certain that Dembray is holed up in his cabin in Wyoming?" Haitham questioned Santos.

"That's my conclusion. His neighbor, McGee, told me that he had loaded his car down with cold weather gear, a rifle, and a shotgun, probably to do some hunting. I said it sounded like he was headed to the cabin in Wyoming and McGee agreed."

"Well, Santos, it looks like our work is cut out for us. We know Dembray is aware that we are after him and that he is well armed."

Santos was curious, "So what do you plan to do, Haitham?"

Haitham smiled, "Not me, Ramon, you." Santos tried to respond, but Haitham held up his hands to stop him. "You know your way around, Ramon. I want you to positively locate this cabin and also confirm that our Mr. Dembray is in the cabin. We will need you to draw a good map of the exact location of cabin, noting all buildings near to the cabin."

"Anything else?" Santos asked with a smirk.

"Yes, take Lt. Walidi with you. He was born in the United States and has an American passport. As a result, he speaks English very well. The two of you will have to figure out some story as to why you know each other and what you are doing in the wilds of Wyoming. I leave that to your imagination. In addition to your map and notes, I also want you to find out when the hunting season begins in Wyoming. If there has to be shooting, no one will pay much attention to it during hunting season."

Santos smiled wryly, "I assumed that I would be given the task of locating our friend Dembray and doing a reconnaissance of his cabin and the area around it. I suggest that Walidi and I first travel to Salt Lake City which is located on U.S. Interstate 80. From the map, it should not take us long to drive to Wyoming and and locate Mr. Dembray."

Haitham was impressed that Santos had suspected he would be involved until Dembray was located. "Once you have located Dembray and done a distant casing of his cabin, I want you to clear out. If at all possible, do not let him get a good look at you. That is critical. Dream up a good cover story for being in Wyoming at this time of the year. I also want the two of you to find a nearby town or city where we can assemble a team of six or seven people without raising local suspicions."

Santos was thoughtful. He had more experience in the United States than all of the rest of Haitham's team. "Can I assume that we have an unlimited budget?"

Haitham faced crinkled into a smile. "I do not think we have any money problems. Mustafa transferred fifty thousand dollars to an account established by the Embassy. Zaki is the only one that can draw from the account."

"Zaki Sa'duni is here in Ottawa?" Santos asked.

"Yes, he wants to see you and me before you depart to make some of the necessary preparations. I can tell you he is anxious to get his hands on Dembray."

Santos was incredulous, "Have you all thought this through? I think it is insane to believe that we can kidnap a professional like Dembray and somehow drag him to Baghdad. Our best bet is to kill him and get the hell out." Santos' voice rose as he spoke. Before Haitham could question him he continued, "Our chances of taking him alive are slim. Even if we do get

269

him alive, we will be several hundred miles inside the United States. Look at the map. Even if we get him across the border into Canada, we still have the problem of somehow smuggling him out of Canada. I say we kill him as quickly as possible and get it over with."

Haitham realized he couldn't argue Santos' point. "I do not disagree with you. I think we can probably bring Zaki around to the same way of thinking, but, and it is a big but, we must try to capture Dembray. If we do capture him, we can at least question him for a couple of hours. If we have something to show for our efforts, it will help us to make the case that there was no way to smuggle him out of Canada on to Baghdad."

Santos did not seem to be too pleased with Haitham's comments, "Perhaps. I just think it is going to be pure shit luck to capture a well-armed professional alive. But I'll leave the convincing of Zaki to you. If I know Zaki, he will want to give it the old college try."

--->==◉ ◉==<---

Pine Springs. October 22, 1982.

Alain put a new clip in his Browning automatic. He looked at his stopwatch and began firing at a standard upper body target from a distance of forty-five feet. He squeezed off the eight rounds in the clip, then looked at his stopwatch. He noted that he had gotten off the eight rounds in forty-six seconds. *Not bad,* he thought to himself. He walked to the target and saw that only one round was out of the black. He thought that was probably good enough for today. He had started firing at twenty-five feet, fired eight rounds, then moved back five yards at a time and fired eight more rounds at each stop. He tried to get off each of the eight rounds within fifty seconds.

He had sighted in his Winchester Model 70 earlier in the day. He chose to sight it in using a four-power scope at a hundred and fifty yards. After pacing off the one hundred and fifty yards and shooting, he was pleased with the very tight pattern of his five shots. It was unlikely there would be any long distance shooting if the Iraqis actually came after him, but he wanted to be ready. He decided to use 150-grain bullets since accuracy was more important than stopping power;

after all, he wasn't going to be shooting at bears. There had been enough rounds fired for one day. He took the guns into the cabin to clean them later.

He was fairly sure the Iraqis would try something. If the responsibility was in the hands of the Iraqi General Intelligence Directorate, he assumed that someone would be sent in to case his cabin. It could take them time just to locate the cabin. The easiest way would be for them to hang around Pine Springs and follow him. He decided that when he did go to town to load up on supplies he would go very early in the morning. He would take a round about route driving back to his cabin.

He took some fine white thread that he had bought out of his pocket. Since his cabin was the last one on the dirt road, he decided to put a few traps along the road. He walked down the dirt road until he was within a hundred yards of Ed's cabin. He tied one end of the thread to a tree alongside the road. He then walked to the other side of the road and tied the other end to a tree at a height of about three feet off the ground. At three feet, any passing vehicle or someone on foot would break the thread. Given the chilly weather, someone breaking the thread might not even notice it. Alain had difficulty making it out at a distance of ten feet. He would check the thread early the next morning when he drove to town to lay in some additional supplies. He walked back towards his cabin and, using the thread, set a total of six traps in a large semicircle at an average distance of two hundred yards from his cabin. He hoped for some snow since footprints would be easy to spot. The most recent snow had not amounted to much and had all but disappeared. The ground was beginning to freeze and, after a few more cold nights, would be as solid as a rock. He would have to pray for snow.

He also had some heavy, black cotton material from the store that sold sewing supplies. The woman who sold the material had given him a quizzical look, but hadn't said anything. He planned to cover the windows in the living room and the kitchen during the evening hours when he had lights on in the cabin. He made an arrangement with some finish nails to easily cover the windows and then remove them.

There was one issue that gave him some concern. He had considered talking to what passed for the local police in Pine Springs, but decided there was no way he could enlist their help without raising questions he could not answer.

He started to walk back to his cabin but stopped to watch the sun set in the distance. The forest this far up was mainly pines which pretty much eliminated any underbrush. He thought that if he had to shoot at someone, he would have good visibility. He looked at his watch and saw that it was just about time for a martini. With the setting of the sun, it got dark fast at this time of the year in the mountains.

--->==◉ ◉==<---

October 23, 1982.

Alain got up early in the morning. Despite eating a large steak the previous evening, he fixed himself ham and eggs, drank two cups of coffee, and set off for Pine Springs at seven o'clock. He stopped before he reached the thread trap. It was intact. He would re-trap the dirt road when he returned from town. In Pine Springs, he loaded up on supplies. Ed had built him a cold shed outside the rear door of his cabin to keep things cool in summer. At this time of the year, it served as a good freezer because no sun hit the shed. It was well built. Ed had bolted it onto a prefab concrete slab so that a bear, human or real, could not haul it away. The shed was about three and a half feet high and it consisted of a heavy gauge plastic insert that fit snugly inside a very well made box of thick oak. There was a plastic cover over the insert and the top was also made of oak. It was hinged and opened up. The top fastened securely with a hasp and padlock. Alain locked it when full. Ed had sworn that the shed was bear proof. So far, Ed's guarantee had held up despite at least two attempts by bears.

--->==◉ ◉==<---

Pine Springs. October 26, 1982.

"Rashid, this has got to be quick. We locate Dembray and get the hell out of here before anyone gets curious about what two foreign looking men are doing in Pine Springs." Ramon Santos emphasized his point to Lt. Rashid Walidi by gesticulating with his fork. They were having breakfast in a small restaurant on the main street in Pine Springs. They had arrived late last night and managed to get rooms in a motel just outside of town. Santos had slept well and Walidi told him that he fell asleep as soon as he got in bed. Santos, who had stopped talking to eat some of his pancakes, looked at Walidi and said, "Rashid, I want to be done and out of here today."

"Fine," Walidi answered without much conviction. "What do we do first?"

"That's easy, we locate Dembray's cabin. Hopefully without him noticing us. I talked to the manager of the motel this morning. I asked him about Dembray's property using the general description that was in one of his credit reports. I told him it was my understanding that the owner of the property wanted to sell it or another property he owned." Santos paused to make sure that Walidi understood.

"Hopefully, he gave you something to go on."

"He was very obliging. He told me Dembray's property was at the end of a dirt road that led north off the main road about three miles east of Pine Springs. The manager had never been to that location, but was pretty certain Dembray's cabin was off the main road at the end of that dirt road."

"What do we do first?" Walidi wasn't going to suggest anything. He knew that Santos was a favorite of Zaki Sa'duni.

"Why, Rashid, we take a long walk." With that, Santos got out of his chair and, motioning to Walidi, said, "Let's go. We will drive through town, locate the dirt road, and find a place to park."

"There are bound to be other cabins besides Dembray's. How do we avoid them?"

Santos looked at Walidi as if to ask him what kind of training he had received from the General Directorate of Intelligence. He decided to be kind. "We will go off road into the pine forests and hope they don't notice us. I hope that today's trip to Dembray's cabin will be the only one we must make, so let's be thorough."

Santos paid the cashier. They left the restaurant and got into their rented sedan. Santos drove through town. He was not sure that Walidi was the best choice for the job. It seemed to take him a long time to comprehend things. He wondered why Zaki thought so highly of him. In Ottawa, Santos had to tell him to turn over anything that would identify him as an Iraqi to Haitham Abd al-Nebi. *Well, you work with what you're given*, Santos figured. If they only spent one night in

Pine Springs, they shouldn't raise too many suspicions among the locals. He also thought the Utah license plates on their car would help if they were questioned by anyone. He steered through the rest of Pine Springs. When they left the town behind, he told Walidi to concentrate on looking for a dirt road that would lead off on his side of the road. They had gone almost three miles when Walidi said, "Here it is."

"Good, let's find a parking place and see what we can see." Santos drove about a mile farther down the main road, pulled off on the side close to a house, and parked. He opened a small athletic bag, extracted a pair of binoculars, pulled out a camera, and handed that to Walidi.

"Do you know how to use one of these?"

"Of course," Walidi replied, somewhat miffed.

"Good, the camera is loaded. Here is an extra role of film. Take pictures of everything. Once the films are developed, we can sort out what will be of use to us when we go after Dembray." As they began walking back to the dirt road, Santos asked Walidi, "Rashid, what do you think of our chances of actually kidnapping Dembray?"

Walidi shrugged his shoulders as he answered, "Our orders are to kidnap him and bring him back to Baghdad."

"Let me put that another way, Rashid. What are the obstacles to kidnapping Dembray, smuggling him several hundred miles to the Canadian border, taking him across, hauling him to some airport, getting him onto a plane, and flying him to Baghdad? This presumes that somehow we can charter an airplane that could fly nonstop to Baghdad. The only other way would be to smuggle him aboard an Iraqi ship. Do you have any idea how often an Iraqi ship calls at a Canadian Port?"

"It would appear to be next to impossible."

"Bravo, Rashid. Fortunately, it is not our worry. Our worry is not to be spotted by Dembray."

Walidi looked at Santos and frowned. "I understand why we must not be spotted, but why is it a worry for Zaki?"

The question confirmed Santos' concerns about Walidi's training and experience in the intelligence business. "In the first place, if Dembray spots us, Zaki would not allow either of us to return. This would leave him short handed. As a senior intelligence officer, he must assume that Dembray is now forewarned; he needs all the manpower he can field. When we return to try and capture this Dembray, we two will probably play roles where Dembray will not get a chance to see us until it is too late for him. Spotting us again after a few days would only serve to alert Dembray and possibly give him a chance to escape. This is something Zaki wouldn't want."

"But Zaki seems hell bent on capturing him alive."

Santos' smile held no mirth. "Sure, he wants him alive. He wants to get additional information out of him. Zaki is too smart to think he has any chance of bringing Dembray back to Baghdad. In short, our goal here is to come up with enough information for Zaki so he can come up with a plan to get our hands on a live Dembray."

They continued walking in silence until they reached the point where the dirt road turned north off the main road. Santos held out his arm to stop Walidi from heading off on the dirt road. "Wait until there are no cars visible in either direction." There were five mailboxes on the right side of the dirt road. Santos pulled a notebook out of his pocket and wrote down the names on the mailboxes. He also made a note about a cabin on the opposite side of the dirt road.

"Okay, no one's coming. Let's go," Santos said as he started walking up the left side of the dirt road. "Try to stay just off the road where there is some growth. We don't want to make it easy to spot our foot prints. I want you to take plenty of pictures. Photograph anything that will help us describe the road up to Dembray's house - the other houses, landmarks like large boulders or anything exceptional. If Dembray is in his cabin, he may come outside. I don't plan to get too close to the cabin unless there is good concealment. The camera has a zoom lens so, if Dembray comes out of the cabin for anything, try and get a couple of shots of him."

After walking about seventy-five yards, they came to a side road that led to a cabin about seventy yards back in the woods. Wisps of smoke rose from the single chimney. Santos made some notes. There was a small wooden sign that had one word on it, Swenson, matching a name back on one of the mailboxes. They continued about half a mile until they came to another side road with a cabin about fifty yards back. There was a Ford pickup parked to one side of the cabin. Santos made additional notes. Using his binoculars, he included the license number of the Ford pickup.

"Funny, Rashid, we have come well over a half of a mile and found two cabins on the west side of the road, but none on the east side. This may be a big help to the team Zaki uses to attempt to capture Dembray."

They walked almost a mile before they came to another short dirt road that led to a small cabin not far from the road. Since there was no smoke coming from the chimney, or any vehicles parked by the cabin, Santos walked to the cabin and looked around, inside and out. When he returned to where Walidi was standing, he began making notes.

"It looks like this cabin is only used in the summer time, there is no sign of life. The generator behind the cabin is cold and the fuel tank is almost empty. This helps the cause. Remind me to check out the first cabin again. I didn't see any vehicles around it, but there was some smoke coming from the chimney."

"Good idea." Walidi hesitated before adding, "I don't want to offend you, but since this cabin is deserted, maybe it could be used as a command post for the team that makes the attempt against Dembray."

"Good thinking, Rashid, that might work out. My only concern would be that it is very close to the road. According to the mailboxes, there are two more cabins on this road. Let's see what we can see."

They walked quietly until they came to the fourth cabin. In the distance, well back from the dirt road, they could see a fairly sizable cabin. A sign on a tree leading to the house read "The Wilsons." Santos noted a man, a woman, and at least one child. It looked like they were packing up to leave. They were bringing bundles out of the cabin and putting them in the back of a Jeep and the trunk of a large car that looked like a Buick. He decided to move on quickly and see if they were still there on the way back. He made notes as they walked. When he finished writing, Santos said to Walidi, "Well, Rashid, it looks like our friend, Dembray, is the last stop on the line."

"Yeah, it looks like at least two of the five cabins could be deserted if the Wilsons are really leaving. What will help Zaki is that the first two cabins are relatively close to the main road. There is a very good chance that we will have some uninhabited area between Dembray's cabin and those first two cabins."

Santos wondered whether to congratulate Walidi on his powers of deduction. Since he couldn't do it and keep a straight face, he decided to change the subject. "We will have a problem. If there is shooting, there may be only one way out. We will check as we leave."

They walked until they could see a cabin in the distance. Santos calculated that it was two hundred yards from them. There was smoke coming out of the chimney. A Jeep was parked alongside the cabin.

Santos motioned to Walidi, "Rashid, I want you to make an arc through the woods keeping about this distance between you and the cabin. As you move along the arc, take pictures. I want you to memorize what you see. We must know if there is a door at the back of the cabin - please note windows, everything. Most important, see if the dirt road ends at Dembray's cabin. I also want some idea of what lies beyond there. I'm going to circle in the other direction to get a good look at the front of the cabin. Let's meet back here in no more than twenty-five minutes."

As they were about to set out, Alain came out of the cabin. Walidi took several pictures of him as he went to the Jeep and retrieved some articles. When Dembray reentered the cabin, Santos signaled Walidi to move out.

The land broke off fairly steeply at a point about fifty yards from the front of Dembray's cabin so Santos was forced to stay closer to the cabin. When he was directly in front, he took a Minox out of his jacket pocket and began taking pictures. He even got a glimpse of Dembray through one of the front windows of the cabin. He looked at his watch and decided it was time to circle back. He stumbled slightly and, as his head moved lower, thought he noticed something. As he looked closely at the space between two trees, he saw a thread was tied between them at a height of about three feet. The ingenuity of the trap made him smile. He assumed Dembray had set a number of them. Walidi had probably sprung at least one. When they arrived back at the meeting site on the south side of the road, Santos asked him if he had taken many pictures.

Walidi smiled, "Yes, and I even got two more of Dembray. He came out the back door, opened a large chest, and took out something wrapped in butcher paper."

"Good work, Rashid. Let's head back. You stay on this side, just off the road, and I will be on the other side. I want you to look for thread tied to a tree on your side that spans the road to a tree on my side. I discovered a trap like that when I circled around in front of Dembray's house. It would appear that Dembray is both a good operations officer and a very smart one. Let's start back."

They walked along at a slow pace. The Jeep and the car were still parked by the fourth cabin. They discovered nothing until they reached a point about a hundred yards east of the second house. It was Walidi who spotted the thread. Santos made a note of the height and its location with respect to the second house. Walking off the road had allowed them to miss the traps on the way to Dembray's. Santos still worried that perhaps Walidi may have sprung one.

"Okay, Rashid, let's get back to the motel, pack up, and head for Salt Lake City. I'm sure Zaki will want to do something as soon as possible, since they are expecting snow here soon. I want you to drive while I make some notes."

Walidi nodded his approval. He wondered if either of them would be involved in the actual operation. He thought Santos' comment that Zaki would not want to take any chances by involving them in the actual operation was a little far fetched.

Ottawa. October 28, 1982.

"I suggest that we go in, we do the operation, and clear the area as soon as we have done our job. I don't think that we can chance any additional casing. Dembray is obviously aware that he is in danger. The best schedule would be to have the operational team arrive the same evening, do the operation the following morning, and all be on their way by noon of the same day."

Ramon Santos looked around at the small group that had been studying the map he had drawn. They had listened to him as he explained his notations on the map and how he thought they should mount the operation. Everyone silently nodded in approval.

He continued, "If we arrive in the evening we can use the excuse that we are stopping for the night, then going on the following day."

"I agree. Are you absolutely certain that, after the operation, there is no other way out to the main road but the dirt road?" Zaki Sa'duni questioned Santos.

"Yes, we both got a look at what lies beyond Dembray's cabin. The dirt road definitely ends at his place. The land beyond the cabin rises rapidly and is rugged. I saw no signs of even a trail. What about you, Rashid?"

Rashid Walidi nodded as he looked at the map Santos had drawn. He was amazed at how accurate it appeared to him. Santos had also made detailed notes, some of which Walidi couldn't even remember. He pointed at a spot on the map.

"I agree. I actually walked a little beyond Dembray's cabin to get a look at the far side of the cabin and to check for any windows. There is nothing beyond the cabin that indicates there is a way out in that direction. In short, the only way out for a vehicle is on the dirt road. I would suggest that, if we go on foot, we go on a route about fifty yards east of the dirt road. Since the forest is pine, there is little underbrush."

Santos caught the use of "we" by Walidi. Had Zaki told him that he would be involved in the actual operation? Santos thought of raising the question of who would be involved but decided that now was not the time. Instead, he nodded at Walidi and then turned his attention to Zaki.

"Rashid's comment is critical to this operation. For some reason there are no cabins on the east side of the dirt road. I assume that the forest there is owned by the government. I suggest that you send a single man to determine if Dembray is in the cabin. His Jeep, parked by the cabin, will indicate that he is there. If it isn't parked by the cabin, then he is probably in town. What I'm suggesting is that we have to consider two possible operations: one if he is in the cabin, and one if he is not."

Both Haitham and Zaki looked at each other as they considered what Santos had said. Finally, Haitham said speculatively, "Since you were there, and know the lay of the land, why don't you detail the possibilities for us, then we can discuss them and do some planning."

Zaki nodded, the movement of his flaccid jowls emphasized his agreement. "Ramon, you mentioned snow. I suspect that if we are going to mount this operation we had better get started immediately, like tomorrow."

Santos smiled, "You have my agreement on that, Zaki. The prediction was for four to six inches of snow to fall yesterday. I don't know if this actually took place, but at this time of the year, at that altitude, we may be dealing with snow. Our best chance of capturing Dembray alive will be if he is in town for some reason and we can ambush him on his way back to the cabin." Santos gestured toward the map.

"At the moment, we can only confirm that these two cabins on the dirt road are occupied." Santos pointed to cabin number one with the smoke and to Dembray's place. "At the fourth cabin, where the family was packing up, there is a sharp bend in the road to avoid a huge pine tree. This would be an ideal point to take Dembray if he is returning from town. We could pile logs in the road to force him to stop. There are plenty lying around in the woods." Santos stopped to let what he had said sink in.

Zaki rubbed his chin, "Yes, let's keep it simple. We can't hang around. We must do what we are there for and get the hell out. If he is in the cabin, we take him in the cabin. If he is in town, we take him on his way back at the spot Santos has described."

"Pine Springs is a small town. There is no way we can stay in the area without arousing suspicion. I agree that we move quickly. My only concern is that I don't think our chances of taking him alive are very good. Considering the way his partner in crime was killed, he knows we are after him. This is reflected by the traps he set to determine if his cabin is under surveillance," Santos added.

Zaki was decisive, "Okay, we will do whatever is possible. Now, let's talk about assignments. Since Walidi already knows the lay of the land, he will be the one who goes in to determine if Dembray is in his cabin. Question, how close must he get to the cabin to determine if Dembray is there?"

"The dirt road ends near his cabin. The cabin can be seen from around a quarter of a mile away. If the Jeep is there, he is in the cabin," Santos answered before Walidi could say anything.

Zaki had a deep appreciation of Santos as an operation officer. He smiled at him and said, "Outline the operation in what you consider the simplest way to mount it."

Santos took a deep breath. "The third cabin is deserted for the winter. It is also set way back from the dirt road. I say we set up a command post in that cabin. It should be easy to break in. We can even leave some money with a thank you note. We should get there early and set up a watch on the road. Walidi will case the cabin and return to the command post. It will take a little less than half an hour for him to hike to where he can see the cabin and return to the command post. If Dembray is there, the hit team will head for the cabin on foot. Walidi will lead them on the east side of the dirt road, far enough from the road that they can take cover." Santos paused to ask Zaki, "How many, and who, will be in the hit team?"

"Since I am not very agile, I will stay in the command post. In addition to you, Walidi and Haitham, we have Sa'id, Anwar and Isma'il. These three, like Walidi, are all specially trained. Incidentally, at the moment they know nothing about this operation."

"That's six people. I think that's enough," Santos said, with little enthusiasm.

Zaki noted Santos' expression with a grim smile. He thought to himself that maybe the soft life had gotten to him. "I have arranged to have a vehicle stolen. The vehicle is one of those off road machines that Americans like so much. It has been repainted and the license plates have been changed. It can easily carry everyone in the operation. It is now parked in a garage in Denver awaiting instructions. The vehicle will be equipped with four assault weapons, an H&K machine pistol, a couple of Browning 9mm automatics, plus a rifle and a grenade launcher."

"Do the weapons all have silencers?" Santos queried Zaki.

"All but the grenade launcher," Zaki smiled at Santos.

"Any tear gas grenades included?"

Zaki smiled at his focus on the task. "Glad you asked. Yes, but only tear gas. Any kind of explosion might attract attention. Gunfire, I gather, must be a common occurrence out there in the Wild West. Anyway, perhaps the only shots anyone will hear will be those fired by Dembray. What we must do now is focus on timing. The key issue now is how soon we can assemble the team in Pine Springs."

Santos looked at his watch. "It's just about ten o'clock. Let's get on the phone and see how soon we can get out of here. If we can get everyone on flights this afternoon or evening, we should be able to hit the road to Pine Springs early tomorrow morning. Let's assume we can do the operation early in the morning of October thirtieth, or the thirty-first at the latest. Haitham, please get someone looking into what flights are available. Salt Lake City is the closest major airport. Three of the team can fly into Salt Lake City. I know there is a flight sometime in the afternoon, but I'm not sure it flies everyday."

"I'll go and have someone check on available flights and get right back to you. Three might have to go to Denver, but I will also check for a flight to any city in Wyoming," Haitham said as he got up and walked quickly out of the room.

Santos wanted to continue with some planning. He decided to get them focused on the operation. He spoke with authority. "Look, we are going to use two teams in the operation, three men in each team. Let's form the teams now. Since Walidi and I have both been there and cased Dembray's cabin, I will lead one team and Walidi the other. Zaki, can Walidi go to Denver with his team and meet up with your man?"

Zaki thought for a minute. "I think that is a good idea. My man is in place now. If Walidi takes the first available flight to Denver, I will have my man meet him at the airport. He has the four-wheel drive vehicle, a Suburban. It was stolen in Kentucky and, as I said before, it has been repainted and now has New York license plates on it. Once we are finished, the team can drive the vehicle back to Denver and leave it in a parking lot. I suggest leaving the keys in the vehicle. The weapons will also be in there. Maybe some idiot will steal it. The police will never believe his story. Walidi, make sure all members of your team wear gloves when in the vehicle and when handling the weapons. The police will discover no fingerprints except those of the owner and others who were in the vehicle. I assume all of them will have good alibis if questioned by the police."

"Good," Santos beamed. He looked at Walidi. "Rashid, you take Sa'id and Anwar with you. You can take delivery of the vehicle and then drive from Denver to Pine Springs. Stay at the Moonlight Motel, the one we stayed in on the outskirts of Pine Springs. Haitham and Ismail will stay with me at the Best Western in town. We will come up with a contact plan after we know about flights."

Walidi nodded his satisfaction. "From the map we may be able to do it in one day."

"It will be a push, and you will have to obey all the speed limits. Getting stopped by a cop could be big trouble." Santos had a fine edge to his voice. "It's about three hundred miles from Cheyenne to Pine Springs. All told, it's a little less than four hundred miles all the way from Denver."

They were interrupted by Haitham's return. He was studying some penciled notes he had made. He spoke as soon as he entered the room, "There is a flight to Denver late this afternoon which gets in a little after seven o'clock mountain time. The best I can do to Salt Lake City is a flight that gets there after ten tonight."

"That is perfect. It means we can spend the night in Denver and Salt Lake City tonight, then all be on our way to Pine Springs early tomorrow morning." Zaki beamed as he spoke, "I will join the team going to Denver. My man will meet us there. We will stay in the motel you have indicated once we are in Pine Springs. Santos, tomorrow night, you and Haitham can come to our motel to finalize plans for the operation. Haitham, when we are done here, you will go and get confirmed reservations: four for Denver, and three for Salt Lake City."

Santos sat rubbing his chin in thought before speaking, "One thing we have not yet considered. What do we do with Dembray's body, or possibly bodies? We may have casualties."

Zaki looked at Walidi and Haitham, "Good point. Let's not make things easy for the opposition. Do you have anything in mind, Ramon?"

"If Dembray is the only body, we can bury him in the snow. It will be days or even weeks before anyone finds him. The problem could be if we have casualties.

We don't want the authorities to find an Arab body. I suggest we be prepared to burn the cabin if we have casualties."

Haitham's expression clearly questioned the proposal. "A fire is certainly going to attract attention."

Santos didn't respond to Haitham's point. Instead, he asked Zaki, "Can your man in Denver come up with an electric timer and a couple of blasting caps? I would want at least a four-hour delay. If we can set the timer for up to ten hours, it would be better. Dembray has a generator. That means he must have gasoline or diesel fuel."

"My man is an expert on explosives. I'll call him and tell him to either buy a timer or rig one with a delay that can be set for up to ten hours."

Santos smiled, "Relax, gentlemen. This is just for contingency purposes."

--➤● ●◀--

CIA HQS. October 28, 1982. 1500 hours.

The three men were huddled in the office of the Chief of Counter Intelligence, Reginald Smythe. The Chief/CI was obviously discomfited. He looked at the other two men in his office, Everette O'Brien, the Chief of the European Division and Sam Clauson, the Chief of the Near East Division.

"You mean to tell me that the Directorate of Operations has come up with zilch on the murder of Samara'i? Come on gentlemen, you must have come up with something, no matter how thin."

Sam looked at O'Brien and said, "I'll answer that. We have, as you know, received several cables outlining various operations Samara'i was involved in that would certainly have upset the Iraqis."

"Yes, but such operational activity does not meet the threshold of assassination," Smythe answered him, his face wreathed in a furrowed frown.

Clauson rubbed the stubble on his chin, his expression reflecting deep thought. "Yes, Reggie, but that might not be how the Iraqis read thresholds. One thing has occurred to me that might be worth considering."

"Like what?" Smythe barked out.

"It's almost as if Saddam was sending us a message. Our problem is to figure out what we did or are doing that has upset him so much. The Iraqis, for some reason, concluded that Samara'i was involved. That is why he was tortured and killed executioner style."

You could almost see the light bulb go on over Smythe's head. "That's a good point. We did get a note from Jane Brophy that her ex-husband had been in Germany at the same time as Samara'i. They obviously knew each other. Why don't you two question her and then have a shot at her ex-husband. Also, do some research on any Iraqi operations that the two of them may have worked on together. Okay, let's get to work."

Not long afterwards, Jane entered O'Brien's office. He had called her and asked if she could stop by his office. She was confused that he would ask her to come see him.

"Thanks for coming by, Ms. Brophy. Have a seat."

Jane sat down gingerly. She was very curious as to why the Chief of the European Division in the Directorate of Operations would ask to see an analyst in the Directorate of Intelligence. She mumbled a thank you and sat down.

"Ms. Brophy, it is my understanding that you were married to Alain Dembray."

"Yes, Mr. O'Brien. We divorced several years ago. I was Alain's second wife."

"Ms. Brophy, I know you have heard about the rather gruesome death of Hashem Samara'i. Did you know him by any chance?"

"No, I don't think I ever met him. I knew of him because Alain had mentioned him to me a couple of times when we were married."

O'Brien considered her answer before asking, "Were Alain and Hashem on friendly terms?"

Jane answered, "I don't think so. Alain never spoke favorably of Mr. Samara'i."

"We have looked at the past assignments of Alain and Samara'i. As far as we can tell, they were never involved in the same operation. They were, however, both assigned to Germany at the same time in 1973 and 1974. I take it from your previous comment that they were not on friendly terms."

"I was married to Alain at that time and I don't ever recall having been at a social function that included Mr. Samara'i. The only thing I recall is that Alain mentioned him to me several times. He said that Samara'i had screwed up an operation against the Iraqis. Alain had a low opinion of Mr. Samara'i's skill as an operations officer."

O'Brien nodded and smiled wryly, "That seems to be an opinion shared by many ops officers. We are taking a hard look at Iraqi operations that Hashem was involved in over the years. I don't mean to pry, Ms. Brophy, but are you and Alain on good terms?"

"Yes, we are on far better terms now that we are divorced than we ever were when we were married. We see each other for dinner once or twice a month and go to shows together."

O'Brien returned her smile. He knew several couples that would be better off divorced. "I tried to call Alain but there was no answer. Do you have any idea where he is?"

"Yes, he is in Wyoming. He has a cabin there that he has spent a lot of money upgrading. He loves the place. It is beautiful, but I am a city girl. I would get bored with it after a few days. He'll probably stay there until the snow gets deep, then come back here for the winter."

O'Brien opened his desk drawer and pulled out a piece of paper. "The FBI has obtained the phone records of Samara'i. He called Alain once last June. It was a very short call, less than a minute. Did Alain ever mention Samara'i's call?"

"No, I don't recall him ever mentioning it."

O'Brien frowned, but continued, "One last question, Ms. Brophy. You had said that Alain was in Germany just prior to the murder of Samara'i. Did he, by any chance, see Samara'i or know why Samara'i was in Germany?"

"Not that I know. Alain was not away long. He was doing some work on a book he is writing about some failed operation. In fact, I called him when I got the news about Samara'i's murder. He was surprised since it hadn't hit the press yet."

"Is there any way we can get in touch with him? I would like to hear his opinion on why the Iraqis decided to waste Hashem."

Jane thought about a few ways, but there was no direct way. "He has a mailbox on the main road if you want to send him a letter. You could try calling one of the establishments he visits when he is in town, but that might take several days since he doesn't go into Pine Springs that often. I usually leave messages for him at the Mountaineer, a bar in the middle of town."

"Well, thanks for your input, Ms. Brophy," O'Brien said, as he got up from his chair and shook hands with Jane.

Jane mumbled something in return. As she left O'Brien's office, she wondered why he had asked so many questions about Alain. She couldn't help wondering if he was in danger.

O'Brien immediately followed up with a reporting to the Chief.

"That's all I got out of Jane, Reggie. She said that Alain spent a lot of time in his Wyoming cabin and was almost always there at this time of the year to close it up for the winter."

Chief Reginald Smythe was momentarily lost in thought. "Our problem, gentlemen, is that Dembray is the only person we have not interviewed who may have some information on Samara'i. We know from the phone records that Samara'i did call him once. Unfortunately, there is no record that Dembray ever returned his call. The call may not be important because according to Samara'i's phone records he called several retired officers during the same time frame. I have called some of them and they all said that Samara'i had called them asking for help and ideas in finding gainful employment. Let's send someone from the closest office we have to Dembray's location. Questioning Alain is our last hope. Every time the director asks me about this case, I feel embarrassed. Let's focus on Dembray and hope he can give us a lead. What's our closest office to his cabin?"

"That would be Salt Lake City, Reggie," Sam answered.

"Good. Get a message to whoever is in charge there. Tell him to go to Pine Springs ASAP and question Dembray. I've got to go to a meeting. Let me know as soon as you find out something," Smythe ordered as he left the office.

Everette volunteered, "I'll send the message to Salt Lake City, Sam. Fred Grant is there and I know him pretty well."

"Okay, Everette, I hope Grant comes up with something." Sam paused in deep thought, then said, "How about finding out when both men arrived in Germany and when Dembray left. If they arrived at roughly the same time, I'll be very suspicious."

"That's not a bad idea, Sam. I'll get the German Station on it. Let's hope we can come up with something before our next meeting with Reggie."

Pine Springs. October 28, 1982. 1600 hours.

Alain was checking on his traps. He looked at the sky and decided to hurry, it got dark fairly early at this time of the year. He was now concerned. The one trap that was blown on the twenty-sixth was on the south side of the road. What concerned him was that he had been able to make out several footprints, one right between the two trees he had used to set the trap. This was a clear indication that a human type animal had blown the trap. His conclusion had been reinforced when he also found footprints on the north side of the road. Since that one blown trap, no others had been blown. Yesterday's four inches of snow had been undisturbed by any human footprints, his being the only exception. He had seen some deer tracks back in the woods on the south side of the dirt road, but no others. He decided that there was a good chance someone had cased his cabin on the day the trap was blown.

As he walked back to his cabin, he looked up at the top ridge of the Wind River Range. He could see Mt. Baldy. It was bathed in sunlight while he was in shadows. When he was inside the cabin, he locked the front and back doors. His Browning 9mm was with him at all times. The shotgun, loaded with five double ought buckshot cartridges, was placed to the right of the front door. He checked his rifle, loaded it with 150-grain rounds, and set it by the back door. Checking both the back and front of the cabin every half hour became a discipline. He decided to get up at first light, do a reconnaissance of the vicinity, and then check out everything down to Ed and Emma's cabin. He thought of talking to Ed and asking him to be alert to anyone coming along the dirt road. He mulled it over for a while but thought he had better not say anything. He checked his watch and decided on an early martini.

Pine Springs. October 29, 1982. 2100 hours.

Zaki, Walidi, Haitham and Santos were making final plans in Zaki's room. After arriving in Pine Springs, Santos and Haitham had made their way to the Moonlight Motel. They had discussed whether to do the operation on the following day or to wait until the thirty-first. Finally, Santos spoke with some heat in his voice.

"We must do this tomorrow morning and then get the hell out of here. They are expecting at least a foot of snow on the thirty-first. We can't chance being snowbound here. We must put as much distance between Pine Springs and us before any investigation is mounted. Once the word gets out that Dembray has been murdered, Pine Springs will be flooded with federal agents."

While Santos spoke, Zaki looked at him with a curious expression on this face. Zaki wondered if Santos was slipping, he seemed awfully worried. Zaki questioned him, "Why are you so concerned? This place looks like the Kurdish mountains. This small town doesn't even have a traffic light."

Santos frowned at Zaki. Pine Springs may have looked like Kurdistan but the resemblance ended with looks. "Zaki, we have already executed one CIA officer. Even if we are able to take Dembray alive, I assume that we will get out of him what we want and then kill him. I can guarantee you that when they find Dembray's dead body, Pine Springs will be crawling with FBI agents. It is in our best interests to get this over with and get the hell out of here. All of you should get back to Canada as soon as possible, then leave for Europe. I will stay in the States. I'll pick up a rental car in Salt Lake City and drive to Chicago where I have some business." No one responded. Santos thought they looked like animals that had heard a noise and were all staring blankly at the source.

"Okay, we do it early tomorrow," Zaki said, shrugging his shoulders.

Santos nodded in satisfaction. "Let's work out the details for the morning. Haitham came up with a good outline earlier. Why don't you fill us in, Haitham?"

Haitham looked at Walidi. "I want you to rub some mud on the license plates. If you can, drive through some wet snow and mud to get the Suburban splattered with it." Walidi nodded his head as Haitham continued, "First light must be around seven here. Santos, Isma'il and myself will be in the Best Western parking lot at seven o'clock tomorrow morning. Plan to pull into the lot a couple of minutes after seven, but no sooner, to make sure we are all there. We will be waiting in a clear area. After we get in the Suburban, we will leave immediately. Hopefully, no one will pay much attention to us. We will drive to the vacant cabin which is a little over a mile from Dembray's cabin. Walidi will immediately head for Dembray's cabin while the rest of us break out the weapons. Question, what do we do if we run into Dembray driving out on the dirt road?"

"For God's sake, Haitham, let's just hope and pray it doesn't happen. We'll either take him alive or kill him on the spot," Zaki said. He thought about it, then added with a sigh, "I guess it depends on where on the dirt road we run into him."

Santos scratched the back of his neck, smiled, and said, "This is either going to be the worst day of Dembray's life or the luckiest."

Walidi sat silently listening to the exchange. *What should they do, slash his tires? No, that would be a dead give away.* He got what he thought was a bright idea. "Two of us could go in first and put logs across the road. Two of us could carry logs that Dembray couldn't handle himself. Santos, you could pull the Suburban off the road and wait twenty minutes. If Dembray doesn't show up, you can drive in and we'll meet you at the cabin."

Zaki was getting impatient and it showed on his face. "*Bismullah.* Will you stop making this operation complicated? It is a simple operation. We want to get our hands on him alive, if possible. If not, we want him dead. Now, let's make it as simple as possible. Tomorrow morning, we will drive to the empty cabin. If we do meet him on the road, we will take him. In the name of God, we outnumber him seven to one. If we don't meet him on the road, we get to the empty cabin. It will be our command post. Walidi will leave immediately to check on Dembray's cabin. It should only take about twenty minutes for him to get close enough to the cabin to determine if Dembray is in it and return to the command post. Once we know that Dembray is there, the two teams will take up their positions. Walidi, Sa'id and Anwar will leave the Command Post and move quickly and silently on the west side of the road to a position to the rear of Dembray's cabin. Walidi, it is important that you stay out of sight. Santos, Haitham and Isma'il will head for the cabin on the east side of road, keeping out of sight, and take their positions in front of the cabin." Zaki looked around at his assembled team, his demeanor clearly indicating that he had much more to say.

"Sa'id is our best man with the RPG. At a given time, someone on Santos' team will fire a shot into the front windows of Dembray's cabin using an un-silenced weapon. The noise will be a signal to Sa'id to fire a tear gas grenade through a cabin rear window. Isma'il, who will have gotten as close to the cab-in as possible without being seen by Dembray, will rush the front door. When shooting at Dembray, go for the legs or shoulders. If we wound him and over-power him, we should be able to keep him alive long enough for us to question him. Since we all will have silenced weapons, the only shots that will be heard will be the first shot fired by Haitham's team, plus any shots from Dembray and the RPG. This should not raise anyone's curiosity. If there are no questions, let's get a good night's sleep."

There were no questions.

--->==© ©==<---

Salt Lake City. October 29, 1982. 2130 hours.
"Why can't you drive over to Wyoming tomorrow morning and try to get back tomorrow night? It's not a long drive. You told me you only have to ask a retired agency officer if he knows anything about the murder of another agency officer. You could go tomorrow morning, spend a couple of hours with this guy and be back here for dinner."

Fred Grant looked at his wife. He had been in the agency for twelve years and was now the agency chief in Salt Lake City. Fred was approaching forty. He was tall, but slightly stooped. His hair had thinned out and his stomach was beginning to bulge. He was a GS-13, hoping to get a promotion to GS-14 within the next two years. He didn't dislike the agency, but sometimes he thought he could have made a better choice of careers. He had met his wife while assigned to CIA HQS in Washington. They had no children and his wife, Janet, was two years younger than him. She was attractive and in good shape, something she worked on regularly. Fred sometimes wondered how she would have handled motherhood.

"Can't do it, Janet. I have appointments until about three o'clock tomorrow afternoon. After that, I'll drive over to Pine Springs and try to see this Dembray. I think I may have met him a few years ago. If I have to stay overnight, I'll leave as soon as I can Saturday morning."

Janet was less than pleased. Being married to an operations officer in the CIA was grounds for divorce. She mumbled, "So be it," and picked up a magazine.

--=◉ ◉=--

Pine Springs. October 30, 1982. 0703 hours.
Walidi saw the men as soon as he turned into the Best Western parking lot. He eased the Suburban to a stop and they immediately climbed in. As soon as they were seated, Zaki began barking out commands.

"Break out two pistols and an AK-47."

Anwar moved immediately to obey the order as the Suburban pulled out of the parking lot.

"Make sure the silencers are attached," Zaki added.

"Two Browning 9mm automatics and one AK-47, all silenced," Anwar exclaimed.

"Give the AK-47 to Haitham. You keep one Browning and give the other to Isma'il."

Zaki watched as Anwar handed the AK-47 to Haitham and one of the Brownings to Isma'il.

"If we see Dembray driving towards us, I want Walidi to keep driving until we are close. If we must deal with him on the dirt road, I want it to be as far away from the main road as possible. When I say go, Haitham, Anwar and Isma'il will jump out of the Suburban and try to take Dembray alive. If he is armed and is going to open fire, don't hesitate to fire at him, but try your best to just wound him. If we overpower him, we will take him to his cabin and interrogate him there. Everyone understand?" Zaki questioned as everyone nodded their heads in unison.

"Okay let's get to the command cabin as fast as possible, Dembray may be planning an early trip to town."

Zaki sat calmly and watched the passing scenery. The trip went quickly. They arrived at the command cabin just before seven-thirty. They unloaded the weapons, Anwar dealt with the cabin lock, and they all went inside except for Walidi. Zaki took the hunting rifle back out to him.

"Take this with you just in case. It will come in handy if this is a trap. Carrying a rifle, you will look like any other hunter. When you see if his Jeep is there, hurry back here."

Walidi smiled at Zaki, took the rifle, and headed towards the road.

→■◎ ◎■←

Alain had gotten up early and done a full circuit of the cabin. He had checked for new footprints and to see if any of his traps had been sprung. By seven o'clock he concluded that there was nothing new. All of the threads he had strung were still in place. After a spare breakfast, while drinking his second cup of coffee, he decided to check on how much gas was in the can he used to fill his generator tank. He went out the back door and picked up the five-gallon gas can which felt like it was near empty. He unscrewed the cap to the tank for the generator and emptied the gas. The tank was nearly full. He made a mental note to take the gas can to town with him the following morning.

According to the morning news, they expected snow to begin falling around noon tomorrow. Somewhere around a foot was expected. He planned to go into town the next morning, do some shopping, buy some gas, and be back home long before noon. As he turned to go back into the cabin, he thought he saw something in the pinewoods off to the west and south of the dirt road. He stared at the spot where he thought he saw movement but saw nothing further. Maybe he was getting too edgy. He went into the house and checked his rifle. He levered a round into the chamber and made sure that the safety was off. He set the rifle back in its position by the back door. He then went to the front door and made sure his shotgun was loaded with one shell in the chamber and that the safety was off. He had his Browning automatic in his shoulder holster. He turned on the television and sat down to finish his coffee.

⇥▬◉ ◉▬⇤

"He's in the cabin. I got a good look at him from where I was. He came out the back door of the cabin and emptied a gas can into the tank of a generator." Walidi had returned as fast as he could, trotting through the pinewoods. He had the rapt attention of the others.

"Any chance he saw you?" Zaki asked.

"I don't think so. I was over a hundred meters from him and his back was facing me most of the time. Right before he went back into the cabin, he did look in my general direction."

"What do you think, Santos?" Zaki asked.

"If he was concerned, I think he would have gotten a weapon and investigated." He considered the situation briefly, then continued, "I don't think it really matters one way or the other. He obviously knows we killed Samara'i. He is hiding out here, hoping we will be unable to find him. In short, he knows we are after him. I say let's get on with it and finish our job."

Zaki looked at his watch, "It is now three minutes after eight. The two teams should be in place and ready to go by eight twenty-five. I will stay here and drive to the cabin as soon as I hear anything. Remember, at eight twenty-five or as soon as possible after that time, Haitham's team on the east side of the cabin will fire an unsilenced shot through the front window of the cabin. This will be the signal for Anwar to fire the RPG through a back window. If this works, we should have a fair chance of taking him alive. I will be there with the Suburban. If we need to, we can load him into it and bring him here to answer questions." He looked at everyone and said, "Okay, go and get this *ibn alf sharameet* (son of a thousand whores)."

The six men got up in unison and left the cabin. Haitham and Santos were each carrying an AK-47. Haitham also had an unsilenced Browning 9mm to fire the signal for Anwar. Isma'il had the H&K machine pistol. They set out at a fast pace on the east side of the road. Walidi and the other two members of his team moved out and broke into double time once they crossed the road. Walidi was armed with a Browning pistol and the hunting rifle. Sa'id carried an AK-47. Anwar had the RPG-7 on his shoulder and held a bag with two tear gas rounds. They arrived at the target with minutes to spare. They crawled to some pine trees about a hundred yards from the cabin, hid behind them, and waited for the signal.

Haitham's team encountered some difficulty as they approached the cabin. They had to work down the slope that descended sharply about fifty yards from the front of the cabin, then work their way up to a point where they could see the cabin. Once they were in place, Haitham motioned to get Isma'il's attention.

"I want you to move out and, using the Jeep as cover, take up a concealed position. When the RPG is fired, it will get Dembray's attention. I want you to go through the front door. Try not to kill Dembray. If the tear gas works, you should be able to get to him and bring him out. When you move, Santos and I will go straight to the two front windows. Santos will be on the right and I will be on the left. Now go."

They watched as Isma'il silently, and quickly, worked his way close to the cabin and, using the Jeep, took cover. When he reached the vehicle, Haitham nodded to Santos, who immediately touched off a short burst from the silenced AK-47, shattering the glass from one of the front windows. Haitham fired one shot through the other window with his unsilenced Browning.

Alain was standing by the sink when the glass from the first window shattered, followed by the report of Haitham's shot through the other window. Alain immediately looked in the direction of the shot. His training took over. Terrorists try to get your attention in your front, but the real danger is at your rear. He ran to the back of the cabin. There was a man moving from behind a tree. *My God,* thought Alain, *he's carrying an RPG.* He grabbed his rifle with his left hand as he opened the back door with his right hand. He brought the rifle to his shoulder and sighted on the man with the RPG who had kneeled down to steady his aim. Alain fired. He saw the man's head jerk as he fired the RPG. The grenade sailed over the cabin. The man who fired it collapsed in a heap.

Alain had no time to think, there was a loud crash as Isma'il broke through the front door. Alain had his Browning out as he moved to the front of the cabin.

Isma'il quickly recovered from the shock of breaking through the front door and raised the H&K. Alain beat him to the punch, firing a shot that caught Isma'il in the center of his chest. Isma'il's reflexes worked perfectly. The shock caused him to pull the trigger. The first round hit Alain in stomach, the impact bending him at the waist. Isma'il's second round caught him just above his right eye. Alain's last view of earth was a blinding flash as the round exploded inside his head. He was dead when he hit the floor.

Haitham and Santos rushed through the front door. They looked first at Isma'il who was lying face down in a pool of blood. Haitham glanced at Alain. It was not a pretty sight. He was on the floor, flat on his back. The right side of his head had been blown away. They watched, fascinated, as Alain's limbs twitched to the unknown tune of death, then lay still. It reminded Haitham of a tarantula he had stepped on. The legs twitched for a few seconds as if the tarantula was trying to get up and scurry away. Santos looked at the two bodies.

"Shit! Zaki isn't going to be too pleased with this."

Right then, Zaki walked through the front door, looked at Santos and shook his head, "Maybe it is best this way. If there were other people involved in the robbery, we now have no way of identifying them. Hopefully, two dead men will be enough revenge for Saddam, but I doubt it."

"Anwar is hurt bad," Walidi barged in hollering. Zaki nodded to Haitham, who went out the back door. There was silence as the living surveyed the dead.

"Go help Haitham, Walidi," Zaki's voice was calm but firm. Walidi immediately went out the back door. In the distance, he saw Haitham unscrewing the silencer from the Browning. He ran to where Haitham was standing and looked at Anwar.

"He was beyond our help," Haitham said with finality.

Walidi looked at his old friend, Anwar. They had trained together in the army. He saw that Haitham was right. The shot that dropped Anwar must have come from a rifle. It had hit him in the chest close to his heart. There was nothing they could have done for him.

"Help me get him into the cabin," Haitham ordered Walidi, as he grabbed one of Anwar's arms.

Zaki watched as the two of them carried, and dragged, Anwar's body into the cabin through the back door. He decided they better move in a hurry.

"Walidi, take everything out of the pockets of Anwar and Isma'il. Sa'id, go out back and see if you can get some gasoline out of the generator. Make it as fast as you can. Haitham and Santos, wipe the prints off all of the weapons and stow them in the concealment in the back of the Suburban."

Sa'id went into the kitchen, found a bucket, and went outside. A couple of minutes later he returned with the bucket almost full of gasoline.

"There is more left in the generator if you need it."

"Fine. Set it down on the floor. I'll let you know if we need more," Zaki said as he went outside. He returned in less than a minute with the device he had gotten from the agent who had provided the Suburban. Zaki had never mentioned his name and no one was about to ask him.

"Put the three bodies in the center of the room. Walidi, spread some of the gasoline throughout the inside of the cabin. If you need more gas, Sa'id can get it. Be careful. Try not to get any gas on yourselves. Leave a trail so you can back out the front door. The rest of you go out front."

Once outside, Zaki spoke to Haitham and Santos, "This device is simple. The timer can be set for up to twelve hours. I will set it for ten. A battery is connected to the timer and detonator inside this innocent contrivance." Zaki held up a smallish plastic cup with a lid that had been further sealed with duct tape. "It is stuffed with rags soaked in gasoline and some black powder thrown in for good measure. The explosion of the detonator should blow the plastic apart and start a nice fire."

Walidi, then Sa'id, came out through the front door. They had poured gasoline almost up to the front door. Zaki toyed with the device before setting it inside the door in a puddle of gasoline. He then turned to instruct the remainder of his team.

"Okay, Haitham, let's go, you can drop Santos and me off in the motel parking lot before you leave. I want you to go with Sa'id and Walidi and make sure they don't get in any trouble. When you get to Denver, I suggest that you leave the Suburban in the parking lot of one of those big shopping plazas and take a taxi to the airport. We have twelve hours before the fire starts. That means about nine o'clock tonight. One last thought - obey the speed limits!"

The trip back to the hotel was uneventful, and quiet. They shook hands before Walidi drove off with the Suburban and his two passengers. Zaki and Santos drove off in the rented Jeep.

"Zaki," Santos said as they drove out of the parking lot, "I'm going to take you to the best restaurant in Salt Lake City. This operation deserves a celebration."

Zaki looked at him, "I hope Saddam thinks so."

-»≡◉ ◉≡«-

Fred Grant had been delayed leaving Salt Lake City. It was already after ten at night when he checked into the Best Western in Pine Springs. He asked at the desk if anyone knew Alain Dembray, saying that he understood Dembray had a cabin near town. No one at the desk had ever heard of an Alain Dembray. Grant expressed his thanks with a wry grin. He was accustomed to such answers so he asked where he could find the police station. It was about two hundred yards down the street on the same side as the hotel. Grant thanked them and walked to the police station.

When he went inside, there was only one person in view, a young man in street clothes talking on the phone. Fred thought he couldn't be much more than twenty-five. He was well built and had regular features. He was clean-shaven with light brown hair. He fixed Fred with clear blue eyes and an expression that asked what the hell he wanted at this hour. He motioned Frank to sit down as he continued talking on the phone. There was no one else in the office. After a few minutes, he said goodbye and hung up. He looked at Fred and asked, "Well stranger, who are you and what can I do for you?"

Grant replied with his best case officer smile, "I am looking for a Mr. Alain Dembray. I understand he has a cabin near here. Do you have any idea where it is?"

The young man was startled. He looked like a rattlesnake had spooked him. He quickly regained his composure and reached for his jacket.

"Are you a friend of his?"

Fred sensed something was wrong. He took his CIA identification out and showed it to the officer who was now gesturing Fred toward the door.

"There was a fire there tonight. You had better come with me. I'll take you to what's left of his cabin." The young man reached to shake Fred's hand, saying, "My name is Albert Simms, Mr. Grant. Sheriff Fontaine is at the cabin now."

They went outside. A light snow had begun to fall. Simms got in the driver's side of a squad car and Fred got in beside him.

"It's a short ride, ten or fifteen minutes."

Simms drove in silence until they turned off the main road onto the dirt road leading to Alain's cabin. "I assume that you are here on official business, Mr. Grant. Would you mind telling me what interest the CIA has in this Dembray fellow?"

Fred seemed alarmed at what Simms had said, "First, call me Fred. Yes, there is an agency interest. Why don't we wait until we get where we're going and then I'll explain our interest to both you and the sheriff? Please, tell me about the fire in Dembray's cabin. Is he okay?"

"The cabin caught fire, maybe an hour or two ago. One of his neighbors, Ed Satterly, saw the smoke and called in the alarm. By the time the fire company got there, they weren't able to save much of the cabin. What is interesting is the presence of three bodies in the cabin. Ed told us that as far as he knows, Dembray had no visitors. He heard a vehicle drive out but didn't see it. That was sometime before nine o'clock this morning. Ed said he was working outside most of the day and didn't see or hear any other vehicle on the track heading towards Dembray's cabin. He said he heard a couple of shots early in the morning, but around here that's pretty normal. We assume that one of the charred bodies is Dembray. Did you know him?"

"Can't say that I really did."

"The sheriff has a crime scene investigator at the cabin. The county coroner is on his way to take the bodies when we have finished the investigation."

When they reached the remains of the cabin, there were two official cars parked along with a fire engine. A Jeep was parked closest to the cabin. The Sheriff was talking to someone in a fireman's uniform. Grant and Simms got out of the police car and approached the two men.

Simms introduced his guest, "I brought you a visitor, Sheriff. He might be able to shed some light on what happened here. This is Fred Grant of the CIA."

Sheriff Fontaine was a squat, thick-trunked man in his late forties. What Grant could see of his face was weathered like old wood. He appeared to be part American Indian. Fontaine spent a brief moment looking at Grant before he extended his hand.

"Glad to meet you, Mr. Grant. The name's Bill Fontaine," he said as they shook. "This is quite a mystery. I hope you can shed some light. All we know at the moment is that we have a badly burnt cabin and three unidentified bodies laying together on the floor of what was the cabin's main room." He said it like he was certain that Grant could explain precisely why there were three very dead men in the remains of a burnt out cabin.

Grant decided that since Dembray was probably one of the dead, he would put what he knew on the table to try and get answers to some of the questions from HQS.

"Yesterday, I received instructions from my headquarters to come here and talk to Mr. Dembray."

Fontaine interrupted him immediately, "Why is the CIA interested in a man living alone in a remote cabin in Wyoming?"

Fred decided to choose his words carefully. He wanted to get enough information as possible on what had happened to Dembray.

"Sheriff, first I would like you and your deputy to keep the fact that Dembray was one of us to yourselves."

"We didn't know he was a CIA officer. His neighbor, Ed Satterly, didn't mention anything about him being with the CIA. Given the circumstances here, I suspect there is something very strange about all of this. Would you please explain how in the hell you managed to show up so quickly?" The change in the sheriff's tone made it clear to Grant that his explanation better be good.

"I'll tell you everything that I know, sir. One month ago, in Hamburg, a retired agency officer was murdered. It was very obviously an execution. We, I mean the agency, have no idea of what this retired officer was doing in Hamburg."

"I think I saw something about that in the newspaper," Fontaine interrupted him. "The paper said he was of Arab descent and the suspicion was that he had been done in by Arabs. What does this murder have to do with Dembray?"

"First, they knew each other. Second, Dembray was curiously in Hamburg at the same time as the murder victim. My headquarters wants to know if the two of them were involved in something that got someone very upset. Simms told me there was someone else in the cabin besides Dembray. Any idea who?"

Sheriff Fontaine found Frank's question very curious. He ignored it.

"Two men, both CIA officers, were in Hamburg at the same time. A month ago one of them was knocked off execution style. Today, a month later, the second CIA officer was done in along with two others. The murders were over 6,000 miles apart. What were they doing for the CIA in Germany that made someone mad enough to kill both of them, and go to a lot of trouble to do it?"

Grant pulled himself erect, "I can assure you, Sheriff Fontaine, that they were not there at the agency's behest. Both men have been retired for a couple of years. These killings are as much of a mystery to us as they are to you. I suspect the identity of the others in the cabin with Dembray may at least shed some light on who did it."

Having made his statement about no agency involvement, Grant wondered if it was true. His thoughts were interrupted as he and the sheriff watched two men emerging from the ruins of the cabin. One was in a fireman's uniform. The two approached the group.

"What did you find out?" Sheriff Fontaine asked.

The man in plain clothes gestured to the fireman, "You go first, Paul."

Paul took off his fireman's hat. His appearance was such that he could have been cast as a fireman by Hollywood. "The fire was definitely set by someone who was alive. Whoever it was emptied most of the gas that was in the generator tank." Paul reached in his pocket, pulled out two charred shell casings, and handed them to the Sheriff.

"One's from a rifle and the other from a 9mm automatic. The rifle and automatic are on the floor which, being thick oak, did not burn through. Both are now useless as weapons. We'll come out tomorrow and take a more thorough look."

"Thanks, Paul. What about you Ernie?"

"Two of the charred bodies have serious head wounds. I'm pretty sure the third one also died of a gunshot wound. I assume the coroner will confirm this when he checks what's left of the bodies."

Fontaine started to ask some questions, but decided to let it wait until morning.

"Okay Ernie, why don't you wait for the coroner. I'm going back to the office to see if we got anything from the APB we put out on the Suburban with the New York plates." He motioned to Grant, "You can come with me, Mr. Grant. We can talk in my office for a few minutes, then go get a beer."

The Sheriff walked to his car and motioned Fred to get in on the passenger's side. They made small talk until they got back to the police station. When they were in his office, Sheriff Fontaine took a seat behind his desk and motioned for Fred to take a seat in front of his desk.

"Look, Mr. Grant why don't you tell me what you know? Maybe what I have learned so far will start to make some sense."

Fred nodded his agreement, "I got a cable from my HQS yesterday instructing me to come here and see Alain Dembray. By way of background, they told me that Hashem Samara'i had been found dead in a parking lot in Hamburg. Samara'i had been tortured by someone who knew what he was doing and then killed by a 9mm bullet that was fired close to his left temple. My HQS is certain that Samara'i was done in by Iraqi Intelligence."

"Why are they so sure who did him in?" Fontaine interjected.

"Samara'i was an American citizen but was Iraqi by birth. He had a record of having operated against Iraq, so they probably had good reason to dislike him. Samara'i retired about three years ago. Dembray and Samara'i had both served at the German station a few years back. Since both men were in Hamburg at the same time just recently, the agency wanted to know if Dembray could shed some light on Samara'i's grisly demise."

"Dembray is still with the agency?"

"No, he also retired a couple of years ago."

Sheriff Fontaine scratched his head, more in frustration than to quell an itch.

"Pardon me, Grant, but we just aren't used to this kind of thing here. It occurs to me the Iraqis must have been real pissed off about something. First, to kill a guy in Hamburg, and then to come all the way here and knock off Dembray. There has got to be some connection between the two murders."

Grant frowned, "It would certainly seem so, but we can't say that conclusively at the moment. Have you come up with anything?" He thought the sheriff was jumping to a conclusion for which they had no proof.

"Let me check on something and then we can go get a beer at the Old Ranger's Inn. They stay open until sometime between one and two in the morning. Given the events of this evening, I could certainly use a beer."

The Sheriff turned on his answering machine. There was only one message of interest. It was from the Best Western Hotel. The hotel planned to question everyone who was on duty early that morning. They would see if anyone could add anything to what had already been provided about the black Suburban.

The sheriff dialed a number, "I'm going for a beer, Molly. I'll see you later." He hung up. "Okay Grant, let's go."

The Old Ranger's Inn was done up in genuine western rustic. It wasn't really an inn, just a bar that looked like it had been copied from a western movie. There was plenty of room, including a dance floor, and it was obvious that they served meals. The sheriff chose a table back in the corner and yelled for two beers. Both men waited to speak until the Coors draft was served.

"Okay, Grant, here's what I know. Ed Satterly phoned in the alarm. It was sometime after nine tonight. The fire truck got there in a hurry and, a little after ten, I got a call from Fred, the fire chief, telling me I had better get my fat ass out to the cabin, Dembray's place. When I asked why, he said there were three bodies in the place. On the way there, I stopped at Ed's place and questioned him. He heard a couple of shots, two or three, but didn't think much of it. He said he later heard a vehicle come off the dirt road and go by his place on the main road. He said he couldn't recall the exact time, but somewhere around nine in the morning. He couldn't give a description of the vehicle because he was behind the cabin chopping wood at the time. He insists that no other vehicle came off the dirt road and passed his house but that one. I called my deputy on the car radio and had him check with the Best Western Hotel on guests that checked out early this morning. There is also a motel you may have noticed driving into town. He checked there as well."

The sheriff stopped to enjoy some of his beer.

"Did your deputy find out anything?" Grant asked.

"We got lucky with the Moonlight Motel. It seems that four guys checked in last night and checked out this morning shortly before seven. The hotel employees said they all spoke English with an accent and they appeared to be Middle Easterners. They were driving a black Chevy Suburban with New York plates. We put out an APB on the Suburban at about ten-thirty or so tonight. So far there has been no response to our APB. That's bad because I'm convinced that whoever was in that Suburban is also directly connected to this case."

"I agree, but given the lapse in time, the New York plated Suburban could be anywhere by now. If the people who did this are professionals, then the Suburban may be hidden or the license plate changed."

"Okay, Mr. Grant, there is nothing more we can do at this time of night. Come by the office tomorrow morning and I'll let you know if anything turns up."

"Thanks for the beer, Sheriff. I'll be there about nine."

Sheriff Fontaine got up, shook hands with Grant, and left the Inn. Grant wandered back to the Best Western wondering what had really happened at Dembray's cabin.

⊷═◉ ◉═⊷

Pine Springs. October 31, 1982. 0830 hours.

Last night's snow had dropped three or four inches on Pine Springs. Grant carefully tiptoed through it from his hotel to the Sheriff's office. Fortunately, pedestrians had succeeded in tramping most of it down. He hoped he would not run into any major snowfall on his drive back to Salt Lake City. When he entered the police station, the sheriff was sitting behind his desk talking on the phone. Grant knocked on his office door. Sheriff Fontaine waved him into a seat and finished his conversation. Finally, he hung up the phone and greeted Grant. "Well, Fred, I've been able to develop some more information."

"Good, I would like to make as detailed a report to my HQS as possible."

Fontaine leaned back in his chair, adopted his Perry Mason demeanor, and began talking. "First, the coroner, on his own hook, got Ed Satterly to look at the bodies. Ed was able to positively identify Dembray by the boots he was wearing which had not completely burned. His left hand was not too badly burned and Ed recognized both the watch on his wrist and an odd ring that he was wearing."

"Well, at least now we can be fairly certain that Dembray was one of the victims."

"Final identification will be up to forensics. Also, the four men, described as Middle Eastern in appearance, who had checked into the motel late in the evening of the day before yesterday, checked out of the motel at exactly six thirty-five yesterday morning. I also have an updated report from the Best Western. They checked with personnel who were on duty yesterday morning."

"Were they any help?" Frank asked.

"Yes. There were three men, also Middle Eastern in appearance, who checked in at the Best Western the day before yesterday. They checked out a little before seven yesterday morning and were picked up by a Chevy Suburban. One of the hotel employees found this curious since they left their Jeep parked in the hotel lot. He did note that the Suburban had New York plates. He paid attention when they returned. The Suburban drove back into the parking lot sometime after nine. Only two men got out and the vehicle left the hotel parking lot immediately. The two men got into their Jeep and also left the lot. The curious thing is that the Jeep had Utah plates. Unfortunately, there is no record of the plate number." Fontaine stopped talking and handed a sheet of paper to Frank. "These are the descriptions we got of the men, the four in the Motel and the three in the Best Western. They are not very helpful."

Grant took the piece of paper and looked at it. He half smiled. "You're right about that." He handed the paper back to Fontaine. "Well, Sheriff, maybe the two other bodies are people from their group that didn't make it."

"I think so. The bad news is that there has been no response to the APB, at least not yet."

"Well Sheriff, thanks for your cooperation. I'm going to drive back to Salt Lake City. I'll file a report from there. That will give you time to get ready."

Fontaine was more than idly curious as he asked, "Ready for what?"

Frank looked at him, not unsympathetically, "Sheriff, once I file this report, within hours you are going to be up to your ass in FBI Special Agents."

-»▪▪■◯ ◯■▪«-

CIA HQS. October 31, 1982. 1600 hours.

Reginald Smythe, the Chief of Counter Intelligence, had the appearance of a cornered animal. The cable from Fred Grant had upset him. He had known Alain fairly well. When he finished reading the cable, he called several people in for a conference. Sam Clauson, the Chief of the Near East Division, had arrived first, followed by Everette O'Brien, the Chief of the European division. Smythe's face was filled with apprehension.

"Sorry to call you gentlemen in late this Sunday afternoon, but we have a serious problem and the shit is going to hit the fan, probably with the evening newscasts. As you know, I sent a message to Fred Grant in Salt Lake City asking him to go to Pine Springs, Wyoming and look up Dembray. I wanted Fred to find out if Dembray could shed some light on Samara'i's untimely death. As it turns out, Grant was too late arriving in Pine Springs. Dembray was killed sometime during the day and his body and the bodies of two unidentified individuals were covered with gasoline and burned along with a good portion of Dembray's cabin."

Clauson immediately asked, "Who were the other two bodies and is it certain that the third body was Dembray?"

By way of answering, Smythe handed each of them a copy of Grant's cable.

"They are pretty sure the one body belongs to Dembray. A neighbor of Dembray's identified his body by the boots, a watch, and a ring on Dembray's left hand. The FBI is now involved and is sending a team to do a thorough investigation."

Both men winced. Smythe continued, "That means they will inundate us with questions and will entertain suspicions as to why two retired agency officers are in Hamburg at the same time and both are now dead. I've called several of my people in and they are now coordinating with the FBI. Unfortunately, we do not have much to go on."

Smythe had other worries to add, "Our problem is that the descriptions of the prime suspects are vague to the point of being useless. It is getting pretty clear that there is some kind of connection between the two murders and that is the theory that will be behind the FBI's investigation." Smythe paused and looked at Grant's cable again while the two officers finished reading.

"In some way, both Dembray and Samara'i were involved in something that angered some Arab or Middle Eastern entity to the degree that this unknown entity went to a great deal of trouble to knock off the two of them." Smythe paused, "We better do our best to put together all the information we can. Sam, I want you to find out the identities of all the Iraqis that flew out of Amman in the past couple weeks. Check with the NSA, but also have our guys in Amman get the Jordanian Service to check on Iraqis who crossed the borders in the past couple of weeks and flew on to other destinations. I'm pretty sure this was an Iraqi operation. Given Samara'i's operational past, the Iraqis are very likely the people who wanted Samara'i dead."

"Agreed, but that doesn't explain why they went to such trouble to knock off Dembray," O'Brien said.

Smythe almost laughed before he answered, "And that is why you are here, Everette. I want you and your colleagues in the European Division to come up with some answers as to why these two were killed by some unidentified entity. Somewhere there is a reason. Organizations do not go to such trouble and expense to knock somebody off unless they have good reason. Sooner or later, the FBI is going to ask us the same question and we better come up with answers." Smythe paused for emphasis, "Don't let me down on this one, Everette. By the way, have you come up with when each of them arrived in Hamburg and when Alain left?"

"Yes, a cable came in yesterday. Alain flew to Germany on June twenty-ninth. I don't know if it is significant, but Hashem's call to him came shortly before Dembray left for Germany. Dembray flew back home on September twelfth. What is curious is that Samara'i did not arrive in Hamburg until August twenty-first. He also flew to Geneva on September ninth and returned to Hamburg on the tenth. There is no record of Alain having flown to Geneva at the same time.

If they were involved in something together there was not much time when they were both in Hamburg."

"Get that information to the FBI tomorrow," Reggie ordered. He was lost in thought for a moment before he turned to Sam Clauson. "Sam, a question for you. Do you think it's possible that Dembray was killed just because of the coincidence that he was in Hamburg at the same time as Samara'i? Another question for you, by any chance did the Iraqis know that Dembray was a CIA officer?"

"You just might be on to something, Reggie. I'll see what we can dig up. Maybe Samara'i spotted Dembray and tried to save his knickers by telling the Iraqis that Dembray was actually in charge of what had upset the Iraqis. Remember, Samara'i had been subject to extensive torture."

Reggie nodded at Sam, "That's as good a theory as any that has come up so far, let's work on it." Reggie signaled the end of the meeting by saying, "Okay, we know what our problem is, let's meet here in my office tomorrow at eleven o'clock."

--+==◎ ◎==+--

CIA HQS. Washington. November 1, 1982. 1100 hours.
Everette O'Brien and Sam Clauson had just joined Reginald Smythe in his office. "Were either of you able to come up with any information or, for that matter, anything that might shed some light on why we have two very dead bodies on our hands?" Smythe asked.

Everette looked at Sam and motioned for him to go ahead. "I sent an immediate to Amman last night asking for the names of Iraqis on flights out from the tenth to the twenty-eighth of October. I got a preliminary response several hours ago. So far, they have nothing that connects any Iraqis leaving Amman with ongoing flights to North America. They reminded me that most flights to North America require a change of planes in Europe. Also, Jordanian immigration only keeps computer records for about two weeks. We did get a list of some fifty-seven Iraqis that were on flights to Europe. We were cautioned that this list doesn't cover all outgoing flights. We are tracing all the names but, so far, have come up with nothing. I also suspect that if the Iraqis did send someone from

Baghdad to participate in the Pine Springs operation, they were almost certainly in alias. In addition, there are two other possibilities. They could have used Iraqi intelligence officers stationed abroad. I suspect the most likely scenario is that since they just wanted to kill Dembray, they may have farmed out the task to some terrorist organization. Abu Nidal would be my guess."

"Thanks for all the help, Sam." Reggie scowled at Clauson, then turned to O'Brien, "What about you, Everette?"

"Samara'i's landlady called the police when he didn't show up for a couple of days. They went through all of his stuff. They didn't find anything that shed any light on the subject except for one thing."

"What was that?" Reginald asked, immediately curious. "Don't keep me in suspense."

"They found four bundles of hundred dollar bills taped to the back of a dresser."

Sam Clauson let out a low whistle. "Samara'i never had forty thousand in cash in his life. Do you suppose he went over to the Iraqis or someone else and didn't do what he was supposed to do? Hashem being bought by some Middle Eastern Service is not far fetched. He was very bitter about being forced to take early retirement."

"Could be, Sam. It has happened before," Reggie said. "Do you have anything more, Everette?"

"Yeah. I had another long talk with Jane Brophy this morning. She told me Alain was genuinely surprised when he heard about Samara'i being murdered. There was nothing unusual about his being in Wyoming in the fall. It's beautiful up there. He stays for a couple of weeks, closes up his cabin, and comes back to Washington. I did ask her about Dembray's reason for being in Hamburg. She repeated the story about the book he was writing. He showed her the copious notes he had made on the operation together with some additional notes on the plot. I brought up Samara'i again and asked if, by any chance, Samara'i could have known that Alain was in Hamburg. She thought for a moment and said that she had no idea if Alain had told him."

"Did she say anything else?" Smythe asked.

O'Brien smiled. It was a smile from eyes that had entranced a number of women in his storied past. "Not really, Reginald. She said she never called him while he was in Hamburg."

Smythe sighed. It seemed logical that the two murders were connected. Why would anyone go to so much trouble to kill two retired CIA officers? He thought of something.

"It seems we are left with the theory that Hashem may have told his torturers that Alain involved him in whatever he was doing that upset them. But, if he did do as we theorize, it certainly did not preserve his life. So where do we go from here?"

"Good question, Reginald," Sam had almost said Reggie. No one called Reginald Smythe Reggie. "If he did tell them, it didn't save him, it only condemned Alain to death. One other point, if Alain knew he was in danger he most certainly would have let the requisite authorities know he was in danger. He didn't even tell or hint to Jane that he was in any danger."

Smythe scratched the back of his head. "Well, let's tell all concerned to report anything new, even if it's negative. As far as I'm concerned, it's the FBI's case."

He was interrupted by a knock on the office door. He opened the door and his secretary handed him a piece of paper.

"This just came from the FBI by fax," she said.

Smythe read the fax and passed it to Clauson. "The FBI found an expended tear gas shell. It was down the slope from the cabin. It was obviously fired from behind the cabin and missed."

Sam passed the fax to O'Brien. "That means that Alain was either involved with Hashem or the Iraqis were led to believe that he was involved with Hashem."

O'Brien snorted. "I find it hard to believe that Alain would ever involve himself in anything with Hashem. The two did not like each other."

"Not even for money?" Smythe asked.

Sam responded, "I can't imagine Alain being involved with Hashem for any amount of money. Also, Alain was well fixed for money. He inherited quite a bit from his parents."

"I have to go along with Sam on that. I know Alain very well and it would take an extraordinarily attractive proposition to induce Alain to involve himself with the likes of Hashem. The two definitely didn't like each other," O'Brien added.

Smythe took the fax from O'Brien and put it on his desk. "Okay, that's all. O'Brien, stay in touch with Jane Brophy, just in case." Smythe escorted them out of his office.

--→==◉ ◎==←--

Baghdad. November 6, 1982. 0900 hours.

Haitham and Zaki were both nervous. It was obvious that Saddam was less than pleased with their accomplishments. Mustafa Naghshabandi sat in a chair opposite them. He observed their discomfort like a prosecutor waiting to question them. Saddam finally spoke.

"You are telling me that with seven people you were not able to subdue this Dembray so you could question him and find out who was behind the robbery?"

Zaki and Haitham looked at each other. Zaki turned to Saddam and said, "I was at the command post. Haitham can fill you in on the details of exactly what happened. Given the location of his cabin and our assumption that Dembray would be on guard after the execution of Samara'i, we were limited in what we could accomplish. I believe we planned as well as we could under the circumstances."

When Zaki finished speaking he nodded to Haitham who looked back at him like an assassin eyeing his prey.

"The plan we drew up was for Zaki to stay in the command post and the rest of us to split into two groups of three men each. Santos, Isma'il and myself were deployed in the front of the cabin. Rashid, Sa'id and Anwar took up a position to the rear of the cabin. Anwar had an RPG. The plan was simple. Isma'il was to burst through the front door when he heard the RPG fired. He was told it was okay to wound Dembray. We only needed him alive long enough to interrogate him."

"I thought I ordered you to bring him here if at all possible?" Saddam said interrupting Haitham, his tone of voice reflecting displeasure.

"We concluded, after a reconnaissance of the area, that our chances of kidnapping Dembray and successfully smuggling him out of the United States were virtually nil. As obvious Middle Easterners in a very small Wyoming town, we stuck out like seven males in a harem. We had to accomplish our mission by staying only one night in Pine Springs. The best we could plan for was a chance to interrogate him," Zaki answered Saddam.

Saddam did not seem pleased. He said nothing, merely nodded to Haitham to continue.

"Isma'il worked his way close to the front door of the cabin. Once he was in place, Santos fired a short burst through one of the front windows with his silenced AK-47. I fired one shot through the other front window with my unsilenced Browning 9mm. My shot was the signal for Anwar to fire the RPG that was loaded with a CS round. We assumed that the CS round would explode inside the cabin filling it with gas. Unfortunately, Dembray apparently suspected the shots fired through the front windows were a ruse to get his attention to the front of the cabin. He fired his rifle at Anwar just as Anwar was about to fire the RPG round. The rifle shot hit Anwar in the chest and the RPG round flew over the cabin instead of into it. At the sound of the rifle shot, Isma'il burst through the front door assuming the cabin would be full of tear gas. Dembray fired his rifle at Isma'il and hit him square in the chest. Apparently, Isma'il's reflexes caused him to squeeze off two shots from his machine pistol. One of the shots hit Dembray in the stomach. Unfortunately, the second shot blew out his brains. We put the three bodies together on the floor of the cabin. We set a timing device to start the fire in the evening, long after we would be out of the area."

Haitham looked at Zaki who took the hint to continue the explanation.

"We had all checked out of our hotels early in the morning, not wanting to return to the hotel after the operation. The two teams met up at seven o'clock in the morning in the Best Western parking lot. We all went in the Suburban. We drove to the cabin that served as our command post. It was about a mile from Dembray's cabin. Since Rashid already knew the area around Dembray's cabin, we sent him to determine if Dembray was home. Rashid was not gone more than half an hour before he returned and confirmed that Dembray was in the cabin. We then mounted the operation as Haitham has already explained."

Saddam slammed his fist on his desk so hard that everyone flinched. "Are you telling me that this is the end? Is there no way we can continue our investigation to learn more about why this operation was mounted by the CIA? I can't believe they would rob our account. Do they need cash? If so, why us? Have you two done any serious thinking on how we can follow this up? What about the ex-wife?"

Zaki stared intently at Saddam. "We have killed two former CIA officers who robbed one of our accounts. Since the CIA already knows it must have been us who killed the two officers, they are going to pay close attention to all of our operatives. Dembray was divorced from the second wife over three years ago. Are we going to risk our officers? Our best hope now is that they conclude that the demise of the two retired officers is the price they are paying for getting the money."

Saddam was still not satisfied. In fact, he was getting red in the face. "You have failed to answer the basic question. Why would the CIA rob one of our accounts?" He turned to Naghshabandi. "What do you think, Mustafa?"

"I agree with Zaki. We are now faced with a very dead, cold trail. Where do we pick up the scent? If we were to continue an investigation, does anybody have the foggiest idea of where to start? We can't very well go to the Banque Suisse and tell them we have been robbed. I think we are forgetting one thing."

"And just what is it that we forgot, Mustafa?" Saddam interrupted him. Haitham thought Mustafa was shrewd to use the all-inclusive we. Mustafa smiled, then answered Saddam's question.

"What we are forgetting is that we have sent a very clear message to the CIA. Killing the two operatives who pulled off the operation has certainly gotten their attention."

Haitham decided he had a point to make. "When we were questioning Samara'i, he made it clear to us that his only contact in the operation was Dembray. We used considerable body pressure to get our information. I am certain that the only person he knew to be involved in the operation was Dembray.

He did say that Dembray received his instructions from an agency officer that he presumed was a member of the CIA's German station."

"There is no way we can identify this officer or take some action against the CIA's installation in Germany?" Saddam asked, a note of incredulity in his voice.

"I'm afraid that is highly unlikely. They outnumber us. Also, we would be operating on what they consider their turf," Zaki answered Saddam's question. "I do have an idea on why the CIA might have robbed our account. First, they must have had a lot of information on the account since they knew how to access it. I suspect they needed the money for a very sensitive operation and they did not want to get the money through their regular budgetary process."

Saddam grimaced. He looked at the ceiling, weighing what Zaki has said. "Okay, so be it. Now get out of here. I have a war to fight."

→▪━◉ ◉━▪←

Goslar. November 11, 1982. 1130 hours.

Kurth von Stiegel was pleased as he exited the bank. He and Ulla would be able to live in luxury for the rest of their lives. He paused to adjust his coat against the chill breeze that was blowing off the Harz Mountains. As he turned to walk towards the Klastorf Inn, where he was to meet Ulla for lunch, he saw two Middle Eastern men on the other side of the street watching him. One man said something to the other man while both kept looking at Kurth. The other man shook his head indicating that he didn't agree with his companion.

Recent events raced through Kurth's mind like an express train. He walked a few meters, then stopped to look in a store window. He could see that the two men were still staring his way. He walked off rapidly, like a man hurrying to get out of the cold. The oddity of two Middle Eastern men appearing in the small town of Goslar, and not only that, but also apparently interested in him, unnerved him. Could they possibly be Iraqis? If so, how did they manage to locate him in Goslar? If they were Iraqis, the meaning was clear. Whoever killed Alain had forced him to reveal Kurth's part in the robbery. He would have to be very careful. The Iraqis hadn't taken much time to square with Hashem and Alain. Plans began forming and reforming in his brain like a flock of birds that lands in a tree then flies off in a different direction. He decided he better get out of town for a week or so, maybe a week of skiing. He would bring it up with Ulla at lunch.

The one Middle Easterner looked at the other after Kurth had disappeared around the corner. "I tell you, Obaid, that man is the actor that was on the television last night."

"You better slow down on the hashish, Hamid. That guy only vaguely resembles the actor." The two turned to walk away, continuing to argue about the unknown man's resemblance to the actor.

⊷⊷⊷ ⊷⊷⊷

Vienna. September 23, 1983.

Jane Brophy had retired from the CIA the previous June. She spent three months taking care of personal affairs. Though the sole beneficiary of Alain's will, she had no idea what he owned besides the house in Norbeck and the burnt down cabin in Wyoming. It took some time to clear out his house in Norbeck and sell it. His brokerage account and local bank account were now in her name. With the proceeds from the sale of his house, his accounts, her accounts, and her retirement, she was quite well off. Now that Alain was gone, she realized how close they had become in the past few years.

Jane had spent some time looking into what she might do to keep herself occupied. She actually had a few interviews that led to job offers. Before making any final decision, she had decided to take a long tour of Europe. There was more than enough money for a pleasant trip. The formal tour began in London. It would end with attendance at the Vienna Opera that evening. After that, she was on her own for a while.

She took some notes out of her pocketbook. Written on them were the phone numbers of the two banks in Hamburg where Alain had opened accounts. She also had the two keys to the safe deposit boxes. She called the first one, the Dresdener Bank. When she gave her name and the number of her account, there was a pause as the clerk checked the account.

"Yes, Ms. Brophy, I'm sorry for the delay, your name being different from Mr. Dembray's. What can I do for you?" The clerk asked politely.

"Can you please tell me how much is in the account?"

"One moment, please."

Jane was more than surprised by the response to her inquiry. She then called the second bank, the Deutsche Bank. She was a bit startled to find out that the account contained almost four thousand marks. She wondered why Alain had opened two accounts. She found the explanation he had given her difficult to accept. He also never mentioned returning to Germany.

She thought of flying to Hamburg but, since she was not pressed for time, she decided to take a train. It would take her through some of the most beautiful scenery in Europe. Given the amount of money in the two accounts, she would certainly be able to afford subsequent trips to Europe. Jane idly poked at the keys to the two safe deposit boxes and wondered what they contained. She had plenty of time before dinner and the opera, so she thought she would walk to the station to make her train reservations. She picked up the keys and put them in her bag.

Acknowledgements

I am indebted to all of the readers who took the time to help me
with my manuscript.

I would like to express my love and gratitude to the many members of
my large, extended family, most notably,
my loving wife.

Made in the USA
Middletown, DE
02 October 2023

39976802R00181